By J.P. CARUSO

The Menagerie

Published by DREAMSPINNER PRESS
www.dreamspinnerpress.com

The Menagerie

J.P. CARUSO

Published by
DREAMSPINNER PRESS

8219 Woodville Hwy #1245
Woodville, FL 32362 USA
www.dreamspinnerpress.com

The Menagerie
© 2025 J.P. Caruso

Cover Art
© 2025 DAGIN
Cover content is for illustrative purposes only and any person depicted on the cover is a model.
Author Photo © J.P. Caruso

Trade Paperback ISBN: 978-1-64108-816-9
Digital ISBN: 978-1-64108-815-2
Trade Paperback published May 2025
v. 1.0

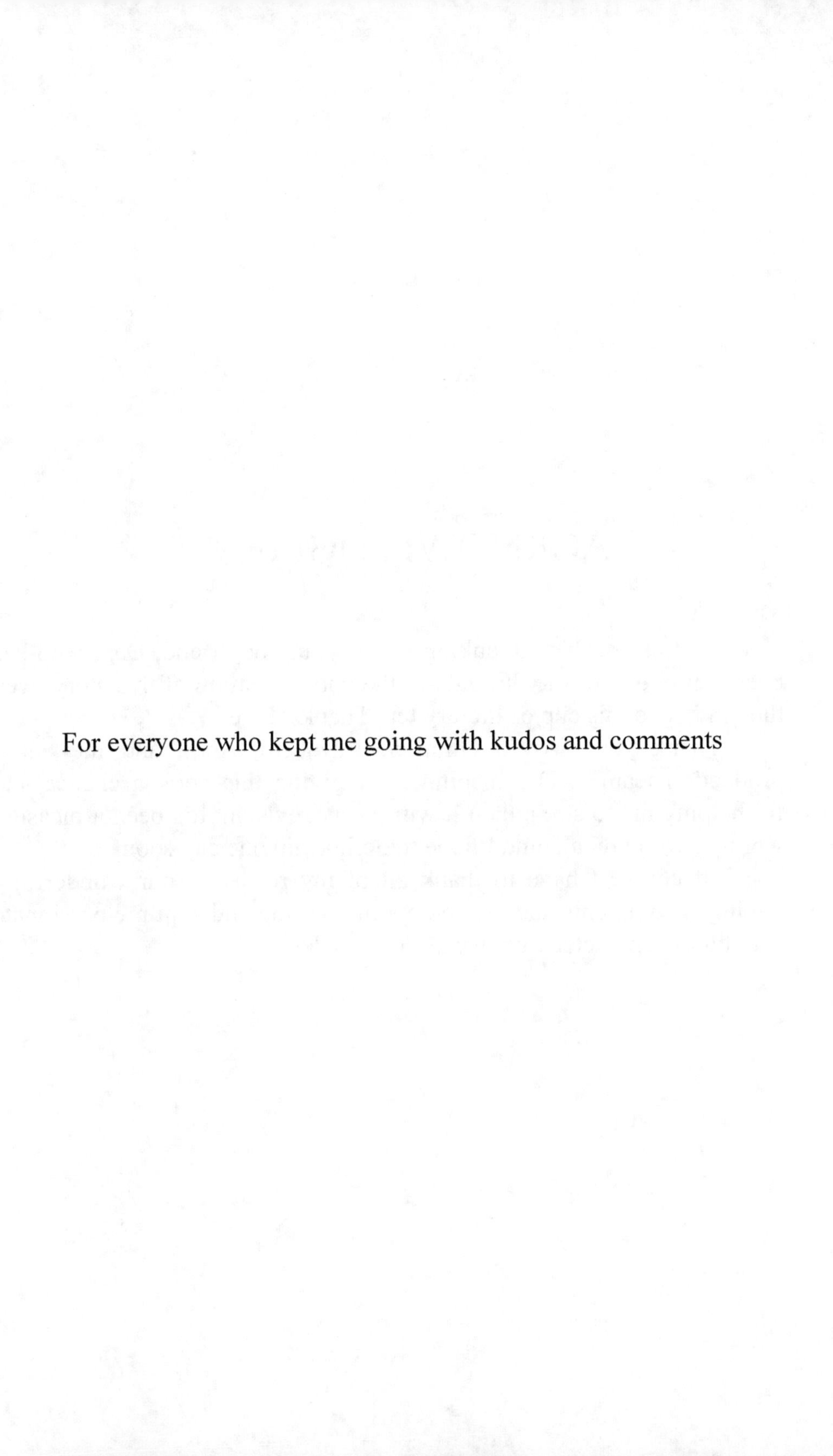

For everyone who kept me going with kudos and comments

ACKNOWLEDGMENTS

I want to start off by thanking my amazing boyfriend, Dan, who has been supportive of me throughout the entire creation of this story even though it's not his cup of literary tea. Thanks, love.

Thank you also to Ginnifer, Elizabeth, Andi, and the entire production team at Dreamspinner for giving this book a chance and for helping me to strengthen it with every revision. It's been a pleasure working with you all, and I hope to do it again one day soon.

Of course I have to thank all of my readers. Your wonderfully unhinged comments and praise kept me writing and kept me passionate about these characters that we all love so dearly.

Chapter 1: The Menagerie

For the first time in his life, Rowan Campbell has a savings account in the quadruple digits. He has a steady and fulfilling job as a paramedic, a small but clean one-bedroom apartment in Boston's Back Bay, and a stable dose regimen of meds to keep his depression and PTSD in check.

He loves his life, finally.

He's happy…

But.

He's happy, but…

There's something missing.

Some itch under his skin that he can't quite scratch through work or hobbies or family gatherings or casual hookups.

It's a random, ordinary Monday when Rowan finally discovers the *something* that's missing in his life.

"Code six-three, 241 West Harrington, nearby units please respond," the tinny voice broadcasts over the ambulance radio.

Rowan shares a glance with his partner, Addison, who nods and picks up the receiver.

"Dispatch, this is Car 47, show us responding. ETA two minutes," she says as she inputs the location in the GPS.

Rowan flips on the siren, feeling the thrill rush through him that still hasn't dissipated in his two years as an EMT and three as a paramedic. He's vaguely familiar with the area, but it never hurts to have the GPS on, especially when a minute or two spent circling around the block could mean life or death.

When they arrive, there's a small crowd outside a whitewashed brick building. Above the crowd is an overhang with illuminated marquee lights circling a black sign that reads The Menagerie in a neat gold script like something out of a modernized 1930s movie.

They grab their gear and a stretcher from the back before signaling to the crowd to move out of the way. As the crowd parts, a petite blond woman in black business clothes and high heels flags them down.

"He's in here," she says, voice serious yet calm, very much unlike most people they deal with.

She ushers them through a heavy cherrywood door and into what looks like a lounge. The interior is dim—both the tiled floors and the walls are black—lit only by blue, purple, and warm white lights that seem to outline all the fixed objects in the room.

Even from the little Rowan can see as his eyes adjust to the dark, he can tell that the décor is chic and modern. It looks as though it would be better suited to the Financial District.

Rowan and Addison make their way up a flight of stairs and into a lounge that is similarly decorated to the one below. Despite the crowd outside, there are still a few people lingering around the edges of the room, huddled together in small groups, whispering to one another. Many of them are in partial states of undress, with robes hastily thrown around themselves.

Down a short corridor, they're led into a small, sparsely decorated room. Rowan barely has time to register the variety of crops and ropes and leather toys mounted to the wall opposite the door when he sees a man on the floor, naked, skin pale, and eyes closed. A woman, also naked, is kneeling over him, fingertips pressed against the pulse point on his neck, eyebrows scrunched in concern.

"What happened?" Addison asks the woman, gently ushering her away from the man.

"We were—I was ch-choking him and… and he… he passed out! He never sa-safeworded, so I thought…. He seemed fine, and then he just… passed out," she stammers.

Rowan kneels down next to the man and grabs his wrist to feel for his pulse. It's weak, but there.

"Did he ever stop breathing after he passed out?" Rowan asks her.

"Yeah. Shit, yeah, he did. I was so fucking scared, but I did CPR on him for maybe a minute? Maybe less? I don't know, it all happened so fast and—"

"Hey, it's okay," Addison soothes. "You did good. He's breathing now, okay?"

The woman nods, covering her breasts with her arms and shrinking in on herself as if only now realizing she is nude.

"Did he fall or hit his head when he passed out?" Rowan asks, doing a once-over to check for physical injuries.

"No. We were already on the floor, and he fell forward into me. I laid him down."

"That's good," Rowan says. "Oxygen."

Addison grabs the emergency oxygen cylinder from her kit and fits the mask over their patient's face, then turns on the flow. The man's eyelids flutter at the rush of oxygen. A promising sign, but he's still not out of the woods. They'll need to get him in the ambulance and to the nearest hospital to find out if there's any lasting damage from the lack of oxygen.

"Has he had any alcohol or drugs tonight that you're aware of?" Addison asks.

The woman shakes her head, then adds, "Well, we had a couple drinks before this, but I think he only had two glasses of whisky. No drugs, but I guess he could've taken something before we met. I don't know."

Rowan lifts his eyelids and shines a flashlight on his eyes to check his pupil response. Still intact—another good sign. It looks like he's going to be okay, but they still need to get him to a doctor.

"They don't allow it here," the woman says, almost to herself. "Choking. But he said he'd done it before and knew how much... how much he could handle, and...."

"We're gonna help him," Rowan promises, setting up the stretcher next to the man and grasping his legs. "Move on three. One, two, three."

They quickly shift the man onto the stretcher and cover him in a wool blanket from their kit before strapping him in.

"Do you want to come, ma'am?" Addison asks the woman as she and Rowan raise the stretcher.

She shakes her head. "I only met him a few hours ago. I don't even know his real name...."

The thought of hurting someone—a *stranger*—and leaving them alone makes Rowan's stomach churn, but he holds his tongue. Anything he wants to say to the woman wouldn't do anyone any good and would just cost their patient valuable time.

They wheel the man out of the room, down the elevator that the hostess points out, and back through the club to load him into the ambulance. Rowan drives and radios the nearest hospital while Addison monitors the man's vitals in the back. All things considered, the call could have gone much worse. They could be driving back without sirens on right now.

But even with the close call, Rowan can't help but think about that wall of toys and equipment. About the darkness of the club and the low, bassy music. About the tingling under his skin and the goose bumps on the back of his neck.

IT SHOULD be a red flag that the first time Rowan hears about the Menagerie is due to a near-life-threatening emergency, but it isn't. His nerves are eased knowing that the man they'd had to bring to the hospital had acted outside of the club's rules, and that even though that was the case, the management made sure he was taken care of.

He barely makes it the full day on Tuesday before he's typing *the menagerie boston* into Google, eyes glued to his laptop screen like he might miss something in the millisecond it takes the page to load.

The first link seems to be what he's looking for. He clicks through to a simple splash screen asking if he's over eighteen. He clicks on "I am 18+" and is brought to a modern, elegant-looking website with a black background and white-and-gold text and an image of a sultry-looking woman's eyes partially covered in a black mask. A golden script reading *The Menagerie* lies directly in the center of the homepage, and underneath: *Boston's Most Exclusive BDSM Dungeon & Club.*

Rowan's heart rate spikes.

He'd assumed the club was of the NSFW variety from the hastily covered patrons and the fact that the man he'd helped had passed out from erotic asphyxiation, but seeing it written plainly on the screen makes it that much more real. And he can't deny that being in the club, even in an official capacity, had done a little something for him.

Okay, a lot of something for him. It's been years since he frequented spaces like that, and he wasn't exactly in the best headspace when he did, but he misses it.

Misses the way the booze and the drugs and the men made him feel. Alive. Sexy. Desired. Like they'd wanted to eat him up when they thought he was a bottom, then submitting with little coaxing when Rowan would pull out his dick and flip them over.

Powerful.

He needs to know more.

Clicking through a few of the pages—About Us, BDSM, FAQ, Gallery, Blog—he learns that the Menagerie is a members-only club that allows its patrons to use their facility and equipment and even book sessions with on staff dominants or submissives.

The gallery shows him the wide variety of rooms available to rent in the club, including a classroom, medieval dungeon, doctor's office, and other themed rooms in addition to multiple standard ones like the one he'd been in yesterday.

Finally, he clicks on the Contact page. The address, hours of operation, and social media handles are all there, along with various pride flags and the words Safe Space for All, but what really catches Rowan's eye is the blank contact form.

Drop us a line.

Rowan doesn't think twice before filling out his name and email address and typing a quick message.

Hi,

I'm interested in becoming a member. Can you send more info, please?

Thanks,

Rowan C.

He hits Send before he can think better of it. Takes a deep breath and closes his eyes, mentally going through his emotional checklist to make sure the impulsive decision isn't a sign of an impending depressive episode. And he isn't irritated, isn't antsy, isn't out of his mind horny— he's okay. His eyes flick to the pill box on his nightstand, Tuesday a.m. and p.m. boxes both empty.

He's okay.

He clicks through a few more pages on the website, reading the latest blog entry and looking at the extensive BDSM educational references. By the time he finds himself reading an article on the best kinds of knots to use for a full-body shibari rig, it's well past midnight.

Fuck.

He has to work in the morning. He closes his laptop, climbs into bed, and tries not to think too hard about how long he'll have to wait for a reply.

But as he's lying there, staring up at the blackness of his ceiling, lit in stripes by the faint blue moonlight shining around the edges of his curtains, he's reminded of the lights in the club and feels the familiar trickle of heat low in his belly.

Feels his cock start to harden as images of strong thighs and sinfully curving spines race through his mind. His legs spread on their own, hips hitching up a fraction of an inch to get any amount of friction on his cock.

He wills himself to calm down because he has to be up in less than five hours, but he's never been good at denying himself pleasure.

More thoughts flood his mind, each making him breathe a little faster, a little shallower. *Sweat-slicked skin. Ragged breaths. A warm mouth. A clenching hole. A hand around a throat.*

And all at once he's going down, down, down the rabbit hole of memories of dark clubs and back alleys and bathroom stalls and hotel rooms far too nice for what they were being used for. Of pushing his body to the limit and his mind well past it. But he's in a good place. He's okay. He can handle it. The thoughts no longer make him spiral into shame and self-loathing—now they make him throb with need.

The phantom taste of a pill on his tongue and a buzzing under his skin is all it takes for his hand to follow his thoughts, down, down, down his torso to slip into his briefs.

The first contact of his cool hand on his hot cock makes him gasp in the quiet. He wants to tease himself, play with his balls and trail his fingertips down the length of his shaft, slide his thumb over the head and draw out the pleasure until he's aching and desperate.

But he's too far gone already, too turned on, too aware that he finally has his shit together and can't risk fucking it all up again by getting sucked back into fantasies.

So he spreads the precome around the head, enough to slick his hand and ease his movements as he strokes himself. He tightens his grip, twisting his hand on each upstroke and flicking his index finger over the head on the downstroke.

In no time at all, he feels his thighs start to tense, then tremble, then quake as he works himself faster. But the friction that he'd loved a few minutes ago is too much, too intense. He wrenches his hand off his cock and spits into it, still a poor substitute for actual lube but far better than precome alone.

The pleasure doubles instantly as he grips himself tighter, hips bucking up into his fist, heat spreading to his limbs. He roves his free hand over his chest, skirting over his nipples and imagining it's someone else, someone grasping at him while he fucks into them faster, faster, faster—

Rowan climaxes with a low groan, coating his fingers and the inside of his briefs in ropes of come, stroking himself through it as his body trembles with the flood of endorphins. Sweat from his hairline trickles down the side of his face, but it does little to cool the heat of his skin.

When he's fully spent and his cock begins to soften, he wipes his hand on his briefs, flinging the comforter and sheets off his upper half to avoid getting them dirty. And he has every intention of getting up and changing into fresh underwear, washing his hands and face, but his eyes won't stay open as his body sinks deeper into the mattress and he drifts off to sleep.

Despite the late night, Rowan wakes the next morning before his alarm goes off. To his surprise, when he checks the time on his phone, he sees an email icon. After swiping open the app, he gawks at the reply from the club, sent an hour after he'd sent his email.

Good evening, Rowan,

Thank you for your interest in The Menagerie! We are always accepting new members. Attached you will find our info sheet, club rules, and application form. If you are interested in applying, simply fill out the PDF application and email it back.

Please know that if accepted, we require all members to submit a driver's license, a credit card to keep on file, and monthly negative STI test results from a physician's office or clinic. While positive results do not preclude membership, there are additional steps we require to keep all of our members safe.

Please reach out with any questions you may have and we'll be happy to answer!

Best,
Clover Monroe
Membership Coordinator
The Menagerie

He's about to download the attachments, but as he stretches out his legs, he remembers he'd come in his underwear last night like a teenager. His lower half is a mess, dried come and spit clinging to the fabric of his briefs. He hops out of bed and showers quickly, despite having more time than usual to get ready this morning.

Freshly changed in record time, he downloads the attachments and opens the info sheet first. Because the one thing that he hadn't learned from the website was the *cost* of becoming a member. And really, that's going to be the determining factor of whether he fills out the application or not. He skims down the page, heart beating perhaps a little too fast for 6:00 a.m. as *Boston's Most Exclusive BDSM Dungeon & Club* rattles around in his head. The word *exclusive* is almost always synonymous with *expensive.*

But when he finds the membership fees several pages down, it's not as bad as he was imagining, though it certainly isn't cheap.

Silver Membership: $100/month
- Allows admittance 4 times per month
- One complimentary alcoholic drink per visit (excludes gratuity)
- Invitation to special events once per month

Gold Membership: $200/month
- Allows admittance 8 times per month
- One complimentary alcoholic drink per visit (excludes gratuity)
- Invitation to special events 2 times per month

Platinum Membership: $300/month
- Allows unlimited admittance
- One complimentary alcoholic drink per visit, all other drinks 50% off (excludes gratuity)
- Invitation to all standard plus additional exclusive special events
- Priority room booking

Rowan swallows as he reads the perks of each membership tier. The thing is, he *could* afford any of them, which is making his head spin a bit. The higher tiers would majorly eat into his savings, but he could swing it if he really wanted to. Only in the past year or so has he started to relax on penny-pinching, something that everyone from the South End is familiar with even if they've long since moved out. But with his steady and decently paying job, manageable bills, and an almost unbelievably padded savings account, he's started to take better care of himself.

Started buying nicer clothes that fit his body better and last longer than a dozen washes. Better skincare and haircare products rather than the dish soap he used to use to scrub the grime off his body. More fresh fruits and vegetables than he's ever had in his life. The occasional latte or album or new pair of sneakers to treat himself, for fuck's sake.

The higher tiers are still a little too expensive for him to justify, especially since he might not even like the place, but he can spare $100 for one month to test the waters. Besides, four visits per month seems like a reasonable amount. While he'd like nothing more than to have hot, kinky sex every night like he used to, that's not practical for him anymore outside of a relationship. And he wouldn't be going anytime other than the weekends anyway.

He reads through some of the other FAQs, which range from *Is sex allowed at the club?—Yes—*to *Is there a dress code?—No, but our members tend to dress in cocktail attire if not participating in a scene.*

Next, he scrolls through the club rules.

There are some that are obvious: *All equipment must be disinfected with provided cleaner after each use; no sexual acts in the bathrooms or locker rooms; no outside food or beverages.* And some that aren't— *No scenes exceeding 4 hours; no bloodplay or cutting; no breath play.* Rowan thinks back to the man they'd helped who had broken this exact rule. He shakes his head. He's done it a few times with partners and gotten off to it more times than he can count, but he never lost sight of how *dangerous* it can be if you don't know what you're doing.

Members will receive two recorded strikes for breaking minor rules before membership is terminated. Membership may be terminated immediately depending on the severity of the rule(s) broken (i.e., if the safety of other members is compromised). Termination of membership is permanent.

Jesus. It's pretty harsh, but Rowan knows that BDSM is all about trust and safety, and that members likely wouldn't be able to fully enjoy themselves if they knew other members were breaking rules left and right with no consequences.

Before he can open the application, his "You're gonna be late" alarm beeps loudly on his phone.

"Shit," he curses, hastily closes his email app, and jumps up to finish getting ready for work.

By the time his lunch break hits, Rowan is itching to open the application. He pulls it up on his phone, zooming in to read the small text. The top portion is all standard name and contact info type stuff, but the bottom half and the second page are far more detailed, most of the questions having several lines to type in longer answers.

Rowan mentally thinks through his answers to the nearly two-dozen questions as he reads through the rest of the application. It's… thorough. Intense, even. His application to be an EMT wasn't this long, and the one to become a paramedic a couple of years later, even shorter.

And it doesn't say anywhere what they're *looking for* in this application. Rowan assumes it's a way of making sure only those who are into this lifestyle join and that they won't damage the club's reputation, but he can't be sure. He could email Clover and ask, but he figures he'll just fill it out and send it off. If he's rejected for whatever reason, he'll ask then.

He can't fill out the pdf on his phone, so he plans on doing it first thing when he gets home in a few hours. But he *can* call his primary care physician's office—because he has one of those now, no longer needing to rely on the underfunded clinics of the South End—and schedule an STI test.

The call is brief, efficient, and Rowan has an appointment for Thursday—tomorrow—before work. He was clean the last time he got tested a few months ago and has used condoms with the sporadic hookups he's had since then, but it never hurts to be sure. And besides, the club requires it.

He finishes his lunch quickly, eager to get through the rest of the day.

Having already thought about his answers to the longer questions on the application, he fills it out in record time as soon as he gets home.

Why are you interested in joining The Menagerie?

Because I want a safe place to re-explore my sexual interests.

Do you have any experience with BDSM? If yes, for how long?
Yes, with past partners. About 5 to 6 years.
Would you describe yourself as submissive, dominant, or verse?
Dominant.
What are your interests in BDSM? Check all that apply.
Rope bondage, leather bondage, toys, collaring, edging, flogging/impact play, rough sex, group sex, exhibitionism, voyeurism.
Are there any areas of BDSM that you are interested in trying?
Roleplay, shibari, sensation play, maybe others.
How important are safewords to you?
Extremely.
Do you have any interest in attending special workshops (alone/in a group) to learn new techniques?
Yes, both.

It takes barely more than fifteen minutes to answer all the questions, and he emails the application back to Clover with a note that he has an STI test scheduled for the morning.

That night he dreams of leather and strawberries.

IN THE morning, he once again awakes to an email from the club.

Dear Rowan,

We are pleased to invite you to become a member at The Menagerie! We feel your interests and experience will make for an exciting addition to our club. Please let us know when you are available for an in-person meeting at the club to complete your membership and fill out remaining paperwork. It should take no more than 30 minutes, though you are free to stay after if you would like.

Best,

Clover Monroe

Membership Coordinator

The Menagerie

Rowan can hear his blood rushing in his ears. Like before, the fast response surprises him—more so after having to review his application. But even if it had taken them weeks to respond, it wouldn't have mattered.

He double-checks the club's hours and sends a final email to Clover, fingers shaking with excitement.

Hi Clover,

Great! I can come in this Saturday at 7pm. Does that work?
Rowan C.

When he receives an affirmative reply barely fifteen minutes later, his heart races. Finally, he has something to look forward to.

He's in.

Chapter 2: Malcolm

When Saturday night finally arrives, Rowan is nearly vibrating out of his skin. He received his test results from his doctor's office this morning—all negative, thankfully—which means that he can stay at the club tonight once his membership is finalized.

He doesn't even fully know what that entails yet, but hopefully he can meet someone at the bar there and spend the night with them. God, just the thought of hooking up with someone who will likely have the same or similar interests as he does has his cock twitching in his jeans.

Since receiving Clover's email two days ago, he's jerked off six times and feels like he could go another six rounds at least and still not be satisfied.

He takes a deep breath and tells himself to calm the fuck down. The long hot shower he takes helps. He makes sure to scrub his body thoroughly, wash his hair, and use some leave-in conditioner so he can style his undercut properly without it frizzing up on top like it usually does on these warm summer nights.

He towels off and considers his wardrobe. He still doesn't have much, but the hand-me-downs from his older brother, Jay, are gone, and he has a mostly full closet of clothes *he* likes and more options than he's ever had before. The FAQ portion of the website said business casual to cocktail attire is common, so he searches for something that will fit those criteria without being too formal.

Freshly dressed in dark jeans and a white button-up, he gathers everything he'll need for tonight and hops in his Honda Civic to make the twenty-minute drive to the club.

He finds a parking spot in the back and circles the building to enter through the front. The club looks much the same as it had when he was here a few days ago, but now he can fully appreciate the ambiance. He approaches the desk at the entryway, nestled before the room opens into the familiar lounge and bar area.

The same blond woman who had ushered them inside the other day is standing at the desk, but this time she's dressed in a slinky black leather dress with a matching choker collar. The blue light of a computer casts a glow on her face, and Rowan notes the cherry-red lipstick and smoky eye shadow. She looks intimidating, but in an entirely different way than she had in her business suit.

He clears his throat.

"'Scuse me?"

She looks up at him through her long eyelashes.

"Hi there! How can I help you?"

"I have a meeting with Clover Monroe at seven, I was just approved for a membership. Rowan Campbell."

"Welcome, Rowan! I'm Camilla. I run the front of house. Follow me."

She leads him past the bar and down the same hallway he'd taken to get to the injured man earlier in the week. She hasn't given Rowan any cue that she recognizes him, which seems odd, but he's sure it's the same woman.

"Did we meet the other day?" he asks, unable to contain his curiosity. "When there was an incident at the club?"

She pauses in front of a door with a plaque that reads Office and eyes him curiously.

"I think I'd remember a face like yours."

"Uh, I was one of the paramedics who responded to the emergency here a few days ago? You showed me and my partner in."

"Oh!" She laughs. "That must've been Clover. My twin. She runs things behind the scenes."

Ah. Twins.

"Oh, sorry."

"Happens all the time." Camilla waves him off and knocks on the door in two quick raps, waiting for a *Come in!* from the other side before opening the door, revealing Clover—identical in appearance to Camilla except for her attire—behind a large white desk.

"Rowan Campbell for you," Camilla tells her sister, ushering Rowan inside.

"Oh! You're the EMT who was here earlier in the week," Clover says as soon as she sees Rowan.

Rowan nods, not bothering to correct his title.

"Please, have a seat. Thanks, Cam."

Camilla leaves with a wink to Rowan.

"Is that how you heard about us?" Clover asks.

"Yeah."

"Not the best first impression, though I'm glad you decided to give us a shot anyway."

"I was impressed by how it was handled, honestly. You'd be surprised how many people either don't call, call too late, or withhold important details from us because they're scared of the consequences."

Clover nods solemnly in response. "I can't even imagine. But you can be sure that won't happen here. Safety is one of our primary concerns, and I'd rather the club get shut down than have someone be harmed because we didn't do enough to help."

"Good to know."

With that, the conversation shifts to business.

Clover gives him the rundown of the club. He learns that there are four levels, each catering to different demographics. The ground floor is mostly professional, with a bar, lounge, and dance floor; nudity and any sexual acts are forbidden on this floor, as it helps ensure anyone who may enter from the street isn't exposed to anything untoward, even though members need to check in at the desk upon arrival.

The second through fourth floors are for sexual acts, with the second floor being open to everyone, the third open only to female-identifying members, and the fourth to male-identifying members. Each floor has its own full bar, several small lounges, a bathroom and locker room, playrooms, and recovery rooms. To Rowan's surprise, each floor also has an area off the lounge specifically for exhibitionists. He makes a mental note to investigate the one on the fourth floor.

Clover is thorough in her explanation of the club rules and membership perks, though Rowan has already read through them all several times. When prompted, he tells her he'd like to try the Silver membership for the month and gives her his license, credit card, and copy of his test results.

Multiple signatures later, he's a hundred bucks poorer and officially a member of the Menagerie.

He shakes Clover's hand as she pages her sister to come get Rowan and show him around.

"The layouts are all pretty much the same, but which floor would you like to tour?" Camilla asks once they are back in the hallway.

"The fourth."

She nods and leads them to the elevator.

"You picked a good night to join, Rowan," she tells him conspiratorially.

"Why's that?"

"*Malcolm* is here tonight."

She says the name like it's supposed to mean something to Rowan. When he stares at her blankly, she makes a small *ah* sound and explains.

"He's… hm. He's basically a god around here. VIP, you could say. Been coming for years. Everyone who sees him in action wants him, even some people not usually into men. Gorgeous, confident, incredible scene partner, etcetera, etcetera."

"He a top?" Rowan asks. Because god or not, if he's not a bottom, Rowan's really not interested. He didn't exactly come here to be the one getting fucked, despite the fact that he does get an itch for it once in a while.

She huffs out a laugh. "Nooo. Power bottom. Think I can count on one hand the number of times he's topped, at least that he's told me about."

That gives Rowan pause. "You're friends?"

"Mm-hmm. Well, as close to it as I think he lets people get, anyway. We've both been here a long time."

Rowan doesn't know what she means by *as close as he lets people get*, but he nods. "So what's so special about him being here tonight if he comes all the time?"

"He booked the Black Room for the entire night."

Again, like that's supposed to mean something to Rowan.

"Black Room?"

He mentally runs through the list of themed rooms that Clover had mentioned but is drawing a blank.

"Unofficially, the *gangbang* room."

"Oh."

Oh.

Rowan feels his cheeks flame up and hates himself for it. He's literally become a member of a sex dungeon and is being escorted by a woman dressed more or less as a dominatrix, and here he is blushing at the thought of a gangbang.

"So… is that something anyone can join in on?" Rowan hedges.

"Yes and no. He's done it a few times in the past, and each time he's picked the participants. You're free to go to the room later tonight to see if he's interested, though it's usually quite crowded, and only a handful get chosen. It starts at eight."

"Got it."

Jesus.

This guy must be a *literal* god if he has to hand select people to fuck him from a lineup. Camilla hasn't said anything about his physical description, but Rowan's picturing some tall, dark, and handsome man with bulging muscles straight out of a Chippendale's calendar. It's not Rowan's usual type. He prefers someone at least a little scrappy and imperfect, but if this guy's as good as he sounds, Rowan can get on board with whatever he looks like.

The fourth floor is styled similarly to the ground floor, all dark walls and décor with golden accents and tastefully placed strips of white and blue lights. About half of the patrons are walking around in various states of undress, and it has Rowan's pulse quickening. A tall, thin man wearing a mesh top and tight leather pants walks past him with a wink before grinding on a group of guys on the dance floor opposite the bar, and Rowan thinks he might like this place a whole lot.

He snaps back to himself when Camilla points out the various playrooms, locker rooms, and changing rooms that her sister had detailed. She also points out the area tucked away into the corner, barely visible if you stand at the right place at the bar, where members can go to watch or partake in public sex acts—the VoyEx corner. Not the most original of names, but it piques Rowan's interest regardless. While full-on sex is prohibited in the main bar and lounge area for cleanliness's sake, since they do serve appetizers and drinks, there's nothing against it there.

He's much more interested in the upcoming gangbang, which really is the best of both worlds.

When the brief but thorough tour is over, Camilla leaves Rowan plunked down at the bar, tells him to ask any of the staff if he needs anything at all, and disappears.

"What can I get ya, handsome?"

Rowan snaps his head up to see the bartender smiling at him. He's beautiful, easily taller than Rowan by a few inches, deep brown skin, short hair styled in effortless-looking sponge curls, chocolate brown eyes. Rowan wonders if it's taboo to ask for a staff member's number.

"Just a beer, please. Whatever's on tap."

The man nods, starts pouring the amber liquid from the tap.

"I take it you're new here…?"

"Rowan. And yeah. Just joined."

Placing his drink on a black cocktail napkin, he gives Rowan a coy smile. "Jeremiah. What's your poison?"

"Thanks. Uh, I'm a top. Dom."

Jeremiah waggles his eyebrows. "Have you heard what Malcolm has planned for tonight?"

There he is again.

"Camilla mentioned it. He really that big a deal around here?" Rowan takes a sip of beer. A little too hoppy for his taste, having grown up drinking the cheapest watery swill anyone in his family could afford.

"Mm-hmm."

Rowan's curiosity is officially piqued.

"What's he like?"

"Quiet, but a bit of a sourpuss when he does talk. Pretty outspoken. He's helped shape some of our policies over the years, believe it or not. Gorgeous too."

That's the second person who's called Malcolm *gorgeous*, and it's not doing anything to dissuade Rowan from picturing some Adonis-like man.

"Think I should try to get in on this gangbang?"

Jeremiah shrugs. "Your call. But if that's your thing, you won't find a better place or a better person for it in the whole city."

Rowan nods slowly a few times, pretending to mull it over in his head as if he hadn't already decided the second Camilla mentioned it that he's going to check it out. If he strikes out, he's sure he can find that guy who winked at him earlier, or even see if Jeremiah's shift is ending anytime soon. After all, he's never had a hard time finding someone to spend the night with when he's wanted to.

"Are you planning on getting another drink tonight, or should I put that in for your freebie?" Jeremiah asks.

"Oh, uh, no, I'm good with this. Thanks." He pauses, tapping the side of the glass a few times. "Do you guys carry Blue Ribbon by any chance?"

To his surprise, Jeremiah huffs out a quick laugh, but it doesn't sound unkind. "We do, but hardly anyone orders it 'cause it's such a shitty beer."

Rowan isn't offended. "I'm a shitty beer kinda guy."

"You're in luck. Turns out so is Malcolm—he's one of the few who drink it, so I always keep a couple cases in stock."

"Oh yeah?"

"Mmm."

That surprises him. For some reason, Rowan had expected him to like top-shelf liquor, so now his mental picture of the guy is all over the place.

Jeremiah makes small talk with him between helping other members at the bar, none of whom catch Rowan's eye. Rowan lets himself get lost in his thoughts, most of which migrate inevitably to this *Malcolm* guy. It's an uncommon name. Rowan doesn't know shit about name etiology or he'd try to develop a picture of him based on his name alone.

He's finishing his drink when he notices many of the members in the bar and lounge migrating toward the end of the hallway and a set of black double doors. He checks the time: 7:58 p.m. This must be what Camilla was talking about.

The *gangbang* is going to start soon.

He discards the empty glass on the bar with a five-dollar bill under it as a tip and heads toward the crowd. There's an excited buzz in the air, like the feeling at a concert after all the openers have left and the main act is about to begin.

Rowan worms his way to the front to find the double doors to the Black Room have been opened and the men have started filing in.

As expected, the walls and floor inside are completely black, the room lit surprisingly well by white spotlights in the ceiling. Also on the ceiling are large hooks, likely designed for suspension rigs. Rowan can practically feel his pupils dilate.

A series of glass cases lined with black velvet adorn the walls, filled with more toys than Rowan's ever seen in his *life*. Everything from cords of every color rope to dildos to bondage gear. The cases are surrounded by open black curtains on either side, the silky fabric catching the light and making them shine.

In one corner is a table set up with condoms and numerous bottles of lube, sanitary wipes, a sink with hand towels, and a mini fridge filled with bottles of water. Rowan hadn't considered the logistics of something like this, but it seems like pretty much everything is taken care of.

In the center of the room is a larger than king-size platform bed, topped with a thick black leather cushion rather than a mattress and sheets.

But the bed is much less interesting than what's in front of it.

Who's in front of it.

Malcolm.

And fuck, when Rowan actually takes him in—this mysterious Malcolm whose reputation preceded him from the second Rowan stepped into the club—Rowan's both over- and underwhelmed.

He's standing at the foot of the bed, weight on one leg, with his arms crossed low over his chest. And Rowan doesn't know how to describe what he sees other than *good* in all the right ways, but definitely not how he was expecting.

For one, he's *short*. He can't be more than five foot six or seven to Rowan's six two, and he'd be lying if he said that the height difference didn't do something for him. And he's…. Rowan doesn't want to say stocky, because that tends to come with a certain sense of unattractiveness, but he's broad around the shoulders and chest, clearly defined muscles half hidden beneath a layer of softness in his arms and belly that Rowan immediately wants to squeeze and watch the skin turn white under his fingertips.

And Rowan had expected bronzed, but Malcolm is *pale*, not washed out but with a healthy glow making all that porcelain skin look smoother than it probably is, if the sparse dusting of dark body hair on his arms and legs and the smattering of scars are anything to go by. But the color of his skin is broken by dozens of blackwork tattoos—not an ounce of color from what Rowan can see.

The first piece he notices is across the man's chest, a trio of lilies—the largest in the center with two smaller ones on either pec—intertwined with two old-fashioned pistols aiming toward his shoulders, plumes of smoke swirling out of each barrel and up toward his collarbones. Next comes his right inner forearm, a skull and crossbones shrouded in black mist.

On his rib cage on the left side is a traditional American-style tattoo—minus the color—of a heart with flowers and leaves peeking out behind it and a curled scroll with the word LISA. It stands out among the realistic style of the rest of his tattoos, and Rowan can't help but wonder who she is and what garnered her a position on one of the most painful parts of the body to get tattooed. Rowan still shudders, thinking of the pain of getting his own cross tattoo on his rib cage.

His eyes are drawn downward. Black boxer briefs are the only piece of clothing Malcolm is wearing, tight enough to cause a slight bulge where the fabric digs into the flesh of his thighs and the V of his hips. On his right thigh, a thin strip of detailed lace is inked beneath the hem of the briefs, wrapping around like a fucking garter belt, a knife expertly tattooed underneath as if actually holding the weapon against his skin. Realistically, the blade would cut through the delicate material, but in the world of ink, this impossible scenario is making Rowan's head spin.

There is a smattering of other, smaller tattoos on his arms and something peeking out on either side of his hips underneath his briefs, and Rowan finds that he desperately wants to get closer to inspect them all.

Malcolm rubs his hands over his face, giving Rowan a perfect view of his knuckle tattoos. It takes a second for his brain to register the words upside down, but as soon as it does—the tattoo spelling THUG LIFE—something in him lurches.

He needs to know more about him.

About this man who's completely blindsided him and who has somehow flawlessly combined feminine and masculine symbols on his body to create an image that isn't wholly one or the other. Rowan wonders if maybe he'd gotten the rougher tattoos first—the knife and the skull and the pistols—then come to terms with something about himself that led him to add the lace, the flowers, the heart with a woman's name on it. Or maybe it was the other way around, or maybe neither is true. Either way he desperately wants to find out.

So far he's spent so much time ogling Malcolm's body and tattoos that he's hardly noticed his *face* at all. And when he finally flits his eyes upward, once again his breath catches. Dark hair buzzed short at the sides and longer on top, curling attractively over his forehead. Thick, dark eyebrows that show so much expression even though he's not actively talking. Sharp nose leading to pouty lips that Rowan both wants to kiss and see wrapped around his cock.

And his *eyes*.

God.

Rowan's always been good with words, but coffee and chocolate and all that other corny shit have nothing on the piercing golden caramel of this man's eyes, and no other comparison does them justice. The whole black-and-white aesthetic he has going on is shattered by the pop of gold. And when his eyes flit around the room and land on Rowan's—for the briefest of seconds—Rowan swears his heart stops.

It's clear that the other men around him have seen him before. Hell, most of them have probably fucked him before. But they seem to be so unaffected by his presence, casually chatting with each other and hardly paying attention to him at all, and Rowan can't help but want to grip each of them by the shoulders and *shake*, because how is no one else having as much of a reaction as he is right now?

And fuck, *gorgeous* is the perfect word, isn't it? Rowan understands why he kept hearing it. He's not hot, not handsome, not beautiful, not pretty. He's a combination of all of those things in different, subtle ways. The intensely hot smolder in his eye, the handsome cut of his jaw, the beautiful curve of his cheekbones, the pretty fluttering of his eyelashes… it all adds up to something that Rowan likes far more than he should.

Just… gorgeous.

Throughout his life, especially during his wilder teenage phase, Rowan has been with nearly every type of guy under the sun. But Malcolm is different. It's like he *is* the sun, or some shit. Like he's what Rowan's been gravitating toward his whole life but never managed to catch up to. Always circling, never getting a chance to meet.

But now he has a chance. To fuck the sun, or whatever.

He can feel his insides bubbling with molten desire, then freezing solid at the realization that he might not get picked, and liquefying all over again at the thought of wrapping his hands around that pretty throat and watching those fucking caramel-gold eyes roll back. Club rules be damned.

Before he can get even more lost in thoughts of all the things he wants to do to the man in front of him, he speaks.

"Aright, let's get the boring but necessary shit over with," Malcolm says.

His voice is a soothing baritone with a hint of gravelly rasp to it. And his accent sounds like he's actually from Boston; Rowan knows from overhearing the other men talk that many of them come from out of state to be here, so it's a pleasant surprise.

Malcolm continues, "First off, if you somehow aren't aware, this is a gangbang, not an orgy. You wanna fuck someone else here besides me, get your own goddamn room."

Rowan barely stifles a laugh, has to cover his mouth with his hand to hide his smile. He already likes this guy. Camilla's words echo in his mind: *Gorgeous, confident, incredible scene partner....*

"Before I go over what's on and off the table, my safewords will be the color system. If you're not familiar with that, green is good to go, yellow is slow down or pause, and red is hard stop. Any questions on that?"

Malcolm looks around the room, and apparently seeing no objections, continues.

"Club rules require frequent negative STI tests. That bein' said, if you've been with anyone unprotected since your last check-in, including oral, get the fuck out. This is a bareback scene, and even if you've got the best dick in Boston, I ain't riskin' anything."

He looks pointedly at the crowd for a heated moment before three or four people exit, tails tucked between their legs.

"Fuckin' Christ," Malcolm mumbles, crossing his arms over his chest, biceps bulging. "Anyone else?"

No one else leaves. Rowan's glad he got his test results back yesterday.

"All right. I'll go over what's acceptable and not before I pick, so anyone not cool with anything can also fuck off. On the 'yes' list for tonight: oral and anal, fingering, rimming, spanking. I like it rough, so don't hold back. All positions are on the table. So is double penetration, provided both'a you don't have Mandingo dicks."

There's a murmur in the crowd and quite possibly in Rowan's chest as well. He vaguely recognizes the name as an old porn star with a massive dick, but his brain is currently stuck on the possibility of fucking Malcolm at the same time as another man.

He's been in a threesome before, once, but the bottom wasn't interested in DPing. Even though Rowan's never seen it outside of porn and he knows how much prep it takes, he can't deny how hot it is.

"Calm down, fuckin' animals," Malcolm mumbles. "Club rules obviously apply for the 'no' list. No breath play or choking, though making me gag on your fingers or cock is fine. No cutting, bloodplay, deep biting, or anything else that will leave a lasting mark, including hickeys. No fisting. No toys. And no kissin' on the mouth. You wanna lip-lock with someone else in here, be my guest, but I'll knock you out if you try to kiss me. Spit's fine, though."

Rowan feels a shiver race down his spine. Well, there goes one thing he'd wanted to do with Malcolm's mouth. But it's understandable. He may be about to get fucked by an as-yet-unknown number of people, but kissing is a fairly intimate act, and Rowan doesn't blame him for not wanting to do it with strangers.

"Also," Malcolm continues, "I can't believe I have to say this, but the only bodily fluids allowed on or in me are spit and come, got that?"

The grimace comes to Rowan's face unintentionally, and he feels himself nodding along with the others.

"We're all here for a good time. But break any of the rules or cross my boundaries—or anyone else's here—and I'll make damn sure you get blacklisted. Enrico'll be happy to throw you out, but I have no problem kickin' your ass myself."

It shouldn't, but the threat goes straight to Rowan's dick. He wasn't lying when he said he liked his partners to be scrappy. He assumes Enrico is some kind of bouncer or security guard, but something tells him that Malcolm could take half the guys in this room if he really wanted to.

"Questions?"

The person next to Rowan raises their hand. Rowan can't help but roll his eyes.

Malcolm huffs out an incredulous laugh, raising his eyebrows at the guy. "This ain't middle school, man. What?"

"Sorry, uh, how many are you picking?"

"Ten."

Rowan can feel his lips parting on their own accord.

Ten people.

Christ.

There have to be at least forty people crammed into the room, and maybe more spilling out into the hallway. That means Rowan only has a roughly 25 percent chance of getting picked, and while he's always been a bit of a gambler, a bit of a risk taker, those odds are still a little slim for his liking.

"And," Malcolm starts, taking a deep breath and exhaling through his nose. "My last Dom moved outta state, so I'm lookin' for a new one. Impress me tonight and we'll talk if you're interested." His eyes sweep the crowd, landing on Rowan's for a beat before moving on.

Rowan's pulse quickens as excited whispers spread through the crowd. Although Malcolm didn't specifically say the words *contest* or *competition* or *tryouts*, Rowan can't help but feel that's what this is. And he's never wanted to win something so badly in his entire fuckin' life.

Fuck. He hasn't even seen this guy in action, he reminds himself. He's purely relying on what others have told him of Malcolm's skills in bed. For all he knows, he could be complete shit and not what Rowan's into at all.

But even as he thinks it, his gut tells him that isn't true. Something about the man is utterly magnetic, drawing Rowan in like a lost sailor to a siren promising dry land. He can only hope he doesn't end up drowning chasing blindly after what he wants.

"Any other questions?" Malcolm asks, eyes sweeping around the room. "'Kay. I'm gonna come around, and if I see somethin' I like, you're in. Not just lookin' for who has the best dick, but if you think it's a selling point for ya, feel free to whip it out."

Most of the people around Rowan scramble to undo their pants and either shove them down to mid-thigh or pull their dicks out straight through the zipper hole. Most start jerking off, and Rowan idly wonders if he should too. He knows he has a nice dick and that he's firmly on the "above average" side of things, but something stops him. Call it his ego, but he feels like he doesn't need to show off his dick to be chosen.

Despite Rowan being fairly close to the bed, Malcolm starts on the opposite side of the room closest to the door.

Rowan can barely hear what Malcolm is saying, but he watches him pick each person, not asking for names but rather *giving* them nicknames based on their physical appearance. Rowan sees each man picked circle around against the wall closest to the bed.

The lucky few.

First is a young white guy with light skin, a tall but lean frame, and blond curls. Malcolm dubs him Shirley Temple, which makes Rowan have to stifle another laugh, though he is curious why Malcolm didn't ask for the guy's name.

Next is a Hispanic man—*Shortstop*, though he's actually the same height as Malcolm—with a medium complexion and black shoulder-length hair. A broad chest and thick legs make him look bigger than he is.

Then Jean-Claude, a deeply tanned probably white guy with short brown hair and more muscles than his namesake, if Rowan is correct in assuming Malcolm was going for a Van Damme reference and the guy's name isn't actually Jean-Claude.

By now it seems clear that Malcolm has no interest in learning anyone's name.

A Korean guy is next, and even Rowan could have guessed what his nickname would be. *Leg Day.* As in, the guy probably never does it if his scrawny legs and massive gym-sculpted chest and torso are anything to go by. He's young, early twenties maybe, with overly styled and gelled black hair and an attractive face. The frat boy look is broken only by the scar running from his temple to his cheek.

Next are Tweedle Dee and Tweedle Dum, who don't look anything alike except for the matching red button-up shirts and black bow ties they're wearing. (*Seriously*? Rowan thinks.) "You two plan your outfits or somethin'? Never mind, I don't care. You're both hot, you're in. Fuckin' Tweedle Dee and Tweedle Dum," he hears Malcolm say. He doesn't actually specify which man is meant to be Dee and which Dum, and Rowan can't decide if that's better or worse than the other nicknames so far.

One of them is Japanese, with a swimmer's build, high cheekbones, and short, neatly coiffed black hair. He's an inch or two taller than the other man, though the latter has at least thirty pounds of muscle on the former. He's white with model-messy sandy hair and a figure that looks sculpted through physical labor rather than at the gym.

After them comes The Rock, and yeah, Rowan has to hand it to Malcolm. He does kind of look like The Rock. An older man, probably in his forties, with a medium complexion and no hair except for a goatee. His musculature rivals that of his namesake, save for the slight paunch around his belly and thighs.

Then comes Cupcake. Rowan has no idea where he got that name from, since the guy is at least six four or six five and built like a strongman. He has dark skin, long black hair in neat twists pulled back into a low ponytail and accentuated with colorful beads, and a short but full beard. It might be the beads, he thinks. Something about sprinkles?

Finally there's Tats, which is the least original of the names. He looks Middle Eastern, with deep olive skin, dark hair that's tied into a bun, and stubble on his face. An athletic body and cheekbones that give even Malcolm's a run for their money. And of course full sleeve tattoos on both arms in a variety of colors and designs.

From the lineup, it's pretty hard to tell if Malcolm has a type other than *big*. Only one of his picks is the same height as Malcolm is—Shortstop—but his musculature makes up for his lack of height compared to everyone else.

Rowan mentally slaps himself for already thinking of these men in terms of the names Malcolm has called them, but really, without names, what else is he going to call them? He'd be thinking much the same things, but probably a little less insulting in most cases.

He thinks briefly of the woman who had choked her scene partner a few days ago. *I don't even know his real name*, she'd said. Rowan suppresses a shudder. There are positives and negatives to being anonymous in places like this, but for Malcolm that anonymity only goes one way. Because everyone sure as hell knows who *he* is, but he doesn't seem interested in learning about anyone else.

There's only room for one more person, if Malcolm sticks to ten people. And with at least a dozen people still milling around between the two of them, Rowan's chances are suddenly a lot slimmer than they were a few minutes ago.

Miraculously, Malcolm passes by all of them and stops in front of Rowan. He gives him an obvious once-over from his shoes up to his hair, then quirks his eyebrows at him.

"Never been with a redhead before. Carpet match the drapes?"

Rowan almost rolls his eyes at him, barely stopping himself. He really hates that question, but he does actually want to get picked, so he's thankful he manages to steel his face.

"Gonna have to see for yourself."

"Oh yeah? Not gonna pull it out like everyone else?"

"Don't need to. Either you're into me or you're not. My dick's not gonna change your mind no matter how good it is."

"You think you're hot shit, huh." It's not a question.

"All the people I've made cry seemed to think so."

Douchey, but true. Rowan knows he's good in bed. Though he doubts he'd be able to make Malcolm cry in a group full of other people, he's filled with the sudden hope that he'll get a chance to try.

He'd love to see those golden eyes filled with tears.

The corners of Malcolm's lips dip into a quick frown as his eyebrows raise, looking *impressed*, and he nods. "'Kay. You're in, then. Better not disappoint me, Red."

"Wouldn't dream of it."

Despite the confidence in his words, Rowan's heart is pounding in his chest. *Red.* He'd been expecting Carrot Top, Chucky, Bozo, Firecrotch… anything along those lines. Red is a significantly better name than the rest of them, but he doesn't let himself read into it.

"All right, the rest of ya, get out."

The size of the crowd had already diminished as Malcolm passed over each person, and the rest file out, the last man closing the doors behind him.

Holy shit.

This is happening.

This is *happening.*

"Been trying to get in on one of these things for *years*," the guy next to Rowan—*Van Damme*—whispers.

"Really?"

"Yeah. Guy's supposed to be super fuckin' hard to please."

"Says who?"

"*Everyone*, man. You new here or somethin'? Can't wait to finally show 'im what he's been missin'."

Rowan doesn't respond, partly because he has nothing to say, and partly because something about the guy's tone makes him want to knock his teeth out. Instead he wonders how many of the others here are in the same boat as that guy, having waited to get invited to a scene like this for ages when Rowan had more or less rolled in off the street and gotten picked the first time.

He turns his attention back to Malcolm, who eyes the lot of them before circling around the bed to face them. The breath Rowan had been exhaling catches in his throat as he waits for the other man to do something. To signal for them to *start*, because he's never done this before and doesn't know how these things are supposed to work.

At once, Malcolm drops to his knees, punching out the rest of the breath from Rowan's lungs and answering his question all in one.

Fuck.

"Well?" he asks, a shit-eating grin on his face. "Who's first?"

Fuck.

The Van Damme look-alike steps up first, shirt already gone and jeans unbuttoned and unzipped. He strokes himself roughly a few times, then with zero finesse, grabs Malcolm by the hair and yanks his head back, rubbing his cock along Malcolm's parted lips. Rowan feels his body jerk forward, his *fight* mode kicking in as it would when he had to protect one of his siblings from a schoolyard bully, but the low groan that pours from Malcolm's throat stops him in his tracks.

Because fuck, this is what he wants, isn't it?

To be *used*.

Fuck.

With that, the floodgates have been opened. The rest of the group starts shedding whatever clothing they have left on, a couple flinging pieces haphazardly on the floor, others stashing them in the cubicle against the side wall that Rowan had overlooked in favor of ogling the sex toys.

He strips down to nothing, quickly folds and stashes his clothes in a cubby in time to see Malcolm take the man's cock into his mouth, lips tight and cheeks hollowed and eyes closed like he's savoring it. Rowan's own cock jumps at the sight, blood rushing down when Malcolm starts bobbing his head.

The Van Damme look-alike throws his head back and groans loudly while curling his fingers in Malcolm's hair.

And fuck, Rowan needs to get closer. It's been barely more than two minutes since he started, but already the other men have circled around Malcolm like vultures, eagerly awaiting their turn. Rowan joins them, shoulder to shoulder with the Tweedles, unashamedly looking at the nine other men around him, admiring their bodies.

He notes, with not a small amount of pride, that aside from Tats, whose cock is a bit longer than his—though skinnier—and Cupcake's, whose is wider around the base, Rowan has the biggest dick of the lot. Most of them Rowan could see himself fucking if they bottomed. He's attractive enough himself to be picky about his sexual partners, but why bother as long as his partner gets him going?

"How's his mouth, man?" the Rock look-alike asks.

"Fuckin' incredible."

Rowan watches his technique. Watches him bob his head and relax his jaw and stick out his tongue and flick his fingers over the head each time he pulls off to take a gasping breath when breathing through his nose isn't enough. Watches him *savor* every moment of having a dick in his mouth. Like a goddamn porn star or something.

It's gotta be good with the groans pouring out of Van Damme's mouth. With how quickly he pulls off with a slap to Malcolm's cheek and the next man takes his place. And Malcolm doesn't bat an eye at each new cock presented to him, taking in each as greedily as the one before it until he's blown most of the group. His jaw must ache, 'cause fuck, Rowan knows his does after a while, after just one dick, but Malcolm's *that* good, apparently.

Rowan's achingly hard. His hand isn't enough. Not when there's a *very* willing mouth a couple feet away that's all warmed up.

He steps up next to the guy with the skinny legs, whose head is thrown back while Malcolm works him over. Feeling Rowan approach, he grins, grips Malcolm's hair and tugs him off, cock slipping out with a lewd *pop*.

"Almost fuckin' came, dude," he says, clamping a hand around the base of his dick. "Can't wait to try his other hole."

Rowan doesn't respond, simply runs his fingers through Malcolm's mussed hair—*soft soft soft*—to get him to open his eyes. When he does, Rowan could laugh at how they widen as he takes in the sight before him. As a redhead with matching pubes and a big dick, he's used to it, but it never fails to kick up his heart rate a notch. Malcolm's head snaps up to gape at him.

"That answer your question?" Rowan asks teasingly.

The only response he gets is a breathy, low *"Fuuuck"* before Malcolm wraps his hand around Rowan's shaft, small hands not able to wrap fully around the widest part of him—fuck, why is that so hot?—and dips his head underneath, eyes closed. Rowan's cock spans his entire face—fuck, why is *that* so hot?—and he lets out a long groan.

Definitely a size queen.

God, even though it's obvious from the fact that he's blown so many people already, the knowledge that Malcolm is this much of a cock slut makes Rowan impossibly harder. Malcolm tongues at the base, hot breath sending a shiver down Rowan's spine before he pulls back and sucks him more than halfway down.

"*Nnnng, shit*," Rowan gasps.

His brain is stuck in a mantra of *hot wet tight hot wet tight* as Malcolm works him over, tongue laving around his head and along the veins in his shaft like it's the best thing he's ever tasted and can't get enough of. And when he finally starts bobbing his head in earnest, lips pulled tight and tongue flattening out beneath, it's heavenly. His fingers, slick from his own spit and the precome from a half dozen other men, wrap perfectly around Rowan's dick, and he pumps Rowan in time with the motion of his head.

He cradles Rowan's balls in his free hand, rolling them deftly and tugging as he pulls back, and it's so fucking *good* that Rowan can hardly think straight.

Shit.

Shit shit *shit*.

Rowan's never been one to blow his load early, but he might right now because he feels like he's going to pass out. And when Rowan tugs on his hair harder and Malcolm opens his eyes, shimmering gold nearly completely blacked out by blown pupils, he nearly does.

Fuckin' incredible is *right*.

But he remembers the first guy who'd wrenched Malcolm's head back and gotten the loudest groan of the night so far, and Rowan wants to get him to top that. He tangles both hands in Malcolm's hair and holds the other man's head still while he thrusts his hips—gently at first, earning him a whimper. Good, but not enough.

When he feels Malcolm's jaw slacken, he pistons his hips harder, faster, until he's fucking Malcolm's face like he's been dying to see someone do for the past however long it's been, balls slapping against his chin. It's not as tight as when Malcolm was in control, but fuck, it's almost better, the fast friction driving Rowan insane. But he wants more, and he'd bet his life that Malcolm does too. So he thrusts in a couple more inches of his length, instantly causing a gurgling cough to bubble up as his cock hits the back of Malcolm's throat.

The other man pulls off with a pant, catching his breath as spit dribbles down his red lips and his chin. Rowan quirks an eyebrow at him in a silent question, and in response, Malcolm wraps his hands around the back of Rowan's thighs and sucks him back down.

"*Fuck*, that's good. Knew you could take more," Rowan tells him.

The calls from the men around them agree.

"Yeah, that's all he's good for."

"Fuckin' slut. Look at him gag for it."

"Wonder if his ass is as greedy as his mouth is."

Rowan drives his hips forward, fucking into Malcolm's mouth, the faintest scrape of teeth every few thrusts making Rowan inhale sharply and fuck him faster, gripping his hair in warning. And each time he pulls, he gets a louder moan from Malcolm. The sounds rattle against his cock like a fucking vibrator, and Rowan's going to come. He's gonna come too soon like a teenager for fuck's sake, and as much as he wants to fill Malcolm's hot mouth with his come or paint his pretty face, he needs to control himself.

"Enough," Rowan says, grabbing the base of his cock and pulling out.

Malcolm's eyebrows knit together, but he pulls off with a pant before looking up expectantly, chest heaving.

"Get on the bed."

"'Bout fuckin' time we got this show started," someone calls out behind Rowan.

He couldn't agree more.

Before Malcolm can even rise up to his knees fully, the strongman guy—Cupcake—hauls him up under his armpits like he's not a fully grown man and dumps him on the bed. He lands on his knees, falling forward and catching himself on his hands with a *slap*! against the leather cushion before he faceplants onto it.

"Fuckin' finally," Malcolm says. "Someone better get somethin' in my ass before I start to get bitchy."

"What d'you mean *start*?" Tats calls out, making a few of the other men laugh.

"Sounds like you're volunteering for the class."

"Stick that ass up for me and I just might."

Malcolm makes a *tch* sound, but arches his back and pushes his ass out to form a sinuous curve, the fabric of his briefs stretched tight across each cheek. And fuck, Rowan's been trying to get a good look at his ass all night, only getting glimpses of it from the side while he was picking people or when he was kneeling and blowing them.

But God if it isn't perfect, even clothed. Muscular with a touch of softness, like the rest of him. And when Tats slaps one cheek and pulls the fabric halfway down the back of his thighs, it's even better, smooth and round with dimples on his lower back and on the sides of each cheek.

Cupcake climbs on the bed in front of Malcolm and slaps his cheek with his cock once, twice, until Malcolm opens and sucks him down. The two Tweedles climb on either side of him, jerking off until Malcolm switches his attention to each of them in turn, supporting himself on one arm so he can stroke one of them while he blows another. His coordination is unreal; Rowan doesn't think even *he* could navigate so much dick. The rest of the men circle around the bed, half watching in front and half in back of Malcolm, all jerking off, some making out with one another. It's hot, but Rowan really doesn't give a fuck about any except one.

His attention snaps back to where Tats is now digging his fingers into Malcolm's ass, whose skin turns white as Tats spreads his cheeks. Rowan has to get closer. He jumps on the bed next to Tats in time to see him run the pad of his thumb over Malcolm's pink hole, and fuck, it's so smooth—the faintest bit of peach fuzz on his ass. He's glad it doesn't look like he waxes or shaves, though, because Rowan's always been more attracted to guys with body hair.

"Beautiful," Tats says, stroking over Malcolm's hole with his fingers.

Rowan watches it twitch at the contact, feeling his own dick twitch at the sight. He pulls Malcolm's briefs the rest of the way down, tugging at the fabric when they reach his knees to pull them off completely and fling them to the floor.

"Lick him," Rowan says. He'd much rather do it himself, but he can be patient.

Tats does as instructed, tongue shooting out to lave over Malcolm's hole in one long stripe.

"*Mmf*!" The whine must come from Malcolm, but with *two* dicks in his mouth, it's muffled.

"No talking with your mouth full," someone says from the front of the bed.

"Fuck you, Tweedle Dum," Malcolm answers, voice hoarse. "Wouldn't hafta if you'd actually use that dick of your—*hnnnn*!"

Rowan can't see, but he assumes some combination of a dick being shoved down Malcolm's throat and Tats burying his face between his cheeks has something to do with the cut-off goading.

Rowan lies on his side to finally get a good look at Malcolm's cock, hard and already leaking precome. He doesn't wanna call it *cute*, because he's pretty sure Malcolm would deck him if he did. It's on the smaller side of average, but it's *thick*, and shit, he needs to taste it.

"Hey, lemme get under him," Rowan says to Tats.

"I want to taste his ass," The Rock look-alike says right after.

Tats pulls off to let Rowan slide underneath Malcolm's hips. It's an awkward position with Malcolm's short legs, but he makes it work.

"You good if I straddle you, man?" The Rock asks Rowan.

"Yeah."

The older man takes the okay and straddles Rowan around his waist, thick thighs encompassing him and hard cock draped over Rowan's stomach. A bolt of heat shoots through him at being surrounded like this, reminding him that soon he's likely going to be buried inside Malcolm at the same time as someone else. He can't wait.

Craning his neck, he finally gets a good look at Malcolm's hip tattoos—vining ivy with thorns on either side of his sculpted V. And the artwork is beautiful, but he's much more interested in his cock. He sucks the tip into his mouth and gets a startled jerk of Malcolm's hips in response, one hand resting on Malcolm's thigh to stop him from fucking into his mouth any farther. With his free hand, he cups Malcolm's balls, rolling them in his palm as a dribble of precome seeps out onto his tongue.

It's sweet, like he's been chugging pineapple juice all week or something. Rowan wouldn't put it past him for something like this. He sucks harder. By now the whimpers are flowing freely from above him, faintly audible over the groans and slick sounds of people jerking off around them.

Rowan feels the bed dip as the men in front of Malcolm change places, but he can't tell who joins.

"Someone get some lube," The Rock says.

Rowan takes that as his cue to reach under and tap him on the thigh so he can shimmy out from underneath. Because as much as he'd like to keep sucking Malcolm's dick until he's squirming above him, there's no way he's going to miss something entering his ass for the first time.

In the few seconds it takes him to switch from lying to kneeling beside him, the Japanese guy—Tweedle Dee? Dum? Rowan has no clue—has taken up position behind Malcolm, bottle of lube in hand. He squirts some onto his palm, warming it between his hands briefly before unceremoniously slathering it over Malcolm's hole.

"Hurry the fuck up and get in me," Malcolm barks.

"So impatient," the man responds, sinking in one long, slim finger. "What, is four hours not enough time for you to spend getting fucked that you've gotta rush through it?"

"Ah! Don't see anyone here rushin' *shit*."

"Hm. How's this for rushing?"

He sinks in two more fingers, and Malcolm's hole swallows them like it's nothing. He must have prepped beforehand, at least somewhat, because someone taking three fingers with only a bit of rimming beforehand can be a pretty tall order unless they get fucked constantly.

Oh, but that's a nice thought. Malcolm being ready to get fucked at a moment's notice. Fucked by Rowan specifically. He files the image away for later.

"Better," Malcolm replies. "But not enough by a long shot."

Rowan's torn between wanting to hear every noise he makes and wanting him to shut the hell up and stop being a greedy brat and take what everyone here wants to give him. He settles on the latter. Malcolm is starting to say something else while he's being fingered open when Rowan brings his hand up and slaps him hard on his left asscheek, the flesh warm under his hand.

"Fuck!" Malcolm cries out.

"Unless you wanna get split in half, you'll fuckin' wait till we get you ready," Rowan tells him.

"Fuckin'—"

Slap!

"—*nnnng!*"

Rowan smooths his hand over the reddening skin, feels the goose bumps pebble up underneath his fingers and the not-so-subtle hitching of Malcolm's hips back against his touch. Looking for more. And that tiny movement is something Rowan's going to be thinking about for the rest of his life.

He slides his hand down Malcolm's crack and presses his middle finger in alongside the other man's three fingers, drawing a gasp from Malcolm. And it's *tight* as he tugs on the rim, definitely not stretched enough to take Rowan's cock right now, but some of the others? Absolutely.

At Malcolm's demand for "More, fuck," Rowan sinks in his ring finger, opening him up along with the other man, who spits into his open hole between their fingers, slicking the way as they stretch him.

"Think he's ready to take the first dick tonight?" someone from up front asks.

"Hell yeah," someone from behind replies.

"I got dibs," Shortstop says, climbing onto the bed from where he'd been standing on the side, lazily making out with the frat boy, Leg Day. His dick is pretty average in length, thickest around the middle, but his balls are large and hang low between his legs.

"'Bout time," Malcolm grumbles.

He pulls off the cocks he's been sucking and jerking and sits back on his heels. No sooner than his ass touches his ankles, he's flipped over onto his back and yanked down to the edge of the bed.

Shortstop slides up behind Malcolm's spread legs, lubing his cock with one hand and fingering Malcolm with the other.

"Ready, baby?" he asks, rubbing the head of his cock over Malcolm's hole.

"Call me baby again 'n you'll be fuckin' your hand tonight."

Rowan snorts.

"You got it, man."

With that, the man presses his dick in slow, but Rowan's eyes snap to Malcolm's face and sees his eyes roll back before they flutter closed. Like he's a junkie getting a desperately needed fix after going through the beginnings of withdrawal. He bites his bottom lip, his two front teeth the slightest bit longer than the rest of them, and Rowan shouldn't find it cute, not when Malcolm's flushed and getting fucked open, but he does.

"Fuuuuck that's good," Malcolm moans.

Rowan can't be bothered to figure out who's speaking when the men around him spew all sorts of filth about how Malcolm looks, but he finds it hard to disagree with any of them.

"Look at how good he takes dick."

"C'mon, fuck him, he's been desperate for it all night."

"Can't let his mouth and hands go to waste."

The guy fucking him picks up the pace, hips slapping lewdly, punctuated only by Malcolm's sharp pants. Until the Shirley Temple guy straddles his shoulders and pushes his cock into his mouth, the sounds now little more than muffled whimpers. The Van Damme and The Rock look-alikes kneel on either side, and Rowan can't see clearly from where he is, but he sees Malcolm's arms move, and the men throw their heads back, evidently both being jerked off simultaneously.

And fuck if that isn't the hottest thing ever.

Rowan's watched a lot of porn. Been to a lot of clubs. Fucked a lot of people. But he never realized how loud sex could be, especially in as large a group as this. Moans and grunts and skin slapping and *Yeah*s and *Fuck yeah*s and *That's it*s fill the air in a filthy cacophony of noise that equally turns Rowan on and annoys him.

Annoys only because he wants to hear more of Malcolm. His sweet little gasps and breathy moans as he's being filled from both ends. And Rowan doesn't know how sensitive Malcolm is, but he dips his head to Malcolm's chest and sucks a pert nipple into his mouth, the sharp inhale he hears over the din answer enough. He tweaks and pinches Malcolm's other nipple, alternating between teasing it and squeezing his pec, reveling in how nicely it fits in his hand.

In seemingly no time at all, Shortstop gasps, "'M gonna come. Fuck, man, can I come in you?"

Malcolm pushes the guy out of his mouth. "You fuckin' better."

"Shit, shit, *shit*—" he gasps, Rowan lifting his head up from Malcolm's chest to see the man's hips stutter as he comes with a long groan.

"Fuck yeah, fill him up."

"First of many tonight!"

"Best cumdump in all'a Boston."

As all the men around them chime in, the white guy Malcolm had dubbed Tweedle Dum (or Dee) grunts from the side of the bed, furiously jerking his cock as he comes on the leather pad.

Malcolm must see it, and he doesn't sound happy about it. "*Jesus.* If you ain't gonna fuck me, at least jerk off on me."

The guy has the decency to look sheepish. "Sorry, man. You're fuckin' hot."

"No shit, Sherlock. Better get it up again before the night's over."

Cupcake laughs low. "Don't wanna disappoint the cumslut. Nine loads just won't do it. My turn next."

He shifts around on the bed, the other man pulling out as Cupcake gets in place. He tugs Malcolm farther down the bed until his ass is right on the edge and throws his legs over his shoulders. With no hesitation, he pushes inside, Rowan noting that his cock is significantly bigger than the last guy's.

Still not bigger than his, though.

And still not too big for Malcolm's apparently *very* greedy ass to handle.

Cupcake sets a faster pace than the last guy, and Malcolm responds instantly, back arching off the bed, eyebrows and toes scrunching.

"Mmm, fuck, like that."

Rowan makes a mental note that Malcolm likes *fast* and *hard*.

The guy fucking Malcolm clearly knows how to use his dick, but his stamina is limited to short bursts every minute or so, and even as an almost exclusive top, Rowan can tell that it's not doing anything for Malcolm after a short while.

With little warning, he pulls out with a gasp, apparently not wanting to finish yet. "Shit, that was good."

"For *you* maybe," Malcolm mutters under his breath.

"You wanna go?" the Japanese guy who fingered Malcolm earlier asks Rowan.

"Not yet."

He does, but he wants to wait. Wants to see what everyone else has to offer before he steps in. Because cocky as it is, he knows he can make Malcolm fall apart on his dick.

The other guy shrugs and climbs onto the bed, nudging Malcolm to roll over onto his stomach and move up until his head is near the edge of the bed. He straddles the back of Malcolm's thighs as he pushes into him in one quick motion, punching out a gasp from him. Rowan rounds to the front of the bed and takes advantage of Malcolm's open mouth by shoving his dick in. It's been neglected for far too long.

"*Mmf!*" Malcolm pants but immediately sets to work. It's as good as the first time, maybe even better due to him being fucked from behind and driven deeper onto Rowan's dick with each thrust.

The guy currently fucking him changes position so he's almost planking above Malcolm, and drives his full body weight onto him with each thrust, the slap of skin loud and sharp as a whipcrack.

"Now *that's* more like it," someone says.

"Look at that fucking ass jiggle," someone else calls out.

Malcolm's eyes are closed as he blows Rowan, but Rowan can tell from the way they're squeezed tight that Malcolm's enjoying himself. Though with his response to the first two guys who fucked him compared to when he'd taken Rowan's dick in his mouth the first time, it's hard to tell what he's getting off on more right now.

Like the first two, the third guy is quick to climax. With a whine, he pulls out and erupts onto Malcolm's raised ass, several streaks of come dripping down his cheeks.

Should've fucked it back into him, Rowan thinks.

Malcolm pulls off Rowan's dick, pushing himself up onto his elbows as he says, "Christ, anyone here actually know how to find a fuckin' prostate?"

Rowan winces. Because it isn't hard. Easier with fingers than a dick and easier when you get to know your partner better, but still absolutely doable. And isn't the point of a gangbang to please the bottom? Either everyone here is selfish and sucks at fucking, or Malcolm really *is* as hard to please as everyone thinks.

He steps down from the bed and circles around to the side to watch. The Van Damme look-alike offers to jerk Rowan off, and he lets him. He's the least attractive of the bunch to Rowan, but a hand's a hand. He turns down his offer to make out.

While he's getting jerked off, Rowan watches as each person takes turns fucking Malcolm. And Malcolm complains about or taunts every one of them.

Shirley Temple is next, fucking him lazily in missionary like he's too afraid of hurting him.

"I remember my first time too," Malcolm coos derisively.

The white Tweedle is next, fucking him doggy style. He keeps too loose a grip on Malcolm's hips and doesn't get enough power to pull him back hard enough on each thrust.

"Thought I'd at least have a coupl'a bruises tonight."

Van Damme steps up after, having made his way around the circle sloppily making out with or jerking off most of the other members, and he fucks Malcolm on their sides, back to chest. Not the best position to be in for any kind of power fucking. With all the bravado he'd shown earlier, Rowan expected *something* impressive. But his fucking skills seem to be on par with his hand job skills—not all that great.

"Always been more of a Seagal fan, anyway," Malcolm grumbles.

Van Damme is replaced by the frat boy, who struggles to keep up a steady rhythm as he takes Malcolm over the side of the bed.

"Not as easy as *Fifty Shades* makes it look, huh, Leg Day?"

None of them get Malcolm on top, which is a shame, because Rowan would bet he'd look amazing, thick thighs straining and abs flexing.

Disappointingly, every single one of them jackhammers into him for a minute or two, most coming and pulling out, others grasping the base of their dicks to stave off orgasm. From the look on Malcolm's face—parted lips, jaw slack, knitted eyebrows, sweat beading on his temples—it's clear that he's enjoying himself, even with all the taunting and the bitching he's doing.

But Rowan wants to see him fall apart completely, and the ferocity of that desire surprises him.

"Beg for my come," the frat boy tells Malcolm when it's clear he's nearing his end. His voice is pitched lower, but it sounds utterly fake. Like he's playing at being in charge. Not something he's used to.

"I don't beg for *anyone*, kid," Malcolm snaps back.

Last up is the guy who looks like The Rock, and he's undoubtedly the best of the lot. He flips Malcolm onto his back and pushes into him swiftly, then hooks his arms under his knees and hoists him up, making Malcolm wrap his arms around his neck for support.

Malcolm's "Fuck yes, finally" sounds relieved as the man uses all those muscles to lift him up and drop him down on his dick over and over with a sharp *slap slap slap.*

It's a good position, Malcolm clearly getting off on being manhandled as much as actually being fucked how he wants to be. Rowan feels the heat begin to pool in his belly and his cock harden fully for the first time in too long. Since it was last down Malcolm's throat in fact.

He strokes himself, watching hungrily as Malcolm starts to sweat above the man, cock hard and bouncing between them.

But it doesn't last. After a few meager minutes, the older man's already nearing his end.

"Sh-shit, I'm coming," he groans, hips jerking erratically and eyes squeezing closed as he lifts Malcolm up one final time and drops him down, clutching his asscheeks tightly as he empties inside him.

Rowan thinks he sees Malcolm sigh as he's lowered back onto the bed.

"Can't believe I actually pay for this shit," he mumbles. "Anyone here able to last more than ten goddamn seconds?" he calls louder. "Or do I gotta resort to the toy wall like last time?"

There are a few grumbles of complaint, but no one speaks up.

And Rowan? Rowan's had enough.

Enough of everyone here being shit at fucking. Enough of waiting for his turn. Enough of Malcolm's fuckin' bratty attitude, justified as it may be. As soon as The Rock steps aside, Rowan spins Malcolm to face him, legs on either side of Rowan's own, the smaller man looking up at him with a quirked eyebrow. He's about to open his mouth, no doubt to say something shitty, when Rowan grabs the back of his skull, wrenching his head back so he's forced to look up at him further.

"Shut the *fuck* up."

Unsurprisingly to Rowan, he does. No one acts like this much of a brat during sex unless they want to be put in their place. And boy does Malcolm *exude* the desire to have the fight stripped out of him.

With his other hand, Rowan cups either side of Malcolm's jaw, squeezing but not getting the reaction he wants. He squeezes again, harder, flesh turning white under his fingertips, but Malcolm doesn't budge.

"Open."

Malcolm's lips finally part, hot breath tickling the webbing between Rowan's thumb and index finger. Rowan gathers his spit on his tongue, opens his own mouth with a raised eyebrow in a silent question as he'd done earlier. Malcolm said no kissing, but with everything he's had done to him tonight, everything he's reacted most violently to, Rowan can say with near certainty that he'll love this.

In response, his eyes widen and he nods, a tiny dip of his head against the tight grip of Rowan's hands, but a *yes* all the same.

Perfect.

Rowan spits into his mouth, pushing in the few droplets that don't make it with his fingers and pressing his jaw shut.

"Good. Keep that warm for me till I'm done with you."

Malcolm's whimper tells him everything he needs to know about how he feels about that.

Rowan pushes him back down onto the bed, the smaller man bouncing up an inch with the force of it, and tugs him by his thighs until he's nestled perfectly against Rowan's hips. And he wants to focus on the sight of his cock pushing into his sloppy hole, pink and open and leaking a steady stream of come from a half dozen other men, but more than that, he wants to watch Malcolm's face.

Wants to see the look in his eyes when he realizes he's about to be fucked properly for the first time tonight.

It doesn't disappoint. As Rowan pushes into the tight heat, Malcolm's eyes widen, his eyebrows shoot up, his nostrils flare, his chest heaves. His mouth stays firmly shut.

Good.

Despite having the largest cock in the room, Rowan doesn't give him more than a moment to adjust as soon as he's worked all nine inches into him. Because he knows full well that Malcolm is a size queen, and that he likes a bit of pain, and that he's been ogling Rowan's dick all night, eagerly sucking it down every time Rowan presented it to his waiting lips.

And finally being inside him?

Fucking heavenly.

He's almost willing to take back the negative thoughts he'd had about everyone else coming so soon with Malcolm's hole gripping him like a vise, but he doesn't want this feeling to end. This heat radiating from his dick through his core and straight out to all his limbs, burning where his hands are wrapped around Malcolm's sweaty thighs. He wants this moment to last forever.

Like he's mentally frozen everyone else in the room, Rowan's focus hones in on Malcolm's face as he spreads the smaller man's legs as wide as they'll go on either side of Rowan's own hips and clutches him around his waist. It's not the best position for hard and fast fucking, but it's perfect for hitting that sweet spot inside him that somehow everyone here has either completely missed or accidentally hit once or twice and never found again.

He tilts his hips down, pulls out, angles up a bit, and *thrusts* back in as hard as he can.

"Mmmmm-hm-hm-hmmm!" Malcolm cries out, loud despite his closed mouth.

It's music to Rowan's ears.

He sets a punishing pace and pumps into him, dragging Malcolm's hips onto his cock for extra power on each thrust so he can wring as much pleasure out of the other man's body as possible. Every thrust is punctuated with a "*Hmm*!" or an "*Mmm*!" and it's fucking perfect. The best thing Rowan's ever heard short of full-out moans, because he knows that with each muffled whimper, Malcolm is keeping Rowan's spit locked inside.

He's *obeying*.

And Rowan wants to reward him.

As good as he knows an endless assault on the prostate can be, he wants him to fully experience everything he has to offer. So he slides his hands under Malcolm's low back and lifts his lower half off the bed, calves hooked over his shoulders and thighs pressed firmly to his chest.

He pulls out and fucks into him, hard, like everyone else should have been doing all goddamn night. More whimpers fill the air. It's incredible how loud Malcolm can be, even with a closed mouth, even with dozens of other sounds competing for space in Rowan's ears.

While the fucking is good, *great* even, Malcolm's dick has been almost completely ignored since Rowan blew him.

"Touch yourself," Rowan tells him.

The reaction is instant. Malcolm's right hand shoots straight to his dick, gathering the steady stream of precome leaking onto his stomach. Rowan watches his fingers, mesmerized by the THUG tattooed on his knuckles. Notes that he's only gripping with three fingers, his ring and pinkie finger simply resting against the shaft as he works himself over. A twist right at the tip. A looser grip on the downstroke.

He catalogs it all, hoping that he'll get a chance to put that knowledge to use either later tonight or in the future.

Somewhere to the side of the bed, he hears an "I'm gonna come!" and snaps his head to see the blond Shirley Temple guy jerking off furiously.

"Get up here and come on him," Rowan growls.

Because somehow, no one's come anywhere except inside or on top of Malcolm's ass yet. And Rowan wants to see him *filthy*.

The guy obeys, hustling onto the bed in time to shoot his load over Malcolm's stomach and cock with a deep moan.

But Malcolm's is louder. His hand works faster over his cock, gripping tight, using the other man's come to slick his motions. And Rowan pistons into him, matching his pace. He can feel the sweat starting to bead on his temples, but he'd rather combust than stop anytime soon.

He's lost track of how long he's been going. Several of the men have climbed on the bed, shoved their dicks in Malcolm's face to take advantage of his free hole, only to have him forcefully turn his head away, lips sealed, and offer his hand instead.

So fucking good.

Apparently, all it takes to shut him up is a big dick and some spit.

"Someone come on his face," Rowan says.

"Gladly," Cupcake replies, joining them on the bed and hovering over Malcolm's face, balls nearly touching his forehead as he jerks himself in quick motions. "Been wanting to do this all night."

In a half dozen more tight strokes, he groans and empties himself over Malcolm's pristine face, thick and so much that it's really a shame he wasn't better at fucking, because it's undeniably hot. His come coats Malcolm's cheeks and chin and lips, dribbling down his neck and pooling in the hollow of his throat as he lets out a keening whine, eyes rolling back in his head.

One by one, everyone who didn't come earlier climbs on the bed and unloads on every part of Malcolm's flushed body, his neck and chest and cock, covering his ink in ribbons of white that melt on his heated skin and drip onto the leather underneath him. And God, he's gorgeous. Moaning each and every time someone releases on him. Moaning louder when Rowan fucks into him deep and squeezes his shaking thighs against his chest.

The quivering starts in his thighs and radiates out to the rest of him, his lower back and his core and his arms all vibrating violently, ass clenching furiously around Rowan's cock. He has to be close. It's a fucking wonder he hasn't come already tonight, but Rowan wants to be the first to get him there. So he drops Malcolm's legs down, Malcolm instantly wrapping them around Rowan's waist as Rowan lowers his ass to the edge of the bed, and hoists him up by the back of his neck so they're mere inches apart.

The angle is awkward—he has to squat down a bit to fuck him like this, thighs burning—but the heat from Malcolm's body and the feeling of him sucking Rowan in deeper is worth it.

Rowan pulls him in close, wipes the residual come from his lips and chin with the hand not wrapped around the back of his neck.

"Show me," he whispers.

This time Malcolm's lips part immediately, giving Rowan a perfect view of the frothy spit filling his mouth. He could have swallowed Rowan's spit. Easily. Could have generated his own to replace Rowan's and he'd be none the wiser, but Rowan knows in his gut Malcolm didn't. Knows that what he's seeing is his own spit mixed with Malcolm's, and fuck if that doesn't almost make him come on the spot.

"*Good.* Swallow it."

With his mouth open, Malcolm's tongue flattens against the roof of his mouth, and with a quick bob of his Adam's apple, his mouth is empty. But better than that is the glazed-over look in his eyes. Rowan knows that look. Didn't think he'd get to see it tonight, not really, because he's been told that it's hard to slip into sub mode with so many people around, so much distraction, but holy shit does it make Rowan impossibly harder.

Fuck, he thinks. *This guy's gonna be the death of me.*

He wraps a hand around Malcolm's cock and quickens his hips, wanting to reward him for being so fucking filthy. Malcolm pants in response.

"Now come for me."

"*Hnnnnng!*"

The moan ripped from Malcolm's throat is hoarse and raw and so loud Rowan's surprised all the glass toy cabinets haven't shattered around them. It drowns out every single other sound in the room, everyone else's groans and grunts and leers and jerking, and Rowan wants to bottle it up and save it for whenever he needs a reason to get hard at a moment's notice.

Malcolm's ass clenches wildly, and his eyebrows knit together. As if in slow motion, his breath leaves him in a rush and his cock erupts in Rowan's hand, coating his fingers with hot come. Rowan strokes him through it, senses finally returning to normal after nearly blacking out everything around him to focus entirely on the man beneath him.

He's only human, and Rowan can't hold back any longer.

The slowly building pool of heat in his belly turns into an inferno as he finally focuses on taking his own pleasure, using Malcolm exactly how he so obviously wants to be used. He pistons into him, body in overdrive, muscles aching. As soon as he feels his balls tighten, he forces himself to pull out and fist his cock, and in two, three, five tugs his vision whites out and he's coating Malcolm's vine-covered hips in come with a deep satisfied groan.

Malcolm drops to the bed, boneless, as soon as Rowan releases the back of his neck to wipe the sweat off of his forehead. And fuck, he's beautiful, sprawled on the bed without a care and dripping come and sweat and fucking *glistening* under the overhead lights like he's made of goddamn Swarovski crystals.

He could spend the rest of the night admiring him, but the night's not over.

"I think it's time to see how much of a cock slut he really is," Tats says.

As if all of that hadn't already proved it a thousand times over.

Rowan would say they should take a breather, give him a break, but Malcolm sits up in one fluid motion, rolls onto his knees and spreads his asscheeks apart, giving Rowan a perfect view of the hole he'd ruined and the come from everyone else still dripping out.

Fuck.

"Well?" he asks. "Who's gonna be the first to double dip?"

"Shit, look, he's practically gaping already," someone behind Rowan calls.

"Nah, but he will be soon," someone else laughs.

"I want him first," Leg Day says.

"Me too," the Japanese Tweedle adds. He lays down on the bed on his back, tugging Malcolm with him until he straddles Tweedle's hips. Without prompting, he sinks down onto the man's cock with a contented sigh, hips rocking in a steady rhythm as he fucks himself.

It's as captivating a sight as Rowan thought it might be, even at a leisurely pace. His eyes rove over every inch of Malcolm, biceps and thighs flexing, abs rolling, head lolling back, cock starting to perk up again after only a few minutes of being soft. And when Leg Day sidles up behind him and presses in two lubed fingers alongside Tweedle's cock, Malcolm's breath leaves him in a rush.

"Fuuuck yeah, keep goin'."

"That's the plan," Leg Day replies.

He works his fingers around the rim, tugging and twisting while Malcolm's rocking his hips against him. By the time he works in a third finger alongside Tweedle's cock, Malcolm is practically whining for him to *get on with it*.

So he does.

Get on with it.

Rowan's transfixed as he watches Leg Day slick his cock and press it into Malcolm's hole beside Tweedle's. It goes in like fucking *nothing*, and shit, Rowan can feel himself getting hard again.

The response from the crowd around them is deafening, a chorus of "Fuck yeah" and "Take it" and "Fuckin' slut" erupting from all sides, fighting over the increase in the slick sound of hands on skin.

And Malcolm fucking keens.

"Oooooooohhh...!"

The long drawn-out noise bursts from the back of his throat as he buries his face in the shoulder of the man beneath him, gripping his biceps.

All the porn in the world doesn't compare to how he looks, how he sounds, as Leg Day pulls out halfway and thrusts in. Malcolm's mouth forms a perfect O, and his eyes scrunch shut as Tweedle finally starts moving as well.

They may have been shit on their own, but together the two find a steady rhythm, one thrusting in as the other pulls out, keeping Malcolm stretched beautifully around both of them. And when Tats makes his way to the front of the bed and presents his cock to Malcolm, he deepthroats it immediately and moans wantonly.

Rowan's mouth runs dry. Falls open. Hangs there for a few seconds before he gets a hold of himself and snaps it shut. Drops back open as one of the men fucking Malcolm comes with a groan and the other keeps fucking him, shaft coated in come.

Rowan feels hot all over. Numb at the fingertips. *Fuck*, he thinks, *get it together. You've seen this shit hundreds of times.*

But he hasn't. Not really. Not in person.

Not with a greedy bottom who cries out in pleasure when he gets both his holes stuffed with cock. Most of the similar porn Rowan's seen focuses on the pain, and Rowan's never been into that. He gets off too hard on his partner enjoying himself to like seeing people in pain.

And Malcolm is definitely enjoying himself. There isn't a shadow of a wince on his face or a trace of an uncomfortable arch in his spine. Raw, open *pleasure*.

Rowan's so transfixed that he misses the other guy coming entirely, only noticing when the men swap out.

Next up are Cupcake and Shortstop, the sheer size difference between the two men almost comical, but fuck if they don't work well together. Cupcake is beneath, Malcolm almost unable to straddle his thick hips properly. But he's clearly flexible enough, legs spread wide enough to reveal Cupcake's pelvic bones protruding between Malcolm's inner thighs.

Rowan wants to taste those thighs. Wants to run his hands over them with Malcolm spread out above him.

He's going to zone out the rest of the night thinking of all the things he wants to do to Malcolm if he could only tell all the other guys in the room to fuck off. But he's here to watch as much as he is to participate, and he forces himself to put aside his fantasies for a rainy day—or a sunny day, or any day, really—and fully take in the beautiful sight of Malcolm surrounded by cock.

The men pair off with whoever's nearby and pass Malcolm around, fucking him two at a time, almost everyone opting to sandwich Malcolm between them, one fucking up into him and the other joining in from behind. Anytime someone slips out, Malcolm barks a command to "Get the fuck back in me," followed by a clipped moan when both cocks are back inside and thrusting into him.

Shirley Temple and the Van Damme guy get creative, both lying back on the bed with their asses and cocks pressed against one another, forcing Malcolm to squat low over them and take them side by side. He groans at the new stretch, uses their legs for leverage, and fucks himself down hard enough to bruise. He rides them until both their ends, miraculously showing few signs of exhaustion despite the brutal pace and position.

God, Rowan wants to wear him out until he can't *move* or even think about it.

And much like earlier, Rowan's tired of waiting. Tired of watching. He's rock hard again and desperate to feel Malcolm around his cock alongside someone else.

Go out with a bang, or something like that.

He climbs on the bed for what feels like the twentieth time tonight, trying to not let his eagerness show but probably failing spectacularly. There's a time and place for being aloof and uninterested, but here and now isn't it.

No, he wants Malcolm to know how badly he wants him.

The little spark Rowan swears he sees in those gold eyes makes him wonder if he's alone in that want.

"Think you can take me with someone else?" Rowan asks him.

"Still waitin' for you to make me cry."

"You're not ready for that."

"*Tch.*"

Every other time Malcolm's been fucked tonight he's been more or less manhandled into position or shown or told where to go. This time, he pushes Rowan onto his back and straddles him, one hand pressed flat to his chest while the other reaches back and strokes him. He doesn't know if Malcolm's hand is slick with lube or come or spit or all three, but he couldn't care less as Malcolm raises up and sinks down onto him with a quiet "*Unhh.*"

And when he leans forward and rolls his hips, taking Rowan's cock all the way in and hovering mere inches above him when he drops back down, Rowan's brain short-circuits. Because he'd fucked him face-to-face before, but they'd still had a fair amount of distance between them. Now he can see everything, and Malcolm's face is almost as captivating as his ass.

He senses another person slide up behind them before he sees him. It's Tats. Rowan's glad—next to Malcolm, he's the most attractive one of the lot, and with his long cock, sure to drive Malcolm crazy.

Malcolm stills above him, and Rowan has exactly zero seconds to prepare himself when he feels the head of Tats's cock slide along his shaft and *push* and—

—and Rowan's gonna pass out. For real this time.

Because *fuck*, all he can think as the other man works himself completely inside is *Tight tight tight tight tight, fucking shit, TIGHT.*

But Malcolm's hole stretches to accommodate both of them while he lets out this beautiful, unhinged moan that cuts off like he ran out of breath right in the middle of it.

"Jesus *fuck*," he gasps.

Yeah. Jesus fuck is right.

It's so good and they're merely sitting still, the three of them panting in unison, and someone needs to move immediately or Rowan's going to blow from the searing heat and pressure around his cock.

Mercifully, Tats begins to move, slowly at first as he acclimates to the feeling. He keeps a steady pace, only increasing incrementally after a few dozen strokes.

And God, it's indescribable. Like Rowan's fucking someone and getting jerked off at the same time. The defined ridge around the head of Tats's cock drags along Rowan's shaft over and over, the sensation ten times hotter than anytime Rowan's jerked his cock alongside someone else's, solely because they're both inside someone else.

But as much as he'd love to lie here and let both of them pleasure him, he wants to *move*.

He raises his knees as best he can, plants his feet, and thrusts up into the tight heat as Tats pulls halfway out.

"Mmmmm fuck!" Malcolm cries out above him.

Perfect.

Rowan wants to hear more of it.

He almost regrets telling him to shut up earlier, because Malcolm isn't being bratty now. Now he's moaning around the two cocks inside him as eight others are being jerked to the sight of him because he's *loving* this. If Rowan could set Malcolm's moans as his ringtone without it being weird, he absolutely would.

But Rowan silently vows to make sure Malcolm never forgets this. He pushes past the overwhelming feeling of needing to come again, past the burn in his muscles, past the urge to catalog every single second of this night, and fucks up into him with everything he has.

He and Tats have a good rhythm. Fast. Hard. Balls slapping against each other's shafts on every stroke, and Malcolm is eating that shit right up, moaning for *faster, harder, deeper, just like that.*

Rowan's pretty sure he blacks out, because before he knows it, Tats says, "*Nnng*, I'm gonna come!" seconds before his pace stutters and his cock twitches alongside Rowan's.

And God, Rowan can feel the wetness and the warmth, and it's almost enough to make him come on the spot, but he doesn't want any of this to be over yet.

Malcolm groans when Tats pulls out, leaving Rowan inside him. No one else steps up to replace Tats, but The Rock look-alike kneels against Rowan's side and feeds his cock to Malcolm like it's a treat, and judging by the eager way he sucks it down, like he's done every single time tonight, it might be. He works The Rock expertly, slurping around the head and using the one hand that's not holding himself up to stroke his shaft in time with his head bobbing. Rowan knows *exactly* how that feels, and it's a miracle that the man manages to last as long as he does.

"Gonna come," The Rock grits out.

And Malcolm wraps his hand around the back of his thigh and pulls him forward, deepthroating him as The Rock's hips stutter and he comes with a groan.

Malcolm licks the man's cock clean, sucking on it until it starts to soften, and The Rock pulls away. Malcolm locks eyes with Rowan, makes a show of swallowing The Rock's load, and for good measure, opens his mouth to let Rowan see there's nothing left. Exactly like Rowan made him do earlier.

And look.

Rowan can share.

Rowan is good at sharing, because he's the middle child of a family of six from a neighborhood where people took care of each other. But he hates it. Now that he has a taste of having his own things, he never wants to have to share anything ever again. And apparently that desire extends to Malcolm too. The entire night has been hot as fuck, but he doesn't want to see him get other people off or see other people get *him* off. He wants to do it himself or make Malcolm do it *him*self under Rowan's watchful gaze.

So he shoots up, pulls out, and coaxes Malcolm onto his knees. He pulls his back flush against his chest as he pushes back into him in one smooth stroke, marveling at the slight resistance he still somehow feels. He squeezes Malcolm's pecs, feels the pounding of his heart reverberating through the taut muscle.

He stills when he's fully seated, Malcolm groaning low and dipping his head forward as if it's the first time a dick's entered him tonight rather than the hundredth.

Rowan slides a hand up from his chest to his throat, skimming his hand along the long column of his neck until he's cupping his jaw and leaning his head back nearly on Rowan's shoulder. He doesn't apply any pressure, keeping his touch featherlight. As much as he'd love to choke him properly, it's against both Malcolm's and the club's rules, and he wouldn't cross those lines for anything.

But the sensation must be doing something for Malcolm if the sharp inhale through his nose is anything to go by. Or the ragged breaths that follow when Rowan starts stroking him with his other hand, Malcolm's cock hard and warm and slippery with come. Rowan ghosts his fingertips along Malcolm's neck and jaw, feels Malcolm clench around him in response and buck his hips back.

"Come *on*," Malcolm growls.

Impatient. Back to being a brat. Malcolm grinds his ass into Rowan's hips the best he can but groans in evident frustration at not being able to get fucked like he wants.

"Hm?" Rowan teases.

"Fuck me, Re—*sh-shit*."

Rowan huffs out a laugh through his nose. "Gonna have to use a different name for me 'less you wanna accidentally safeword."

"Nng!" Malcolm groans, bitten-off curses spilling from his lips as Rowan pulls back and pushes in, pace slow but thrusts hard.

Rowan can hear the struggle in his voice. The knowledge that if he calls him Red like he did earlier, like he clearly wants to again now, Rowan's going to stop. That Rowan *has* to stop.

"Or better yet, I could make you call me sir. Or master."

It's not really the time or place for it—this isn't a *scene* scene, not like that—but he wants to see Malcolm's reaction to it. And Malcolm nods, a quick dip of his chin to his chest. It's too neat. Too practiced for Rowan's liking. No fight, no resistance, none of the fire he's seen all night. None of the desperation, which means he's only doing it to get what he wants.

But…

I can count on one hand the number of times he's topped.

"But something tells me you've called loads of people that. Fuckin' bottom brat like you's used to those. They don't mean *shit* to you."

"Fu-fuckin' Firecrotch," Malcolm grunts.

"No. You've given everyone here shitty nicknames all night. When I make you come this time, you're gonna say my fuckin' *name*."

"Fuck y—hah!"

Rowan wraps his free hand around the base of Malcolm's cock, tight enough to stave off the orgasm he can sense building from the rippling of his walls.

"It's *Rowan*. That's the only thing that's gonna let you come on my cock tonight."

He strokes Malcolm but keeps his grip tight, right to the edge of what he knows is painful.

"I can feel how fuckin' close you are. Cock dripping over my fingers. Slutty ass tightening around me. Didn't think you'd still be able to clench after all the cock you took tonight."

"Fuck me, si—"

Breathy, but monotone.

And while the instant switch from cursing him out to near begging is insanely hot, it's not what Rowan wants. Judging by the lungfuls of air Malcolm is gulping down as Rowan slows his hips more, angling up to brush against his prostate, not what *he* wants either.

"Name's not sir."

"M—"

Rowan grips him tighter around the base, stills his hips to a torturously slow crawl.

"I said *no*. My name or I pass you off to one'a these fuckin' pussies and let *them* try to make you come."

It's a bluff. A boldfaced lie. Rowan doesn't trust any of these people to treat Malcolm as well as he knows he can, as well as he already *has* tonight, and they've hardly exchanged any words in the mere hours they've known each other.

But the threat is enough.

Malcolm's voice is low, barely audible over the pants and groans and slick sounds of men jerking off around them. If his head wasn't dipped back onto Rowan's shoulder, Rowan might have missed it altogether.

But it's there.

He hears it.

"*Rowan….*"

A tiny rasp of a thing, whispered in one single syllable rather than two. And God if it isn't the hottest fucking thing he's heard in his life.

"Again."

Rowan speeds up his hips, loosens his grip on Malcolm's cock and pumps him in time with his thrusts, angling up to hit his prostate on every stroke.

His name comes easier this time. Louder. Breathier. Properly, with two syllables.

"Rowan."

He pistons into Malcolm, driving his full length into Malcolm's ass hard enough to bruise his cheeks and Rowan's hips alike. The cock in his hand twitches as he strokes and twists and flicks his fingers over the tip.

"That's it. Again."

"Rowan, *please*—"

He thought it'd be harder to get him begging, whimpering his name in pure desperation, but really, it wasn't difficult at all. Like he'd been waiting for someone to make him do it. *Doesn't beg for anyone, my* ass, Rowan thinks.

Everything is a blur, all of Rowan's senses going into overdrive as he gives everything he has to the man in front of him. He can feel him shaking, vibrating under his ministrations, muscles taut like a bowstring poised to snap the second it's touched the right way.

"Once more. Then you can come."

That way.

"Rowan!" Malcolm cries out, voice hoarse but the name loud and clear on his lips, body quaking through the orgasm that Rowan can feel as sinuous pulses around his cock and sticky wetness in his hand.

He's so good for him, *perfect*, and Rowan fucks him through it, echoes of his name dripping from his lips like a chanted prayer.

The pure ferality of Malcolm, the *god* of the Menagerie, moaning out Rowan's name in front of a room full of men he had reduced to base physical characteristics rips Rowan's own orgasm from him. He spills inside Malcolm hard, come mixing with the release of nine other men.

"Fuck yeah," someone calls out. "Put 'im in his place."

"Such a good fuckin' slut."

"Gonna jerk off to that for weeks."

Echoes of the same sentiment come from all around them, along with groans and grunts as more men finish. In his periphery, Rowan can see their come splattering onto the bed, but he couldn't care less about it when Malcolm slumps against him, back heaving against Rowan's chest, slick with sweat.

He rocks his hips gently against Malcolm and strokes him through the aftershocks of his orgasm, conscious of not hurting him in case he's oversensitive. And Christ, he must be after having been fucked almost nonstop for hours.

The crowd starts to clear as the men leave one by one to clean themselves off and re-dress, chatting excitedly, until it's only Rowan and Malcolm left on the bed.

"Did so good," Rowan whispers low in his ear. "So perfect. God, you're incredible."

It might be a little much, but he means it. And shit, Malcolm never discussed aftercare, but he must need *something*, so Rowan talks to him in a low voice about how good he was and how Rowan can't believe he's real and pets over his chest and arms and sides until Malcolm stops shaking and his breathing slows. Only then does he pull out, a gush of come following and dripping down the backs of Malcolm's thighs.

This is definitely the end of the night, but Rowan wishes he could keep going. Keep being inside Malcolm and making him come on his tongue and fingers and cock over and over until he's worn him out this much all on his own.

He hopes he'll get to try. Hopes he wasn't imagining their connection. Their *chemistry*.

Because there's something there, right? You can fake a lot of stuff during sex, even if you're a guy with a dick, but you can't fake everything. Not blown pupils or dripping sweat or full-body shudders or any of the dozens of miniscule facial expressions Malcolm made while Rowan was touching him.

But he doesn't get to dwell on it any longer, Malcolm slumping onto his knees, still partially leaning back against Rowan's hips and thighs. Rowan places a steadying hand on his upper back and shuffles around on his knees to look at him. His eyes are closed, nostrils flaring slightly as he breathes. Rowan watches his chest rise and fall, counts his breaths, notes his fingertips flexing where they're pressed flat onto the soiled bed.

"You okay?" he asks gently.

Malcolm nods with his eyes still closed, then clears his throat. He blinks up at Rowan, the gold catching him off guard as Malcolm's pupils shrink in the light and make something stir in Rowan's rib cage.

"'M good, man."

Rowan watches him for a few seconds more, trying to gauge whether he's actually okay or not. He watches Malcolm's abs flex as he reaches his arms above his head in a stretch, the popping of his spine audible even over the chatter of the men and the shuffling of their clothes as they dress.

There's nothing to suggest he isn't okay, at least not right this second, so Rowan rolls off the bed, wincing at the mess he picks up along the way, and crosses the room to the supply table. He grabs a bottle of water from the fridge as well as two washcloths, wets one in the sink and tucks both under his arm when someone slaps him on the back.

Startled, he whips around to find Leg Day grinning at him.

"You were so hot out there, dude."

Out there, like they had a pickup game of basketball rather than a fucking gangbang.

"Uh, thanks?"

"Any chance you wanna meet up next time you come? I'd love to try that thing out for myself," he says, flicking his eyes to Rowan's still very exposed dick.

He's hot. He is, even with his skinny legs and the frat boy thing he's got going on, and Rowan wants to kick himself for what he's about to say, but he's gonna say it anyway.

"I'm not really lookin' for anything right now."

The guy laughs. "It doesn't have to be anything serious, dude. No one comes here looking for the love of their life."

Rowan's eyes wander over to the bed, to where Malcolm is now sitting up straighter and stretching his neck from side to side. He said he didn't want anything serious, but really, the guy talking to him isn't who he wants. Rowan watched him all night, watched *everyone* all night, some more than others, inevitably, but no one as much as Malcolm. God, how could he? That would be like going to some museum and looking at the pedestals instead of the sculptures or the frames instead of the paintings. It wouldn't make sense.

And when Malcolm's gaze sweeps the room and lands on Rowan's before snapping away, he can't help but wonder again if the feeling is mutual.

"Sorry," he finally says.

He barely registers the guy leaving, only catching the tail end of his "Whatever, dude," when he sees the Van Damme look-alike approach the bed, hover, say something to Malcolm. The little pang Rowan felt earlier in his chest migrates to his stomach, barely more noticeable than a mosquito bite, but there and persistent and making Rowan pay attention. Malcolm shakes his head, and the other man leaves with the start of a scowl on his face.

What…? Had he been propositioned the same way Rowan had and turned the guy down?

The wetness seeping into his skin from the washcloths he'd tucked under his arm snaps him back to his senses and reminds him of why he came over here in the first place. Shaking his head at himself, he discards one of the washcloths, now both damp, and grabs a dry one before returning to the bed.

"Here," Rowan says, cracks open the seal on the bottle of water and hands it to Malcolm.

The other man looks at him with wide eyes, slightly parted lips. Like Rowan handed him a bar of gold he'd mined and smelted himself rather than a bottle of water he'd gotten from the mini fridge a few feet away.

"Thanks," he mumbles.

Rowan can't help but watch the pretty bob of his throat as he chugs nearly the entire bottle. When he's finished, Rowan hands him the washcloths. Normally, he'd do it himself—clean up his mess, so to speak—but Malcolm is still a stranger, even if he'd been filled with Rowan in more ways than one, and that's something that some people find too personal.

He gets the same incredulous look as before, but Malcolm takes the washcloths from him and wipes his face, Rowan turning to get another bottle of water to give him some semblance of privacy as he starts wiping down the rest of himself. When he returns, Malcolm seems to be finished, pulling on his briefs straight from the floor with little finesse.

"Do you need anything?" Rowan asks, handing him the other water bottle. "I mean, aftercare-wise?"

He takes the water with a nod and replies, "'M good."

Rowan waits a beat, eyeing him again to make sure he actually *is* okay after such an intense session. But the other man doesn't give him any indication that he needs or wants anything else from him.

That's that, then.

The swell of disappointment in Rowan's chest at Malcolm's silent brush-off stings more than he cares to admit. He'd hoped that he'd done enough to get his attention—made an impression worthy of a second go and maybe more after that.

But he lets it go. Maybe Malcolm really is as hard to please as everyone said he was. And maybe the orgasms Rowan had fucked out of him were plain old Tuesday night lazy jerk-off orgasms rather than the mind-blowing experiences he'd thought they might have been.

Defeated, he gets his own bottle of water and washcloth, wipes off his junk quickly before tossing the cloth into the hamper and finding his pile of clothes. He pulls on his briefs, then downs half of his water, surprised at how thirsty he is after a couple of hours of on-and-off exertion.

He's pulling on his button-up shirt over his tank top when he hears Malcolm's voice from across the room.

"Ay, Shirley Temple."

Rowan's head snaps up as Malcolm calls out to the twinky blond guy who fucked him fourth, maybe fifth. Utterly forgettable. Nothing impressive by any account.

"Me?" the guy asks. Timid. Weak.

"Yeah, you. C'mere. You lookin' for a sub?"

The blood in Rowan's veins boils. Malcolm would eat that man alive and not get a damn thing out of it.

"Uh, I mean…." The guy's gaze flicks to Rowan—barely ten feet away, watching the exchange like a hawk—like even *he* knows that he shouldn't be the one Malcolm is talking to right now.

And Rowan wants to respect his decision. He does, honestly. Wants to be the bigger person and not be a possessive fucking *creep*, especially over a literal stranger, especially when he'd already resigned himself to this being a one-night stand bang, but there's no way in hell that kid rocked Malcolm's world enough for a repeat.

The words tumble out of Rowan's mouth before he can think better of it. "No fuckin' way."

Both men snap their attention to him, Malcolm looking curious, maybe a little smug even, and the other man wide-eyed and jumpy. Scared.

Rowan stalks up to Malcolm, using every inch of his height advantage and gazing down at him. The smirk on Malcolm's lips widens.

"'Scuse me?"

"No fucking way did that kid impress you more than me."

"That so? What makes you say that?"

"The fact that you refused to blow anyone while my spit was in your mouth. The fact that you came super fuckin' hard on my dick. *Twice*. The fact that you know *my* name and you're still callin' *him* Shirley Temple."

"Maybe I'm lookin' for someone a little less rough."

Rowan stares at him.

I like it rough, so don't hold back.

He searches his eyes and finds nothing readable in the steely gold, somehow so different from a few minutes ago when they'd locked eyes on the bed. He takes a steadying deep breath.

"If that's actually true, then fine, I'll leave. But I highly fuckin' doubt it."

Malcolm's eyes flash. "Good."

Rowan's eyebrows knit together, but he can still feel the heat in his own eyes. "Good?"

"Wanted to see if you'd fight for me. Fuck off, Shirley Temple."

The man turns and all but runs out of the room.

"A fuckin' test?"

"And you passed with flyin' colors."

It's not the best way to start off any kind of a relationship, sexual or otherwise. And Rowan could be mad about it—he probably should be—but he finds that he really doesn't want to be.

"Pretty shit test," he muses instead, feeling the surge of angry heat dissipate. "You wanted to *really* test me, shoulda picked that guy who looked like Dwayne Johnson or someone I couldn't fight in my sleep."

Malcolm laughs, a short, clipped thing that sounds like he doesn't do it very often, and Rowan instantly wants to hear it again.

"So, *Rowan*, you lookin' for a sub?"

And that's the thing.

Until a few hours ago, he wasn't. The thought hadn't even crossed his mind as a possibility. He was only looking for a way to blow off some steam, feel good about himself while he was feeling good. But now that Malcolm has brought it up as a possibility, a for-real possibility and not a fantasy rattling around in Rowan's brain, the idea of this being a regular thing between them is utterly tantalizing.

But if they're going to do this, he should be honest with him. Rowan's never been a true Dom in his life. He's always taken the lead in his sexual relationships, both long-term and one-night stands, and he's had kinky sex more often than vanilla in all of those. But a casual, purely sexual relationship with a stranger entirely about satisfying specific needs?

That's new. That's *different*.

And he wants it, but only if Malcolm is okay with Rowan being fairly new to the game.

He's apparently been silent for too long, having been lost in his thoughts.

"Well? Yes or no, tough guy?"

"I've uh… never really done it in an official capacity before."

Malcolm laughs and rubs a hand across his mouth. "Ain't like you need a license to rail me, man."

Rowan feels his cheeks flame but manages to hold on to a scrap of dignity and roll his eyes for good measure. "No shit. I just meant most of this is new to me, at least outside of relationships and hookups. Y'know, in case you wanted someone more experienced."

Malcolm curls his lips under his teeth. Looks at Rowan like he's sizing him up. He takes a slow, steady breath, and Rowan's worried he's going to tell him to fuck off after his admission. But instead, he surprises him, speaking earnestly.

"You seemed to know what you were doin'. You respected my boundaries and had the foresight to know you'd need to stop if I called you 'Red.' You helped me come down at the end, which doesn't usually happen in group scenes unless I ask someone ahead of time. And you could gauge what I wanted in *one* session in a room full'a people—that's pretty fuckin' rare. All that tells me you're experienced enough. The rest is just logistics."

Despite the sexual nature of his words, the sincerity in Malcolm's voice and eyes sends a tingling warmth through Rowan's core, and he can't help the smile that forms on his lips.

"Okay. Then yeah, let's do this, Malcolm."

The other man winces. "Mal."

"What?"

"That's *my* name, Red. Hate it when people call me Malcolm. Pretentious as fuck."

"But why—"

"You think people're gonna line up around the block to fuck a guy named *Mal*?"

Rowan shrugs. "If they knew how tight your ass was, then yeah, probably."

Malcolm—*Mal*—smirks. "Yeah. You're gonna work out fine."

Chapter 3: Wants and Needs

Mal.

The name rattles around in Rowan's brain like a pinball in an arcade machine.

Mal, Mal, Mal.

It suits him. Much more than Malcolm, at least from the little he knows about the man. Now that he thinks about it outside the haze of horny desperation, Malcolm sounds so formal, like the kind of person Rowan had been picturing before he met him.

Before he fucked him.

Malcolm sounds like the kind of guy who would kick someone off his yacht if they dared to wear flip-flops rather than those expensive boat shoes that Rowan knows nothing about.

Like the kind of guy who'd only want sex at 9:00 p.m. every other Wednesday night for exactly twelve minutes.

Or maybe like the guy the mob would send after you to break your fingers if you refused to pay off your debts.

But Mal.

Mal sounds like the kind of guy that vibes with everything Rowan's learned about him in the short time he's known him.

Like the kind of guy who likes shitty beer, probably because he grew up drinking it like Rowan did and never bothered to switch to anything better.

Like the kind of guy who says *ain't* and *fuckin'* and *bitchface*.

Like the kind of guy who can get fucked by ten guys and still want more.

Yeah.

Rowan thinks Mal is a much better fit. He likes how the name feels in his mouth, how it rolls off his tongue, though he hasn't actually said it out loud yet. He's about to test it out properly when Mal himself snaps his fingers in front of Rowan's face.

"Yo, you space out on me, man?"

Fuck. Yeah, he definitely did.

"Sorry, what?"

"I asked if you were hungry. I know a place."

Rowan's stomach lurches at the thought of spending time with him so soon. "Yeah, starving."

"Cool. Meet me at the bar in twenty. Need to clean up."

Rowan nods and checks his phone: 11:43 p.m. It's much later than he thought it would be, but thankfully he doesn't have to work tomorrow. He finishes buttoning his shirt and is about to head toward the door when he notices Mal grabbing a handful of washcloths and a spray bottle from the supply table and spraying down the bed.

Rowan knew the rule about cleaning up, so it's not surprising. But what *is* surprising is that the nine other men whose mess is on the bed up and left without so much as pretending to offer to help clean up. Actually, given the way most of them acted during the gangbang, he probably could have predicted it.

He rolls up his sleeves quickly and goes to the supply table to grab his own washcloths and the hamper from under the table and bring them over to the bed, where he silently starts wiping the come and lube and sweat from the leather pad.

Mal gives him that same incredulous look he gave him when Rowan offered him water earlier. It makes Rowan's heart break a little. How has he done this multiple times, according to Camilla, and been forced to bring himself down from orgasm *and* clean up the whole mess afterward?

"You don't gotta do that," Mal says.

Rowan shrugs. "You shouldn't have to do it yourself. 'Specially when most of it's not yours."

"Pretty sure that fuckin' pile's *yours*." Mal points to a large pool of come directly in the center of the bed where he and Mal had finished.

"Didn't hear you complaining at the time."

"Yeah, well, jizz is hot in the heat of the moment. Now it's just fuckin' gross."

Rowan hums in agreement and scoops up the mess with a cloth, wincing as he dumps it into the hamper and letting Mal spray it again before he wipes it clean. Silently Rowan hopes the club provides an industrial-strength cleanser. Working together it only takes them a few minutes to thoroughly clean the bed, making it look like new save for the subtle sheen from the washing fluid.

With a muttered, "Thanks," Mal dumps the cleaning supplies back on the table. "All right, see you in a few."

"'Kay."

Rowan watches him exit the room—still in nothing but his briefs—admiring the way his back muscles flex as he walks. He feels a stirring in his groin, like he hadn't come twice in the span of a few hours. He can't help but wonder if it's the newness of Mal that's getting him going like this, or if this is what it's going to be like as long as they're… *whatever*. Dom and sub. Fuck buddies. Though Rowan's pretty sure you need to *be* buddies first before the term "fuck buddies" is actually appropriate. Right now they're just people who have fucked and are going to make plans to fuck again.

Probably. Hopefully.

The point is, Mal's hot, and Rowan already wants more.

When he hears the door to what is presumably the changing room slam shut, Rowan realizes he's been standing by himself in the Black Room. He tugs at his shirt, regretting having gotten dressed now that he's going to be out in public again. He'd planned on going home, showering, and passing out for at least ten hours, but Mal had completely changed those plans. And Rowan's immensely looking forward to spending more time with him, but he feels gross, having only given himself a cursory wipe down before he'd put his clothes back on.

He heads to the bathroom down the hall, marveling at the warm cream-colored walls and soft lighting and cleanliness. Rowan hadn't been expecting a gas-station bathroom, exactly, but this is some five-star hotel shit.

Mercifully, a basket full of travel-size toiletries sits on the sink counter. Rowan washes his hands, splashes some cold water on his face—careful to not drip onto his shirt—and towels off with one of the rolled hand towels stacked in neat rows. He takes a miniature bottle of mouthwash and gargles with the entire thing, spitting it in the sink after a minute or so. There are a wide variety of deodorant sticks and sprays, including the same Old Spice that Rowan uses at home. He applies a fresh coat, smooths out his shirt, and pockets the rest of the tube, not wanting to waste it.

Somehow, his hair is still mostly fine despite everything that happened tonight, so he simply wets his fingertips and flattens down the curls at his temples that are starting to get a little too long to be left ungelled.

Returning to the lounge, he sees that there are still a decent number of people milling around, which isn't surprising since it's only around midnight on a Saturday night. He wanders to the bar, seeing that there are several empty barstools and that Jeremiah is still working.

"Don't *you* look freshly fucked," Jeremiah says to him with a devious twinkle in his eyes as Rowan plants himself on a barstool. "I take it you got in?"

Rowan can't help the corners of his lips turning up. "Yeah."

"Good for you. Malcolm's picky as hell." He leans closer and drops his voice. "Which is also good for *me*, since I always make a killing in tips from his rejects."

Rowan laughs, picturing the scenario perfectly. Dejected men slumping down at the bar, throwing their money at the next pretty thing they see after being turned down by Mal, probably not for the first time. He's reasonably sure at least two of the men at the bar were in the room with him when Mal picked.

"Anything I can get for you?"

"No thanks, just waiting on Mal—uh, Malcolm."

Rowan stops himself from saying *Mal* because he isn't actually sure if the other man wants people knowing his nickname. Clearly everyone here refers to him as Malcolm, so it's a safe bet to stick with that when they're not in private. The little flip in his stomach returns tenfold at the thought of already having a *thing* between the two of them, but it's likely that Rowan's reading too much into things.

To his surprise, Jeremiah's eyebrows shoot up to his forehead. "Oh?"

"Oh... what?"

Jeremiah's lips pull back into a secretive smile as he takes a black cloth from behind the counter and wipes away a condensation ring on the bar. "Just surprised, is all."

Man, for a guy who's seemingly *extremely* open about things, everyone is secretive as fuck about Mal.

"Why?"

"He's usually a one-and-done guy when he's not subbing for someone long term."

Once again Rowan's unsure if he should mention their soon-to-be Dom/sub relationship, but he figures they're going to be seen together at the club, so it couldn't hurt to share with a staff member.

"Ah, we're kinda...."

"Hooo-ly shit," Jeremiah laughs. "First day at the club and you've managed to snag the most sought-after fish in the pond."

Yeah. He kinda did, huh? Unless Mal decides sometime between now and whenever that Rowan's not up to his standards and seeks out someone else. It seems he'd have plenty of options.

Rowan gets that now too. Why apparently everyone wants a piece of him. There's something deeply satisfying about getting to tame someone like Mal. Like Malcolm. To take this wild, feral thing and bump him down a notch or two because that's exactly what he wants.

And Rowan hasn't *really* tamed him. Not yet. Probably won't ever be able to, and that thought renews all his vigor in an instant before Jeremiah speaks again.

"Should've taken a swing at you when I had the chance."

"Hands off, Jer," Mal's voice sounds from behind Rowan.

Rowan spins on his stool to see Mal, taking in his fully clothed figure for the first time. He looks good, wearing black jeans with wide holes in the knees, a plain black shirt, and a light-colored jean jacket. He's evidently freshly showered, the tips of his hair still misty and tousled like he'd only run his fingers through the length of it rather than brushed it properly.

Rowan suddenly feels gross in comparison and desperately wishes he had showered instead of pulling his clothes on over his dirty body. But if the once-over Mal gives him is anything to go by, he'd say he still looks presentable.

"Relax, like I'd be able to pry him from your claws anyway."

With an exaggerated eye roll, Mal turns to Rowan. "You ready?"

"Yeah."

"Cool. Let's go, Red. Later," Mal calls over his shoulder as he turns and heads toward the elevator without so much as waiting for Rowan.

Rowan scrambles off the barstool with a quick goodbye to Jeremiah and half jogs to catch up with Mal as the elevator doors open with a *ding*.

They ride the elevator in silence and then make their way through the first floor—which is packed with people. When they pass Camilla on the way out, Rowan sees her eyes flick up to them for a moment before she does a double take, head snapping up and mouth dropping open like a cartoon character. Instantly after, she bites her bottom lip—visibly fighting a smile—and waggles her fingers at them. Mal flips her off behind his back as Rowan turns and gives her a small wave, at least *trying* to be polite. She and Mal might be friends, but Rowan definitely isn't, and he doesn't want her to think he's being rude.

As soon as they're through the double doors and into the warm summer air, Mal pulls out a cigarette and lights it, taking a deep drag before turning to Rowan for the first time since the bar.

"You smoke?" he asks, offering the cigarette to Rowan as the smoke swirls out from his lips.

"Trying to quit, but yeah."

"*Tch.* Been sayin' *that* shit since I was thirteen."

Rowan huffs a small laugh. He takes the butt and places it between his lips to take his own drag, trying not to think too hard about where the cigarette had been. He hands it back, shivering as their fingers brush and mentally kicking himself for not being able to blame it on the weather.

"C'mon."

Mal shoves his free hand in his jeans pocket and starts walking down the street at a quick pace, making Rowan once again have to take a few half-jogging strides to catch up. He's thankful for his long legs being able to keep pace with Mal, who would put the old ladies who power walk in the mall to shame. If he hadn't been there himself, Rowan almost wouldn't believe this is the same guy who got fucked—and DPd—by ten others. Barely a hitch in his step.

Rowan pushes down the surge of heat he can feel building again, and thinks that Mal is going to be the death of him.

It's only a five-minute walk to the restaurant, which they pass in comfortable silence. The place is little more than a tiny diner with a neon Open 24/7 sign flickering in the window and a rusty bell that dings when they enter.

Something bluesy is playing on the jukebox, and the air is filled with the telltale smell of fried food and something that might be cinnamon. A plump older woman with rosy cheeks and salt-and-pepper hair in neat pin curls is wiping down the counter when she notices them enter.

"Mal, baby!" Her voice is a soothing low rasp with a hint of sweetness to it.

"Hey, Sheils."

"The usual?" she asks once they reach the counter.

"Yeah, please. And whatever he wants," Mal says, gesturing to Rowan.

"Uh...."

Rowan frantically looks up at the overhead menu, consisting of two large blackboards with specials handwritten in chalk. He has no idea what Mal's usual is, though he has to admit he really likes the idea of him having a "usual" at a small place like this. A Mom-and-Pop type place like you'd see every couple of blocks in the outer limits of the city.

"What can I get ya, hon?" the woman asks. Her name tag reads Sheila.

Fuck, right. Food.

His eyes flit across the menu, seeing typical diner staples and breakfast items served until noon.

"Uh… I'll have a BLT and fries, please."

"What kind of toast?"

"Wheat?"

Sheila nods but doesn't write down his order. Rowan always had to write stuff down when he worked at his sister Aubrey's diner, even a simple order like that, so he's impressed.

She fills and hands them two large plastic cups of ice water and tops off the coffee of the lone man at the opposite end of the counter before disappearing into the back.

Mal takes both drinks and nods to a round booth in the back corner of the diner. "C'mon."

They sit opposite each other, the cushioned seats much more comfortable than Rowan would have expected. Mal takes a few deep gulps of water before setting the cup down on the table with a *thunk*.

It strikes Rowan that this is probably weird. Being here in a diner with a guy he'd fucked with nine other guys with the intention of getting to know him better so he can fuck him again. Mal's not saying anything, but the silence aside from the overhead music is driving Rowan a little crazy, so he racks his brain for something to say.

"You come here often?"

He winces. It sounds like a bad pickup line. Mal merely raises his eyebrows at him and leans back against the booth seat, exhaling hard through his nose.

"Yeah. Usually once a week."

"After you go to the club?"

"Yeah. Haven't been in a while, though."

"How come?"

Mal rubs absently at his eyebrow. "Long story."

"Oh, okay."

He wants to point out that they have time for a long story, but it's the universal sign for "I don't want to talk about it" that has Rowan stopping himself.

They sit in silence while waiting on their food, and it isn't uncomfortable, but Rowan's dying to ask him *anything* about himself. As it is, the only sounds audible over the faint jukebox music are the sizzling of the grill and the occasional clanking of plates and silverware. But he wants to try to make Mal laugh again. Wants to find out what else he's into and how this thing is going to work between them.

And despite the silence, Rowan decides this is definitely weird as hell. Being here with a guy he'd done a bunch of filthy shit with, watching him pick at his nails and occasionally take a drink of water. It's like he's a completely different person in the club versus outside of it.

Rowan wonders if the person he's seeing now is Mal. Not Malcolm. In the club, he'd been loud and bratty and crass and witty and everything that made the connections in Rowan's brain light up like a Christmas tree.

Now he's calmly quiet, fidgeting every once in a while, locking eyes with Rowan for a moment before hastily pulling away to stare into an empty corner of the diner. Rowan thinks about what Jeremiah had told him about Mal—about *Malcolm*—when they'd been chatting at the bar. *Quiet. Bit of a sourpuss. Outspoken.*

It seems pretty accurate from what he's gathered so far. But he wants to know more. Know everything.

It should probably worry him that he's already so intrigued by the guy, so desperate for any scrap of knowledge about him. But he checks in with himself, and he's not angry or restless or desperately horny— well, no more than usual—like he is when he's about to go through a major depressive episode, so he's okay.

He's curious, is all.

And he's about to ask Mal what he does for a living or make some kind of small talk when Sheila's suddenly next to their table balancing four plates on her arms.

"The usual for Mal," she says, placing down a stack of banana pancakes, sausage links, bacon, eggs, home fries, and marble rye toast cut into triangles.

"Thanks, Sheils."

Rowan's eyes nearly pop out of his skull, not only because it's a *fuckton* of food, but also because apparently this woman likes Mal so much she's willing to make him breakfast food well outside the cutoff time for it.

She places the final plate, a thick BLT with a pile of steaming fries, in front of Rowan.

"And a BLT on wheat for…?"

Mal answers for him. "This is Rowan."

"Rowan…?"

Rowan clears his throat. "Campbell."

"Campbell?" She narrows her eyes at him. "Are you related to Hank by any chance?"

Fuck. Leave it to Hank to somehow infect a small diner all the way in the Back Bay with his bullshit.

Rowan heaves a sigh, hoping he's not going to be chased out with a broom or, more likely, a shotgun. "Unfortunately. He's my dad."

"Ah. Well. Can't be helped, I suppose. I know well enough not to judge someone for the sins of their father." Sheila squeezes Mal's shoulder as she says it, while keeping her eyes on Rowan. "You seem like a nice enough boy, Rowan. I hope I'll see you around again."

"You too."

Rowan is confused as hell by the entire exchange. When Sheila leaves, Rowan looks to Mal with an, "Uhh…." but the other man shrugs and stuffs half of a sausage in his mouth.

"Haven't eaten anything but a protein shake all fuckin' day," he says, as if in explanation, barely chewing the food before grabbing his utensils to roughly cut up his pancakes then drown them in syrup.

"Really?"

Mal gives him a *You serious?* look while shoveling up home fries with his fork. Oh. Yeah, duh. Rowan had already almost forgotten what they'd done. *And* how much prep it takes to do a big bareback scene like that, or do any kind of anal play really. Usually douching is enough, but apparently Mal hadn't eaten all day as an extra precaution.

"Oh. Right." He feels the heat creep into his cheeks and forces himself to focus on his own food instead, suddenly famished.

While it's hard to screw up a BLT, he has to admit that this particular sandwich is delicious. Fresh-tasting produce, a pile of crispy bacon, bread that's soft in the center and crunchy on the outside. The fries are good too—not overly greasy or salty like a lot of places make them—and with some sort of spice blend on top that makes him wolf them down about as fast as Mal's devouring his own food.

When Rowan's mostly done with his sandwich and Mal slows down, less ravenous and more grazing, Rowan feels like it's safe enough to at least ask some basic questions.

"So what do you do?"

"Wha' do I do wha'?" Mal replies, mouth full of food.

"For a job? Or, like, are you a student or something?"

Mal snorts in the back of his throat mid-swallow, somehow not choking in the process, and wipes his face with a napkin.

"I'm an accountant."

Rowan barks out a laugh before he can stop himself. In return, Mal gives him a flat stare.

"Somethin' funny, Firecrotch?"

A chill runs down Rowan's spine, as if someone had dumped a bucket of ice water on his head.

"Wait, you're serious?"

"The fuck would I lie for?"

"Like a sexy accountant or a real accountant?"

Mal rolls his eyes. "A real one, jackass. I'm good with numbers."

"Oh. Jesus, sorry. Guess I just… can't picture you doing anything corporate." Rowan's eyes flick down to Mal's knuckle tats and back up to his face in time to see his eyes roll.

"They let me work from home."

"Oh. That's good."

"Mmm."

He doesn't ask Rowan what he does in return. But sue him, Rowan's proud of his job and wants to show off a little bit.

"Did you hear about the guy that got choked out at the club last week?" Rowan asks.

Mal nods his head in recognition. "Yeah, fuckin' moron. Shit's forbidden for that exact reason."

"I was the one who had to come get him."

"Oh yeah?"

Rowan nods. "He was in pretty rough shape."

"You a paramedic or somethin', then?" Mal asks, flooding Rowan with a surprising rush of warmth.

"Yeah, actually. Most people guess EMT."

"There's a difference?"

Oh.

"Yeah. Paramedics can do more treatments before the patient gets to the hospital than EMTs can. Putting in IVs, prescribing drugs if we know the patient's history, that kinda stuff."

Mal picks up the final piece of bacon on his plate with his fingers and folds it into his mouth. "Got a bit of a God complex, huh?"

Rowan shrugs. "I like helping people."

Mal doesn't reply with anything other than a quirk of his eyebrows. He wads up a napkin and wipes his hands before sitting up straighter in the booth, clearing his throat.

On to business, then.

Rowan decides to speak first. "So, uh, how does this work, exactly?"

"Dom/sub shit?"

"Yeah."

"It's different for everyone, obviously. But for us, it'd prob'ly be a once or twice a week thing at the club." Pausing, Mal asks, "What membership level do you have?"

"Silver." Rowan doesn't know why, but a twinge of embarrassment creeps into his cheeks. Thankfully, Mal doesn't seem fazed by it.

"'Kay. We'll do once a week, then. Saturdays good for you? Same time?"

"Yeah, that works."

"You really never had a sub before, huh?" Mal asks after a brief pause, nibbling on the crust of a toast triangle.

"Not anything long term, just a coupl'a exes and hookups."

"Nothing at the club?"

"Uh, well I joined today, so no."

"No shit?" Mal's eyebrows quirk up again. Rowan likes how expressive they are. "Figured you were new since I hadn't seen you around, but I didn't peg you for a first-timer."

Rowan doesn't tell him that he's not really a first-timer when it comes to the club scene. Only the nonsketchy, legitimate, *legal* club scene. Instead he brilliantly says, "Well, you've got a dick, so you wouldn't need to peg me."

The flat stare he gets in response makes him bite his bottom lip.

"That your way of saying you bottom too?"

"No… well, I *have*, and I like it every once in a while, but mostly I top. What about you?"

"Eh. Get an itch to top occasionally, but I like havin' somethin' up my ass too much to do it all the time."

"Cool."

Cool. As if that's not Rowan's wet fucking dream. He's sure his face is doing something stupid, but Mal doesn't react, so maybe he's merely mentally drooling.

"So you've had Doms before? Long-term ones?" Rowan asks once he regains his composure.

Something in Mal's expression seems to close off at that, eyebrows knitted together slightly and eyes flicking to the side.

"Yeah. Nothin' worth sharing."

"Got it."

It's easy to forget that, despite what Mal and Rowan had done together and how they're talking to each other now, they're still strangers. And some things don't need to be shared. Skeletons in the closet and all that. Rowan gets it. His own closet's practically a fucking graveyard, so he doesn't resent Mal for not wanting to open up about personal stuff that doesn't directly involve Rowan.

"You kinda said a few things you like earlier, but what else are you into?" Rowan asks, changing the subject.

"Want my laundry list of kinks, Red?"

Rowan shrugs. "Kinda, yeah."

"Gonna be here for a while."

"This place is open twenty-four seven, isn't it?"

That earns him a smirk and a quick huff of air through Mal's nose, and Rowan feels his chest puff up a tiny bit at having made Mal laugh again.

"Got a point there. I said I liked it rough, so that includes pushin' me around, manhandling, overpowering me, all'a that. Bein' held in place and forced to do whatever the Dom says, obviously consensually. I'm not into that nonconsensual playacting shit. And havin'—"

"Wait, wait, wait, hang on," Rowan says, fishing for his phone in his pocket and swiping to open his Notes app. "Gonna write this down."

"*Tch.* Fuckin' Boy Scout, huh?"

"You expect me to remember everything you tell me? You said it was a long list."

Mal's eyebrows bounce up in a way that says, *That's fair*. "You ready, Nancy Drew?"

"Yeah," Rowan says once he's typed out what Mal's said so far. "So manhandling and being rough and shit, is that something you'd want all the time, or just when you're in a certain mood?"

Biting the inside of his cheek, Mal takes a second to respond. "More often than not, yeah. Not really in this for tender shit."

"'Kay."

Rowan dutifully types *no tender shit*, though he can't help but think back to how Mal crumbled into him and let himself be petted and talked down at the end of the gangbang.

"I like impact play a lot. Crops 'n belts and all that are good occasionally or when I'm pretty deep in it, but I like regular slapping and spanking best."

That gets Rowan to stop typing. "Yeah, you seemed pretty into it earlier."

Mal bites his lower lip. Rowan's eyes lock on to the plush lip when it springs back from his teeth slicked with spit.

"What can I say? You got big hands, man."

It takes most of the willpower Rowan has left to not vault over the table and show him everything he can do with his big hands.

To his credit, Mal continues, apparently without the need to jump Rowan in the same manner.

"Bondage is a big one too."

"What kinda bondage?"

"All of it—leather, ropes, cuffs. Collars. Chains sometimes. Either partial or whole body, but I'm not into any kinda gimp suits or shit like that."

"'Kay. I'm mostly familiar with padded cuffs, but we can try out some of the other stuff."

At Mal's nod, Rowan types out a note to remind himself to do some research later on. He'd been particularly interested in reading about shibari before he'd joined, and he can only imagine how good Mal would look with ropes digging into his skin.

"Do you like being tied down to stuff or just tied up so you can't move?"

"Both. Depends on what we're doin'. But it goes with the whole manhandling thing. You tie me up and throw me around, I'm gonna be ready to blow pretty much immediately."

Fuck.

Mal continues, "Though it's equally satisfying to be held in place and not given what I want."

"Yeah. For sure." Jesus, this guy really is gonna kill him. "What about other kinds of toys?"

"'M good with most stuff. Plugs and beads are my favorite. Dildos every once in a while, but I like the real thing better. I'm good with, like, nipple clamps, pumps, and gags too, but nothin' that causes a lot of pain. And no fuckin' chastity devices or CBT either."

Rowan stops writing. He knows what chastity cages are, but, "CBT?"

"Cock and ball torture."

Involuntarily, Rowan winces. "Eww, yeah, all set with that."

"Good. Some Doms wanna show how fuckin' tough they are by causin' pain. Which is fine if the sub's into it, but usually they're just lookin' for a reason to be a dick."

"I'll take your word for it." Rowan catches Mal's eyes, decides—unrelatedly—to change the background color of his list to golden yellow. "Seemed like you liked dirty talk too."

Mal downs the rest of his water. "Gotta. That's half the fun."

"What kind do you like best?"

"Got a bit of a humiliation and degradation kink, but nothin' extreme. Praise too, but prob'ly after we get to know each other better. Kinda fuckin' disingenuous or whatever right off the bat."

Rowan forces himself not to drool at Mal's words. Even though it's turning him on, he can't help but be a bit embarrassed by how he'd talked Mal down at the end of the gangbang. It clearly wasn't a dealbreaker at least. And was probably more of an exception to that rule given that it was a part of what Rowan thought he might need for aftercare and not part of the scene itself.

"How about outfits or role-play?" That's an area Mal hasn't touched on yet.

"Outfits, yeah. Not usually something I like to bring up right away, but since you asked, I like jockstraps a lot. Panties too, if I'm in a certain kinda mood."

"Oh." *Fuck.* The mental of image of Mal in a jockstrap or lacy panties sears itself into his mind. He's absolutely going to be jerking off to it later.

"That a good 'oh'?"

Rowan remembers how to swallow after a few seconds. "Yeah. Very good."

"You bi? I like panties, but I ain't a chick."

"I'm gay. I'm not into overly femme guys, but I bet you'd look fuckin' hot in pretty much anything."

He watches Mal's eyelids half close, gold barely showing through the sultry gaze. Like he knows exactly how fucking hot he is and exactly how much he's affecting Rowan with a few suggestive words.

"Not into role-play, though," he says, snapping Rowan back to himself. "We can do somethin' if you're into it, but it's usually too fake for me."

"N-no, not really. I'm good."

"'Kay." Mal pauses, then states casually, "Big into choking too, but that's obviously off the table for us."

Rowan nearly drops his phone. He knew it.

Mal had practically melted into him when he'd so much as grazed his fingertips over his neck. The thought of actually getting to apply pressure and feel his pulse in his fingertips and watch his eyes roll back—*fuck*. He wants it. But it's unrealistic to expect it, and not only because it's forbidden at the club. Choking and breath play is the ultimate sign of trust in a Dom/sub relationship, at least to Rowan. Your partner's life is *literally* in your hands.

"Right," Rowan manages, clearing his throat. "Uh, me too, for what it's worth." The seemingly approving look Mal gives him nearly sends Rowan to the floor. "What, uh, what about planning out scenes?"

"A general idea's good, but I like to be surprised," Mal replies as if he hadn't sent Rowan's brain into a tailspin. "Don't need to practice every fuckin' thing you say."

"You want me to pick stuff to do each session, or do you wanna tell me ahead of time?"

"Mmm… bit of both. I'll text you before Saturday and let you know any specifics I'm feeling, and you can fill in the rest."

Sounds pretty perfect to Rowan. That way he knows whatever they do will be something Mal will like, but with enough freedom to keep things interesting and not so rigidly structured.

"That works. Are your safewords always the color system, or did you do that only for the gangbang?"

"Colors, yeah. Hate actual words. Don't need to be callin' out my fifth-grade math teacher's name while I'm gettin' fucked. You good with that?"

Rowan snorts but doesn't say that he could pick something that's *not* his old teacher's name. He's fine with colors, though. It makes it easier.

"Yep. How about if you're gagged or something—do you have a clicker, or is that somethin' the club has?"

Rowan's never actually had to use one before, but he did read about them during his short research phase while he was applying.

"I have one. I'll bring it each time just in case."

"Cool. Do you usually use stuff provided by the club or bring your own?"

Mal rubs a hand across his face, and Rowan fixates on the ink on his fingers a little longer than strictly necessary for the quick gesture. Thinks back to the sight of them wrapped around his cock, guiding him into his mouth—

"The club has pretty much everything, but I do have my own collection'a shit that I like using. Occasionally I'll use some of the club's stuff if they have a model I like better."

"'Kay. I'll prob'ly have to take a look at what they have next time so I know what the options are."

Mal nods, and Rowan's struck with another question.

"How do you wanna deal with room reservations, by the way? I don't have the booking app that Clover mentioned yet, but I can get it later."

"It'll be easier if I do it. I get priority for pretty much everything."

Rowan feels his eyebrows shoot up at that. Guess he really is a VIP.

"That a membership perk?"

"Eh, kinda. Been there for ages, and the twins are pretty good to me."

Damn. He's insanely curious, but they still need to stick to business.

"Cool. And what about aftercare? You didn't say much about it earlier and kinda seemed surprised by it."

Mal shifts in his seat and bites the inside of his cheek, making his lips pucker to one side. Rowan's suddenly filled with a twinge of dread that he doesn't actually do any kind of aftercare, which can be incredibly dangerous. Thankfully, Mal replies quickly.

"Depends on the scene, I guess. But uh, usually just staying close, talking me down. Soft touches if we do any kinda impact play. Pretty much what you did earlier."

"'Kay. How about cleanup? Do you wanna do that yourself?"

The wince on Mal's face is almost enough of an answer in itself. "Yeah. Don't need anyone wipin' my ass till I'm a geriatric."

Rowan snorts in response and makes a note in his phone. "Got it."

"What about you?"

"About me… cleaning up?"

Another eye roll. "I meant, what kinda shit do *you* like? This is a two-way street."

Oh. Right.

"Uh…." Rowan taps the tabletop a few times, putting his phone down.

What *does* he like? He's tempted to say *Everything you did earlier was fuckin' perfect*. And it was, but he wants to be more specific.

"I'm into pretty much all the things you are, in terms of toys and kinks and shit. Nothing extreme or gross. I like being in control, obviously, but only if it's earned. I like when my partner puts up a bit of a fight. But I get off hardest on making my partner feel good."

"Lotta people say that."

"I'm not a lotta people."

"*Tch*. Can say that again," Mal says, a flash of teeth peeking through the corner of his upturned lips.

That was probably a compliment. Mal seems the type to give indirect compliments like that rather than straightforward ones, and Rowan's completely okay with it. It lets him know he's not alone in his… *whatever* he's feeling toward the other man.

"How do you feel about edging and orgasm denial?" Rowan asks, and he swears he can see Mal's pupils dilate.

"Love it."

Fuckin' perfect.

"Cool. That's good. Kinda one of my favorite things."

"Oh yeah?"

"Yeah."

"So you like longer sessions, then?"

"Uh, how long do you consider long?" Rowan asks.

"Few hours," Mal replies. "Club limit's four hours, though."

"I'm good going for that long. I have decent stamina."

Mal huffs a small laugh. "Yeah, unlike everyone else tonight. Think that Van Damme guy lasted, like, five thrusts."

Rowan's lips curl into a smile. He doesn't *really* like shitting on people, but the other men who were part of the gangbang were pretty terrible across the board for a long list of reasons.

"Yeah. Kinda surprising for an *exclusive* club. Thought people'd be better."

"You'd be surprised," Mal muses. He pops a stray home fry into his mouth, and Rowan has no idea where he's putting all that food. "Thought you were gonna deck that blond kid at the end."

"I don't like sharing."

It's the wrong thing to say, judging by the quick pulse of Mal's eyebrows toward his nose.

"To be clear," Mal says, steeling his face. "We ain't exclusive. Either way. I'm good with barebacking for everything as long as we're both clean, but if one of us fucks someone else before our next test, we use condoms. That good with you?"

"Yeah, of course. Sorry, didn't mean it like that."

He is okay with it. Really. Though even as high as his sex drive is, it's unlikely that Rowan's going to want to fuck anyone else, knowing what's—*who's*—going to be waiting for him come Saturday.

Feeling like their discussion is coming to an end, Rowan closes his Notes app and swipes to his contacts, asking, "What's your number?"

Mal tells him, and Rowan enters each digit silently yet punctuated by the rapid staccato of his heart. He types out Mal's first name, realizing as he does that Mal knows his last name, but not vice versa. "Hey, what's your last name?"

"You a fuckin' phone book or something?"

"Just asking."

Mal huffs and looks away, and Rowan's starting to pick up on his mannerisms, including avoiding eye contact when he's hesitant about something.

"Savaryn," he mutters, like it's something to be ashamed of.

And maybe it is, based on what Sheila had said earlier. Sins of the father. Rowan wonders if Mr. Savaryn is as shitty a dad as Hank was.

"Thanks" is all he replies, opting not to make a big deal of it. Because it isn't. Family's what you choose for yourself, not what you're born into.

He obviously can't take a picture of Mal, so the contact icon remains, sadly, a flat green circle with MS inside. He sends Mal a quick text so he has Rowan's number too. It hits him now, with Mal's number safely saved in his contacts and a one-line convo going, that this is actually real. He's actually gonna get to fuck him again, hopefully multiple times if he doesn't screw anything up.

"All set, guys?" a young girl with a cloth apron tied around her waist asks as she approaches their table.

"Yeah, thanks," Rowan replies, pushing his plate toward the edge.

"No problem. Sheila says it's on the house," she says, stacking their plates and cups into one heavy-looking pile and casually hauling the dishes away in the crook of her arm.

He hears Mal sigh as she walks away. There's definitely a story there, but Rowan figures Mal won't tell him even if he asks.

"You good?" Mal asks.

Rowan nods, shoves his phone back in his jeans pocket. They exit the booth, and Rowan heads straight for the door.

"Hang on a sec," Mal says over his shoulder as he approaches Sheila. She's sitting down behind the counter, placing pastries on a three-tiered stand next to the register.

Rowan can't hear what they're saying, but they talk for barely a minute, Mal shoving a wad of bills into Sheila's apron despite her best efforts to push the money away. Sheila places a wrinkled hand on Mal's bicep, rubbing up and down twice, squeezing once. Familiar. Rowan *can* hear Mal's faint, "Bye, Sheils" before he turns to leave.

It's interesting—Mal's use of nicknames. It seems like they're either meant to convey affection—Jer, Sheils—or utter indifference—Shortstop, Leg Day. He can't help but wonder which Mal means when he calls him Red.

"How much do I owe you?" Rowan asks once outside.

Mal lights up another cigarette. "Don't worry about it."

"You sure?"

A puff of smoke billows out from Mal's nostrils, reminding him of the tattoo inked across his chest and shoulders. Tantalizing. Rowan wants to see it again. And get a closer look at the rest of his tats without the distraction of nearly a dozen other bodies surrounding them.

"Yeah."

"Uh… thanks."

Call it a Southie thing, but Rowan hates having people pay for him. Even when he didn't have money, he was always determined to pay his own way by any means necessary. But he lets it go, making a mental note to pay Mal back in some way later on.

They walk back to the club, this time idly chatting, ironing out minor details of their arrangement, talking shit about some of the guys from earlier, pointing out random bits of graffiti that not even the Back Bay is exempt from. This time, Mal's pace is more leisurely, and it takes them twice as long to get back.

"Are you good to get home?" Rowan asks once they reach the front doors.

"Not a fuckin' princess, man."

"Relax, I'm only checking. You *just* got railed by a buncha guys, then ate your weight in food. Wanna make sure you're not gonna pass out on the way home or anything."

"*Pft*. Yeah. 'M good."

"'Kay."

"I'll text ya. Later, Red."

"Bye, Mal."

Rowan watches him cross the street and enter a dark sedan parked at the curb. Nearly as soon as he closes the door behind him, the engine roars to life, the headlights flare on, and the car peels down the road.

MAL DOESN'T text Rowan for the next five days. He wants to kick himself for expecting it, for wanting it, but that's not their arrangement. Instead, he goes to work, does chores around the house, runs a few miles each day, watches more BDSM porn than he has in his entire life, finds some legitimate websites with advice on being a good Dom, and scours them when he can get his dick to calm down for long enough.

It's all to distract from the persistent buzzing under his skin. Anticipation.

Finally, on Thursday night, his phone dings with a message, the entirety of which he can read from the notification on the lock screen.

[MS] *you still good for saturday?*

Rowan scrambles to unlock his phone and type out a reply.

[RC] *Yeah! 8pm?*

[MS] *yeah*

[RC] *Cool. Is there anything in particular you want to do?*

[MS] *want you to be rough with me. got a taste of it last time but i wanna see what you got*

As soon as the words reach his brain, heat pools in Rowan's belly as he types out a reply.

[RC] *I can do that. Anything else?*

[MS] *didn't get to feel you open me up. or do you not eat ass*

[RC] *I do. And I will*

[MS] *good. We'll take it slow this time n ramp shit up later*

[RC] *I'd like that*

Rowan doesn't want the conversation—as short and businesslike as it is—to end, but he also doesn't want to press his luck. They're not close enough for lengthy conversations that aren't about their arrangement, and he doesn't want to be annoying and risk pushing Mal away.

[RC] *See you Saturday!*

Rowan follows the words with a smiley face emoji, and regrets it almost immediately. Though he wasn't expecting a reply, a few minutes later, he gets another text from Mal.

It's an emoji rolling its eyes.

Stupidly, it brings a smile to Rowan's face. He can't wait for Saturday.

Chapter 4: Two Pieces of a Puzzle

"WHAT'S UP with you?" Addison asks when Rowan punches in on Friday morning. "You've been brooding for *days*, and now you come in with a big smile on your face."

"I haven't been brooding," he snaps back, forcing away the smile he didn't know he'd been sporting and opening his locker to unload his backpack. He'd been not-so-patiently waiting for Mal to text him all week, is all.

"You've spoken, like, *half* the words this whole week that you normally speak in a day."

Rowan gives her a flat stare. "Just got some stuff going on."

"Uh-huh. What's his name?"

"Why do you assume it's a guy thing?"

Addison laughs, carrying a box of supplies to the back of the ambulance and starting to restock things they're running low on. She speaks frankly, in a way they've gotten comfortable with over the course of their two-year partnership. "Rowan. You're like a golden retriever normally, so when something's buggin' you, it's painfully obvious. And you told me yesterday everything was fine with your family. Ergo, guy thing."

Rowan grabs his duffel and loads it in back next to the box of supplies, Addison swiftly restocking gauze and antiseptics while watching him in her periphery.

"You suck sometimes," he mumbles.

"Mm-*hmm*. So, name?"

He hesitates. Because telling Addison about Mal feels a lot like making it a Thing, which it isn't supposed to be. It's *not* a Thing. Well, it's a *thing*, lowercase *t*, but not a capital *T Thing*. There's a difference. And he really needs to develop a goddamn poker face before he turns thirty.

"It's no one," he tells her, settling on a half-truth. "Just a booty call for tomorrow."

She pauses her restocking. "Oh, I thought you were done with Grindr. Wanted something more serious."

Fuck. He did tell her that, didn't he? And he *did* want that for a while. Thought that maybe he could make up for all the anonymous sex of his teens and early twenties with an actual relationship. But it's hard to meet people when your entire social circle consists of your siblings, whose own social circles are barely more diverse. So he'd resigned himself to just… nothing. Well, except the occasional Grindr hookup, because he's not *that* okay with being single.

Until the Menagerie, that is.

Until Mal.

He's not stupid. Definitely not naïve. He knows that his impending Dom/sub relationship with Mal isn't going to turn into anything more. And hell, he might not even *want* it to be more. All he has to go on is a fuck and a meal. A couple of texts. Nothing really. So technically, saying it's a booty call isn't a lie.

"Changed my mind."

Addison gives him a skeptical look but doesn't comment further.

They finish prepping the ambulance for the day ahead, Rowan making sure to keep the conversation firmly away from his weekend plans. By the time they get their first call and roll out of the station, siren blaring, Rowan's run out of things to say.

It's probably unhealthy how much he's looking forward to seeing Mal again.

ON SATURDAY morning, Rowan wakes up a full hour before his alarm. Sue him, but he's a little excited.

He wastes no time preparing a shake for breakfast—frozen fruits, handfuls of fresh spinach, protein powder, milk, and almonds all blended into a sweet drink that he chugs in between dressing in his running clothes.

When he leaves the house, he's only intending to run a mile, maybe two, to get his blood flowing. But he gets lost in his thoughts, rows of apartments and houses passing by in a blur, giving way to small shops as his legs carry him on his longer route, and before he knows it, he's hit five miles as his apartment building comes back into view.

It feels good.

Despite the heat and the sweat dripping from his temples when he's back inside his apartment, he doesn't bother to do more than splash some cool water on his face and run a wet cloth over his neck and shoulders. He's planning on taking a much longer shower before he leaves tonight.

By lunchtime he's already half hard in his sweats, but he forces himself to ignore it, not wanting to have trouble getting it up again tonight. It likely wouldn't be an issue, but he's not chancing it. *Especially* not for his and Mal's first time alone.

Damn.

He's gonna get to fuck him again in a few short hours.

The anticipation of it makes him feel like an eager teenager again. Idly, he wonders if he's ever looked forward to seeing anyone as much as this. Not likely. Even in his past relationships, few and far between as they were, he remembers feeling like it was a chore to see his partner rather than a gift. Something to look forward to. Hopefully, it's a good sign that that doesn't seem to be the case with Mal, even if they're only going to be fucking.

When he deems it late enough and he's tired of pacing his living room and twiddling his thumbs, he showers thoroughly, styles his hair, and dresses similarly to last time, dark jeans but this time with a dark gray button-up shirt, leaving the top two buttons undone. He likes showing off the small patch of skin there with the soft curls of his chest hair peeking out through the lapels of the shirt and the low neck of the white tank top he's wearing underneath. It makes him feel hot. Desirable. Like a goddamn adult man and not the barely legal waxed teen he'd been when he last frequented clubs like this.

The time passes by in a blur, and before he knows it, it's seven twenty and he's out the door.

It's a bit earlier than necessary for him to get there and be ready to go by eight, but since Mal hasn't texted him again and since he started the gangbang right at 8:00 p.m., Rowan wants to make sure he won't be late.

The drive over feels like it takes hours, as he hits every red light possible. There was only one light he might have been able to make, had the person in front of him not slammed on their brakes the second it turned yellow. He mentally curses them out, then forces himself to loosen his grip on the steering wheel and take a few deep breaths. The last thing he needs tonight is to lose control. It would make for a terrible scene for both of them, and Mal might not give him another chance if he blows it.

The rest of the drive passes without incident, and when Rowan finally pushes through the familiar double doors and approaches the front desk to check in, Camilla is once again stationed behind it. Tonight she's in what looks like a black jumpsuit that's unzipped nearly down to her navel, showing off her cleavage. Her eye makeup is strikingly gold and sparkling, accenting her wavy icy blond hair.

Her face lights up when she sees him. "Heeeeyyy!" she calls, voice lilting.

"Hi, Camilla."

She wastes zero time in interrogating Rowan.

"Sooo, looks like you and Malcolm hit it off last time." There's a knowing smile playing on her face that makes Rowan's cheeks flush.

"Yeah, kinda." He rubs at the back of his neck.

"Are you gonna be his new Dom, then?"

"Unless it turns out I suck at it, yeah."

Her smile widens to a full-on Cheshire cat grin, eyebrows raised nearly to her hairline in excitement.

But to his surprise, she doesn't say *You'll be great,* or something optimistic along those lines. Instead she says, "If you do, he'll let you know."

Somehow that makes him feel better. Because the truth is, he *could* very well suck at it, or not be what Mal wants at all. Camilla clearly knows that, and she also apparently knows that Mal would be honest with Rowan about it if that were the case. And something about that blunt truth is significantly more comforting than any reassurance she could have given him.

She types something quickly on her laptop. "You're all set. Malcolm reserved the Gold Room for you two tonight. Fourth floor, as I'm sure you could've guessed. He isn't here yet, but he can show you to it when he gets here."

"Thanks," he says, fighting to keep his own smile at a normal level and not match her excitement.

"Nooo problem!"

He heads toward the elevator and can't help but feel like he was being tested. Sized up, maybe. Idly, he wonders how close she and Mal are, and if he told her anything about their time together last week, or if she intuited it from seeing them walk out together.

On the fourth floor, the lighthearted teasing continues from Jeremiah at the bar.

"Back for more, stud?"

At this rate Rowan's pretty sure his blush is going to be permanently imprinted on his skin. He might have to change his hair color so it doesn't clash. Something dark, maybe.

"Wouldn't you be?"

Jeremiah laughs, the movement causing the thin golden chains dangling from his ears to catch in the light in a way that reminds Rowan of Camilla's glittering eyeshadow. Now that Rowan takes him in properly, it almost looks like they coordinated outfits, Jeremiah wearing black slacks and a black button-up with the top three buttons undone, revealing a glimpse of sculpted abs. Once again, Rowan wonders if he would have hooked up with him had he not gotten into the gangbang.

"I meant what I said last time—that Malcolm's a one-and-done type guy," Jeremiah says.

Recognition trickles through Rowan slowly at first, then all at once like a deluge. That must mean….

"You actually hooked up with him?"

"Looong time ago, but yes."

That gets Rowan's brain whirring. *How long ago? Who initiated? Who topped, if anyone? Was it kinky or vanilla? Why did it only happen once?*

The litany of questions must be written all over Rowan's face, because it elicits another chuckle from Jeremiah.

"Don't think too hard about it. We were tipsy and bitchin' about how we hadn't had any good dick recently."

Yeah, Rowan's definitely gonna think hard about that. Despite all the burning, invasive questions flitting through his mind, the main one he wants an answer to is, "Was it good?"

A flash of brilliantly white teeth accompanies Jeremiah's answer. "Very."

He's gonna think about that *really* hard.

"Blue Ribbon, right?" Jeremiah asks after a beat.

It's really a wonder how everyone here seems so nonchalant about wreaking havoc on Rowan's imagination. But he really should have expected as much from a sex club.

He blinks, willing away images of strong thighs wrapped around a taut waist, and feels himself nodding, too distracted to feel embarrassed by his drink choice. "Yeah, thanks."

Jeremiah nods, retrieves a bottle from a fridge under the counter and uncaps it in one smooth motion. He places a cocktail napkin and glass on the bar top, then expertly tilts the glass and pours the beer so the foam reaches the rim without spilling over. It reminds Rowan of his own bartending stint, however brief, the memory less than fond. He shoves the thoughts away, not wanting to taint his night with memories of his past.

Rowan nurses his drink rather than downing it like he's tempted to and risk losing his faculties. He swivels on his stool and takes in the club properly for the first time tonight.

Blue- and white-tinted lights stream down onto the dance floor and illuminate a crowd of writhing bodies dancing to the low, bassy music. A few couples make out in corners only marginally darker than the rest of the club. Small groups of people crowd around both the high-top tables and low-top booths, glasses clinking with sporadic toasts between bouts of laughter and snippets of conversation.

His eyes drift back to the dance floor and lock on to a guy in a tight tank top, biceps bulging and body rolling in a way that makes Rowan have to spread his thighs a little bit wider. He watches him dance, making his way toward Rowan one beat at a time.

He's so focused on the guy's bedroom eyes and the cut of his jaw that he barely notices the wave of people around him splitting and rejoining as someone moves through the crowd. He sees a hand snake around the man's shoulders, causing him to turn in place. And then there's Mal, easily a foot shorter than the other man, pulling him down by the neck and saying something in his ear.

Rowan jolts upright, willing the music lower unsuccessfully of course—so he can hear what Mal could possibly be saying to him. A few seconds later, the man runs his hand down Mal's arm and squeezes his bicep once before melting back into the crowd.

And then Mal's making his way toward Rowan, and the lights are shining on him, casting pretty shadows across his cheekbones and making his eyes glisten, and God, he looks fucking *ethereal*, and Rowan's wondering how he ever looked twice at the other guy.

"Yo."

Rowan ignores the pulse of excitement that courses through him, the weeklong build of anticipation of seeing Mal again finally releasing as a tingling he feels all the way out his limbs.

"Who was that?" he blurts out, rather than offering a normal greeting.

Mal turns as if he'd already completely forgotten about the guy he'd spoken to.

"Him? Dunno, Jason… Jackson? No fuckin' clue."

"Oh. So you don't know him?"

Golden eyes rake down Rowan's body like he's being scanned. It makes the hairs on his arms and the back of his neck stand upright.

"Fucked him a few months ago. Kind of an airhead, but he's got a big dick."

"Bigger than mine?"

Mal scoffs, but there's an amused smirk on his face. "Got a complex?"

"Just scoping out the competition."

"*Tch.*"

Mal plops down on the stool next to Rowan, nodding to Jeremiah when the bartender makes eye contact with him. Mal's dressed similarly to last time, dark jeans and fitted maroon top with a white denim vest, the sleeves fringed like they've been cut off. Rowan likes it. But now that he knows Mal's an honest-to-God *accountant*, he's having a hard time imagining him in slacks and a button-up. Though Mal had said he works mostly from home, so maybe he has no need for fancier clothes.

Frankly, Rowan would much rather imagine him naked…

… or he could wait, like, an hour and see it for himself again in person.

Yeah, that sounds much better. Saliva pools in his mouth at the thought, dredged up from the carnal part of Rowan's brain that hasn't been able to catch a break since he walked through the doors a week ago. He hones in on the glass as Mal takes a sip of his beer, watching the amber liquid disappear into his mouth.

He can't believe a few hours ago he thought he'd have a problem getting hard again.

"How was your week?" Rowan asks after watching Mal take two more sips of beer.

Mal places the glass down but keeps his hand wrapped around the base of it, one finger tapping the side like he's trying to decide what to say. Which is weird because it shouldn't be a question that really requires any thinking.

After a moment longer, he finally says, "Fine."

"That's good." He waits for Mal to ask him about his own, but after another long sip, he realizes he probably isn't going to. "Mine was good."

"That's good," Mal mimics the enthusiasm in Rowan's voice, though it's definitely put on.

Rowan can't get a read on the guy, and it frustrates the hell out of him. For someone willing to share extremely intimate details about himself, he seems unable or unwilling to talk about anything mundane. Maybe he hates small talk, but *fuck*, if they're gonna do this, they need to at least be able to talk like normal humans. Rowan's about to say something when Mal takes another deep drink of his beer and he's struck with a different thought.

"You're not gonna get buzzed off that, are you?" he asks, gesturing to Mal's half-empty glass. He's thinking about how Mal hadn't eaten last time; if he's drinking on an empty stomach, he could easily get buzzed enough to lose his faculties and make it so they can't do a scene tonight.

"Nah. Been drinkin' practically since I was in fuckin' diapers. And I never do scenes drunk. Shit's dangerous, even if you know what you're doin'."

Rowan knows as much both from his recent research and from his wilder younger years, and he's immensely glad to hear Mal agree with it.

He continues, further putting Rowan's concerns to rest. "Was gonna have you look at the gear they've got so you know what's available for the future. That's gonna take a bit."

Rowan finds himself nodding as Mal speaks. "Sounds good."

They drink in silence for a few minutes, save for the music overhead, but Rowan can't help sneaking glances at him out of the corner of his eye. Picturing him naked. Sweating. Spread open. Begging for cock. Rowan's, mainly. Jason-Jackson's and Jeremiah's too.

He's not as subtle as he thinks, and Mal catches him. "The fuck are you starin' at, Red?"

Rowan feels his cheeks heat up, glad for the partial darkness and the blue lighting. He's embarrassed to tell him what he's *really* thinking, so he settles on a half-truth.

"Sorry, just… Jeremiah, ah, told me you two slept together."

The bartender's ears must have been burning, because a moment later he appears, asking if they need anything else.

"You tellin' people my shit, old man?" Mal says, though it's lighthearted.

Jeremiah rolls his eyes. "Puh-*lease*. Like you give a fuck about anyone knowing how much of a slut you are."

Mal snorts in the back of his throat but doesn't deny it as he downs the last few sips of his beer.

"Old man?" Rowan asks when Jeremiah leaves to help someone else. "He can't be more than, like, thirty-five. How old are you?"

"He's thirty-nine. I'm twenty-eight."

"Oh. Cool. I'm twenty-seven."

Mal's eyes rove over Rowan's face. "Got a bit of a baby face, man."

"Uh… thanks?"

"It's the eyes." Mal doesn't say what he means by that, or if it's a good or bad thing, but as soon as Rowan takes the last sip of his own beer, Mal turns to him fully and says, "You good?"

When Rowan meets his eyes this time, they're lidded, *hungry*, and Mal looks like he wants to eat him alive. And Rowan's all too eager to let him.

"Yeah."

Mal throws some cash on the bar, Rowan leaving his own tip next to it before he follows Mal past the dance floor and nearly all the way down the long hallway of closed doors to a room labeled The Gold Room.

The room itself is much smaller than the Black Room, though similarly furnished. The walls are black, but with gold pinstripes evenly spaced between, making the room all but shimmer from the overhead lights. There's a supply table with a sink and mini fridge in one corner, an adjustable play bench in another corner, cases of toys lining the walls, and a queen-size platform bed topped with the same thick black pad in lieu of actual bedding. Rowan wonders if any of the rooms have *real* beds and thinks that he'd really like to fuck Mal on a proper bed at least once.

Mal closes and locks the door, something Rowan hadn't noticed him do for the gangbang, then opens the toy case closest to the wall.

"C'mere."

Rowan joins him and stares at the wide variety of toys. This cabinet seems to be filled with dildos and vibrators, and they look like the expensive sort, not the cheap stuff you'd buy from the seedy sex shops Rowan had frequented in his younger days. There are a range of sizes, from small and thin to nearly the size and length of Rowan's forearm, which makes him wince. Mal pulls out a clear glass dildo that looks like a smooth stack of beads with a slight curve to it.

"This one's my favorite," he says, handing it to Rowan.

"Kinda small for a size queen."

"Fuuuck off." Mal laughs. "'S a good warm-up. Feels like beads."

Rowan puts it back. "Any others you like?"

"Eh, used most of 'em except the fuckin' massive ones. They're all pretty good, but like I said, the real thing's better." He glances at Rowan's crotch, tongue darting out over his lower lip.

Rowan huffs out a laugh through his nose, if only to keep himself from pushing Mal to his knees to let him have a taste of *the real thing* right now.

"Do you like vibrators?" Rowan asks.

"Vibes are good. Not big on the feeling inside unless it's right on my prostate, but everywhere else outside is pretty sensitive."

"Good to know."

Rowan's mentally cataloging everything Mal says. It shouldn't surprise him that he seems so in tune with his body and knows exactly what he likes and what he doesn't like, but it does. It's a pleasant change from what he's used to, anyway. In the past, Rowan's had partners who barely knew how they liked to be touched, or had a hard time communicating it, so Rowan couldn't get them off as well as he would have liked. And sure, given enough time he can figure anyone out, but that's not exactly feasible for a one-night stand.

He's lucky, really, that he was able to pick up on Mal's tastes so quickly last time. It led him here, after all.

Glancing at the cabinet again and eyeing the litany of cock rings in all shapes and sizes, some with and some without ball rings, he asks, "How about cock rings?"

"Eh, they can be good for edging. Usually they annoy the fuck outta me."

"Got it." But a thought strikes him. "Did you like it when I cut you off from coming last week?"

"Yeah. Shit was hot. I'm big into edging and orgasm denial in general, so it was a good surprise."

Somehow Rowan's brain manages to make him feel both relieved and turned on at the same time.

Mal points to a set of fleshlights and masturbators. "You ever use those?"

"Fleshlights? Once, but it's kinda shit compared to an actual hole."

Mal snorts. "Got that right. Can be fun if you're gettin' fucked at the same time, though."

And fuck if that thought doesn't go straight to Rowan's dick. He's definitely going to have to remember that for the future.

Mal points out a large, long set of silicone anal beads, each bead nearly two inches in diameter. "These are my favorite. Got my own set at home immediately after I used 'em for the first time."

It's almost funny how willing Mal is to talk about sex—how *eager* he is to talk about it—when he wouldn't even have a casual, polite conversation a few minutes ago.

"You wanna use 'em tonight?"

Mal looks like he's considering it. "Nah. We'll keep shit pretty vanilla for tonight."

Rowan nods, thinking that even anal beads are pretty vanilla. Actually everything they've looked at so far seems vanilla. Though he knows from the experience he *does* have that you don't need toys to have filthy, kinky sex, they certainly help.

They move on to the next cabinet, this one containing cuffs, collars, and gags.

"Prob'ly get a lot of use outta these," Mal says.

"Yeah?"

A shrug from Mal. "I like bein' restrained. Got my own set of cuffs that I like better, though. I'll bring 'em with me."

"What's different about yours?"

"They're fur lined. The plain leather's hot as shit, but after a while, the chafing gets to be too much, and it takes me outta it. The club doesn't really keep any toys with fabric like that since it's hard to clean in between uses." He gestures to a cabinet to the right that they haven't looked at yet. "'Cept the ropes, but those are easy to wash."

"That makes sense." Rowan looks around at the other toys in the cabinet. "You like being gagged?"

Rowan swears he sees Mal's eyes flash. "Yeah."

"Any in particular you like or don't like?"

"Can't go wrong with a ball gag. I like the breathable ones, though," Mal says, pointing to one gag in the selection of at least ten that has a bright red ball perforated with small holes.

Rowan nods. "What about with clothing?"

The look Mal gives him is somehow appraising and feral all at once. "You got a thing for ties or somethin'?"

"Somethin' like that."

Mal quirks his eyebrows at him but doesn't inquire further, then moves on to the next cabinet, which has every type of crop, whip, cane, paddle, tickler, and flogger that Rowan's ever seen, and more than a few that he hasn't.

"Jesus," Rowan says, ogling the collection. He picks up one paddle, seeing that it's smooth on one side and metal studded on the other. "You ever use stuff like this?"

"Early on, when I was figurin' shit out. Told you last time, but I don't like a ton of pain."

A thought strikes him then, given the intensity of some of the toys. "I thought the club had a no-blood policy? Some'a this shit would definitely make someone bleed if you used 'em hard enough."

"Yeah." Mal taps on a placard inside the cabinet that Rowan hadn't noticed until now. A review of the rules, it looks like. "Kinda gotta be on the honor system that you won't do it. Not like Clover comes in and inspects all the subs before they leave."

Rowan snorts a laugh at the image of the professional, buttoned-up Clover checking for rule-breakers every night. "Makes sense. Kinda gross to use some of the same equipment with that being possible, though."

Rowan's far from a germaphobe, but his standards for cleanliness have skyrocketed since leaving his home in the South End, and he's not keen on going back.

Mal nods in agreement. "Yeah. 'S why I bring a lotta my own stuff. All theirs is treated leather or synthetic shit that's easy to clean, but I don't trust some'a the dickbags that go here, even if the club cleans everything themselves regularly."

That puts Rowan somewhat at ease. He has a small collection of his own toys that he'd be willing to bring as well, though he suspects that everything he has, Mal does as well.

"So when we get to using this stuff," Rowan starts, "do you usually pick out what you wanna use in the beginning, or pull them out as you go?"

"In the beginning. Makes it easier to keep the scene going rather than stoppin' to look for specific toys." He pauses, eyes scanning the various cabinets. "I know where pretty much everything is, but it's not practical to take me out of it to explain which cabinet a certain toy is in."

Take me out of it. He's talking about subspace. Talking specifically about *Rowan getting him into it.*

Fuck. It might not happen tonight, it being their first time alone, but the thought of getting Mal so lost in pleasure that he reaches that high? Fucking delicious. It happened once at the gangbang, briefly—a tiny glimpse of that hazy fog of pleasure in Mal's eyes that Rowan's been thinking about nonstop since.

Rowan's cock stirs in his jeans. He's thankful for the tightness of them, otherwise it'd be embarrassingly obvious.

The next cabinet is filled with neatly coiled ropes in all colors and lengths, as well as various hooks, clips, and bindings. A quick glance to the ceiling shows what looks like an adjustable bar lined with hooks, presumably to tie someone to. It sends another bolt of desire through Rowan, as does the long coil of cherry-red cotton rope that catches his eye among the plainer colors. He'd love to see the color against Mal's skin, digging in and breaking up the pale expanse of his chest and arms and legs.

"You ever use rope?" Mal asks, as if sensing what the image is doing to Rowan.

"Yeah, but nothing fancy. Just some wrist and ankle restraints."

"There's a workshop comin' up in a few weeks on it."

That piques Rowan's interest. "Like shibari?"

"Yeah." Mal pulls a mass of black rope from the hook that had been badly coiled and expertly untangles and coils it in quick figure-eight motions. He looks almost like he's offended at whoever used it last having put it away so poorly, and Rowan can't help but agree. "One of next month's special events. We can go if you're interested."

Rowan's stomach flutters wildly at the thought of learning a new skill, especially a new skill that would greatly benefit them both. *And* at the thought of spending more time with Mal, though he doesn't know if it would replace his usual session with him or be in addition to it. Either way, he's a thousand percent in.

"Yeah, I'd like that. Lemme know when it's coming up and we can figure it out."

"I'll text you the details later."

Rowan watches Mal wrap the end of the rope around itself three times, securing the effortless loops he'd made. He tugs both ends, as if checking his work. Then he looks up at Rowan through his dark lashes, rope pulled taut between his hands, and wets his bottom lip with a quick flash of his tongue.

All at once, there's a shift in the air, an electric charge lingering between them. It drives Rowan to move, a magnetic pull he couldn't resist if he wanted to.

Rowan steps forward, plucks the rope from Mal's fingers, and places it back on its hook, never once breaking eye contact. He's much more interested in the way Mal's lips part and his eyes rake him up and down.

God, Rowan wants to kiss him. How the hell could he not? Plush lips parted ever so slightly, pink against his pale skin. And it's such a natural buildup to sex that without it, it feels like he's revving a car engine while it's still in park. Not going anywhere. But it's firmly off the table, and Rowan's going to have to find another way of working Mal into a frenzy.

Without the help of nine others.

The challenge of it spurs Rowan into action.

"Get undressed," he says, voice low.

He feels his back straighten of its own accord, raising him to his full height. Legs hip-width apart and weight evenly balanced between them. Chest puffing out slightly. He doesn't know if there's a word for it, this feeling of getting into character, but it feels natural. Feels like if he's keenly aware of how his body looks and feels, if he has control over it, then he'll have full control of his mind as well. And, hopefully, Mal's.

Mal's eyes flash, and a hint of a smirk graces his lips as he toes off his shoes and socks and kicks them to the side. He locks eyes with

Rowan and grips the lapels of his vest, slowly shrugging it off first one shoulder, then the other. As much as Rowan would love to see Mal do a slow, sexy striptease for him, he's been dying to get his hands on his skin again for a week now.

"*Faster.*"

A huff of a laugh through Mal's nose is his only response. He reaches behind him to tug his shirt off over his head, taking even longer than he had with the vest.

So that's what kind of night it's gonna be.

Not on Rowan's watch.

The second the fabric clears his head and that shit-eating grin sees the light, Rowan grabs his arms—still swathed by his shirt—and pulls him flush against his chest.

"Can't even trust you to follow a simple fuckin' instruction, can I?"

"Guess you'll have to—"

Rowan shuts him up with a sharp squeeze to his biceps through the soft fabric, enjoying the firmness of them. "When I want you to answer something, *you'll know.*"

He doesn't give Mal time to say something else shitty, spinning him in place and then walking him the two steps to the bed before shoving him forward onto it with a *whump*, arms pinned underneath him, ass perfectly aligned with Rowan's crotch.

"*Nnng—*" the soft moan is barely audible from where Mal's face is pressed into the mattress, but it's beautiful.

With a firm push to Mal's lower back, a silent command to *stay*, Rowan sinks to his knees and hooks his fingers in the waist of Mal's jeans. The fabric is almost too tight for him to fit his hands under on either side, but he manages enough to give a firm tug downward over the swell of Mal's ass. He's expecting the same black briefs Mal wore last time, maybe a different color.

He's not expecting to be met immediately with bare skin.

But it's *not* bare skin. Not completely. There's a thick black band stretched across Mal's lower back, sitting below his dimples, another band wrapped around each cheek, framing his ass perfectly.

Fuck.

He hadn't thought he'd get to see Mal in a jockstrap so soon. It throws him off completely, keeping him frozen in place for far longer than it should, to the point where Mal shifts above him, hitching his hips back.

Rowan snaps out of it, yanking the jeans down to Mal's ankles. Naturally, Mal moves to kick out of them, but Rowan stills him with a firm grip to his calf, the idea of him being bound by his own clothing far too tempting to pass up.

"Tell me if you need to move, understand?"

"Y-yeah."

God, hearing the hitch in Mal's voice so soon shouldn't be that hot. If he needed any confirmation that Mal likes being pushed around, this is definitely it.

Now, with Mal where Rowan wants him, he can focus on the smooth expanse of his ass, accentuated by the dark straps. Rowan notices a tattoo he hadn't seen before on the back of Mal's left ankle, two small snakes serpentining up nearly to his calf, one larger than the other. It looks older than some of the others, ink starting to fade into the cracks of his skin. He brushes his fingertips over it briefly, then runs both hands up Mal's legs, pausing a moment when he passes the tattooed band of lace with the knife on his right thigh.

Rowan never thought he'd be one of those people obsessed with tattoos, but something about Mal's strike a chord with him. They look good against his skin, like they're part of it, where Rowan's always thought his own single tattoo looks pasted on. If he didn't have a job to do—making a wreck out of the other man—he could spend hours tracing the ink with his fingers and, if Mal would let him, his tongue.

But now he continues his trail up Mal's legs to his ass. Last time he hadn't gotten a chance to properly worship it. This time he's gonna make up for that.

He slides his hands past the straps and curls them around to take a cheek in each hand… and *squeezes*. The firm flesh gives under his grip, dimpling and turning white where his fingertips dig in. He kneads Mal's ass, fully enjoying how it feels in his hands, the perfect size. The feeling of it and Mal's quiet hums from above have his cock hardening in his jeans, and for a moment, he's tempted to pull it out to relieve some of the pressure, but if he does this might be over far sooner than it should be.

So he settles for spreading his own thighs as best he can, careful not to kneel on Mal's jeans pooled on the floor, keeping his legs in place.

Under his hands, Rowan feels Mal clench his ass, the cheeks tightening and making Rowan lose his grip. A "Get on with it," it seems. But Mal's in no position to be making demands.

Smack!

Rowan slaps his right cheek *hard*, red immediately blooming across pale skin, a gasped "Mmm!" coming from the bed.

He spanks Mal again on the other cheek for good measure, feeling goose bumps pebble up as he smooths his hands over the heated skin. One of these days, now that he knows Mal's penchant for spanking, he's going to turn his entire backside red.

But now—now, he finally spreads Mal's cheeks apart, revealing the tight pink hole that Rowan's been dying to get inside of again.

He hears his own breath hitch, which means Mal probably does too, but he doesn't acknowledge it. Maybe cutting him a little slack for being eager.

"See somethin' you like, Firecrotch?"

Maybe not.

To add insult to injury, Mal clenches again, hole winking, enticing him to touch. Enticing him *in*. Fucking *taunting* him.

Rowan rises up, slips one hand under the back band of Mal's jockstrap and the other under his chest, and hauls him up swiftly so his bare back slams into Rowan's clothed chest. He drags his hand along Mal's chest, trailing fingertips up the cords of Mal's neck to grip his jaw and turn his head halfway toward himself. Lips and nose pressed against his ear, Rowan can smell his shampoo, something minty and sweet.

"Call me that again," he says, tone measured, "and I'm gonna get that fleshlight and make you watch me get myself off while you sit here, hard 'n empty. Got it?"

For good measure he grinds his cock into Mal's ass, letting him feel exactly what he would be missing out on.

He feels Mal nod, ear brushing his lips and sending a tingling sensation through Rowan.

"Good."

With that, he shoves Mal back down on the bed and returns to kneeling behind him, snapping the bands of the jockstrap on his way down. And while he doesn't love the idea of rewarding him for being a brat, he's tired of waiting. He spreads Mal's cheeks again and licks a hot, wet stripe from the edge of the jockstrap up to his hole, the clean musky scent spurring him on as much as Mal's gasped, "Hah!"

He repeats the movement several more times, Mal's noises fading to little more than contented sighs as he acclimates to the sensation. Which means Rowan needs to change it up.

He squeezes Mal's asscheeks, pulling them apart as much as he can, pressing his face in between so he can suck on Mal's hole. That gets Mal breathing heavy again. Beautiful. Rowan wants to keep him vocal, so he alternates between sucking, licking with the flat of his tongue, and tracing around it with the tip.

From past experience, he knows he's capable of bringing someone to tears with his tongue, but tonight's not the night for that quite yet.

Still, he can't help wanting to tease Mal.

He pulls back to run the pad of his thumb over his hole, watching it quiver under his touch.

Suddenly he's bombarded with images of Mal's hole dripping with other men's come as it had been last week. And fuck if it doesn't turn him on knowing he'd been filled to the brim, fucked empty and filled again and again, loving every second of it.

He needs to get something inside him right now. Rowan pries apart his hole with his thumbs and delves his tongue inside, the phantom taste of come he imagines almost masking the taste of his own spit as he works his tongue deeper inside.

"Fuuu-*uhhck*!"

He wishes his tongue was longer so he could hit his prostate. But with how hard Mal's clenching around him, practically cutting off his circulation, he doubts that he would be able to push in far enough even if his tongue was sufficiently long. He withdraws his tongue and licks over Mal's hole, tiny kitten licks to give him a breather.

A breather that Mal evidently doesn't want.

"Come *on*," he growls, shoving his hips back.

Smack!

Rowan's hand connects with Mal's asscheek in a sharp spank that echoes in the room.

"Hah!"

He runs his hand over the pink skin, warm to the touch. Feels the skin pebble up with goose bumps under his fingers.

"You said you wanted me to eat you out, so quit bein' ungrateful."

"I'm not—"

Smack! Smack!

Two quick blows, one on each cheek, and Mal is gasping a bitten-off moan instead of whatever lameass excuse he was going to give for mouthing off again.

"You *are.* Now shut the fuck up."

As soon as the words are out of his mouth, Rowan dives in again, sucking and licking Mal's hole like it's the best thing he's ever tasted. And fuck, it might be. He pulls back for a brief moment to catch his breath, then spits directly on Mal's hole, watching the thin white trail run over the rim and down the back of his balls. He thinks again of last week when Mal had been leaking, lets a groan escape that he hadn't planned on, then licks up his spit and imagines it's his own come, and it feels *filthy* but somehow hot as hell at the same time.

Mal's already so pliant under his tongue, almost fully relaxed despite the position and despite this being their first time together, and it sends a pulse of heat through Rowan as he continues to work him over. And by the time Mal's full body is shaking, nearly vibrating with the tenseness of his muscles, and Rowan's jaw and knees are starting to hurt, Rowan knows it's time to move on.

God, he needs to get inside Mal again. As much fun as he's having teasing Mal, he's teasing *himself* in the process, knowing there's a warm, wet hole in front of him that he gets to sink into once he's prepped.

Lube.

He needs lube right now.

"Stay," Rowan tells him with a firm push to his lower back.

He crosses the room to the supply table, grabbing a new travel-sized bottle of lube—a white-and-green bottle with Good Clean Love *bio-nude* printed on the front. Definitely not the KY he's used to, but this brand touts that it Works the Way You Do thanks to some sort of Bio-Match technology, and Rowan's a little skeptical, but he figures if anyone's gonna have good quality lube, it's gonna be a sex club.

He should have gotten the lube before they started, given what Mal told him earlier, but they kind of went from zero to a hundred, both clearly eager to get on each other again. Next time, Rowan tells himself, he'll be better prepared.

From the short distance away, he takes one more moment to admire Mal, upper body still pressed into the mattress, thick legs straight except a tiny bend at the knees so they don't lock and risk him passing out. He's fucking beautiful, and Rowan's dick twitches in his pants at the sight of him waiting for him.

He doesn't look as long as he wants, but long enough to commit the sight to memory to jerk off to later.

When he takes his place back behind Mal, he runs a hand along his lower back, above the jockstrap, and asks, "You good?" to check in.

"Yeah," Mal replies.

"Good."

And as much as Rowan likes him in this position, with his legs still so close together, he can't open him up as much as he needs to.

He nudges the back of Mal's thigh with his knee. "Take 'em off," he says, though Mal had already clearly received the memo, as he steps out of his pants, pushes them off one foot after the other, then kicks them to the side.

As soon as they're off, Rowan grabs the back of Mal's right knee and hauls it up on the bed, stretching Mal wide and giving him much easier access to his ass. And Mal *goes* with it, huffs out a breath of air, maybe of surprise but definitely not of anything resembling disapproval.

Rowan wastes no time in running a palm between Mal's cheeks, over the slick hole he'd had his mouth on minutes ago. And the other man all but whimpers at the contact, much firmer than Rowan's tongue had been.

"Fuckin' love this, don't you?" he asks rhetorically.

He's not expecting a reply—he doesn't need one to know what the answer is—but Mal makes another one of those strangled "*Mmm!*" noises that makes Rowan's dick twitch.

"Yeah. Course you do." He huffs out a laugh, preps two of his fingers with a generous coat of lube, and circles his hole with his fingertips. "Bet you couldn't fuckin' *wait* to feel me again. Bet the second your ass went back to normal after the gangbang, you shoved every toy you had up there, just to see if any of 'em felt like me." Rowan punctuates his cocky rant by sliding his index finger in to the last knuckle.

"*Hnnng!*"

"I know they didn't."

Rowan pumps his finger in and out slowly, letting Mal adjust despite his already shoving his hips back to get Rowan deeper. Perfect. He indulges him after a few moments, adding in a second finger if only because Rowan would have done the same thing if he owned a fleshlight. Tried to mimic the feeling of Mal's ass around him, only to realize that nothing could beat it.

"You said it yourself," he continues, squeezing Mal's asscheek with his free hand and feeling Mal jerk in response. "You prefer the real thing."

He can barely see it from where he's kneeling, but he glimpses the back of Mal's head bob twice in a nod. Hears his breath practically echo in the room with how hard he's breathing from two fingers.

"And you know what, Mal?" Rowan asks as he scissors his fingers, spreading them wide to help stretch Mal's rim and inner walls. He lets the question dangle in the air, lets Mal ruminate on it for a minute as he works him open, delving deep inside.

Finally, when he senses Mal is nearly ready for another finger, Rowan crooks his two fingers up and spears them directly into Mal's prostate, with a swell of pride as he finds his mark perfectly and rips a keening moan from Mal's throat.

A loud "Hah!" turns into a low "Ohhhh!" as he presses harder into the sensitive gland.

Rowan barely contains a moan of his own as he promises, "I'm gonna fuckin' *ruin* you for everyone else."

And Mal's whine grows impossibly louder as Rowan continues petting over his prostate in long, firm strokes that he knows would drive anyone wild. "Yeah. Wanna hear you," he croons.

With his free hand, Rowan tugs down the fabric of the jockstrap covering Mal's cock, the material damp from how much he's been leaking. And fuck if *that* isn't the hottest thing. He pulls out Mal's cock and balls, feeling the weight of him in his hand as he pumps him, firmly but rhythmically, in time with the press of his fingers against Mal's prostate.

It's a weird angle, but Mal *mewls* and twitches in his hand and—

"Fu-fuck, I'm gonna—"

Rowan pulls his fingertips away and tightens his hand around Mal's cock, not wanting him to come so soon. Though he can't deny how hot it is that Mal has nearly come from a brief prostate massage and hand job. Can't deny how *hard* it makes him thinking of edging Mal one day, milking his prostate until he's leaking all over himself and ready to blow, only to be denied that pleasure over and over.

Fuck.

But for now, he asks, "You wanna come now?" and resumes his fingering, steering clear of Mal's prostate.

Mal's back heaves once, twice. "N-not yet."

As much as he'd like to, Rowan's not gonna tease him anymore. He slips in a third finger, stretching him thoroughly and letting himself enjoy the feeling of the tight heat around his fingers. The heat of him in his hand, precome leaking from his tip nearly down to the fucking floor, a shiny gossamer trail proving how turned on Mal is right now.

Rowan could stand to fit in another finger, knowing how big he is compared to most guys, but he's greedy.

Selfish.

A pretty shit quality for a Dom, and Rowan will work on that later, but he's been *dying* to get inside Mal again, like an addict awaiting his next fix, and it should bother him, it should *worry the fuck outta him*, but he's hard as a rock and he doesn't care.

Rowan rises up, gripping and spreading Mal's asscheeks as he does and rutting his still-clothed, hard bulge against him, not caring that lube and his own spit smear on the front of his jeans.

With both hands, he grips Mal's biceps and hauls him up, back once again pressed to Rowan's chest, eliciting a sharp inhale from Mal.

And as hot as the faux restraints are, Rowan wants him fully naked. He pushes the scrunched-up fabric of Mal's shirt down his arms and lets the garment drop to the floor.

With Mal completely naked, Rowan takes the opportunity to run his hands up Mal's sides, over his abs and pecs and back down across the subtle indents of his rib cage. Exploring him. Normally, he'd spend as much time as he wanted feeling him up, but he's all too aware that even that can be seen as too intimate, which isn't what they're here for.

Maybe one day they can dip into that territory—once they've known each other for longer than a week, that is—but for now Rowan makes his appreciation of Mal's body known with two quick loops, a squeeze here and there, a raking of blunt fingernails against his skin. And then he's done. But before he stops, he can't help but notice the way Mal's head has started to dip back, a breathy rush of air escaping his lips, particularly when Rowan had brushed over his nipples.

The fact that Mal evidently has sensitive nipples sends a surge of heat to Rowan's dick, and he files that knowledge away for later. He'd already suspected as much from the gangbang, but the confirmation of it now is a welcome fact.

Rowan spins him in place, less rough than he had been initially, but still firm in his movements. Mal shifts easily, and once they are face-to-face, Rowan tells him, "Undress me."

Mal smirks and raises an eyebrow. "Can't do that yourself, Fire—"

Rowan threads his fingers in Mal's hair and tugs his head back, forcing him to look even further up at him.

"You wanna try that again?" Rowan asks rhetorically, eyes narrowed, watching with laser focus as Mal swallows, Adam's apple more pronounced than ever with his neck craned back.

Then there's that tiny nod of his head again, and in one quick motion, Mal's fingers come up to start unbuttoning Rowan's shirt, working from the top down. He pushes the fabric off Rowan's shoulders, lets the garment fall to the floor along with Mal's own clothes, then reaches for the hem of Rowan's tank top.

"Pick it up," Rowan orders.

Mal pauses, glancing up at Rowan with a questioning look, eyes widening when he sees that Rowan's serious. Slowly, he dips in place, keeping eye contact as he retrieves Rowan's shirt from the floor.

"Fold it and put it on the bed."

A hitch in his breath, but Mal obeys, quickly shaking out and folding the garment, if a little unevenly with it still being unbuttoned, and places it on the corner of the bed.

"Good. Keep going."

Rowan hadn't planned on this, but something about it gets his blood racing. The power imbalance of having Mal pick up and fold Rowan's clothes while his lie crumpled on the floor. It does something for him, is all. And the way Mal's breath stutters when he pulls Rowan's tank top over his head and immediately folds it tells him he's most likely into it too.

Mal moves to start on his jeans, but Rowan pushes at his shoulders to get him on his knees instead, seeing that he'd intentionally landed on his own pile of clothing as Rowan hoped he would.

And God, seeing him on his knees in front of him, looking up expectantly, has Rowan's cock growing impossibly harder.

"Shoes first."

Mal sucks his bottom lip into his mouth as he unlaces Rowan's shoes one at a time, Rowan stepping out of them himself. He doesn't love his feet being touched, so when Mal moves to take his socks off, he stills him with a hand to his head and toes them off himself.

Without being told, Mal folds his socks in half and turns at the waist to place them atop Rowan's shirts.

Fucking perfect.

"Now you can take my pants off."

Mal deftly, silently unbuttons and unzips Rowan's jeans, hooks his fingers in the front pockets, and tugs them halfway down Rowan's thighs. He brings one hand up to half circle Rowan's hard dick, feeling him through his briefs.

Even that simple touch feels fucking great, but that's not what he told Mal to do. So with his hand still curled in Mal's hair, he *pulls* once again, tearing Mal's gaze away from his lap.

"Didn't say to feel me up, Mal."

And Rowan half expects him to grope him again, but something about the way Mal's cheeks flame instead gives Rowan pause. Almost like he's not used to people calling him *Mal* in bed, and his brattiness was thrown off. That's something to delve into later, given that Mal told him to call him by that name when they'd talked after the gangbang. Insisted on hating being called Malcolm, even.

For a second, he's tempted to pause. To check in and make sure he didn't cross a line. To be *soft*.

But the way Mal's fingers dig into Rowan's hips at the band of his boxer briefs, knuckle tattoos vibrant against his pale skin, makes him reconsider.

Want you to be rough with me, Mal's text echoes in his head.

"You done bein' a fuckin' brat, or do you actually want me to fuck a fake pussy instead of your ass?" Rowan asks.

A beat, then two. Mal doesn't respond.

A sharp *tug* at the roots of his hair. "*That* would be one of the times I want you to answer."

A pause then "No." Grumbled. Annoyed.

Two can play at that game.

"*No* you're not done bein' a brat, or *no* you don't want me to fuck the toy?"

Rowan can practically feel the resentment radiating from Mal as his muscles tense beneath him. So different from the near embarrassment he'd shown a few moments ago at being addressed by name. Yet now Mal answers, "Don't want you to fuck the toy," through gritted teeth.

"'S what I thought." Rowan huffs out a low laugh, cupping Mal's chin with his thumb and pointer finger and tilting his head up to meet his eyes. "That mean you'll be good for me?"

And, yeah, okay, a small part of him does wish that Mal would be good and do everything he says. But a much larger, *harder* part of himself wants him to keep going. Wants him to keep being the petty, whiny, mouthy brat that he is when he's naked and make Rowan work for it.

But he can't let him know that. Not right now at least.

In lieu of a verbal response, Mal nods against his fingers, curtly, clipped almost, if that's possible with a gesture. Rowan takes it as a win.

"Good. 'Cause I missed this greedy fuckin' mouth of yours," Rowan tells him, dragging his thumb along Mal's lower lip. Mal cranes his neck to follow the trail of Rowan's hand, until he sucks the digit into his mouth, tonguing over Rowan's first knuckle. "Yeah. Want you to get my dick nice and wet, just like that." He lets him suck on it for a few seconds more before pulling it out of his mouth and wiping his thumb on the side of Mal's cheek. "Got a job to finish first, though."

At once, Mal's fingers tug Rowan's jeans the rest of the way down his legs, waiting for Rowan to step out of them before folding and placing them on the bed.

He curls his hands into Rowan's briefs and tugs them down, Rowan's cock bobbing out and hanging hard between his legs. In a flash his briefs are with the rest of his clothes, and Mal's eye level with Rowan's cock and looking *hungry*, eyes half lidded. Mal drops his jaw and presses his tongue against his bottom lip, inviting Rowan inside.

Rowan holds his cock at the base, pumps himself once, and rubs the tip along Mal's outstretched tongue, watching as Mal's eyes flutter closed at the taste. His lips close around the head, ready to suck, but Rowan drags his cock to the side, watching rapt as Mal's cheek bulges before it pops out the side of his mouth. He feels the hot puff of air as Mal exhales, but it's cut short when Rowan sticks his cock back in. A groan vibrates through Mal's lips as Rowan repeats the action, growing stronger as Mal sucks a little harder each time his mouth is filled.

And God, when Rowan finally relents and stops teasing both Mal and himself and presses his cock deeper inside, it's as good as he remembered. Better even, now that they're alone and there's only the sounds of Rowan's steady breaths and the wet slurp of Mal working his cock with his lips and tongue. He looks so fucking perfect with his lips stretched wide and eyes scrunched tight and…

… oh.

Oh, that's not right. Rowan shifts his hand from where it has been resting, easily nestled into Mal's hair, and cups his cheek, runs his thumb across his temple.

"Look at me," he says, voice even.

And when Mal's eyes flutter open and he looks up at Rowan through his dark lashes, lips tight around his cock and still languidly sucking, well, Rowan can't help but tell him how good he looks.

"Fuckin' perfect like this."

Mal hums around him, the vibrations tingling through the head of his dick and making Rowan's breath hitch. And the little shit must love that, using his tongue to push Rowan's cock against the side of his mouth so that Rowan can feel it bulging through his cheek, which, okay, *fuck*.

Rowan dips his head back for a second, long enough to get his bearings as Mal works him over expertly. He's forced to look down at him again when he feels a hand curl around his shaft and Mal's mouth pull off a few inches.

Prying Mal's fingers off and pushing them away with a flick of his wrist, Rowan tells him, "Said I wanted your mouth, not your hand."

He thrusts back in the few inches that he'd slipped out, feeling the back of Mal's throat close around the tip of his cock and the sputtering choke that follows. Mal's hands jerk up involuntarily and clutch at Rowan's thighs.

"Keep 'em in your lap," Rowan says, voice stern. And when he pulls them back down, hovering over his dick, Rowan adds, "But don't fuckin' touch yourself," for good measure. Mal's fingers clench, but he dutifully places a palm on each thigh.

Rowan feels more than hears Mal's slight whimper at the direction, little more than a tingling sensation around the head of his cock. Then Mal gets to work in earnest, dutifully sucking him down, head bobbing and hands clawing into his thighs, little red crescents forming in his skin from Mal's blunt nails. Rowan lets him work on his own for a long few minutes, growing harder with each passing second and each dribble of spit that runs down Mal's chin.

And he's so fuckin' pretty like that. *Gorgeous.* Eyes lidded but still open like Rowan told him, focused on him.

"Fuck," Rowan breathes as Mal's tongue delves into his slit. "Wish you could see yourself like this."

Frankly, Rowan wishes he had better than 20/20 vision. Wishes he could see in HD with the way Mal's devouring him right now and looking like he's loving every second of it.

Rowan sinks his fingers into Mal's hair, the only warning he gives him before thrusting into his mouth, cock hitting the back of his throat and making him splutter before Rowan pulls back. He keeps his cock in his mouth, just the tip, and lets Mal catch his breath.

The feeling of Mal's hot breath on his cock sends a wave of pleasure through him and a spurt of precome to dribble out from his tip. And Mal outright *whines* at that before suctioning his lips around him again and locking eyes with Rowan, lidded and hazy as he lets Rowan's cock sit in his mouth.

Waiting.

Waiting for Rowan to fuck his face like they both want.

And holy *fuck*, he's perfect.

A curl of Mal's tongue on the underside of Rowan's tip is all the motivation he needs to fist his hands in Mal's hair and slam forward into the wet heat of his mouth. He gives him no break this time, cock sliding in easily and Mal expertly keeping his teeth out of the way and taking nearly Rowan's full length down his throat.

The hot suction of Mal's mouth around him is heavenly, but the blissed-out look on Mal's face is so much better. Rowan keeps Mal's head mostly still between his hands as he fucks into his mouth, watching his eyes droop the more of his cock Rowan stuffs inside. By the time Mal's struggling to keep his eyes open and is breathing hard through his nose, Rowan's groin is pressed firmly to his face.

"*Unh,*" Rowan moans, drinking in the sight of Mal with his mouth full. "Fuckin' made to suck cock, huh?"

He keeps thrusting in deep, hands sliding out of Mal's hair to cup his cheeks on either side, fingertips pressed against the underside of his jaw to feel him swallow around Rowan's cock. Feel the shifting of his muscles as Rowan holds him still. Mal gags, coughs, throat tightening around Rowan's dick before he pulls out, and Mal moans openly, a beautiful "*Hnnnn!*" sound that lights Rowan's belly on fire.

"Yeah, *God*. Tell me, Mal."

Another thrust, not as deep but *fast*, driving himself in to the root and back out again. And then another strangled sound from Mal, like he wants to answer Rowan but can't do that with his mouth full. Rowan grips his cock around the base, pulling out and rubbing the tip across spit-slick lips.

And when Mal works his lips around his head, like he's sucking on a goddamn lollipop, well. That's really all the answer he needs, but—

"Tell me how much you love this," Rowan demands, curling his hand around Mal's jaw and coaxing his mouth open to circle his cockhead around Mal's tongue.

Mal closes his lips around his tip in a filthy semblance of a kiss. "Fuckin' *love it.*"

His words, sultry and low and gravelly from having his throat fucked, bypass Rowan's ears and go straight to his dick, making his stomach clench and his balls tighten like he's about to *blow* for fuck's sake.

And he's gonna risk it, risk coming early, but, well, Mal said he wanted him to be rough. Said he *fuckin' loves* having a cock in his mouth. So Rowan's gonna give him what he wants.

Once again, he grips Mal's hair, lines his cock up, and slams home, fucking his mouth fast and hard like he's gonna do to his ass later on. A teaser. A promise.

"*Hm-hm-hm-hm!*" Mal groans with every thrust as Rowan's cock hits the back of his throat and his balls slap against his chin.

His hands fly up to clutch at Rowan's calves, and Rowan lets him, knowing that he probably needs the leverage and also that Rowan doesn't want to stop to tell him to keep his hands in his lap.

God, he's so fucking perfect.

And *fuck*, it's too much. Someday he'll have Mal suck him off and swallow his come, but now he needs to stop. Needs to be inside his other hole again.

"Get up," Rowan tells him, pulling out and dislodging Mal's hands from his legs.

Mal obeys instantly, almost *too* eager, and Rowan would comment on it—whether to praise or chastise, he has no idea—but he'd be lying if he said he wasn't equally as excited. Still, Rowan notes the slight wobble in Mal's knees as he rises up in front of him.

Once Mal is at his full height, Rowan bends and hooks his hands behind Mal's thighs, feeling the swell of his ass above, and lifts him quickly, then dumps him backward onto the bed—away from Rowan's clothes—his weight manageable but still making his quads strain with the effort. Mal's wide-eyed expression is fully worth it when he hits the pad with a *thump*, his surprised look quickly shifting to lust.

And seeing him like that—splayed on the bed, chest and cheeks flushed, cock hard where it's once again concealed by the jockstrap— nearly makes Rowan dizzy with want.

"Anyone ever tell you how good you look on your back?"

Instantly, Mal's face flushes a beautiful crimson to match the color on his chest.

With a low chuckle, Rowan keeps his eyes on him and climbs on the bed between his legs, which part automatically for him. He settles in a wide, kneeling stance pressed against Mal's ass. He ruts his cock against Mal's, spreading his precome and Mal's spit against the already-damp fabric of the jockstrap. The feeling is both electric and *primal*, settling somewhere deep in Rowan's gut.

"Yeah," Mal replies, hitching his hips up in a slow grind, abs flexing tantalizingly. "They all did somethin' about it, though."

Yeah. He needs to get on him right the fuck now.

"Changed my mind," Rowan tells him. In one swift motion, he pushes Mal's knees to his chest then off to the side, using the momentum of the motion and one hand under his lower back to flip him onto his front. "Think I like you on your knees better."

"Fuck—"

"That's the plan, but do you think you deserve it?"

Mal huffs out a breath that sounds entirely too self-satisfied for their current positions. "Think you're gonna fuck me whether I deserve it or not."

Smack!

Rowan slaps his right asscheek hard, hand stinging with the effort. "Ah!"

Rutting his cock against the back of Mal's thigh, Rowan spanks him again. "I got a whole wall full'a toys that can get me off, Mal. Don't need your slutty ass."

And boy if that isn't the biggest lie Rowan's ever told in his life. Because he does, in fact, very much need Mal's ass. Is very much going to fuck him whether he deserves it or not. Even if Mal had done nothing but disobey him this whole time, he'd still fuck him at the end 'cause he fuckin' loves it too. They *both* fuckin' love it.

But he has a role to play, and that role right now demands making Mal beg for it.

Mal props himself up on his forearms and arches his back, sticking his ass out like he had at the gangbang. Right before the first guy fucked him. Rowan has to grip the base of his dick to stave off the desire to come from the sight and memory alone.

Instead, he casually snaps the straps of the jockstrap, enjoying the way Mal's ass all but jiggles with the force of the elastic snapping back into place.

"*Pft*. Look at you. So fuckin' desperate, huh?" Rowan shoves two fingers deep inside him, pressing against his prostate once before pulling away and focusing on simply dragging his fingers in and out.

"*Hn*!" Mal's head dips to the bed, legs widening on their own.

Like he's fucking *presenting* himself to Rowan, and fuck if that doesn't make his dick throb.

"Yeah, you are. Fuckin' obvious, really." Rowan reaches over to grab the lube he'd thrown on the corner of the bed and slicks himself up while he fingers Mal. "But I wanna hear it. Just like last time."

There's only a brief hesitation before Mal replies in a quiet voice, "Fuck me."

His tone is nowhere near as desperate as Rowan knows he's feeling right now, if the breathless whimpers he's letting out and endless straining of his muscles are anything to go by.

So Rowan withdraws his fingers and grinds his slick cock between his cheeks, the tip catching on the rim of Mal's hole, making the other man whine.

"Not good enough."

"Fuck." Mal grits out, and Rowan sees him ball his hands into fists on the bed. "Come on."

One final slick thrust and Rowan pulls away, sitting back on his heels until he's completely separated from Mal's body.

"Nah, you know what I wanna hear, Mal."

Instead of the verbal begging Rowan wants, Mal widens his knees again so Rowan has a perfect view of his pink hole closing around nothing. Where it *should* currently be closing around Rowan's cock.

"Cute how you think that's gonna work," Rowan tells him.

He slides off the bed, turning and making for the toy wall. In reality, he's not going to get any of the toys. Their talk beforehand made it clear that Mal wants this session to be mostly vanilla, so he's obviously going to respect that. But Rowan can fake it. Can bluff for the sake of riling Mal up and getting him to beg for his cock.

"Rowan…."

There it is.

That quiet muttered word that's still somehow loaded with annoyance and resignation, but most importantly, with *desire* underneath it all.

"Hm?" he hums, turning to look at Mal, who's not looking at him, head still dipped low to the mattress.

"Fuck me, Rowan." Louder, but still too quiet.

Rowan returns to the bed, climbs back on, and kneels at Mal's side. He cups his chin in his hand, turning Mal's face to look up at him. "Didn't quite hear you." With his free hand, Rowan strokes himself in long, slow pulls.

Mal's entire focus is on Rowan's cock, lips parting again as if remembering how it felt in his mouth. As he watches Rowan jerk himself, his features relax, brows no longer scrunched together, eyelids no longer narrowed. It takes nearly a full minute, but he's done fighting.

"I want you to fuck me, Rowan." This time it's perfect. Breathy and with an edge to it, but sincere enough that Rowan will give it to him.

He walks on his knees back around behind Mal, then clutches above Mal's elbows to haul him onto his knees and pull him back against his chest. He crosses Mal's hands behind his back and switches his grip to fit both of his wrists in one hand—and fuck, he *can* fit both of them in one hand—freeing his other to line up his cock.

"Good. That wasn't so hard, was it?"

As soon as the first inch is inside Mal, Rowan reaches around to tweak his nipples, the hard buds hot under his fingertips.

"*Unnnnhhhh—!*"

And *God*, as he presses in deeper, it feels like Mal is sucking him in, and he can't help releasing a low groan, matching Mal's.

"Yeah, that's it, Mal," Rowan tells him. When he's halfway in, he pulls back out and then works himself deeper, pinching Mal's nipple between his fingers.

"Fuck," Mal curses, breathy and low, when Rowan's fully seated.

"Yeah," Rowan agrees.

He slides his free hand up Mal's chest, fingers skirting over his pecs and clavicle and up to his neck, like he had at the gangbang. He feels more than hears Mal's sharp inhale at the contact, all the much hotter now that he knows that Mal is into choking. But he continues his trail up, cupping Mal's jaw and turning his head to the side as he thrusts leisurely into him, feeling Mal open up around him.

"So fuckin' tight for me," he says in his ear as Mal shudders and clenches around him.

"Shit…."

And it's nice, this slowness. Appreciating each other and getting accustomed to being connected again. But Mal said he wanted rough, so that's what Rowan's gonna give him. And if Rowan's being honest, he wants to fuck Mal into next Tuesday.

Wants to ruin him like he promised.

In one swift move, he slides both his hands to Mal's arms, wrenches them behind his back as he had before, and crosses them over one another.

Rowan holds him in place there, fucking into him hard three, four times, the slap of his skin against Mal's deafening in the mostly quiet room.

"*Guh!*" Mal exclaims, breathless.

Yeah, that's more like it.

Rowan switches his grip to once again hold both of Mal's wrists in one hand and uses his other to shove at Mal's midback to force him down onto the bed.

He falls with a soft thud and a surprised but satisfied-sounding groan.

"Fuck," Mal swears again.

"Be good and stay just like that for me."

Mal squirms underneath him, arms shifting as if testing out Rowan's strength. Rowan almost lets him go, having not expected the resistance, but keeps his hold and tightens his grip, pushing Mal's wrists into his lower back right over the band of the jockstrap.

"Mal…," Rowan chastises. "That's not being good."

With his free hand, he spanks Mal twice on the side of the thigh, the muscle tensed on the second hit.

"*Ohhh, fuck.* May-maybe I don't wanna be good."

"Nah. I think you do." Rowan pulls back his hips and snaps forward. "I think you wanna be real good."

"*Hnn….*"

Rowan starts up his leisurely pace once more, keeping a firm grip on Mal's wrists with one hand and squeezing his asscheek with the other. And fuck, he feels *incredible*, even at this slow pace, and Rowan's not quite sure how he manages to keep talking through it.

"That wasn't a no, Mal. 'Cause I'm right, huh?" Rowan changes his thrusts into a heavy grind, circling his hips while he's fully seated, feeling Mal's walls stretch to accommodate him.

A low whimper and a shifting of Mal's hips is all he gets in response.

"Yeah." Rowan laughs through his nose. "Big, tough, Thug Life Mal Savaryn wants to be good and be rewarded with a nice thick cock."

He's talking out of his ass, to be honest. Doesn't know *shit* about Mal's background other than that he'd been somewhat embarrassed about Rowan knowing his last time, that his dad was probably a piece of shit, and that he's got a pissy attitude and halfway violent tattoos. But it does *something* to the other man, judging by the instant spike in Mal's breathing. He'd be willing to bet there isn't a drop of gold left in his eyes, completely blacked out by blown pupils.

"I know you want it rough, Mal. And I'll give it to you…." Rowan cuts off with a sharp, quick series of thrusts before returning to his slow, *slow*, pace. "But you gotta ask for it."

And then there's the tiniest whispered, "Rowan…." Softer than it had been earlier, and fuck if that doesn't kick Rowan's own heart rate up a notch or twelve.

"Mmm. You told me what you wanted earlier, before I started fucking you. Now should be no different."

He *had* asked him to fuck him a few minutes ago. Told him via text that he wanted it rough. But now Rowan wants to hear him beg. Like he'd done at the gangbang. Like he said he never did for anyone.

And Rowan can probably get him there, if he just—

"Mmmm!"

Perfect. Changing the angle of his hips enough to hit that sweet spot, drag over it in slow, teasing pulls. Rowan keeps Mal's wrists pinned but drags his other hand over the curve of his spine, sweat beading over his smooth skin.

"Come on, Mal. Only good boys get the cock they want."

Press. Drag. Whimper.

Then, finally, "*Please….*" A sweet, low whisper that's music to Rowan's ears.

"Please what?"

"Please fuck me."

"I am fucking you." A roll of the hips, as if to prove his point.

"Fu-fuck—"

"Gonna have to be more specific, Mal."

Rowan can't help it—saying Mal's name. Loves the way it rolls off his tongue, hangs in the air, makes the other man blush. He can see the color spread over the back of his neck and to his shoulders as he fucks into his tight heat.

A low groan, then, "*Please* fuck me harder."

Perfect.

Rowan complies, pulling nearly all the way out before slamming back in, the slap of his hips against Mal's ass like a gunshot.

"Mmm!"

He knows what Mal wants. He wants it hard *and* fast, but he only asked for hard, so that's all he's gonna get. He keeps his thrusts slow, a long few seconds between each sharp, hard thrust. And it's good, it's *so good*, but Rowan's hoping he'll realize that he needs to ask for *exactly* what he wants soon, because this is driving him crazy.

"Fu-fuck, *please….*"

Thrust.

"What is it, Mal? This not doin' it for you?"

Thrust.

"Faster… *please.*"

Thrust.

"Faster, huh? Shoulda said so."

Rowan quickly adjusts his grip, holding one of Mal's wrists in each hand, still crossed over one another, and immediately starts up a punishing pace, fucking into him hard *and* fast like they've both been craving.

"Fuuu-*huuuh*-ck!" Mal keens, breath punched out with every drawn-out syllable.

Fuuu-huuuh-ck is right. Rowan's in heaven; he's gotta be. Because nothing on earth could possibly feel better than Mal clenching around him, taking in all of him over and over and pushing his hips back in time with Rowan's thrusts and moaning so beautifully for him.

Heat spreads quickly from his groin to his core and to his limbs, that sweet burn that means he's getting close—*already? Fuck*—and he's gotta change something or else he's gonna come early, merely minutes after he'd started fucking Mal for real.

Rowan pauses his thrusts, letting go of Mal's wrists and sliding his hands up to the crooks of his elbows. In a quick jerk, he tugs him up off the bed, nearly flush to his chest, Mal's surprised gasp cut off quickly by his loud moan as Rowan slides deeper inside him. The lube from his ass spreads around Rowan's pubes, sticking to Mal's skin where they're pressed together.

He feels Mal's biceps flexing against his fingers as he holds him mostly upright and resumes fucking into him, just as rough but not quite as quickly as before, now that he's supporting the full weight of Mal's upper body.

"Feel so fucking good," Rowan grunts over the rhythmic *slap, slap, slap* of skin and the wet *shlick, shlick, shlick* of the lube that's dripping down the back of Mal's thighs.

Mal mutters a long string of curses in return, head dipping forward and showing off the full length of his spine and the deep V between his shoulder blades from where his arms are pulled taut behind him.

"Thought about this all fuckin' week," Rowan tells him. "About how fuckin' perfect you were last time and how… how good you'd be again, just for me."

"Mmm, fu-fuck, me too."

And shit, hearing the sentiment echoed in Mal's voice makes Rowan's whole body shiver with want, and God, he's slipping, switching out of that Dominant headspace and into regular desperate-to-get-off headspace, but hopefully Mal will cut him some slack. If the near-constant gasping and moaning pouring from his lips is anything to go by, he probably has.

But he's gonna blow soon, so fucking soon, it's a miracle he's lasted this long. And he wants Mal to get off first.

He fucks into him close to a dozen more times, aiming to hit his prostate each time, or at least have his cock drag past it. Fucking his full length in *deep* is so utterly satisfying that it takes everything he has to keep his grip on Mal's sweaty arms and not let him fall completely.

He scrunches his eyes shut for a moment, letting the pleasure wash over him before wrenching them back open. He dips his head, watching his cock slide into Mal's perfect ass over and over, and he's suddenly struck with a thought. Probably the best idea he's had while balls-deep in the hottest guy he's ever seen.

"How attached are you to this jockstrap?" Rowan asks, breathless.

"'M not. Got… *unh*… got plenty more at home."

"Can I…?" He tugs slightly at one of the straps.

"Fuck yeah, do it," Mal replies instantly, like he's on the same wavelength as Rowan and doesn't even need him to finish his sentence.

Fucking perfect.

Rowan lets go of one of Mal's arms, then the other so he falls back down onto his hands and knees, fists the sides of the straps, twisting his wrists so the fabric wraps around each hand for a better grip, and *pulls*, the *riiiiip* of the seams starting to give nearly as hot as Mal's keening whine as Rowan plows into him. The straps are stretched to their limit as Rowan uses them to pull Mal back onto his cock, slamming into him with abandon.

"*Nnngggg, shit,* just like that!" Mal groans, letting himself be moved however Rowan wants.

He's perfect. He's perfect, he's perfect, he's *perfect*, clenching tighter and moaning freely and holy shit, Rowan's gonna come. He wraps the straps around his hands once more, stretched nearly to the point of tearing, and speeds up his hips until Mal's moans devolve into half-gasped "*Aah*s!" and "*Mmm*s!"

By the time Rowan's about to blow, Mal chokes out, "*Rowan… I need….*"

And fuck, hearing his own name on Mal's lips again nearly pushes him over, but he keeps his composure long enough to realize that Mal's saying he needs to come. He's asking permission, for fuck's sake, and *holy shit*, he's perfect.

"Yeah, Mal, *do it*. Make yourself come on my cock."

Rowan barely registers the sight of Mal's hand disappearing underneath his body before he's clenching violently around him and his back is arching up beautifully, beads of sweat rolling down the curve of his spine and over his shoulder blades.

"Fuck fuck fuck fuck *fuuuck*—"

His low groan spurs Rowan to fuck him faster, faster, chasing his pleasure on the tail of Mal's own, his body squeezing around him. And in barely a handful more thrusts, Rowan feels the telltale tightening in his groin, the thrumming in his fingertips, and the wild beating in his chest, and then the release, sharp and quick and *sofuckinggood* as he empties inside Mal.

Pleasure spikes through him, coming in shorter and shorter waves as his hips slow to a crawl. Rowan stays nestled inside Mal as long as he can, until the relentless twitching of Mal's walls becomes too much for his softening, sensitive dick.

In the haze of his orgasm, he wonders if Mal is into overstimulation— being made to come over and over until he's coming dry. He'd look so hot like that—Rowan's sure of it. He makes a mental note to ask him about it later on down the road. Mentally highlights and circles and underlines it too.

Now he pulls out gently, stroking over Mal's back and sides despite the patches of sweat making an easy slide across skin difficult.

As soon as Rowan's out, Mal collapses onto his stomach, face pillowed in his arms. A jolt of concern rips through Rowan as he drops to his knees next to Mal's upper body, hand hovering above his mid back.

"Mal? You okay?"

A positive-sounding grunt is his only answer.

"C'mon, man, talk to me."

Thankfully, Mal turns his head to face Rowan, eyes bright if half closed.

"Sorry," he mumbles, voice hoarse. Then clearer, "I'm good. Was good, jus' fuckin'… tingly."

"Good tingly?"

"Yeah."

Rowan lies on his side, running a hand over Mal's shoulders and back. He thinks back to what Mal said he needed for aftercare—*talking him down, light touches for any kind of impact play*. While he only spanked him a few times, he was pretty rough for most of the night. He lightens his touch, fingertips barely ghosting over Mal's skin but still firm enough to not be ticklish, if Mal is.

There's a tiny trickle of warmth in his belly at the thought of this gorgeous, sexy, confident man being ticklish that Rowan forces down because it's a little too much… *something* right now. A little too much.

"You did so good, Mal," Rowan tells him in a low voice. "I'm so proud of you."

A barely-there hum is Mal's only response, and Rowan takes it as a good sign.

"Loved seeing you get so turned on. And being good for me, asking for what you needed." He strokes through Mal's hair, the strands damp with sweat but not deterring Rowan in the slightest. "I'm so lucky you trusted me enough to do this with you. See you like this. Fuck, you're amazing."

The words tumble out of Rowan's mouth like they had last week, largely unplanned but no less sincere. Probably *too* sincere, if he's honest, but he's sure Mal will tell him that later if that's the case.

A few quiet minutes pass, Rowan continuing to whisper to him while listening to the other man breathe and come down from the vigorous fucking they'd done.

And Rowan himself takes longer than normal to get his breathing and his heart rate under control, the sheer excitement of the night causing his heart to still beat erratically. He feels sated in a way he hasn't in a long while, even more so than he did after the gangbang. An intense, deep sense of satisfaction at a pretty mind-blowing orgasm. But more than that, at being able to make Mal come again on his own. Being able to make him *good tingly*.

Eventually Mal takes a deep breath through his mouth and blows it out through his nose before pushing himself up onto his knees, dipping into a quick child's pose, then settling onto his heels, palms pressed flat to the bed. Exactly like he had done after the gangbang. Rowan can't help but wonder if the position is somehow grounding for him. A way of easing himself back into his surroundings.

Rowan's suddenly aware of his own body, muscles sore like they are after a tough workout. He'll definitely need to stretch later. He tenses his quads while still lying on his side, feeling the pearls of come and lube making his pubes stick to his groin. With a groan he rolls off the bed, knees wobbling a bit as his feet touch the floor, and grabs washcloths and water bottles for himself and Mal.

They hydrate and clean themselves off, Mal pulling a face as he wipes between his asscheeks, undoubtedly getting a cloth full of lube and Rowan's come. Rowan's never had someone come inside *him* before, but he knows how messy lube alone is and never envied his partners when they inevitably had to clean up Rowan's mess themselves.

Now clean, they wipe and sanitize the bed together, considerably less messy this time than it had been after the gangbang. The ease of cleaning the leather pad almost makes Rowan wish he had one at home, but he still much prefers the softness of a real mattress and sheets to the somewhat clinical feeling of the pad.

Mal retrieves his clothing from the floor, giving them a cursory shake off while Rowan retrieves his own pile of clothing, partially from the bed and partially from the floor where they'd been knocked while he and Mal fucked.

Rowan throws on his briefs and tank top while he watches Mal turn his clothing right side out. The jockstrap hangs loose around his hips from where Rowan had stretched it out, and he feels a slight pang of guilt about it, even though Mal had told him he could pull on it. But he still doesn't seem to mind, eventually pushing it off and letting it fall to the floor before crumpling it up and tossing it in the trash bin under the supply table.

"You hungry?" Mal asks as he comes back to the bed and scoops up his clothes.

"Starving."

"Cool. Meet me at the bar in twenty."

Rowan gives him a thumbs-up rather than replying verbally, which earns him an exaggerated eye roll as Mal turns to leave the room, this time fully naked.

He can't help but balk. *And* admire the view of Mal's backside as he swaggers out the door. Completely at ease. Confident. Rowan's gone through phases of shame and pride in his own body throughout his life. Now he feels good. He's healthy, not overexerting himself. Eating regularly. Taking his meds. Staying stable. Staying *sane*. And all that has led him to his current figure, toned in the ways he likes but with enough bulk to know he's not going to wither away.

Shaking his head to clear that line of thought, he makes his way out of the Gold Room and toward the changing room, the thumping bass from the bar fading away as he retreats farther down the hallway.

In the changing room, there are a few people in varying states of undress going about their business, though Mal isn't among them. Rowan wonders at that while he finds an empty shower stall, grabs a neatly-rolled towel and a travel-sized bar of soap from the basket outside and stashes them on the cedar bench inside the stall before closing the heavy curtain.

The stall looks pristine, white subway tiles lining the interior of the shower, gleaming golden fixtures. It's a bit much for Rowan's taste, but he can't deny that it looks good. Expensive, as he'd expected.

He peels off his tank and briefs before turning on the water and setting the temperature to something shy of molten. And when he steps under the spray, it feels *heavenly*, the water pressure a perfect downpour against his neck and chest. It feels so much like a massage that he bows his head and lets the water rain over him and cascade down his back, soaking him instantly and washing away the last remaining evidence of his and Mal's time together.

The idle chatter of the other men fades away until there's only the pleasant sound of rushing water and the memory of Mal's moans in his ears. He lets himself relax fully, feels his tense muscles ease with the heat and the pounding water as he replays everything that just happened in his mind.

Mal is so fucking perfect in a way that Rowan's never encountered before. Sure, he's had some great sex in the past and been with partners who knew what they liked and had a good time, but Mal is… *different.* He's confident and completely unashamed of what he likes, and from the start it drove Rowan crazy in the best way. And Mal knows exactly how to push to get what he wants, but in a way that never makes it feel like he's the one calling the shots. Well, no more than a sub normally is in a Dom/sub scene.

He can't help but wonder exactly how much Mal's done this. How many people he's been with. When he started experimenting with things beyond vanilla. How long it took him to figure himself out and learn what he likes. How to *get* it. Because despite Rowan's own confidence when it comes to sex, it's obvious that Mal's light-years ahead of him in the BDSM scene.

But Mal seems fine with Rowan being somewhat lacking in experience. If anything he seems almost eager to show him the ropes, and Rowan can only hope that the trend continues the more they do this. Hopes he doesn't reach a plateau and make Mal lose interest.

Rowan starts scrubbing himself clean and thinks that really, it's exactly that kind of thought he's always needed to kick his competitive nature into overdrive, his determination to be the best fucking Dom Mal's ever had.

Tonight Mal had clearly enjoyed himself. He seemed to oscillate between pushing back against and obeying Rowan's orders, which to be honest, Rowan's not sure is a good or a bad thing. He's going to have to do some more research later and talk to Mal about whether he should be aiming to keep him in subspace for the whole session, or if it's normal to dip in and out of it. So far he's really only seen short glimpses of it. First at the gangbang and then a few times earlier tonight.

For now he assumes that it's normal to slip in and out of that submissive headspace, especially since they're still getting used to each other. He dwells on that, knowing that at the very least he's not making up their chemistry. They seem to *fit*, and that thought carries Rowan through the rest of his shower.

When he gets to the bar this time, exactly twenty minutes later, Mal's already waiting for him.

THEY FIND themselves at the same diner as before—Sheila's, Rowan notes, the name making sense after meeting the woman herself last week. This time Mal declines his "usual" when Sheila asks him about it, instead ordering a burger and fries, a bowl of chicken noodle soup, and a slice of apple pie. Rowan orders a turkey club with chips, and they claim the same back corner booth as last time.

Once again, Rowan ogles the large amount of food when it comes. He's not one to judge how much or how little food someone eats—God knows he's had his own issues with food throughout his life, not only from growing up poor and having to scrounge when he could, but also when he was actively fighting his mental illness and his meds. But it does make him worry that Mal is purposely starving himself. He'd said as much before the gangbang, and Rowan's not his parent or guardian, but he doesn't want it to be something that Mal thinks he *has* to do before their scenes.

"Do you…," Rowan starts, then trails off, unsure how to phrase his question without sounding patronizing. His eyes sweep Mal's features, sharp but with full lips and cheeks, his body toned with muscle and a layer of fat, minimal as it is. He looks healthy, but Rowan knows far too well that health isn't only skin-deep.

"What?"

"Do you always… fast all day before scenes?"

Mal looks taken aback by the question, his eyebrows shooting up.

"Fuck no, man. I love food." As if to prove his point, he takes a hulking bite of his burger, chews quickly, and swallows. "Only did it for the gangbang 'cause you never know what you're gonna get. How rough the people're gonna be, how they might react. People don't like to talk about it, obviously, but accidents happen, and that shit's awkward enough with one person, never mind ten."

Relief floods through Rowan.

"Okay. That's good."

That earns him another single raised eyebrow from Mal.

"Just had to make sure you didn't think I expected it or anything. I don't want you to pass out in the middle of a scene."

"Been doin' this long enough to know how to take care of myself, man." Mal's tone is clipped. Serious.

"Right, yeah," Rowan says immediately. "Sorry, didn't mean to imply you didn't."

He gets a grunt as the only response as Mal scoops up a large spoonful of soup and slurps it loudly.

They eat together in silence, same as last time. It's not awkward, exactly, but Rowan feels like he's one strike away from blowing this whole thing. He dives into his food, equally as delicious as his meal last time had been. The diner is definitely a hidden gem, and he's thankful it hasn't been driven out of business by a smoothie bar or yoga studio as places like this often are in the Back Bay.

When Mal has finished most of his food, he surprises Rowan by pushing the slice of apple pie toward him, the scent of cinnamon filling Rowan's nostrils.

Still, he questions, "Uhh…?"

A quick eye roll from Mal has Rowan's face heating up. "Try it," he says. "Shit's like crack, I swear."

The scratch of the plate against the table as Mal nudges it closer to Rowan feels a bit like an olive branch after the awkwardly tense past few minutes, and Rowan's all too happy to take it.

He plucks his unused fork from the table and scoops off the point of the slice, making sure to get some of the fresh whipped cream neatly piled on top. He can feel the *snap* of the crust as his fork cuts through it and see the amber filling start to topple out onto the plate before bringing it quickly to his mouth and stuffing the bite in.

At once his tongue is bombarded with apple and cinnamon and allspice and butter and a dozen other things he can't even begin to describe. Hands down, it's the best pie he's ever had, even beating Addison's famous handmade desserts that all their coworkers rave about.

"Holy fuck," Rowan says before he's even swallowed.

"Told ya."

There's a small smile playing on Mal's lips that reaches his eyes, and that tiny look alone is almost sweeter than the apple pie itself. He grabs his own fork, scoops up a large chunk, and shovels it into his mouth, eyes fluttering closed at the first taste like Rowan suspects his own had. Rowan puts his fork down on his plate, assuming Mal had only intended on having him try it.

"You don't want more?"

"Oh, I didn't think you wanted me, yanno, double dipping."

Mal gives him a flat stare as he takes another bite. "Just had your tongue in my ass 'n your dick in my mouth, man. 'M not worried about *cooties*."

Once again, Rowan feels his face burn but immediately digs in for another bite as if the act of eating will help the flush dissipate from his cheeks faster.

"'Anks," he mumbles, mouth full. Then, when he finally swallows, "You were pretty adamant about the 'no kissing' thing last time. I didn't wanna overstep." Even though he'd had Rowan's literal spit in his mouth during the gangbang, somehow sharing food seems more intimate than that.

Mal pauses, fork halfway between the plate and his mouth, and bites his cheek quickly before releasing it.

"That's different," he says, quieter than Rowan would have expected. "Too personal."

"I get it."

And he does. As much as he'd love to get his lips on Mal's, kissing *is* personal. More so than sex, sometimes. Though if he ever does get the chance to kiss him, God knows he'll take that privilege and fucking *run* with it.

When the pie is nothing more than miniscule flakes of pastry on the plate, Rowan figures it's time to bring up what he's been wanting to talk about this whole time.

"So, what'd you think?" He can't help the nerves tingling through him in asking, despite the fact that he's still here and Mal hasn't kicked him to the curb yet.

"About tonight?"

"Yeah."

"It was good. Fuckin' *great*, if I'm bein' honest, 'specially for a first scene, but I think we can do better as we ramp shit up."

Nodding in agreement, Rowan adds, "Yeah. I don't mind vanilla stuff, but I'm definitely looking forward to some'a the stuff we talked about last time."

"Mmm. We'll stick with exploring some kinks for now, maybe work in some restraints next time."

Rowan doesn't want to dwell on why, but relief floods through him at hearing *next time*. Because there's gonna *be* a next time. And fuck if that doesn't nearly get him hard again right here in the diner. That and the image of Mal being restrained by something other than loose clothing.

He takes a—hopefully unnoticeable—shaky breath, reminding himself to get a grip. It's not like he's not gonna get another chance at fucking him. They *just* established that that will very much be happening.

"I meant to ask earlier, but what do you wanna get out of our time together?" Rowan tries not to sound too much like he's quoting from the BDSM material he'd found, but Mal sees right through it.

"Did some research, huh?" Thankfully, he doesn't sound put out by it. "Good."

"Good?"

"Practice is the best experience, obviously, but there's a shitload'a books out there on it if you wanna get really deep in it."

"Really?" Obviously there's books on it. *Idiot*, Rowan thinks at himself.

Mal nods. "Yeah. Read a bunch of 'em."

"You like to read?" He doesn't know why that surprises him. Mal's clearly very smart and well-versed in this stuff.

Mal's lips twitch to the side like he's chewing his cheek again. "Yeah. Audiobooks, though."

"Oh, cool. I can never concentrate on those. They put me to sleep."

"Yeah, well…." He clears his throat. "I can text ya a list of books if you want."

"That'd be great, actually."

"As for your question," Mal starts, pausing to take a sip of his water. "I wanna get outta my head. Let someone else make the decisions for a change since I do that shit enough every day. And I wanna not feel guilty for likin' what I like. Had some shit Doms in the past that tried to make it seem like wantin' to get pushed around in bed made me a bitch the rest'a the time."

There's a story there, and Rowan wants to press, but he figures Mal is still more willing to share his food and his body than his past.

Rowan simply nods in understanding. As much as he's a stickler for being in charge of things, there have definitely been times in the past where he's wished someone else would take the reins and tell him what to do. And while there's not as much stigma around topping as there is bottoming, anything that strays even slightly from vanilla sex is looked down on by some people.

So he gets it. And he's glad Mal told him.

"How 'bout you?"

Blinking, Rowan's brain stalls. "I, uh… guess I never really thought about it…." He winces. "I know that's a shit answer."

Mal gives him a shrug as he dumps a few ice cubes from his water into his mouth and crunches them loudly. "Better than you makin' somethin' up." Then he stuffs one of the few fries left on his plate through his lips, and Rowan's not even sure he's finished chewing his ice yet. "Don't gotta figure it out right now long as you're not actively disliking the shit we do."

"No, I—" Rowan starts, then pauses to rack his brain. He wants to be able to give Mal an answer, something more concrete than *I dunno*. But what *does* he want from this, outside of some good—*great*—sex with a hot—*gorgeous*—guy?

He thinks about his past, about the clubs and the drugs and the booze and too many nameless men. About flying off the rails and losing control and being *so sick* but not knowing it. About his diagnoses and his family's desperate, relentless attempts to keep him stable, keep him alive, despite the hell he gave them for it.

With all that in mind, he finds that the answer to Mal's question, to what does he want, comes to him easier than he thought it would.

"I've kinda hurt a lot of people in the past. Family mostly, but exes and strangers too. Not physically, but emotionally. I wanna make someone feel good for a change. Be the one takin' care of someone and worrying about them instead of myself. I mean, I kinda do that shit every day at work, but there it's… clinical, I guess. Not really personal, even though I do care about all my patients. And I obviously like bein' in control, think that shit's obvious by now, but I like havin' to work for it, not just be *given* it 'cause someone feels bad for me. Makes me feel like I have a purpose, I guess."

Done with his speech, he finds Mal looking at him curiously. Like he's a puzzle he'd thought he'd finished but found a dozen more pieces to and doesn't quite know what to do with them. Rowan can only hope that when he figures it out, he'll like what he sees.

"I get that," Mal says eventually.

While Rowan hadn't exactly been seeking his *approval* in his answer, it feels good to have some semblance of it nonetheless.

Then Mal adds, casual as ever, "Sounds like we're a good match."

And fuck if that doesn't release the floodgates of… *something* in Rowan. Some tingling warmth he doesn't know how to name emanating from his core and radiating out to his limbs, pooling neatly in his fingertips and making them twitch where they sit on the table. He tries to hide the unintended gesture by wiping his fingers on the paper napkin he'd balled up next to his empty plate, but Mal's amused-looking smirk tells him he wasn't all that successful at hiding his reaction.

Sue him. He'd been thinking the same thing, and to have the sentiment echoed back is overwhelming. Rowan lets himself bask in the feeling.

They fall into another comfortable silence, each picking at the scraps of their food. Right before midnight, a shared look passes between them, a mutual *You good?* that has them both stacking their plates at the end of the table and gathering their things.

Barely a minute later, the same busser as last time comes to their table to collect their empty dishes, once again assuring them that it's on the house. As they slide out of the booth, Mal sighs and reaches into his back pocket, but Rowan stops him with a hand on his elbow.

"I got it. You paid last time."

Mal doesn't protest, simply nods his thanks.

"But uh, I have no idea how much any of that cost," Rowan tells him.

"Twenty-eight fifty," Mal replies instantly.

Stunned, Rowan asks, "You just… know that?"

"Been comin' here forever, man. Give her a good tip."

And with that, Mal heads to the door, raising his hand in a wave to Sheila across the diner as he does. He pulls out a cigarette while he's halfway out the door and quickly lights it before the door is even fully closed behind him, the flame glowing bright among the streetlights and the neon signs hanging in the windows.

Then he's disappeared from view, and Rowan approaches Sheila at the counter.

"Hi, Sheila," he says.

"Hi, honey. How was everything?"

"Great! The pie especially. Probably the best I've ever had."

Sheila's eyes light up at the compliment. For a split second, she reminds him of his mother in one of her manic baking sprees, making something deep inside Rowan ache until he shoves the feeling down so he doesn't do something crazy like ask the woman for a hug.

"Glad to hear it. You need somethin' else?" she asks.

"Oh no, just wanted to pay."

"Bah," she exclaims, waving him off with an exaggerated arm gesture. "I told him no."

"I appreciate it, but Campbells always pay their debts." He pauses, thinking back to the diner last week when she'd asked his last name, and rolls his eyes. "Hank excluded, obviously."

She huffs a laugh at the last bit, clearly knowing it to be true somehow, but nonetheless seems to relent and pulls out her order pad to scribble down their orders before sliding him the slip across the counter. Exactly like Mal had said, the total inked at the bottom is $28.50, tax included. Something a lot like admiration sparks in Rowan's chest. This feeling, he doesn't try to push away.

He hands Sheila two twenties and decides to ask one of the two main questions he has right now. "Can I ask why you don't charge us? Or… Mal, I guess."

Her connection to Hank can wait, far less intriguing than her connection to Mal.

Her lips pull back into a closed-lip smile, though the kindness never leaves her eyes. "Mal's done a lot for me," she says, plugging their order into the surprisingly modern-looking register and slotting Rowan's bills inside. "I'll spare you the details, but he's a good boy. One'a these days I'll get him to stop payin' me again."

She holds out several bills and coins to take as change, but Rowan waves her off. Rowan doesn't really know what Mal's idea of a good tip is, but he only has forty bucks in cash on him, so that'll have to suffice. It's over twenty-five percent anyway. With a grateful smile, she stuffs the cash in the lidded tip jar that's surprisingly full.

"I doubt that," Rowan tells her, getting the sense that Mal wouldn't take any kind of charity from her—or anyone, for that matter—unless he was truly desperate. Kind of like Rowan. He wonders if Mal's Southie too.

His brain finally catches up, dwells on the *again* in her last statement, and wonders if there *was* a time when Mal was truly desperate and sought out Sheila's help. He figures if Mal ever wants him to know whether that's true, it'll have to come from the man himself and not from Sheila.

Sheila chuckles through her nose. "Me too, Rowan. Have a good night, okay?"

"You too."

Rowan exits the diner into the humid night and sees Mal leaning against the window, cigarette dangling loosely down by his side, eyes fixed on the light-polluted sky. The fluorescent neon glow from the signs hanging in the window illuminates his profile in a pretty collage of red and blue, melding into purple across his temple. Briefly, Rowan's taken aback by the sight of him, practically glowing like he had been when he first saw him tonight, and he's frozen in place, drinking in the view.

When Mal notices him, he doesn't comment on the deer-in-headlights response. Instead, he wordlessly holds out his cigarette.

As Rowan gets his limbs to move and takes a deep drag, smoke filling and burning his lungs, he thinks he may have found a few more puzzle pieces too.

CHAPTER 5: THE LOVING DOM

ON SUNDAY morning, Rowan wakes to the warmth of the sun on his face and the faint chirping of birds from the nearby trees. Despite the exertion and excitement of last night, his body feels sated, relaxed in a way he hasn't in a long time.

He has nothing planned today aside from laundry and meal prep for the week. And seeing how long he can go without jerking his dick raw at the memories of last night. As soon as he thinks about it, there's a slow spreading heat in his belly and groin, his cock plumping up at the thought of Mal on his knees, mouth tight around him, eyes dark with arousal.

It's enough to get him to reach beneath his comforter and grope himself through his briefs. He's already half hard and well on his way to losing the bet he made with himself, but fuck it, he's feeling good and in no hurry to end that any time soon. He keeps his touch light, teasing almost, and lets his thighs spread and his body sink further into his mattress as the memories of last night flit through his mind like an old film reel, slightly hazy but clear enough to remember the important details.

Like how Mal looked up at him with the coil of rope pulled taut between his hands. Like how he whined so beautifully nearly every time Rowan touched him. Like how he asked *permission* to come, then immediately came around Rowan's cock.

God.

Rowan's partial chub perks up as he palms himself, and all too quickly he's achingly hard and the indirect touch isn't enough. He slips his hand under the waistband of his briefs, breath catching when he finally circles his cock. With a firm grip, he gives himself two long pumps, and he's so turned on but hasn't even been hard long enough for there to be enough precome to ease his motions. He rolls to the side with a huff, hand still down his briefs, and pumps the bottle of lube he has laid on his nightstand.

He hadn't intended on jerking off this early in the day, but now that his hand's slick with lube, it's become a *thing*, and he's going to indulge. He shoves his briefs halfway down his thighs with his clean hand, the band catching on his cockhead and making it slap back against his belly. As soon as he gets his hand back on his cock, the heat of it makes the lube nearly melt off.

But fuck, it feels good. His eyes slip closed as he gives himself over to the steady flow of oxytocin through his body as he strokes himself.

Unsurprisingly, his thoughts drift again to Mal. He wonders if he's at home, lying in his bed, thinking about last night. Wonders if his hair's mussed up or if he's one of those people who look neatly coiffed even in sleep. Wonders if his muscles are aching and if he regrets letting Rowan shred his jockstrap. But he especially wonders if Mal had woken up with morning wood, and if it was a slow, lazy spreading of heat like Rowan's or a raging inferno that had him shoving his hand down his underwear as soon as he was fully conscious.

Wonders if his hole is still loose from last night. God, Rowan can picture it perfectly. One hand on that plump cock of his, pumping away but needing something in him. Needing to feel *full*. Other hand snaking down between those fucking thick thighs and two fingers sinking into himself. A hitch in his breath.

Rowan makes a tight ring with his thumb and index finger, slipping it down over his cock from tip to base and imagining he's sinking into Mal. It doesn't compare, of course, but the mind's a powerful thing, and if he squeezes his eyes shut harder, he can almost, *almost* make himself believe that it's Mal riding him, sinking down onto his cock like he had at the gangbang.

God, he has to get him in that position again. As hot as it is seeing every inch of his cock enter Mal's perfect ass, he wants to see Mal's face and all of those subtle expressions he makes that continue to sear themselves into Rowan's memory.

Eyes scrunched tight, brows knitted together, bitten lower lip releasing into a perfect O as he clenches around Rowan's cock—*fuck*.

Rowan grips tighter, precome finally flowing freely enough to further slick his motions, but he's so turned on that he barely notices, toes curling and legs shaking as he comes, pleasure spreading through him in waves. He lies in the aftermath, come cooling on his belly as his breaths even out, as his body goes limp from the exertion.

Unexpectedly, his phone chimes multiple times in quick succession. He snatches it from his nightstand, worried that someone's dead or hurt or in jail, but relaxes when he sees they're all texts from Mal. Lets the slow trickle of warmth in his belly sit there before he tells himself to stop being a fucking idiot and open the texts like a normal person.

He's clumsy typing in his passcode with his left hand and fails it twice before finally managing to unlock it and swipe to his texts.

[MS] *the ultimate guide to kink edited by tristan taormino*

[MS] *the new topping/bottoming books by janet hardy + dossie easton (good to read both even if you're not a switch)*

[MS] *the loving dominant by john warren*

[MS] *those are good to start*

[MS] *lotta crap out there too so if you read anything else read some reviews first*

The books Mal said he'd send him, of course. Before he replies, he hauls himself out of bed to wash his hands and his stomach and put on a fresh pair of briefs. When he's done, he types out a quick reply.

[RC] *Thanks! I'll check those out*

He looks over the list again. The last title surprises him. After all, isn't *loving* kind of the opposite of what you'd want from a Dom? Sure, some people might be into that, but from what Mal has told him and from their few times together so far, it seems like he wants Rowan to be rough with him. Aggressive, almost. Make him beg and work for his release.

He pulls out his laptop and searches all the titles on Amazon, starting with *The Loving Dominant*, and adds them all to his cart, barely blinking at the price. He still has a few days left on his thirty-day Prime trial that he'd started a couple weeks ago, so thankfully he gets free two-day shipping.

Biting his lip, he picks up his phone, contemplating sending something else to Mal. He wants to text him more. Wants to have a conversation about how Mal first found the books, when he read them, how often he seeks out new material, if at all. Wants to ask him what else he likes to read besides kink books. But instead, he gets a brief flashback to the gangbang, to something Mal had said to one of the men, and he laughs to himself a bit and doesn't think before he types:

[RC] *I recall you saying something about fifty shades at the gb, that any good?*

He punctuates the text with a smiley face emoji wearing sunglasses.

Mal's response comes immediately.

[MS] *fuck off*

Rowan laughs, a pleasant lightness spreading through his chest imagining Mal rolling his eyes at the text, but it's cut short when he realizes that he fucked up, because now there's really nowhere for this conversation to go without Rowan forcing it.

So instead, he settles on sending another trusty emoji—this time a hand making an ok symbol—and laments not trusting himself and asking Mal more about his reading, or anything else that would keep them talking.

Sighing, he rolls out of bed and heads to the bathroom to pee, brush his teeth, and wash his face. He skips a shower because it's Sunday, he has nowhere to be, and he'd showered last night at the club.

He makes his way to the kitchen, lured by the scent of freshly brewed coffee, thanks to the timer on his coffee machine. It might not be the fanciest model, but he'd grown up with a dingy, yellow-stained coffee maker that you had to slap the side of halfway through brewing to get it to stop sputtering. Now he has a milk frother, though he's only ever used it a couple of times.

He pours himself a cup and takes a long sip, eyes slipping closed at the taste. It reminds him of the diner—Sheila's—though he hasn't actually had their coffee, given that he's only been there twice with Mal, both times late at night.

He wonders if Mal likes coffee.

WHILE HE'S eating lunch a few hours later, to his surprise (and delight), Mal texts him again.

[MS] *shibari class is gonna be on saturday the 8th at 6*

[MS] *that work for you?*

Rowan sucks the juice from the tomato in his sandwich off his fingers, wipes his hands on his sweatpants, and swipes to his calendar app. That's more than a month from now, meaning he and Mal will have several scenes before then. It should be enough time to get to know him a little better *and* for him to gain some more confidence as Mal's Dom.

[RC] *Yeah, that's perfect*

[RC] *How long is it?*

[MS] *should be 2 hours*

[MS] *we can still scene if you're up for it after*

[RC] *Yeah definitely*

[RC] *Probably not with rope though, I wanna be able to practice before we use it for real*

[MS] *yeah it'll be better if you practice*

[MS] *i'll bring some of mine to take home if you want*

There's a flutter in Rowan's stomach that he blames on the copious amount of sriracha he'd squirted in his sandwich.

[RC] *That would be great!*

[RC] *Thanks*

Unsurprisingly, Mal doesn't respond to Rowan's text or the sunglasses emoji he tacks on, so he sends another text, this time determined to keep the conversation going.

[RC] *Btw, is there anything you wanna do next time?*

It takes Mal a few minutes to respond.

[MS] *let's use the beads i showed you*

[MS] *i'll bring those and my cuffs too*

[MS] *and i wanna get you off with my mouth*

The texts come one after the other, barely any time between them, each one like a punch to Rowan's chest that nearly gets him hard again.

[RC] *Ok. Any position you wanna be cuffed in?*

[RC] *And do you wanna be cuffed the whole time or just part of it? Like how long can you go for w/o being uncomfortable*

[MS] *behind my back*

[MS] *and i can go a while but let's work up to that. probably use the beads first then cuff me for the rest*

[RC] *Got it*

Rowan taps the side of his phone, debating sending his next text. Mal had said this was a two-way street—their Dom/sub relationship. And he knows that, but he still feels a bit weird asking for things he wants. So far everything they've done he's enjoyed, and honestly he'd rather let Mal take the metaphorical reins while they're still getting used to each other.

From the bit of research he's done online so far, he knows that for some partners, their ultimate goal is to know exactly what the other wants and needs at any given moment, and to deliver that. Rowan doesn't know how realistic that is for them, or for pairs in general, but the idea of getting to that level of comfort and trust with Mal makes him giddy.

He sends the text.

[RC] *How do you feel about ass to mouth btw?*

[MS] *as long as it's my own ass it's hot*

[MS] *don't really trust mfers i don't know*

[MS] *why, you wanna do that?*

[RC] *Well yeah I wasn't thinking of anyone else's*

It's pretty hard to focus on anyone else's ass when Mal's is right in front of him.

[RC] *And yeah if you're cool with it*

[MS] *yeah*

His excitement simmers, the week-away anticipation stagnating when he remembers something Mal said to him in the diner last night: *I think we can do better.*

[RC] *Hey so when you said we could do better yesterday, is there something more you want from me?*

[RC] *I mean obviously I'm gonna get better and learn you as we go but like is there anything specifically I can do next time?*

Waiting on Mal's response, he takes another bite of his long-forgotten sandwich.

[MS] *be rougher*

As his phone lights up on the table, Rowan's fingers clench, soft bread dimpling in his hands.

[MS] *and meaner*

A sharp squeeze and a cucumber slides out onto his plate. Rowan drops the rest of his lunch with it, quickly picking up his phone as Mal texts him again.

[MS] *seemed like you might've been holding back a bit*

[MS] *don't*

[MS] *assuming you like that and you're not more of a soft dom*

And yeah, Rowan won't lie. He *did* want to be rougher. *Meaner,* as Mal put it. He wants to see how far he can push Mal, how desperate he can get him, how quickly and completely he can make him lose it. Like a deep-seated itch he only now realized was there but he can't quite scratch yet. With shaking fingers, Rowan types out his reply.

[RC] *I was worried it'd be too much*

[MS] *that's typical for new doms*

[MS] *and it makes sense while we're still getting the hang of things*

[MS] *don't get me wrong yesterday was fuckin hot*

[MS] *wouldn't still be talking to you if it wasn't*

[MS] *but i can take a lot more than you gave, at least within the confines of the shit we talked about after the gb*

[RC] *Okay. Are you looking for rougher/meaner in terms of what I do physically or just for dirty talk or both?*

[MS] *both*

[MS] *i like a bit of humiliation/shaming like i said before*

[MS] *and having you threaten to take shit away last week was hot. not always the best route to take with subs especially if they got abandonment issues or whatever but it's good with me*

[MS] *don't wanna be fucking human furniture though cause i do like pushing back still*

Rowan has to pause to look up 'human furniture,' which he instantly regrets. He swipes back to his text conversation with Mal.

[RC] *Yikes at the human furniture shit*

[RC] *And okay I can do that. You said you liked being praised too, but not right away right?*

[MS] *yeah. i'll ask for something like that outright, usually the day of the scene if i'm in a certain kind of headspace*

Though they've talked pretty extensively about sex and play at this point, it still catches Rowan off guard to hear Mal talk so openly about it. It strikes him that Mal knows exactly what he likes and doesn't like, exactly how he reacts to certain things (and most likely *why* he does), and is completely comfortable sharing that with him, still a near stranger. He knows how to read his own moods and determine what kind of treatment he wants from his partner, and it's something that Rowan both admires and envies. Hopefully, as he keeps doing research and keeps playing with Mal, he'll find his own balance.

[RC] *Sounds good. Looking forward to next week!*

[MS] *me too*

The flutter comes unbidden to Rowan's stomach, and he lets it linger as long as it wants to.

They have their plan, then. Mal wants Rowan to cuff him this time. Bind his hands. Come in his mouth. Be rougher with him. Meaner.

Rowan can't fucking *wait*.

WHEN THE books he'd ordered from Amazon finally come in on Tuesday, he tears open the package and immediately starts reading *The*

Loving Dominant. The cover is a little trashy, looking like a blurry still from a vintage porno, but both Mal and the reviews online had said it was great for new Doms.

He learns a hell of a lot from reading it. First and foremost that there's actually a *difference* between being a top and being a Dom—namely that the latter demands some kind of power exchange with a sub. And he might have known that instinctively, but actually reading it makes him realize that he has much to learn about this whole lifestyle.

It makes Rowan reflect on why he's doing this with Mal when before he met him he hadn't had much of an interest in it at all. On why he's so intrigued by being in control and exerting that control over someone who allows him to do so.

Given the title of the book, it's not surprising that right out of the gate, it talks about what actually makes someone a *good* Dominant. And from it he learns that people who put others first, especially when it comes to pleasure, tend to make good Doms.

The book's author suggests that for him the pleasure of being a Dom comes from the desire to give pleasure to his sub beyond what regular, vanilla sex could accomplish, and to give himself the ability to be in nearly complete control. And when Rowan does some introspection, he finds that both those ideas jive pretty well with him and his reasons for enjoying being a Dom, even with the little experience he has with it so far.

It feels like a confirmation of sorts. Validation, maybe. That he's not some psycho who gets off on pushing people around, but that the desire to do so comes from the intense, core-deep *need* to please. He's never wanted to cause pain or take something from someone that wasn't freely given. Never wanted to do anything that couldn't directly be traced back to his innate need to help and take care of others. It's why he'd wanted to be a doctor when he was younger. Why he's now a paramedic.

Like he'd told Mal, he wants to *heal*, not to *hurt*.

There's a line in the very beginning of the book that piques his interest and stays in the back of his mind as he devours page after page. Something about sexual appetites being a lot like chocolate sauce on pizza; it's not for everyone, and people may not understand entirely *why* they like it, but it doesn't make their desires any less real or valid.

Rowan thinks that chocolate on pizza sounds pretty gross, but then again he's sure that some people would find some of his and Mal's sexual desires gross. Like the fact that they met at a gangbang at a sex club and subsequently agreed to meet up once a week to have filthy sex. Or that Rowan actually likes pineapple on his pizza.

The metaphor makes his brain twist a bit, but what it comes down to is that people have different appetites and that he shouldn't feel weird about the kinds of things he wants, even if they're not *that* out there.

As he reads he finds that the book covers everything from the psychological impact of BDSM play, to examples of types of play, to tips on specific techniques, to suggestions for cleaning up after scenes. It's short but thorough.

There's even a section that describes the appeal of being a submissive that Rowan reads carefully and makes a mental note to ask Mal about later on. It talks about how a person could find enjoyment in essentially becoming subservient to another and to willingly subject themselves to some sort of pain or discomfort for the sake of physical and mental sexual gratification.

He thinks about Mal asking him to be rough. Be mean.

Admittedly after the spike of arousal had subsided, Rowan had been concerned about Mal asking for him to treat him that way. Namely he'd been concerned about *wanting* to do that to him. Do that *for* him as much as for himself. But the more he thinks about it, the more he realizes that what the book is saying very much holds true to himself regarding his desires—that they come from a good place, not from a dark place.

It's not a long read. He's nearly finished by dinnertime, partly due to him skimming or entirely skipping the portions of the book detailing things that he and Mal had already agreed they weren't into: pet play, golden showers, and other things that Mal had aptly described as "weird shit" during their first talk.

Different appetites, whatever. Not for the first time, he's glad they're on pretty much the same page when it comes to their interests.

There is one part that gives him pause over all the rest, though. Makes him sweat a bit and shift his weight back and forth on the couch.

One bullet in a long list of things you should do with your partner before your first scene; many of which he and Mal had done, but one that Rowan hadn't really known about and that Mal didn't bring up.

Talking about any psychological problems.

While the book mentions claustrophobia as an example, Rowan's mind obviously jumps straight to the diagnoses he's been dealing with since he was a teenager.

Depression. Later, PTSD. Touch of anxiety.

His heart races, the steady throb of which he can feel in his fingertips. He *barely* knows Mal, but does he have to tell him about this? Does he owe it to him? Is it unfair to either of them for Rowan to hide it? After all he's stable, hasn't had a major episode in at least a year, and stays on top of his shit. Keeps all his emotional ducklings in a row and checks in on himself more than his overbearing but well-meaning siblings had when he was younger and out of control.

And after a long, long while of pacing his apartment, opening and closing the fridge, reading and rereading that bullet point in the book, he decides that it's his own business. If something comes up down the line that could potentially impact Mal, he'll tell him.

That's what this shit's all about, right? Honesty, communication, trust? It has to be. If the situation calls for it, he has to be willing to reveal parts of himself that sometimes scare him to someone who might be scared *of them* in order to keep them both safe. While Rowan's a far cry from being dangerous anymore, it's always a possibility. He could always slip up and miss the signs and be too engrossed in the siren call of false pleasure or vindictive anger to realize that he's on a slippery slope to a physical and emotional crash.

And he vows silently to keep himself in check and one thousand percent ensure that he doesn't do anything that would compromise this new and evolving relationship with Mal. To flat-out tell him about his illnesses if he needs to, or to end things altogether if their play becomes too much for him to handle.

That's how Rowan becomes a *Loving Dom.*

ON SATURDAY night, Rowan is once again checked in by Camilla.

"So," she says by way of greeting, "I hear you're coming to the shibari class next month."

Rowan blinks at her, still not entirely used to her blunt attitude. "Hey. Uh, yeah. Did Malcolm tell you that?"

Even after only a couple weeks of calling him *Mal* in private, it still feels weird to go back to using his full name when talking about him in public. He makes a mental note to ask him if he still wants to be called his full name in front of other people.

"Mm-hmm, he booked a spot for the two of you, so you're all set. Normally for special events like that, you need to go through the app."

"Right, I remember Clover saying that when I joined." He folds his arms over his chest, looking for something to do with his hands. "How often do those come up?"

"A few times a month, usually. There's an Events tab on the app that you can check out."

"Got it."

She rapidly types something on her computer before looking back up at him with a radiant smile. "All set, same room as last time."

"Is that his usual or somethin'?"

She purses her lips to the side momentarily, one sharp cheekbone casting a shadow across her jaw. "Mmm, sorta. From what I remember, he sticks with one room per Dom and switches when he gets a new one."

"Huh."

Interesting. Rowan wonders if that's typical for subs in general or a quirk of Mal's. It almost sounds like something you'd do when you break up with someone and start dating someone new. Which, in a way, their Dom/sub relationship kind of is. Mal had been with someone before Rowan, and probably someone before him, and while there isn't the same romantic connection as you'd have with a traditional dating relationship, there must still be some of that lingering discomfort about fucking someone in the same place as someone else.

But maybe not. This is a sex club, after all. A place of business transactions.

Rowan dwells on it throughout his customary single beer, not even bothering to finish it completely. He makes idle conversation with Jeremiah, rejects the advances of an attractive silver fox, and keeps a mental tally of how many people an enthusiastic twink makes out with on the dance floor.

Barely fifteen minutes later, Mal appears by his side and skips a drink altogether, opting to lead Rowan straight into the back rooms with little more than a "Hey" and a nod.

In the Gold Room, Mal flings his messenger bag down on the bed and unzips it in three quick movements, opening it like a briefcase. Inside are numerous bulging pockets, the contents of which Rowan can't see, plus several toys nestled in the middle.

"Brought some shit," Mal tells him unnecessarily.

He pulls out a pair of black leather cuffs, each a little over two inches wide with a silver buckle on one side and a D-ring on the other, connected by a sturdy-looking metal connector that clips on to each ring. As Mal had told him before, the inside is lined with short black fur that looks almost like velvet. Next to the cuffs he places a long string of silicone anal beads, identical to the ones they'd looked at last time in the toy cabinet. Finally he places down a bottle of strawberry-flavored lube.

"Strawberry, huh?" Rowan comments. "That your favorite?"

"The other flavors taste like ass, man. And not in a good way."

Rowan mentally slaps himself for nearly forgetting. Forgetting that *tonight*, he's gonna fuck Mal's mouth after he fucks his ass.

He's gonna *come* in his mouth after he fucks his ass.

He remembers how greedily Mal had swallowed each load at the gangbang, how delicious he looked with come coating his tongue and lips and dribbling down his chin.

"I'll take your word for it," Rowan tells him, finally.

He feels his dick give an interested twitch as he picks up the cuffs to examine them. He unclasps them from one another, turning one over in his hands, feeling the softness of the fur and the smoothness of the leather and the cold bite of the metal clasps. He flicks open the clasp, testing it several times to get the feel for it. Going through the motions. *Pull, flick, clasp, tighten. Repeat. Pull, flick, clasp, tighten. Repeat.* He practices a few more times, until his fingers slide over the material confidently.

Comfortable in his ability to open the cuffs quickly should the need arise, Rowan places them aside. Looks up to find Mal staring intently at him.

"You good, Boy Scout?"

The flush comes to Rowan's cheeks against his will at having been clocked on his brief dalliance in the Boy Scouts because of some damn *cuffs*.

"Yeah."

Mal half zips his bag and places it atop the supply table on the other side of the room.

When he returns, Rowan asks, "Since this is gonna be a bit more involved than our last scene, do you want me to check in throughout? Like, ask for your color?"

Mal chews his cheek in consideration.

"I normally don't ask for that unless it's a scene that I think will push me to my limit or it's somethin' I haven't done before. But is that something you wanna do?"

"Maybe?" Rowan replies, hating how uncertain he feels.

"Gotta be on the same page about it, Red. One way or another."

It's a bit jarring—hearing the nickname so close to their scene—but it solidifies the desire he has to check in with Mal throughout.

"I'd like to, at least for today. Does it take you out of it?"

"Eh, yes 'n no. It makes me have to pause and think about how I'm feelin', so there's gonna be that moment where you kinda take a bird's eye view of yourself and everything goin' on. But at the same time, it's reassuring that if something's wrong, you're in a safe place to fix it."

Of all the things Rowan likes about Mal, his honesty and intelligence are creeping higher up on the list every time they meet. Rowan takes a deep breath, thinking through his words.

"Just don't wanna go too far, y'know?" he confesses.

"Yeah, I get it," Mal says with a shrug. "Lotta new Doms find it hard to get over the fear of causing pain. *Unwanted* pain anyway. And then when they get over that, they gotta wrestle with another part of themselves—morals or whatever—that tells 'em they shouldn't *like* causing pain, even if they only like it in a controlled setting and they're not just a fuckin' psychopath."

Rowan remembers a bit from *The Loving Dominant* that said something about domination, sadism, cruelty, and brutality becoming confused, and he thinks it's a pretty apt description of what Mal's talking about.

"Hope you don't think I'm a psychopath."

Mal scans him, and Rowan's never felt quite so much like a worm in a petri dish.

But the illusion shatters with a swipe of Mal's tongue across his lower lip. "Nah," he says, lips quirking to one side. "Think you're kind of a freak, though."

Unable to help it, Rowan laughs. Because there was no judgment or vitriol in Mal's tone. Only a sort of camaraderie that stems from *'cause I am too.*

"Yeah," Rowan agrees. "But so are you."

That little side smirk appears again, and it shouldn't get Rowan going as much as it does. "Yeah."

"How 'bout I check in if it seems like something might be too much?"

Mal nods. "That works. Not afraid to use the words on my own either, so you don't gotta worry about me waiting to be prompted or whatever if somethin' starts crossing a line."

Rowan knew as much, but hearing it confirmed again for him helps dissolve that last little bit of tension that had his shoulders and neck stiff all day.

"'Kay, good."

As Mal moves to lean back against the edge of the bed, right in front of Rowan, there's that electric charge in the air again. That *shift* that Rowan's body understands instinctively on a primal level. And when Mal lifts his chin to smirk up at Rowan? Well. The electricity surges, heat and steam and sparks flying.

Against his own desires, Rowan doesn't touch him yet. Doesn't reach for him. First, he unbuttons the cuffs of his shirtsleeves, neatly folding each side up to his forearms, watching Mal's eyes track his every move. He doesn't remove anything, much more interested in getting Mal naked again.

For a moment, Rowan considers making Mal undress himself again.

But this time, he wants to do it. Wants to unwrap this gorgeous man like the fucking gift he is and watch him watch *Rowan* savor every goddamn second of it.

And yeah, Mal said that he wanted to be treated rough, and Rowan's gonna give that to him, but the temptation of the buildup to it is stronger than his desire to give in immediately.

He turns Mal in place, slotting his chest against Mal's back, gripping him by the biceps. Held in place, he hears Mal take a deep breath in, one, two, three seconds, followed by a jagged exhale as he tilts his neck to one side.

Like this, the cords of muscle running down Mal's long neck pulse mere inches from Rowan's lips, and he's struck with the sudden urge to lick, suck, bite. Mark him up. Someday maybe, when they've talked about it. But for now, he noses behind Mal's ear, breathing in that same minty scent he'd smelled last time, pressing his hips forward into his ass and letting Mal feel him grow hard. With the way he's started hitching his ass back against Rowan's crotch, he must feel it. *Good.*

Rowan might be willing to play into Mal's desire to be degraded—and if he's being honest, his own desire to do it to him—but he'll be damned if he doesn't let the other man know how much he's enjoying this too.

But he'd enjoy it more, if….

He shifts one hand down to grip Mal's hip, stilling his movements. Squeezing enough to feel the sharpness of his hip bone even through his jeans. Rowan moves his other hand from Mal's bicep to curl around Mal's chest, palm resting flat against his sternum, fingertips skimming his neck. He shifts the hand on Mal's hip around Mal's waist to unbutton his jeans. Rowan feels Mal's hands wriggle underneath, attempting to take over in getting them off, but Rowan quickly slaps them away.

"It look like I need your fuckin' help?" he growls in his ear, popping the button.

"Dunno, can't see ya."

It's a taunt. A good one, because it almost works. Almost gets Rowan to spin him in place and tear his clothes off. Shove him to his knees like he did last time.

But it's what Mal wants, and Rowan's not gonna give in that easily.

Because Mal also likes being denied.

"Shame," Rowan tells him. "Clasp your hands behind your back."

He loosens his grip to let Mal do as he's told, but unsurprisingly he doesn't.

"Make me."

With a turn of his head, Rowan can see Mal's smirk in profile. That shit-eating grin he seems to sport whenever he knows he's being a brat.

And listen. Rowan's got a much better handle on his temper than he used to, but two taunts in a row reach *right* up to the limit. Almost but not quite boiling over. It's Rowan's pettiness that does him in, really. In one swift motion, he wrenches Mal's arms from his sides to behind his back, bending at the elbows so he can grab his own forearms.

"Need me to wipe your fuckin' ass for you too, Princess?" Rowan growls.

"May—"

"Finish that answer and I walk out that door." With a final squeeze to Mal's arms, after Mal finally locks his hands in place, Rowan resumes his previous task.

No faster than before, he drags Mal's zipper down and pries apart the fabric enough to free the tip of his hard cock under his briefs. He ignores it, though, focusing his attention on the lowest button of Mal's shirt.

Each tiny *pop* of a button releasing gets Mal squirming in front of him. Impatient. By the time Rowan is on the last button above Mal's pecs, he hears a low huff of breath.

"You got somewhere to be?"

Mal doesn't respond, and this time, Rowan presses.

"Tell me, Mal. Am I wasting my time here?"

"Wasting *mine*."

Rather than the trickle of annoyance he should probably feel, Rowan feels like laughing, the sound coming out low in his throat.

"Oh yeah? What would you be doin' if you weren't here right now?" Rowan asks, sliding the smooth fabric of Mal's shirt off his shoulders and tugging at his arms until they release.

With a careless flick, he tosses the garment on the floor behind him, then runs his hands lightly over Mal's sides. *Bare,* no undershirt or tank beneath it, which feels sluttier than it should.

"Findin' someone who'd actually fuck me sometime this century," Mal says, sarcasm dripping from his tone.

"Try again."

Because it's obvious that Mal would not, in fact, be going out and finding someone else. Rowan knows that much in his fuckin' *soul*. They're too good a match for that, and while they've firmly established that they're not exclusive, Rowan's confident enough in his abilities as a partner to keep him coming back—even if his confidence as a Dom isn't quite there yet.

"Maybe go find that Jason guy."

The guy at the bar last week. Beefcake with bedroom eyes. Dick that may or may not be bigger than Rowan's. "Thought it was Jackson?"

"Same shit."

Rowan snorts in the back of his throat and runs his palms over the taut planes of Mal's stomach, delving beneath his open jeans and feeling the heat of him.

"Can't even remember his name. Sounds like you had a great time with him."

"Don't need to know someone's name to get dicked down."

"Mmm. But you know mine. Made sure'a that." With that he curls his hand around the base of Mal's cock through his briefs in a slow, teasing stroke.

"*Hhhh*—" Mal breathes.

"Know what I think you'd actually be doin'?" Rowan asks but doesn't wait for a response. "Think you'd be sittin' at home, jerkin' off. Coupla beers, maybe a few hits on a joint if you smoke. Thinking about how much you wish it was me."

"Can jerk my dick just fine, man," Mal huffs, defensive. He doesn't deny it, though.

"Can't fuck yourself just fine, though." Rowan slides one hand around Mal's hip to the curve of his ass, rubbing a fingertip between his cheeks through his briefs.

"Got toys."

"Mmm. It's not the same with toys, though, is it, Mal?" he asks, slipping his hand under Mal's briefs and squeezing his asscheek, still lazily stroking him as a wet spot starts forming in the fabric from the tip of his cock.

Rowan likes this banter. *Loves* it, if he's being honest, and wants to keep it going as long as Mal will tolerate.

"Toys can't touch you," Rowan purrs in Mal's ear, hands leaving his cock and ass to stroke up over the heated skin of his sides, his chest, his shoulders. "Can't hold you down." A firm grip to muscular biceps. "Can't treat you how you wanna be treated."

In one swift motion, Rowan shoves Mal's briefs and jeans down off his hips, making him gasp at the sudden exposure.

"Isn't that right, Mal?"

"*Hn*…. They got some fancy fuckin' toys nowadays."

"If they had a toy that could do all this, you'd'a bought it already. Instead, you spend three hundred bucks a month to come here and have someone do it to you."

Mal's already well and truly lost this argument, but Rowan can still sense the fight in him. The urge to push and the need to be *right*. But more than that, to be in control and then have that control stripped away.

"Maybe if—"

"*Enough.* On the bed. Ass up," Rowan tells him, nudging him toward the bed. "Finish stripping first."

Mal does as he's told, shedding his boots, socks, jeans, and briefs and tossing them in the direction of his shirt on the floor. With practiced ease, he positions himself on the bed, resting on his elbows with his knees spread wide. From above, Rowan can see the sinful dip of his spine and the pronounced muscles of the back of his thighs, begging to be grabbed.

"Look at you," Rowan says, more to himself than to Mal as he gives in and squeezes each thigh in turn.

"Don't got eyes in the back of my head," Mal replies anyway.

Smack!

A sharp spank under one asscheek, red already starting to blossom on his skin as Mal's surprised gasp fades away.

"There's an idea," Rowan muses, soothing over the heated skin. "Get a big fuckin' mirror in here. Make you watch yourself fall apart."

"*Hn….*"

Smack!

"Hah!"

"See how desperate you look till you get what you want."

"N-not fuckin' *desperate*," Mal mumbles, but the way he's rocking his ass back against Rowan's hands tells a different story.

"We'll see about that."

Rowan reaches for the beads that Mal placed on the bed earlier, the weight of them a pleasant heft in his hand. Grabbing the strawberry-flavored lube, he pops the cap and squirts a drop on his thumb, surprised to find that it's clear, not red as he'd thought it might be. With the pad of his thumb, he circles Mal's hole, not pressing inside but simply testing the resistance—it's tight, he can tell that much, which means Mal must not have prepped much beyond whatever his cleaning routine is.

But before he fingers him open, he circles the rim a few times with his thumb, a pleased hum coming from Mal. And Rowan knows he's supposed to be mean. Supposed to push him and shit, but he can't help dipping forward and pressing a kiss straight to Mal's hole, feeling the muscles quiver against his lips and tasting the artificial strawberry of the lube.

Sweet.

Unlike Mal's grumbled, "You just fuckin' *kiss* my asshole, man?"

And well. *Yeah.* He fuckin' *wanted* to, all right? But he's not gonna say that. Mal might kick him to the curb if he did. So he doubles down, sucking on the puckered hole before licking a long wet stripe over it.

A sharp inhale from Mal tells Rowan he's not as put out by it as he originally seemed.

"Yeah," Rowan tells him, pressing another semblance of a kiss to his hole. "Can do whatever the fuck I want."

"Nng… 'cause I let you."

"Yeah. You let me. 'Cause you fuckin' love it."

There's nothing Mal can say in response that wouldn't be a flat-out lie, and Rowan knows they both know it. He lets the sentiment linger in the air between them and sets to work, lubing his fingers quickly, along with Mal's hole, focused on getting him prepped enough to take the beads.

As he stretches Mal, Rowan grows harder in his jeans, the tight heat around his fingers a promise of what's to come.

When there's little resistance and Mal's making these beautiful, gaspy little noises, Rowan withdraws his fingers and grabs the string of beads.

"Think you're ready for these?" he asks, dragging the strand of beads over Mal's slick hole.

"Fuck yeah."

"How bad d'you want 'em?" Rowan teases, circling the first bead around Mal's hole and putting the tiniest amount of pressure against it.

"C'mon, been dying for 'em all day," Mal replies, pressing backward in an attempt to get more of the bead inside.

And yeah, okay, that's pretty convincing, but….

"Bet you have." He walks around to the side of the bed, Mal rising up on his hands and turning up to him expectantly. "Show me. Get it wet," he orders, holding the first bead to his mouth.

Mal's lips part, pressed lightly against the silicone bead. The sight of the bead obscuring his mouth makes Rowan's own lips water, and his cock jump as he imagines Mal stuffed with a ball gag.

Slowly, Mal opens his mouth wide enough to suck the tip of the bead in, all but kissing it as his lips close around it and push it back out, saliva gleaming against the matte black.

"Said get it wet, Mal. You call this wet?"

He doesn't give Mal a chance to respond, pressing the bead back up against his lips. This time, he takes the whole thing in his mouth, lips closing tight around Rowan's fingers where they grip the bead by the stem. The look in Mal's eyes as he works his tongue around the bead is utterly devious, his tongue hot as it flicks against Rowan's fingertips.

Heat pools in Rowan's belly as he lets Mal suck on the bead and his fingers, feeling the spit start to trickle down his wrist.

It's surely wet enough now, but Rowan's selfish, and he's not done watching Mal suck and lick the beads like candy. With his other hand, he presses his thumb against the side of Mal's lips, stilling them.

"Another."

He watches as the realization dawns on Mal and his eyes widen before slipping half closed. His mouth drops open enough for Rowan to shift his grip and shove the next bead inside. This time he keeps his fingers outside and covers Mal's mouth with his palm, careful to not block his nose, the stem of the second bead slotted between his index and middle fingers.

"*Hnn…,*" Mal groans.

Mal's tongue darts out to lick at Rowan's palm once before slipping back inside, his jaw working and cheeks hollowing as he sucks—a tantalizing reminder that Rowan's going to be coming in that mouth by the end of the night.

"One more," Rowan tells him, watching the pretty bob of Mal's throat swallowing once, twice. "Give me a nod or shake."

A firm dip of his head, and a third bead is popping in, Mal's jaw slackening at the weight of them.

"Mmm," he hums, mouth full.

Rowan squeezes at his cheeks, forcing him to look up at him. His eyelids flutter but remain open, the slivers of gold standing out against his skin—pale where it isn't flushed—and Rowan swears he can feel his own eyes dilate further.

"You're ready for 'em now," Rowan tells him, tugging the whole string out with a sharp tug as soon as Mal relaxes his jaw.

Mal gasps, panting with his mouth open. A dribble of saliva runs over his bottom lip, and Rowan swipes at it with his thumb and pushes it back inside Mal's mouth. Mal greedily tries to suck on Rowan's finger, but Rowan pulls his thumb out and circles back behind Mal, palming his asscheek roughly.

Eager to get the show on the road, Rowan quickly lubes up the first bead and presses it against Mal's waiting hole. There's little resistance as he pushes it inside, mesmerized at the way Mal's hole seems to swallow the bead.

"*Hnng…*," Mal moans, dipping his head against the bed.

"Took that one right in, huh?" Rowan tugs on the bead, watching rapt as it starts to emerge. "Keep it in."

Mal shudders lightly but dutifully clenches and sucks the bead back inside. The act looks *filthy*, and it's definitely doing something for Rowan.

"Next one," Rowan warns, quickly lubing the second bead and pressing it inside after the first.

"Mmm…."

Good, but Rowan wants more.

He circles the rest of the string of beads, making the short silicone strand between the beads circle Mal's rim, tugging on it enough to expose the end of the bead inside.

"Shit!"

Better.

Rowan's hand rubs in a soothing motion over Mal's ass as he pushes the next two beads inside in quick succession, Mal's breathing growing harder with each one. He teases him, tugging the fourth bead halfway out before shoving it back inside, watching rapt as Mal's hole adjusts and eventually swallows it greedily, closing back up like nothing happened.

"Last one," Rowan tells him, again circling the strand around Mal's hole to draw out more of those gaspy little moans from him.

"Fuck… *do it*, c'mon."

"All together, these are almost as long as me. You sure you don't want my cock instead?"

With a slow but firm tug, Rowan pulls the fourth bead back out, the scent of strawberry permeating his nose.

"*Nnnng!*"

"Seem to enjoy this just fine. Why bother with the last one?"

A slick *pop*, and the third bead's out.

"Shit… fuckin'…."

When Rowan starts tugging the second bead out, Mal lets out an honest-to-God whine that sends a spike right through Rowan's core.

"No!"

The word makes Rowan freeze.

"Color?" he asks quickly, hoping the panic swelling in his chest isn't evident in his voice.

"*Green*, shit, fuckin' green. Just need…."

Rowan's relief is instant, washing over him like a tidal wave. Briefly he pictures himself leaning in, kissing Mal's cheek and smoothing his hands over the backs of his perfect thighs, cooing at him that it's okay. That he'll give him what he needs.

But that's not what Mal wants. Not what he asked for. So that's not what Rowan gives him.

"What you need," he starts, tugging the second bead out completely, to Mal's audible dismay, "is to quit fuckin' *whining* and let me play with you how I want."

He reaches between Mal's legs with his free hand, stroking his cock leisurely and finding that he's hard as a rock. Good.

The beads are slippery with lube, making Rowan fumble them in his haste to position them back at Mal's hole.

Two.

Three. Four.

Three. Four. Three.

Two.

He pumps each bead in and out, marveling at the way each one disappears so easily. Equally marveling at the effect it has on Mal—a constant stream of moans and whimpers that makes it hard to tell if Mal likes the beads going in or coming out more.

Either way, it's a delicious melody in Rowan's ears. It makes him want to reward Mal with what he's been near begging for since the start.

With a quick swipe of his fingertip to coat the fifth and final bead in the lube already dripping from Mal's hole, Rowan ultimately presses the last bead inside.

"Fuuu—" Mal whimpers, body stilling save for a subtle quaking in his thighs.

Color Rowan impressed. He gives Mal a moment to adjust to the new fullness before again twirling the looped end around in a wide circle, tugging Mal's rim. Mal gasps, arms collapsing beneath him, head buried in between as he shoves his ass back at Rowan.

Smack!

"Mmm!"

"Finally got what you wanted, huh? Only minimal bitching," Rowan states, slapping each asscheek twice more in quick succession, watching as Mal's back arches beautifully and his legs spread another inch apart.

Mal simply lets out a shuddering breath in response.

"Mmm," Rowan hums in appreciation. He palms himself once, painfully hard from the lack of direct stimulation all night.

And really there's no need for that. Not when he's got such a willing partner right in front of him. He climbs on the bed, only pausing to kick his boots off before swinging his legs up beside Mal.

Mal looks up at him, eyes bright but back still arched and tense, no doubt from the fullness of the beads.

"Come here."

There's a brief hesitation before Mal crawls the two feet toward him, circling around to Rowan's side and pausing next to his thighs.

"Straddle me."

Again, that moment of hesitation, Mal eyeing Rowan's pristine jeans.

But Rowan doesn't want hesitation. He wants to be *obeyed*. He rakes his hand through Mal's hair, tugging once his fingers meet the roots.

"Didn't shove the beads up your ears, Mal. Let's go."

He doesn't wait for Mal to respond before tugging harder toward his lap. Mal fumbles with a mumbled, "Fuckin'…." as he swings a leg over Rowan's thigh and settles below his lap with a wince.

"Fuckin' *what*?" Rowan challenges, yanking him up by the ass until he's firmly seated above his cock.

"Gonna ruin your—*nnng*!"

Mal groans deep as Rowan grinds his hips up, driving his hard cock between his cheeks.

"You're *gonna* do what I tell you," Rowan replies, gripping Mal's hips almost hard enough to bruise and dragging him forward in a filthy grind. "*Move.*"

He drinks in the sight of Mal's eyes rolling back as he starts a smooth rocking of his hips, abs flexing and cock bobbing. Each roll a perfect, smooth drag across Rowan's hard cock, punctuated by a stutter and a gasp as the beads are pressed deeper inside Mal.

"Tell me how it feels," Rowan commands.

"Fu-*full,* fuck…."

"Wanted all of 'em in you so fuckin' bad."

He grabs Mal by the back of his neck, yanking him down so Mal has to slap the bed next to Rowan's shoulder to keep from completely collapsing on top of him. Mal's eyes widen, nostrils flaring, but he keeps up that delicious grind all the while without even being told.

"This what you wanted, Mal?" he demands, watching the other man's eyelids flutter and a bead of sweat trickle down his temple.

"Want… want y-your…," Mal starts, hips stuttering as much as his words.

Rowan slaps the side of Mal's thighs, fingertips digging into the taut muscle and cutting off Mal's words. He forces him to resume his grinding, feeling more than seeing the hitch in his breath at the way the beads must shift inside him. At the way the scratch of his jeans, soft as they may be, must bite into his heated skin.

Rowan reaches around Mal's side, thankful for his long arms when he finds the loop on the end of the beads. He tugs Mal completely on top of him, feeling the heat and heft of his body like a weighted blanket, comforting despite the heady atmosphere around them. Mal hitches his hips, grinding his hard cock into Rowan's as Rowan tugs the first bead out.

"Mmm…," Mal whimpers, burying his face in Rowan's shoulder and muffling the sound.

With his free hand, he drags Mal's head up by his hair. "Wanna hear you, Mal."

A smooth tug and the second bead is out, Mal's groan this time loud and clear.

"That's it. In this room, your noises are *mine.*"

Pop. Moan. Pop. Moan.

The next two beads in quick succession.

"Ooooh, fuck…."

Mal's thighs quiver around Rowan's waist as he twirls the string of beads around his rim, teasingly pulling at the last bead.

"Last one. Think you deserve my cock yet?"

Mal scrunches his eyes tight, nodding vigorously against Rowan's chest, rustling the fabric of his shirt.

"Oh yeah? Whatcha done to deserve it, huh?"

Rowan shifts his grip on the beads and presses another one back inside.

"Fuck…." Mal pants above him, fingertips clawing into Rowan's biceps as he continues to rut his cock into Rowan's lap. "I…."

"You what?"

Rowan pops another bead back in, circling his fingertip around the pulsing rim as soon as the bead is nestled inside. Wishing it was his cock probably as much as Mal does.

"I… fuckin'…."

"Haven't done *shit*," Rowan finishes for him. He slips a finger in Mal's hole, rubbing along the bead inside him and pressing it toward his prostate. "Been a brat all night, as usual."

A *whoosh* of breath escapes Mal's mouth, and Rowan can feel the moisture from his breath dampening his shirt. But there's no reply. No rebuttal defending his actions. Only a subtle shaking from his prostate being stimulated and his hard nipples brushing against Rowan's shirt like Rowan wanted.

"Lucky for you I'm feelin' generous today."

He tugs the string of beads fully out, one by one, quickly replacing them with two of his fingers to feel the flutter of Mal's hole clenching.

"Fuck!"

"Off," Rowan orders, withdrawing his fingers and shoving at Mal's shoulder.

With shaky legs, Mal climbs off Rowan and slips from the bed to stand on the floor, hard cock peeking out over the edge of the mattress, a thin trail of precome dripping tantalizingly.

Rowan swiftly sits up and rolls off the bed himself, then sinks to his knees in front of Mal, tongue darting out to taste the salty drop.

"*Nnggg….*"

Rowan sucks hard at the tip, not taking the rest of him in his mouth. He swirls his tongue around and delves into the slit when he feels Mal's hands card through his hair. He drags himself off Mal's cock and catches his wrist in a firm grip before he has a chance to pull away.

"Uh-uh," he chastises.

He shoves his hand away and rises to his full height, Mal straining up at him even before Rowan wrenches his head back to force him to look farther up.

Rowan tuts at him. "And right after you said you deserved my cock, too."

The glint in Mal's eyes crackles with charged electricity, sending a tingling trail straight to Rowan's dick.

"Don't matter if I deserve it."

There it is. That cockiness that piqued Rowan's interest from the start.

But now it pisses him off.

"Wanna bet on that?"

Rowan reaches around, sliding his palm over that perfect ass and shoving two fingers back inside Mal's hole, tugging upward so Mal has to raise up onto his tiptoes. Nearly eye to eye with him, now.

"Could get you off any number'a ways beside my dick," Rowan says.

To prove his point, he pumps his fingers in and out, crooking up and brushing against Mal's prostate on each drag. It's obvious that Mal's trying not to let the mask slip. Trying not to show how affected he is by Rowan's touch when he's trying to be smug and make a point. It's even more obvious that he's failing.

Rowan releases the hand in Mal's hair, trailing down the side of his face and ghosting over his neck long enough to feel the throb of his pulse point. He doesn't miss the way Mal's eyes flutter at the contact.

"Ain't gonna get what—*fuck*… what ya want if ya don't," Mal tells him, despite the way he arches into Rowan's touch.

He's right, of course. The bastard.

"Seem awfully worried 'bout my dick for someone who said he didn't need it earlier."

Mal's hands wander down to Rowan's crotch, palming him through his damp jeans. "Don't need it," he argues, pressing with the heel of his hand. "Want it, though."

Rowan huffs out a sarcastic laugh and shoves Mal's hands back down by his sides. "Course you do. Fuckin' slut."

He swears he sees Mal preen at the name. Totally unashamed.

He tugs at Mal's slick rim, adding another finger, which he takes in easily. Perfectly stretched and ready for Rowan's cock, thanks to the hefty beads.

"Got somethin' to do first, though," Rowan says, withdrawing his fingers and wiping them on Mal's ass before grabbing the cuffs from the edge of the bed. "How tight do you want 'em?"

"Third hole," Mal says, offering Rowan his left wrist.

Rowan inspects the cuffs, runs a thumb over the third hole where the leather is softer and more worn than the rest, evidence that the cuffs have seen some use. Evidence that Mal's been with other people he's trusted to bind his hands.

Trust.

That's what this is all about.

What all the reading and the research he's done on the subject has told him is vital to any kind of Dom/sub relationship.

And already Mal trusts him enough to put himself in a nearly helpless situation. He doesn't doubt that the man could still hold his own in a fight even with his arms tied behind his back, but the sentiment stands. There's a swell of *something* in Rowan's belly that he'll examine later, when he doesn't have a naked and hard Mal waiting in front of him.

Probably more carefully than he needs to, Rowan unfurls the first cuff and wraps it around Mal's slender wrist, looping the strap through the eyelet and fastening it at the third hole. He folds both hands over the cuff, checking the fit, and feels Mal's fingertips graze slowly, deliberately, across his wrist.

Looking down through his lashes, Rowan sees Mal watching him with half-lidded eyes, the gold of them so fucking bright even in the relative dimness of the windowless room.

Another light stroke of his fingertips, this time directly over Rowan's pulse point. Where Mal would surely feel the rapid rush of blood in his veins if he pressed a little harder.

"Good?" Rowan asks.

"Yeah."

As Rowan's clasping the second cuff on Mal, the room seems to grow twenty degrees warmer, and Rowan's sure it has everything to do with the heated look Mal's giving him. His gaze keeps him rooted in place, nearly causing him to fumble in tightening the cuff fully. He recovers quickly, hoping that Mal didn't notice his near slip-up.

The smirk forming on his lips tells Rowan he isn't so lucky.

Rowan grips his shoulders hard and spins Mal in place, tugging him back against his chest.

"Somethin' funny?"

"No, *sir*," Mal mocks.

Yeah, *that* shit's not gonna fly.

Rowan tweaks both of Mal's nipples between his fingers, tugging on the hard buds until the other man is writhing in his arms, spine creased and head dipped back against his shoulder. It's then that Rowan grabs both of Mal's wrists and deftly clasps the connector on to each side, locking his arms behind his back.

"This is a good look for you, Mal," Rowan tells him, testing the connector with one hand and resuming his assault on Mal's nipples with the other.

Mal groans, chest puffing out as he presses into Rowan's touch.

Even in their close proximity, Rowan marvels at the way Mal's back muscles flex and his shoulder blades shift as he squirms. He lets himself explore Mal's body, running over defined pecs and taut shoulders and down the deep curve of his spine, his skin warm and slick with the cooled sweat from the first half of their session.

He ends his journey again at the cuffs, tugging once more on the connector between Mal's wrists, the light jingle of metal sending a jolt straight to his painfully hard cock.

Rowan feels a surge of desire race through him and abruptly spins the pair of them in place, shoving Mal face down onto the bed.

"*Fuck!*" he gasps.

Rowan ruts against his ass, utterly shameless in his need to watch his clothed cock slide between slick cheeks, further dampening his already ruined jeans. But God, the sounds Mal makes when Rowan grinds against him and tugs his arms taut are completely worth it.

"Gonna fuck you just like this."

In a flurry, Rowan unbuttons his shirt and flings the tails out of his way as he pulls out his cock through his jeans and coats himself in lube. He doesn't bother asking Mal if he's ready. Hell, *Rowan's* been ready since last week.

But the urge to tease Mal some more is stronger than the urge to be inside him again. He presses his cock to his own belly, letting the weight of it fall down and slap at Mal's hole, the slick sound like a gunshot in the quiet room.

"*Unnhhh….*"

Rowan grips himself around the base, slapping at Mal's hole over and over until it's pulsating wildly and the lube is nearly tacky.

"Fu-fuck…. C'mon, fuck me!" Mal whines, raising his upper body up off the bed as best he can.

Smack! Rowan slaps the side of his thigh once before shoving him back down, hand pressed tight to his mid back.

He knows better than to shove his cock straight in when Mal hasn't been properly fucked yet tonight, even if some dark part of his mind is growling at him to *take* and that *Mal would probably fucking love it.*

Instead, he inhales, exhales, matching his own breath to the steady rise and fall of Mal's back as he presses the tip inside, Mal's hole swallowing it greedily like the beads earlier.

"Ohhhh, *fuck*…."

Inch by inch the tightness and the heat grows increasingly overwhelming, a droplet of sweat finally making an appearance, dripping down Rowan's temple but doing jack shit to cool him. It's hard to think that anything could quench the inferno threatening to engulf him—every tiny clench of Mal's walls around him kindling in the fire.

Fully seated, he gives both himself and Mal a moment before starting a languid pace. A few thrusts to acclimate. When he feels Mal starting to get twitchy—hears his groans shift from breathy to impatient—he knows he needs to get a move on. And for once he fully agrees with him.

But he can't resist the urge to watch his cock splitting him in half. He pries apart Mal's cheeks, slick with lube. Hones in on the way his hole stretch-stretch-*stretches* to accommodate him as he fucks into him.

"Fuckin' *made* to take my cock."

"Don't… *unhh*… fla-flatter yourself," Mal breathes, fumbled words surely belying his true thoughts on the matter.

Rowan snaps his hips, driving into him hard.

"Not flattery if it's true."

He picks up his pace, settling into that hard-fast-good rhythm that they both crave. The sight of Mal face down on the bed, wrists cuffed behind him and unable to do anything but *take* whatever Rowan's giving him spurs him on, and before he knows it, that heat is building inside him far too soon.

He slows again, forcing himself to focus on the tiny *unh, unh, unh* from Mal each time Rowan's hips connect with his ass. But he wants to hear. Wants that push and pull that makes their fucking feel more like fighting in the best way.

Rowan tugs at the connector between the cuffs, the metal cool in his hand, and *pulls*, Mal's arms straightening out and the dip in his spine forming a beautiful valley down his back.

One day Rowan's gonna lick and suck every inch of that spine.

"Finally…," Mal breathes, though it's barely more than a whisper.

Rowan's distracted with the tight heat around his cock and the vine tattoos curling around Mal's hips and ending before the dimples of his lower back, but he registers it a beat later.

"Fuck you say?"

He tightens his grip on Mal's hip, whiting out the black ink with the force of his fingertips.

"Told ya I wanted it rough."

"Yeah," Rowan agrees, gripping Mal's elbows and pulling his arms back until his shoulder blades nearly touch, driving into him hard.

"Mmm!"

"You did say that." He tugs him up, chest completely lifted off the bed, held up only by Rowan's grip on him.

For a blissful minute, he fucks into him, an obscene, slick *slap* filling the room with each thrust, punctuated by Mal's satisfied groans.

As fantastic as it feels, he doesn't want to give in to Mal's demands so easily.

"Know what I want though, Mal?"

He releases Mal's arms, shoving him off his dick and back down onto the bed, his surprised yelp intoxicating as he twists and lands on his side.

Rowan flips him fully onto his back, and with a sharp pull, yanks at Mal's thighs until his ass is on the edge of the bed, sweat-slick back sliding across the leather pad and making a grating *squeak* noise.

"Not to fuck me, apparently," Mal quips, though it's obvious he's winded from the maneuvers.

Rowan slaps the outside of Mal's thigh.

"Fuck!"

"Gonna slap that fuckin' attitude right outta your mouth one'a these days."

And oh, *there's* a thought. Seeing Mal's face with cheeks as red as his asscheeks have gotten the few times he's spanked him.

But would Mal—

"*Do it.*"

Fuck. He wants to.

But…

"Nah. You don't get to ask for shit."

He heaves Mal's legs onto his shoulders and pulls Mal's body up to near sitting, one hand secure around the back of his neck. And Mal folds into it, sending heat straight to Rowan's cock and flooding his mind with images of other positions he could manhandle him into.

"You get to watch me fuck you how I wanna fuck you," he tells him, guiding his cock back inside Mal's slick hole but only putting in the tip.

"*Uhn…,*" Mal moans softly, eyes fluttering closed.

Rowan curls his nails into the back of his neck.

"Open. Or you're not gettin' any more."

Mal groans but opens his eyes, the shimmer always catching Rowan off guard when their eyes connect after a long while apart.

"Good," Rowan tells him. "Watch."

Gold eyes drop to where their bodies are connected, and Rowan thrusts his full length inside in one long, slow motion that has Mal groaning and his eyes fighting to stay open, brows knit tightly together.

"Now squeeze."

At once, Mal's walls clench around him like a vise, releasing after a second before tightening right back up. Fucking *milking* Rowan's cock, for fuck's sake, and it's driving Rowan insane.

"Oh fuck…," he gasps, forgetting himself and getting lost momentarily in this wild new pleasure he's sure no one else has made him experience.

Mal's calf flexes against his shoulder, and Rowan snaps out of the mini trance Mal's ass had lulled him into.

He wraps his free hand around Mal's cock, gathering the precome leaking onto his abs and slicking his hand, stroking him in time with his thrusts.

"Ohhh *shit*...," Mal moans again, throwing his head back and pinching Rowan's fingers against his upper back.

Rowan tears away the hand on Mal's cock and smacks the inside of his thigh, leaving a slick red handprint in its wake.

"What'd I just fuckin' tell you?" he snaps, slapping Mal's other thigh to match.

Mal exhales heavily but looks down again, biting his bottom lip, probably to keep himself from saying something Rowan's gonna make him regret. Only then does Rowan grasp his cock again and resume his thrusts, slow but deep and hard and *so fucking good*.

"Yeah...," Mal breathes. "Fuck, *faster*...."

Rowan huffs a laugh. "Thought I told ya you didn't get to ask for anything."

He pulls out completely, thrusting in to the root and withdrawing fully again. Driving every inch of his cock into the slick heat of Mal's hole.

"C'mon."

"Told you, Mal. I'm gonna fuck you how I want." Two sharp snaps of his hips. "Gonna get my cock nice and wet, then shove it down your fuckin' throat and make you quit bitchin'."

"*Nnggg*...."

Rowan drives into him, balls slapping obscenely against his ass.

"Can beg if you want, though." Rowan locks eyes with Mal, who snaps his gaze up from where it had been dutifully trained on Rowan's cock. "Might get ya somewhere."

And he must be desperate, cock pink and hard and leaking precome all over Rowan's fingers, because he barely wastes any time before whispering, "*Please*...."

The best sound in the fucking world.

"There you go. Such a good slut." Rowan rewards Mal and stops torturing himself, slamming his hips into him at full force.

The slap of their bodies is loud and slick and nearly a better mix of sounds than Mal's gasped moans.

"*Fuck*! There...."

Rowan switches from full-length thrusting to short, fast strokes over Mal's prostate, bending his knees to angle up and drive the tip of his cock into the sensitive spot. And fuck, it's doing as much for him as it clearly is for Mal, the other man flushed and panting beneath him, legs shaking where they're propped on Rowan's shoulders.

Barely a minute later and Mal's entire body is trembling, no doubt straining with the effort of holding the position and from the assault of Rowan's cock on his prostate and his hand stroking him in firm tugs.

"Fu-fuck… gonna… need—*Rowan!*"

God, it'll never get old. Hearing Mal gasp his name.

"C'mon, Mal," he goads, slamming into him with a force that nearly has his own vision whiting out. "Lemme feel that ass tighten."

"Fuuuuck!" Mal cries, ass clenching wildly and cock spurting forcefully enough to paint his own pecs in come.

"Yeah, God, that's it." Rowan strokes him through it, the sight of Mal covered in his own come bringing back delicious memories of him from the gangbang. "Fuckin' filthy. Look at you."

And Mal can only whisper another "Fuck…" before Rowan's pulling out and letting Mal's legs fall to the floor and his back fall onto the bed.

Rowan climbs up as well and hauls Mal onto his knees, then positions himself between them, lying back but half propped up on one elbow. Mal widens his stance, arms still bound behind his back, and moves to dip down to take Rowan's cock into his mouth. But Rowan stops him, swiping his hand through the streaks of come on Mal's chest and stroking himself to coat his own cock in the mess.

Then he grips Mal's hair and tugs him down so his mouth is hovering inches above his cock, lying flat against his belly.

"Taste yourself on me."

Mal lets out a fucked-out little whine and leans down to lick a hot, wet trail from Rowan's balls to the tip of his cock. He licks him several times more, cleaning his own come off Rowan's cock and moaning with each swipe of his tongue.

The sensation is nice, but it pales in comparison to the sight of Mal swallowing his own come. Of him pausing each time before he slips his tongue back into his mouth to show Rowan the white streaks coating the pink. He mouths at Rowan's cock the best he can without the support of his hands, knees widening to allow him to dip down farther.

"C'mon, *suck* me," Rowan growls, lifting his cock with his free hand and slapping Mal's cheek with it until the other man opens his mouth and turns to catch the head between his lips. "There ya go. Didn't think I'd need to tell a cock slut like you to do your fuckin' job."

There's some kind of garbled response in the back of Mal's throat, but Rowan grips his hair to keep him from lifting off.

It's clear that Mal's struggling in this position, his balance thrown off without the use of his arms.

Rowan pulls him off his cock, the wet *pop* dulled by the thrumming in his ears, but he asks, "Color?"

"Green," Mal responds instantly, lips slick and red.

Satisfied, he shoves him back down. And Rowan can see that Mal is still hard and dripping between his legs, still moaning and breathing ragged breaths through his nose as he sucks Rowan's length. Barely the first few inches, actually.

"Took all of me last week. You outta practice already?" Rowan taunts.

Mal merely grumbles something in the back of his throat in response, a brat even with his mouth full. Rowan swings his leg around and shoves at Mal's lower back with his heel, pressing him farther down onto his cock.

Mal sputters and chokes, swallowing around Rowan's cock, driven deep into his throat, the spasming muscles sending a spike of pleasure through Rowan.

"Mmm, *fuck*, that's better."

As soon as Mal widens his stance and pulls back enough to catch his breath with a fucked-out sounding groan, all bets are off. Rowan grips Mal's hair tight, guiding his mouth as he fucks up into it. And Mal rolls with it, mouth suctioning impossibly tighter around him, hot and wet and perfect.

Rowan wants nothing more than to scrunch his eyes shut and get lost in the feeling, but he can't keep his eyes off Mal. Not only because he needs to make sure he's still okay. But also because his cheeks are flushed and his hair is sweaty and he's absolutely fucking gorgeous. Rowan brushes his thumb across his cheek, willing him to look up at him.

Eyes bright and shiny and—

That telltale heat swoops through Rowan as he sees the first prickles of tears in Mal's eyes.

Still waitin' for you to make me cry. What Mal had said at the gangbang. Except he didn't think it would happen so soon. But it's not enough. He wants the tears to fall.

He thrusts deeper, pulling Mal's nose flush with his pelvis, cock sliding down the back of his throat.

A muffled cough, then—*there*.

The first tear, a perfect fat drop pooling at the inner corner of his left eye. It catches the light as it rolls over the lower lid and runs down Mal's flushed cheek, leaving a pearlescent streak in its wake before it disappears beneath his chin. The next drop pools and falls quickly, rolling off Mal's sharp nose and landing in Rowan's pubic hair—mixing with Mal's spit and Rowan's sweat.

It's filthy, and Rowan's so fucking hard and about to burst with the need to come.

"Look at me," he says, voice a rasped whisper.

Mal pulls back off his cock an inch or two to crane his neck up enough for his golden eyes to lock onto Rowan's, and Rowan feels the breath leave his lungs in a swift *whoosh* that has him inhaling sharply.

And fuck, he's beautiful, like Rowan knew he would be. Eyes wet and shining and starting to turn red around the rims, but pupils still blown wide—a testament to how turned on he is. How much he loves this. *Perfect*.

"There you go," Rowan tells him, unable to hide the reverence in his voice. Unwilling too. "Knew you'd look fucking perfect crying on my cock."

As the tears form and spill, form and spill, Rowan stills Mal with a hand in his hair. With the other, he swipes at the tracks running down his cheeks, gathering the remnants of the liquid on his thumb and pushing it into Mal's mouth alongside his cock. Rowan feels more than hears the other man's moan—the vibrations traveling from his cock to his hips and making him cant up into Mal's talented mouth, slick with spit from laving his tongue over Rowan's thumb like it's a fucking lollipop.

Rowan can't settle for imagining the taste. Pulling his thumb back out, he wipes again at Mal's cheek, replacing the tears with Mal's spit. He sucks his own thumb into his mouth, the saltiness of Mal's tears and his own precome mingling into a bitter taste that hits deep in Rowan's core.

The reaction from Mal is instant, ragged breaths pattering against Rowan's pelvis and eyes nearly rolling back in his head as he resumes sucking Rowan with a newfound fervor.

Rowan doesn't know exactly what about the gesture got Mal's blood pumping—having Rowan's fingers in his mouth or swapping spit or simply the fact that Rowan's managed to make him cry after only two sessions—but hell if he isn't gonna do it as often as possible.

Mal lets out a strangled whimper as Rowan thrusts up into his mouth, cock once again hitting the back of his throat. Balls tightening, belly clenching, thighs shaking on either side of Mal's face as he works furiously to bring Rowan off, and in no time—

"*Fuuuck*, that's it. Gonna...."

The only acknowledgment Mal can give him is a soft "Mmm" as his eyes roll back then close tight, the remainder of the tears that have formed spilling over in a pretty cascade, and...

That does it.

Rowan's hips jerk as he erupts into Mal's mouth, unsure if his own groan or Mal's is louder.

Gripping the back of Mal's head, he keeps him there, jacking his hips to get deeper inside, keep feeling that warmth and that suction that's driven him wild from the start.

And Mal moans right on through it, keeping his eyes open and lasered onto Rowan's until he swallows, the back of his throat rippling around Rowan's cock.

Rowan's breath leaves him in a rush as his body stops vibrating and he comes down from the high of his orgasm as Mal sucks him clean. Cock finally softening, he pulls out of Mal's mouth, a trail of spit still connecting the tip with Mal's slick lower lip that nearly makes Rowan get hard all over again. The way he gets Rowan going is *insane*.

Rowan sinks down onto his knees, face-to-face with the flushed man as he runs a hand through Mal's sweaty hair. Tilts his head up. Locks eyes with him and sees the blown pupils start to shrink, hazy look slowly dissolving to clear caramel-gold.

And he wants to kiss him.

He *can't*; he knows that. But fuck, Rowan's gotta be a bit of a masochist, because having to deny himself that is easily the hardest thing he's done, especially when Mal's lips are pink and slick and parted just *so*.

"Okay?" Rowan asks.

Mal nods, blinking slowly and rolling his shoulders.

And Mal's still hard.

"You want the cuffs off, or do you want me to get you off again?"

"Cuffs," Mal tells him, voice low.

Shuffling behind him, Rowan quickly unclasps the latch between the cuffs, freeing Mal's hands. One at a time, he raises Mal's hands and removes the cuffs, the fur slightly damp from the thin sheen of sweat that's accrued from their session.

Once Mal is free, he rolls his wrists and shoulders, tilts his neck from side to side. Rowan holds the back of his elbow and helps him to his feet, guides him to the bed and lets him get comfortable on his back before he slicks his hand and brings Mal off again in smooth, slow jerks.

When he's panting and sated, Rowan helps him come down.

A privilege he still can't quite believe he gets to be a part of.

THEY'VE MADE going to Sheila's diner a tradition of sorts, and it brings a welcome sense of familiarity to their sessions, coupled with an anticipation that has Rowan floating the entire walk there.

Because here, tucked away in the corner booth under the fluorescent lights, Rowan can actually get to know Mal's mind rather than his body. Here he's more than a bratty sub—he's a wholeass *person* that Rowan's been dying to get to know since he first locked eyes with him at the gangbang three weeks ago.

And sure, he knows some of what Mal likes sexually. Knew some of *that* shit before he'd even spoken two words to the guy, so it's easy to think he knows a lot about him. But so far everything he's learned has been carefully curated, filtered, sterilized almost, in a way that makes him realize he doesn't know the other man at all. It's like he's still getting Malcolm, this caricature that he's sculpted to present to the outside world so he doesn't have to get too close with anyone.

Rowan wants to know *Mal*.

The guy who's friends with the Monroe twins and Jeremiah and a sweet old lady who runs the diner they've come to frequent.

The guy whose tattoos are equally delicate and threatening.

The guy who shares pie and cigarettes with an almost-stranger without batting an eye.

That's the guy Rowan wants to get to know, and he has no problem admitting that, even after only two scenes alone with him.

"SO, WHAT'S the verdict?" Rowan asks, pouring the packet of oyster crackers into his tomato soup.

"Was good," Mal replies after he finishes a bite of his sandwich. But he doesn't bother to look up from his food, diving in for another bite immediately.

It's a relief, but it does little to dispel the feeling of being a kid and waiting on his teacher to pass back the test grades.

"That's good. I'm glad, I mean."

Fuck, he's such an idiot. He shoves the corner of his grilled cheese into his mouth after dunking it in the tomato soup. But the bite of food, delicious as it is, isn't enough to keep him from opening his big mouth again.

"Was uh… there anything you didn't like? Or that I could do differently?"

In reality he knows that it's good for them to talk about this shit. Get everything out in the open so there's less chance for miscommunication and dissatisfaction and so they can learn each other and keep getting better every time. He suspects that the twinge of embarrassment in asking will fade eventually.

For the first time since they got their food nearly five minutes ago, Mal looks up, an amused smile on his face.

"You this much of a teacher's pet in school too?"

The embarrassment becomes a full-on deluge, Rowan's ears and face and neck undoubtedly flushing to clash with his hair.

"Not… I mean, I just—"

"Relax, Red. Just fuckin' with ya. Woulda been concerned if you *didn't* ask that at some point."

Rowan exhales a heavy breath and unclenches the facial muscles he didn't know he'd clenched in an effort to chill out. Hell, less than an hour ago he had a mind-blowing orgasm with a smokin' hot guy and is currently eating homemade grilled cheese and tomato soup, and he's tenser than a guilty defendant on trial.

"I liked everything you did," Mal says, as if sensing Rowan finally relax.

And that… well, it's got Rowan feeling all sorts of things he doesn't want to name right now. All of them soft and warm and pleasant.

"Yeah?"

"Mmm. You stuck to the acts we talked about beforehand. Checked in when you thought I was telling you 'no' or thought it was too much. Kept the dirty talk to shit I told you I liked."

A thought strikes Rowan even through Mal's praise of his performance.

"When I said I was gonna slap your face and you told me to do it, what's…." He pauses, trying to figure out how to phrase his question. "We were obviously in the middle of the scene, so like… how much can I take what you say during that time seriously? I mean, I obviously wasn't gonna do it right then, but is that something you'd be open to me doing in the future, or was that just heat-of-the-moment type shit?"

Mal sucks his bottom lip into his mouth, wetting it with his tongue. "In general, you should assume that anything we don't explicitly talk about is just dirty talk. Kinda like you sayin' you'd leave the room if I didn't comply. We both know it's not gonna happen, but it's hot. The face slappin' thing, though… I *did* mean that."

God, Rowan feels his cock jump at the thought. "Yeah?"

"Yeah. You were right for not doin' it. We've only talked about spanking and impact play on less sensitive areas. Legs and chest and ass like you stuck to tonight."

Rowan is glad he wasn't too tempted to give in to that desire earlier. "I read one of those books you recommended. *The Loving Dominant.* Said some people write up an actual contract for this type of stuff."

"Yeah," Mal tells him. "I have with Doms in the past who wanted everything written out. 'S fine if you wanna do that—we can draw somethin' up in writing. I never thought it was that necessary since the shit I'm into isn't overly intense. Nothin' that could cause significant pain or situations that could be traumatizing or anything."

From what he's read and from his few scenes with Mal, both their interests do fall on the more vanilla side of the BDSM landscape. "No, I'm good. Fine with talking stuff out. Just still need to check when things happen that I obviously haven't dealt with before."

Mal nods. He lets a beat of silence linger, a thoughtful look on his face, before telling Rowan, "You *get* it. Usually takes people a lot longer to suss this shit out, but you're good at readin' me. If I felt like you weren't getting it or you needed a firm set of boundaries, I'd say we should write something. But that's not the case."

There's that flush again, this time spreading all the way down to his fucking *toes* with a cascade of warmth that has nothing to do with the redness of his skin.

"It helps that you're pretty open about what you like," Rowan tells him.

Mal grunts noncommittally. "You'd think so. Had some Doms in the past who'd flat-out ignore obvious cues, let alone subtle ones."

Rowan's not surprised. He thinks back to the man he'd helped at the club barely more than a month ago. How his partner hadn't noticed all the signs of someone slipping out of consciousness, some of which should be obvious even to an untrained eye.

"Used to it from work, I guess," Rowan tells him.

"Didn't know paramedics fucked their patients," Mal quips back, amusement in his eyes.

"Only the hot ones," Rowan jokes. Mal's tiny side smile feels like a victory before he continues, "Nah, I mean that, like, half the time the people we help are either unconscious or close to it, so you kinda have to be good at reading body language and shit if they can't tell you what's wrong."

Mal hums thoughtfully. He stuffs some BBQ chips inside the corner of his sandwich and takes a bite, the crunch of it reminding Rowan that his oyster crackers are probably soggy in his soup by now.

As Rowan's scooping them out with his spoon, Mal says, "The one thing I'd say is that there were times when you could'a gone further."

Rowan raises an eyebrow at him. "Oh yeah?"

"Mmm. Not complainin', but you could'a made me work for shit more. Not given in so easily."

Rowan shifts in his seat. "Pretty fuckin' hard denying you *anything*, Mal."

As soon as the words leave his mouth, Rowan wants to kick himself. Because that's a whole lotta *too much too soon* that's probably going to make Mal uncomfortable. Hell, it makes *him* uncomfortable with how sincere it is.

But thankfully Mal blows right past it. "Push and pull, man. I get off on being denied shit, and you get off on doin' it. The payoff's more satisfying havin' to work for it."

"Yeah," Rowan tells him. "I know. Just… need to get outta my head."

Maybe there's something off about Rowan's tone, because Mal's eyes narrow a fraction before he speaks again. "You feel guilty or anything?"

It seems to come out of left field, and Rowan's sure the surprise shows on his face. "Guilty? No… why?"

"Not anxious or depressed or anythin'? Now or last week?" Mal presses.

Mal couldn't possibly know about his depression, but even with the moments of uncertainty he's felt so far being Mal's Dom, Rowan knows that nothing he's felt with him even comes close to those days of feeling like the absolute scum of the earth.

Rowan shakes his head. "Nope."

Seemingly satisfied with his answer, Mal takes another bite of his sandwich, then speaks with his mouth full. "Wanted to make sure you weren't droppin'."

Oh. Right. He'd been so focused on Mal the past two sessions that Rowan hadn't even considered the possibility of dropping himself. Of the two of them, it *is* more likely that the newbie would be more emotionally compromised after a scene than the seasoned pro.

Regardless, there's a flutter in his chest at Mal's concern.

"Oh," Rowan says. "Kinda forgot that was a thing, honestly."

"Less common than sub drop, but it happens."

Mal meets his eyes, and the intensity that Rowan sees there turns the flutter into a full-on palpitation.

"You start feelin' like that after our scene's over, tell me. Or text me if it's later in the week or somethin'," Mal tells him, voice serious.

Rowan wants to say *thank you* and he wants to say *I like learning this stuff with you* and he wants to leap across the table and kiss the tiny fleck of mustard off the corner of Mal's lip because sure, Rowan's clinically mentally ill, but he's also apparently fucking crazy and way too into this guy he's basically only hooking up with.

What he says instead is nothing, and what he does is nod and take another bite of his grilled cheese.

Mal mirrors his nod, seemingly satisfied. "Anyway," he says, "don't be afraid to push me more's all I'm sayin'. Gotta trust yourself that you're not gonna fuck it up. But that'll come with time. Already pretty damn good at it for a newbie."

That same rush of tingling warmth he's felt countless times tonight spreads through Rowan once more.

Mal was right. You can learn a lot of shit from books, and Rowan has so far, but nothing beats actual experience. And nothing feels better than hearing your sub say you *did a good job*. The irony isn't lost on Rowan—that as the Dom, the one who's supposed to take care of *Mal* and tell him *he's* doing a good job, the opposite feels just as good.

A two-way street.

Chocolate sauce on pizza.

THEY WORK through their meals, snippets of meaningless conversation sprinkled in.

Mal unzips his messenger bag to check something on his phone, Rowan catching the light glinting off the metal clasps of the cuffs he'd unceremoniously tossed inside after their scene.

"Is there anything of the club's that you actually use?" Rowan asks, recalling that Mal said he mostly brings his toys and equipment.

"Eh," Mal shrugs. "Not really? Basically just the rooms and benches and shit. People are fuckin' gross, man."

Rowan thinks that the club isn't nearly as gross as it would be if it weren't in a fairly posh neighborhood. In fact it's been pretty spotless every time he's been there. Though he does remember the thorough toy cleaning and maintenance instructions he'd read in the book earlier in the week and thinks that Mal's probably right despite Rowan's recollection of the club's toy-cleaning standards when he'd signed up.

Still.

"Must be kinda used to gross, though," Rowan comments. "You're Southie, right?"

Mal's eyebrows quirk up.

"Your accent. I am too."

"No shit?"

"Yeah. Lived on Hampton Street."

"Huh," Mal says, looking thoughtful and—if Rowan's reading it right—a little impressed. "Lived, like, a mile from there. On Baker."

"Damn, small fuckin' world."

A smirk settles on Mal's face. "Knew you seemed like a scrappy fucker."

Rowan snorts in the back of his throat. "Why, 'cause I was gonna fight that guy at the gangbang?"

"Just in general. Don't really take shit from what I've seen so far."

With a shrug, Rowan replies, "Yeah, guess so. The result of being the middle of six kids."

"Fuck, I thought *Savaryns* bred like cockroaches."

"Don't think that's the right expression."

"Whatever, Red." Mal tilts his bag of BBQ chips up and empties the crumbs into his mouth, crunching loudly. "Left that shithole so I didn't have to deal with that shit anymore. Bein' fuckin'… dirty all the time. Usin' other people's stuff. Can finally use my *own* shit and not hafta share it with anyone."

Rowan's heart gives a little kick in solidarity, having felt the exact same when he'd moved into his own place after having to share everything he's ever touched his entire life.

"I get that," Rowan tells him. "Kinda seems like a waste of money, though. Why even go to the club at all? Why not bring people home with you?"

"Keeps shit separate," Mal grumbles. "I don't need some random guy comin' over to my place when we're just fuckin'."

Rowan tries not to take that personally. He gets it. They're not dating. They're *just fuckin'*. Even if he is a step above *some random guy*, at least in his own opinion.

"Makes sense," Rowan says instead.

They sit quietly for a few more minutes, but there's a gnawing *something* inside Rowan that he doesn't quite know what to do with.

But he shoves the feeling aside, remembering that he'd been meaning to ask Mal something about what he'd read earlier in the week.

"Have you always been a sub?"

If the shift in topic surprises him, Mal doesn't let it show. "Pretty much. Why?"

"Just curious."

"Curious 'cause you wanna try it, or you wanna know why I like it?"

Maybe someday Mal's perceptiveness will stop catching Rowan off guard.

"Why you like it. I mean, I know I like being in control and shit and that I get off on pleasing people, but I don't think I'd like submitting as much."

Mal hums softly. "Think I kinda scratched the surface before, but I like shutting my mind off for a bit. Not having to worry about normal day-to-day shit and just *existing*. Pass off the choices to someone else. Someone I know won't fuck me over."

It makes Rowan's cheeks tingle that Mal can already tell that about him from a few sessions together, and he can't help the smile it brings to his face.

Mal continues, "It's more than physical for me. Obviously shit feels good, but being comfortable enough to admit that I like giving up control and to actually *do it* takes that pleasure to another level. 'S like… being *free*, y'know?" He takes a deep breath, making his nostrils flare out. "Used to have to hide a lot. You're Southie, so you gotta know what that's like."

"Yeah," Rowan replies. Even if he'd been pretty open about his sexuality, he still had his fair share of run-ins with local homophobes.

"So doin' this feels more like my authentic self, if you wanna get all psychological about it. Makes the pleasure more intense knowing I'm safe and am gonna be cared for even if I fuck up or don't meet the other person's expectations or whatever."

Rowan wonders what it is about Mal that makes him almost downplay his knowledge about this stuff. Wonders if it's that lingering Southie mentality that it's not worth shit to be emotionally aware or smart in ways other than what relates directly to life on the street.

He hopes he finds out one day.

They settle into a short silence, the clinking of dishes and the muffled coughs of the few late-night patrons and the sizzling of the grill filling the air between them. Rowan glances toward the counter and sees Sheila adjusting her name tag, reminding him of another thing he'd wanted to ask Mal.

"Oh hey, I meant to ask you the other day, but do you want me to call you Malcolm at the club? Like in front of Camilla and Jeremiah or whatever?"

Mal bites his lip, rubs at his eyebrow. "Don't really give a shit, but…. Yeah, prob'ly."

The *yeah* tells Rowan that he does, in fact, give a shit. At least some part of him does.

"'Kay. Is there a… reason for it?"

Again Mal fidgets. Bites the inside of his cheek. Averts his gaze. He's clearly uncomfortable about it, and Rowan quickly backtracks, not wanting to scare him off.

"Don't hafta tell me if you don't want. Was only curious," Rowan says.

"Not exactly dinner conversation, man," Mal replies in a low voice, not looking up from his food.

"That's cool. Sorry."

That urge Rowan has to pry is intense, but he shoves it down. Apparently not far down enough to stop his next question from tumbling out.

"Have you had all your Doms call you Mal, then?"

"Just—" Mal starts, stopping himself.

The *Just you* hangs in the air between them for a long moment. Unspoken, yet palpable. *Visceral* in a way that has Rowan's blood rushing in his ears and his belly churning.

"Uh… no." Mal continues. "Felt weird havin' you call me Malcolm, so…." He trails off, far quieter than he had been during his long explanation.

"Oh. Cool."

Cool. Like Rowan's heart isn't hammering a mile a minute, thinking about the way Mal had blushed so beautifully when Rowan had called him *Mal* during their first scene. He tries not to let it get to him. Not to make it so obvious that Rowan knows that Mal thinks of him as different somehow.

Not some random guy, even if in this tiny way.

WHEN THE bus girl comes to take their empty plates, Mal asks her to bring them a slice of key lime pie and the slip. She nods but insists that Sheila said their meal is once again on the house.

Mal grumbles and asks her for a blank order slip, which she rips off from the pad tucked inside her apron and leaves to fetch their pie. He takes out a pen from the front of his messenger bag and quickly scribbles down their orders and the prices from memory, pie included.

"Be back in a sec," he says, grabbing his wallet and swiftly sliding out of the booth.

Rowan watches him make his way toward Sheila and slap the bill on the counter in front of her, presumably along with some cash. The old woman doesn't even flinch, simply sighs and continues filling the pastry display with muffins and scones. Rowan can't hear their conversation, but he sees Mal plant both hands on the counter and dip his head forward as if exasperated. Eventually Sheila seems to relent, punching their order into the register and taking Mal's money.

Rowan's *dying* to know what the story is there, but his wandering thoughts are halted when the bus girl places a delicious-looking slice of key lime pie and two forks on their table.

Rowan thanks her, waiting for Mal before he digs in. He paid for it after all. The least he can do is wait for him. It's easily more restraint than he's had to display all night, remembering how good the apple pie was last week.

When Mal returns, Rowan gives him a questioning look, but the other man shrugs it off with a shake of his head.

AS THEY work through their dessert, they make light conversation. When prompted, Rowan tells Mal about all five of his siblings in turn, highlighting their best qualities rather than dragging them to a stranger. In turn, Mal tells him about his job and that he'd gotten his associate's degree in bookkeeping when he was in his mid-twenties, something he casually mentions no one in his family had done before.

Small things. Normal things. Nothing nearly as heavy as the subjects they'd broached earlier, but still Rowan has to fight to keep the smile off his face.

When they finally part ways in the parking lot of the club half an hour later, Rowan's jaw and cheeks ache from the effort.

Tonight felt good. Tonight felt like *progress* in cracking that titanium shell that Mal has around everything that's not strictly related to physical pleasure. Rowan only hopes that things keep going this well.

Chapter 6: Mistakes and Promises

Rowan's next two scenes with Mal go as well as their first two. They use the cuffs both times, Mal jigsawing into near impossible positions that get Rowan's heart thudding and his dick throbbing. They test out the glass dildo that Mal had shown him before their first scene together, which pales in comparison to the silicone beads they'd used the second time, and a set of clover nipple clamps that make Mal keen the loudest he ever has. Rowan had dutifully filed that particular fact away for later use as soon as Mal nearly came from Rowan tugging on the chain connecting his overly sensitive nipples.

It really is amazing that after only four sessions alone with him, he already feels in tune to Mal's desires. To his body. His reactions. Like the way his thighs shake when he's on the verge of coming, or the way he bites his bottom lip when Rowan strokes over the tip of his cock. The way his eyes roll back any time Rowan's hands ghost over his neck.

He never thought he could be so completely and thoroughly satisfied with a sexual partner. Even in the past with hookups or fuck buddies or the couple of people he's referred to as his *boyfriend*, he's never felt like this. Just… gratified in every way. And sure, he's never delved this deep into his sexuality before, so there's obviously an element of newness that explains some of it, but the rest is solely Mal.

And yeah, there isn't a romantic connection between the two of them, but there's *something*. Not a friendship yet, but definitely a kinship, if anyone uses that word anymore. Two boys from the South End who overcame some shit, got out, and now get to live their lives the way they want. At least that's true for Rowan, and he assumes that's pretty close to Mal's story from the snippets he's told him.

Dirty. Closeted. Abused, probably, in some way or another.

The hallmarks of too many kids in the South End, though many of them wind up on the streets or in jail or six feet under. They don't make it out like Rowan did. Like Mal did.

Somehow their paths never crossed when they were growing up, but Rowan wonders what it would have been like if they'd known each other. Would they have been rivals? Friends? Fuck buddies? Boyfriends? It makes his head spin thinking about the smallness of the world and about how someone who lived a mile away from him growing up carved out his own path in the world and still somehow wound up at the very same club as him.

He wonders, too, if he'd even have stayed a member of the Menagerie at all if he hadn't been picked by Mal that first day. Would he have found someone else to spend a few hours with instead? Would he have committed to being someone else's Dom? Or would he have gone home empty-handed and canceled his membership the next day?

It's all a little too much to think about. For now, Rowan counts his lucky stars that he gets to have this.

ROWAN FINDS himself looking forward to their diner "dates" almost as much as their actual scenes, because that's when he learns the most about Mal.

He doesn't like tomatoes—*No fruit should be both sweet and bitter. Shit should be illegal.*

He actually enjoys his job as an accountant for some sort of tech company that Rowan doesn't completely understand—*Pay is decent and my bosses are actually smart enough to listen to me when I tell 'em they're wastin' money on somethin'.*

He *is* capable of having a friendly conversation, as long as he gets something in his ass first— *Don't ever get a tattoo on your hips, man. Shit's fucking painful. Yes, way more painful than the ribs, Saint Mary.*

And in turn, Rowan tells Mal as much about himself. As a middle child of six, Rowan's never really liked being in the spotlight. He doesn't tend to offer up much information about himself unless there's a specific goal in mind, but with Mal, it's effortless.

As easy as when he used to have meaningless conversations with his brother Jay in their childhood bedroom, passing a joint back and forth. But now it's meaningful conversations with Mal in Sheila's diner, passing whatever dessert Sheila whipped up that day back and forth.

He tells Mal about how he became a paramedic—how he loves helping people and making a difference, even though his job can be stressful and mentally draining at times.

He tells Mal more about his siblings—Aubrey and Jay and Clara and Rory and Marc, each with their own set of quirks that are as frustrating as they are endearing.

He tells Mal about how he wants his next apartment to have a balcony so he can grow tomatoes—*They* are *good, what the hell do you mean you don't like them?*

He doesn't tell Mal that he's clinically depressed. As much as he wants to let Mal into his life, some things aren't meant to be shared casually over strawberry shortcake.

SOMEWHERE IN between the second and third sessions—Rowan absolutely does *not* know the exact day without looking back at the message—they've started texting more. Not really *Hey, how was your day* type things, but little things. Mostly kink-related things, but conversations nonetheless. That first week alone, they talked four times, on and off for several hours throughout each day.

And it made him so fucking glad and honest-to-God giddy that he wonders if he really *is* a teenager with his first crush and not a twenty-seven-year-old man with a membership to a sex dungeon.

Don't get him wrong, Rowan knows he's being an idiot—expecting something *more* to come of his conversations with Mal, which would theoretically then bleed into his scenes with him. It's beyond wishful thinking, and pretty dishonest if he's being frank. Because he's wanting something more than what Mal wants to give him, more than what they've established they're going to give to each other.

Every time Rowan had a friends-with-benefits situation when he was younger, Aubrey had always warned him that it would end badly, that someone would catch feelings and shit would get awkward and one or both of them would get hurt.

Clearly, he hasn't learned from his big sister's advice.

He should nip this shit in the bud and probably go out and fuck some other people to get over his hang-up on Mal. But… he doesn't *want to*. And that is what scares him more than anything. The fact that his notoriously high libido is satisfied with only one hookup per week is astonishing, even with his usual daily jerk-off sessions still intact. There's something there about quality over quantity, but Rowan doesn't want to let himself think about that for too long.

But as well as things are going, there's one frustrating caveat to all of this. To the texting and whole "getting to know one another" thing that still keeps Mal out of arm's reach. It's that for the most part—when they're not within the confines of the diner—Mal really only seems to want to talk about sex. And look, if that's all Mal is willing to talk about? Rowan's gonna talk about sex. A lot.

On a random Tuesday afternoon, he texts him the first thing that pops into his head.

[RC] *What's your favorite position?*

[MS] *prison guard*

His response is immediate. He knows Mal works from home, but it's still a pleasant surprise that he's paying him the attention he should be paying to Excel spreadsheets.

[RC] *???*

[RC] *Never heard of that*

[MS] *you did it last week*

[MS] *prison-guard-07.gif*

The gif of straight-up porn catches Rowan off guard, though it really shouldn't given who he's talking to. But now that he sees it, Rowan does remember it well. Mal on his knees with Rowan fucking into him from behind, holding his arms tight to his lower back as if he were in handcuffs. It was hot as shit, and Mal definitely seemed to enjoy it.

[RC] *Ah, gotcha*

[MS] *or on my knees with my face pressed into the bed*

[MS] *like riding a lot too*

[MS] *my actual favorite though is missionary while i'm gettin choked*

[RC] *Too bad we can't do your actual favorite*

Rowan's not expecting a reply to that.

[MS] *yeah*

[MS] *got big hands man*

[RC] *Should have you ride me again though. Haven't done that since the gb*

[MS] *yeah*

[MS] *next saturday?*

[RC] *Definitely*

Rowan thinks the conversation is over, but Mal follows up with a less-than-common question of his own.

[MS] *what's yours*

[RC] *Assume you mean for topping? Guess it depends*

[MS] *yeah. depends on what*

[RC] *If I'm fucking someone I care about or not*

[MS] *why does that matter*

[MS] *fucking is fucking*

[RC] *Thanks Shakespeare*

[RC] *It does matter. To me at least*

[MS] *sap*

[MS] *so what you only fuck people in missionary if you love them*

Well. No, but it does feel more special that way. But he's not gonna tell Mal that. They kinda-sorta fucked that way during the gangbang, but that was about as far from romantic as you can get.

[RC] *Not what I meant*

[RC] *I like missionary or spooning the best if there's feelings involved*

[RC] *And just doggy if it's a casual thing*

[MS] *you got a different favorite for bottoming*

[RC] *I don't really do it enough to have a favorite*

[RC] *Probably riding though so I can still be in control*

Rowan doesn't tell him that it's been over a year since he last bottomed, and even longer since he really enjoyed it.

EACH TIME his phone vibrates or lights up with a message from Mal, it gets Rowan's heart racing. Standing in line at the grocery store, winding down from a run, folding laundry… normal, everyday things are made all the more enjoyable when he sees Mal's name on the screen. Every conversation throughout the week is a tiny sip of Mal that Rowan drinks in like a man lost in the desert—tiding him over long enough to make it to the oasis of Saturday night but never enough to fully quench his thirst.

[RC] *You ever been fisted before?*

[MS] *what the fuck*

[MS] *why*

[RC] *Sorry, just read something about it and was curious*

[MS] *once*

[RC] *No shit?? Did you like it?*

[MS] *fact that i only did it once should speak for itself man*

[MS] *but no not really*

[MS] *wasn't that bad i guess. the stretch felt kinda like a big toy, but the guy kept wiggling his fingers and it was weird as fuck*

[RC] *Jesus*

[MS] *that's not something you wanna do is it?*

He can practically hear the grimace in Mal's tone, and it makes him smile.

[RC] *Fuck no*

[RC] *The gaping aspect can be kinda hot, but I don't like it to that extreme*

[RC] *Reminds me of this guy with a prolapsed anus we had to drive to the ER once*

[MS] *you know you fucked up if it don't go back in on its own*

And was that a… joke?

Like an actual, unprompted, ha-ha *joke?*

God, Rowan likes him *so much.*

DESPITE HIS best efforts to keep himself under control these past few weeks, Rowan's blossoming… *whatever* on Mal is so embarrassingly obvious that even Addison has picked up on it and hounds him relentlessly because of it.

She catches him texting Mal on one of their rounds, turning his phone out of her view so she can't see the photo of the new vibrating plug that Mal bought.

"That your 'booty call' again?" she asks, not even trying to hide the smugness in her voice.

"Shut up," Rowan tells her, because he is a mature adult fully capable of keeping his emotions in check and *not* a hormonal teenager.

"You've been seeing this guy for, like, a *month* now, Rowan. That's not a booty call anymore."

"We fuck once a week. Saturday at eight. That's a booty call."

"Uh-huh, and me and Char are just roommates."

"You're *married* to them. And that's different," Rowan shoots back.

"Domestic partnership," she corrects. "But no, the point stands."

"We've only fucked, like, five times so far. It's nothing serious."

But he wants it to be. Not *going steady* serious, 'cause it's way too early for that, but he'd be a filthy liar if he said he didn't want anything more than what they've got going on right now. Or at least a shot at something more.

Hell, he'd settle for a kiss.

"I can count on zero hands the number of times I fucked someone *five times* and didn't end up dating them for at least a year," Addison says matter-of-factly.

Rowan bristles, unsure exactly why he's being so defensive about the whole thing. Well, he knows why. Despite that they've started talking more between sessions and spending longer and longer at Sheila's diner at the end of their sessions, he has no idea if Mal feels anything between them or not.

They've got great physical chemistry. Their bodies fit together in a way that feels effortless and, well, *special* for lack of a better word. Hell, Rowan's had some great sex in his life, but it's never been like this. Easy. Fun. Deeply satisfying during and after. And all that while *sober*, for fuck's sake, which is more than Rowan can say for many of his past hookups.

"It's different with guys," Rowan says instead.

"I know you don't believe in that sexist BS."

Rowan sighs. "No. But even if I *did* want something else—which I don't—we agreed on a casual thing. And I'm not gonna ruin fantastic sex 'cause I caught feelings."

"Fantastic, huh?" Addison laughs.

"You have no idea."

"Well, you better lock that shit down before someone else snatches him up."

"Again, not gonna happen."

"You never know," Addison insists in a singsong voice.

Her refusal to drop the subject is getting on Rowan's nerves.

"I *do* know. The only thing we talk about is sex. We don't hang out outside of hookups, and we don't even kiss when we're fucking."

He leaves out the fact that their fucking requires much more vulnerability, communication, and trust than what she's probably assuming.

"All right, all right, down, killer," she says.

Mercifully, a call comes in right then, abruptly ending their conversation. Rowan's never been so glad for someone to be injured.

THE CALL is Rowan's least favorite kind. Domestic abuse.

They race to the scene—a narrow, rundown house on the outskirts of the Back Bay. Two police cars light up the dismal gray area with flashing blue lights that always make Rowan's nerves fray—a harsh reminder of all the times he's run from those exact lights in the past and the one time he couldn't.

He pushes aside thoughts of police and actions that aren't entirely his own and climbs out of the ambulance with Addison in time to see a burly man being handcuffed against a squad car.

On the porch steps is a young woman, early- to mid-twenties, maybe, hunched in on herself and staunchly ignoring the police officer trying, presumably, to take her statement.

But Rowan has authority here.

"Paramedics! Clear the way," he calls.

The cops begrudgingly make way for them and hover a few feet away as Rowan kneels at the woman's side. She's thin and pale, her long, straight black hair splayed across her shoulders and casting a dark curtain over her face.

Rowan does a quick external exam of what he can see, noting that she's cradling her arm in her lap.

"Hi, I'm Rowan. Can you tell me where you're hurt?"

She shakily holds her right arm out. "Just my arm."

Rowan quickly pulls a pair of gloves on, asking, "No head or back injuries?"

"No. Aside from…." She gestures to her left eye.

For the first time, she looks up, and Rowan is struck by her eyes. Teary, rimmed red, mascara starting to run down her cheeks, a bruise already starting to form around her left eye socket.

But shockingly golden. Bright and piercing even brimmed with tears.

Fuck, she looks *exactly* like Mal. Her coloration, slim build, facial structure… down to her cheekbones and the curve of her jaw. And of course those gold fucking eyes. So similar to the ones that *Rowan* had made cry a few weeks ago for an entirely different reason that it nearly makes him forget himself.

"Can I…?"

She nods, brushing back the bangs covering her forehead.

Rowan gently prods around her temple and eyebrow with his thumb, careful not to hurt the already swollen area.

"This'll be a nasty black eye in a couple days, but there's no external bleeding or broken bones, so there's not much I can do about it at the moment. Can I see your arm?"

Once she extends it, Rowan slowly turns her palm face up.

But he pauses, seeing the small tattoo inked inside her wrist. Two curving snakes, one larger and curled around the smaller of the two. Similar to what Mal has on his calf.

It can't be… can it?

Mal hasn't said anything about any siblings, and Rowan hasn't asked, still too worried of overstepping. But as he thinks about it, he remembers something he'd said at the diner after one of their first sessions when Rowan mentioned being one of six kids: *I thought Savaryns bred like cockroaches.*

Rowan can't help but wonder if she's a sister or a cousin of Mal's.

"What's your name?" he asks.

"Amy."

She doesn't offer a last name, and Rowan doesn't pry, despite that he's itching to.

"Do you want to tell me what happened to your arm?"

As she talks, Rowan lightly prods her arm with his fingertips, feeling the bones of her forearm and wrist, mentally cataloging each as he feels it.

"My boyfriend… he just gets upset sometimes. He drank too much tonight. And I said…." She sighs deeply, shaking her head before continuing. "He hit me. Grabbed my arm and pushed me. I shouldn't have… should'a just…."

She sighs again.

"It's okay, Amy. It wasn't your fault," Addison tells her, a comfort and solidarity that, as a man, Rowan can't provide.

She nods, wincing with a light hiss when Rowan touches one spot on the side of her wrist.

"I don't think anything is broken, but you may have a bad sprain. I can put a brace on it for now, and we can take you to the hospital to get it looked at, or you can go yourself if you don't want the medical expense of the ambulance ride."

The worst thing about his job is seeing the defeated look in his patients' eyes when he mentions the ambulance cost. Sometimes he doesn't. Not if it's a life-or-death situation. But something like this, where it's clear that the person will be okay for a while and where they look like they'd be crushed with the cost of it, he makes sure to let them know they're not obligated to go with them.

"I'll be fine. 'S not the first time this shit's happened."

Her face hardens. Clearly, she's tougher than Rowan initially thought. Again, he's reminded of the now-familiar scowl he's grown to look forward to seeing every week.

Addison gets a cold pack from her kit, snaps it to activate it, and hands it to Amy.

"Here," she says, gesturing to her eye. "It'll stay cold for about an hour and will help reduce the swelling and bruising."

The half nod she gives Addison confirms for Rowan that this really isn't the first time this has happened, and that she's probably well aware of how to care for her injuries.

"Do you have somewhere to stay tonight? Somewhere else?" Rowan asks.

It's not his job. But Rowan knows too well that the cops don't give enough of a shit about people like her to do anything to help.

She nods. "Yeah. I'll call my brother. Can stay with him."

Rowan's head is swimming.

"Okay, that's good. You have a way to get there?"

"He'll come get me. He always does."

It's as good an answer as he can hope for. He puts a temporary brace on her wrist and tells her to take some ibuprofen to help keep down the swelling, and to get to a doctor as soon as she can.

"Thanks," she mumbles.

Not for the first time in his career, Rowan wants to squeeze her shoulder or pull her in for a hug and assure her that it'll be okay, but it's not his place. Definitely not in a case like this.

"No problem" is what he says instead, before packing up his kit and heading back to the ambulance with Addison.

ON THEIR drive back, Addison asks him, "You okay?"

Rowan's caught by surprise. "Yeah? Why wouldn't I be?"

"Kinda zoned out there for a minute looking at her arm. Seemed like you knew her, maybe."

Goddammit. He really needs to work on his fucking poker face.

"I don't know her," he says. "Just reminded me of someone. I hate those calls."

Addison accepts his reasoning, and they ride in silence the rest of the way back to the station.

ROWAN DOESN'T hear from Mal at all the next day, a Thursday, which until about a week ago, wouldn't have been unusual. But he can't stop thinking about the young woman with the probably-sprained wrist and the same piercing eyes as Mal. Nearly the same tattoo, if in a different location.

It's definitely not a coincidence, right? Or is his mind so overflowing with thoughts of Mal that he's started to seep into every aspect of Rowan's life? Seeing connections where they aren't? Every shade of brown and gold morphing in Rowan's brain to fit the shade he's constantly thinking about? There's some phenomenon that has to do with that, but Rowan can't be bothered to look it up.

He wants to text him. Wants to breach their mutual understanding of just-fuckin', just-sex talk, and ask him how his day was with the hope of finding out if his suspicions are true.

Is Amy his sister? Did Mal pick her up and let her stay with him? Is she still at his home? Did she make it to a doctor? Has this happened before? It seemed like it had, recalling Amy saying, *He'll come get me. He always does* when Rowan asked if she had a way of getting to her brother.

He doesn't text Mal.

Instead he goes for a run, each step pounded into the pavement tamping down all the questions rattling around in his head.

ON FRIDAY night, Rowan receives a text from Mal. His stomach drops, thinking he's going to be canceling their session for some reason, but is relieved to see that isn't the case.

[MS] *wanna switch things up a bit tomorrow if you're cool with it*
[RC] *Sure, what do you have in mind?*

[MS] *want to try out more praise this time. been great with the meanness but not feeling it for tomorrow*

The past few weeks, Rowan's been gaining more confidence in his ability to be a mean Dom—and his enjoyment of it—but this is something new. And honestly it's not like it's gonna be all that difficult, he doesn't think. Getting to tell Mal how good he's being for him *outside* of aftercare? Yeah, that shit's gonna be a breeze. Rowan practically has to bite his tongue during their sessions to keep himself from blurting that stuff out and ruining the mood.

[RC] *Yeah definitely*

But it can't have been a spur-of-the-moment decision that Mal wanted this now. He's told Rowan before that he'd only ask for it when he was in a certain headspace, and Rowan wonders if it has anything to do with Amy—if they *are* related, after all.

[RC] *Any reason why?*

It takes Mal a long few minutes to respond.

[MS] *just some shit goin on*

[RC] *You wanna talk about it? Either now or during our scene tomorrow?*

Rowan had read that some subs like working through shitty days during their scene. But Mal's answer comes immediately.

[MS] *no*

Right. Too personal. Just fuckin'. Rowan gets it.

[RC] *K*

[MS] *wanna try out some edging too*

He lets the quick change of subject pass, intrigued by the prospect of edging Mal. By now Rowan definitely has a good enough handle on getting Mal to come and knowing his tells for them to try edging, and he's immediately on board with it.

[RC] *Definitely*

[RC] *You mentioned a fleshlight last time we talked about edging, want to use that too?*

[MS] *yeah that'd be good. got one of those clear cock sleeves and a vibe i can bring*

[MS] *and a blindfold if you're cool with it*

That's a new one. He's about to question it when Mal's explanation comes through.

[MS] *usually like to do that when there's more praise than normal. blocks everything else out*

[RC] *Yeah sure*

He's read enough about sensory deprivation to know that it can make everything much more intense—physical feelings and emotions alike. But in the back of his mind, Rowan does wonder if Mal doesn't like making eye contact when someone tells him he's being good.

[RC] *Do you like/want to be tickled when I'm edging you?*

[MS] *no. just pull away before i cum*

[RC] *Got it*

[MS] *some people like or need it, but i hate being tickled*

[RC] *Glad I asked then*

[MS] *might want to use the cuffs again too, but not sure atm. you mind if we figure that part out right before?*

[RC] *Fine with me, just lmk*

[MS] *cool*

Rowan sends Mal a thumbs up emoji.

[RC] *Enjoy the rest of your night*

You sure you don't want to talk? he wants to send.

He doesn't.

[MS] *you too*

"You've been coming here over a month now, right?" Jeremiah asks as he places a foaming glass of beer in front of Rowan.

It's a slower Saturday night, the music turned down to a level that allows easy conversation across the bar.

"Yeah, why?"

"No reason. It's nice to see Malcolm stick with someone again. Leave some for the rest of us for a change." He laughs.

Rowan huffs a short laugh of his own. "You guys all talk about him like he's a mythical creature or some shit. He's just a guy."

If Rowan's directing that particular message to *himself* rather than to Jeremiah, no one needs to know that.

But the smile never falls from Jeremiah's lips, and the glint never fades from his coffee-colored eyes, and Rowan gets the feeling once again of being dissected.

"You like him."

Rowan nearly spits out his drink. Having Addison clock him is one thing, but someone so close to Mal? Someone who knows him, who's *friends* with him? Yeah, that shit's a little too close to home for comfort.

"I like *fucking* him," Rowan clarifies, purposefully not taking another sip of his drink to avoid looking like he's hiding behind it.

"Course you do. Everyone likes fucking him."

"So… what? The fact that I keep showing up for some great ass means I have a crush on the guy?"

Jeremiah holds his hands up in mock surrender. "No need to get defensive about it."

"I'm not."

Like he wasn't defensive about it with Addison all week. Jesus Christ, he really is in deep.

"Reading people's seventy-five percent of my job, honey," Jeremiah tells him, like he's explaining something obvious to a child rather than something supposedly secret to a grown man. "Got it written all over those big green eyes of yours."

This time Rowan *does* hide behind his drink. Hides whatever the fuck his eyes are doing that make it extremely obvious to everyone around him that he's got a *thing* for Mal. Malcolm. Whatever.

As the minutes tick by, Rowan grows anxious.

That sudden drop in his stomach he'd felt last night when Mal texted him now settles in slowly, not a roller-coaster plummet but a gradually rising tide. Something he only really notices the longer he waits, the longer he watches other club members dance and flirt and pair (or triple) off toward the back rooms. As the thumping bass fades out into a different thumping bass.

When Mal finally arrives, he's almost twenty minutes late and is the most dressed down Rowan's ever seen him. He still looks good, still looks hot, but now he looks comfortable. Fucking… *domestic*, almost. In a long-sleeve gray Henley and some form-fitting black joggers. Usual boots nowhere to be found, instead replaced with navy-and-white Saucony sneakers.

It's kind of unfair how he can pull off both the dressed-up and laid-back looks effortlessly.

"Hey," Rowan greets. "Thought you might'a been ditching me."

"Sorry, hit some traffic. C'mon."

His tone is off. Tight, maybe. Definitely a far cry from the cockiness Rowan's used to from him.

"Everything okay?"

"All good."

Rowan knows immediately that it's a lie, and as Mal turns to lead them back to the private rooms, he grabs his forearm to tug him back to face him.

"Mal, you sure you're up for this?"

The blue and white lights flash across his eyes, highlighting sharp cheekbones and plush lips. A furrow in his brow that Rowan wants to smooth over with his thumb.

"Yeah," he says, features relaxing as he heaves a sigh. "Had a rough couple'a days. Just wanna forget about shit for a while."

Rowan searches his face. What he's looking for, he can't say, but he doesn't see anything immediately concerning. And he can't exactly blurt out, *Do you have a sister who was abused by her boyfriend?* Because he may be dense at times, but he's got *some* sense of timing.

"Okay," he says instead, once again letting Mal lead the way to the Gold Room.

As he's done each time the past few weeks, Mal tosses his bag onto the bed and quickly pulls out their chosen supplies for the night: a black, padded blindfold, cuffs, and the clear masturbator he'd mentioned. It's only a few inches long, with an opening on either end and smooth ridges lining the inside. Rowan picks it up and turns it over in his hands. The opening is small, sure to be tight around Mal's cock.

Mal pulls out a vibrator too—a smooth black silicone one that's roughly egg-shaped, with two buttons on the bottom for controlling the speed. Rowan knows that Mal doesn't like vibrators in his ass, but that he likes them everywhere externally. And Rowan absolutely plans on using that fact to his full advantage.

The cuffs are the same as they've used a few times now, but rather than a clasp that connects them together, Mal brought a matching set of thigh cuffs as well. *That* gets Rowan's heart rate going for the first time tonight, worry over Mal's well-being momentarily pushed out of the limelight.

"Want your thighs cuffed?" Rowan asks, though it seems obvious.

"Yeah," Mal replies, taking the cuffs from Rowan and turning them to show the D-ring on either cuff, each with a longer clasp already attached. "Makes it so I can't use my hands. Changes it up a bit."

"Gonna have to get creative with positions, I assume."

"Not as much as you'd think. I'm pretty flexible, so most positions are still on the table except me basically standing upright." He pauses, snorts a quiet laugh that lifts Rowan's mood. "'Less you wanna fuck Nosferatu."

"Well…," Rowan muses, once again taking the cuffs from Mal. "You do have the same complexion."

"Oh, fuck off, Campbell."

He turns away from Rowan, but Rowan catches the smile on his face before he succeeds in hiding it. Rowan snorts, going to grab a new bottle of lube from the supply table while Mal fiddles with the blindfold.

"You wanna wear that the whole time? And the cuffs?" Rowan asks, returning to Mal's side.

"Can put 'em all on at the beginning, but bind me after we get warmed up."

"'Kay."

Thinking forward to what they have planned for the night, Rowan adjusts the sex bench opposite the bed so that the back is upright and there is plenty of room to accommodate them both. They haven't used it together yet, and hell, Rowan's *never* used one before, and it takes a moment fiddling with the metal pins to get them to lock in position, but he figures it out quickly enough.

Everything is in place. They know what the plan is. Rowan's got a good sense of how things are gonna go, but…

He hesitates.

Because this part he's a little unsure how to navigate. It's been easy enough to strip Mal down or order him to strip himself and get right to it. But while he's grown considerably more comfortable being an asshole, to put it bluntly, he's not quite as sure how to do *this*.

How to be gentle. Well, gentl*er*. But not too gentle. They're not making love here, for fuck's sake. And Rowan's a little worried that he's gonna slip and skirt that line rather than continuing to play his usual dominant role.

He wants to kiss Mal. Fuck, he keeps coming back to that, but what could possibly be a better way to praise Mal than with his lips and tongue?

Stop it, he tells himself. *You're just gonna let yourself down.*

It's then that Mal takes initiative and gets things started. He can clearly tell that Rowan's a little out of his depth with this, and he toes off his own sneakers and socks and nudges them under the platform of the bed.

Rowan snaps back to himself. Right. He's got a job to do. He's here for a reason. To help Mal let loose, and in turn to let loose himself.

Exploration. Fun. Orgasms. He's got this.

Rowan unbuttons the two fastened buttons on Mal's Henley, revealing a sliver of his toned and tattooed chest. He grabs the hem of the shirt, keeping his touches light, tugs it slowly over Mal's head, and this time, tosses it on the corner of the bed rather than the floor.

Whatever's going on with Mal, he doesn't want to do anything to make him feel worse. He wants to make him forget for a few hours.

As he kneels to tug down Mal's joggers, he's met with the unexpected sight of cherry-red silk and lace.

"Oh…," he breathes.

A rush of heat shoots straight to his cock, making him light-headed and glad as hell that he's kneeling.

"You wear these for me?" Rowan asks him, dragging his joggers the rest of the way down and coaxing Mal to step out of them, eyes trained on Mal's panties the whole time.

"Yeah," Mal tells him. "Said you'd like 'em."

"I do. Look so good on you."

With a palm to each hip, he turns Mal around, still kneeling behind him. Drinking in the sight of those perfect cheeks framed in lace.

He'd read something once about how a Dom should never get on his knees for his sub. But that person clearly didn't know what the fuck they were talking about, because down here, he feels *invincible*.

Feels untouchable as he runs his hands over Mal's asscheeks, squeezing and watching the skin turn white against the bright red of the panties. Feels *alive* when he slips his fingertips under the lace-trimmed bands and sees the tiny pink indents where they dig into Mal's skin.

As he tugs the fabric to the side, Mal starts to press back against him, hands planted on the bed in front of him.

"*Uh*-uh," Rowan scolds. "You just stand there and be good for me."

For once, Mal listens the first time. And if he hadn't already made it clear that tonight wasn't going to be their usual, Rowan would have been able to tell from that fact alone.

Before he leans in, his gaze drops to the two snakes tattooed on the back of Mal's ankle, side by side, one slightly smaller than the other. His mind races, but he buries his face between Mal's cheeks and lets himself forget.

The panties get in the way of him fully going to town, so he keeps his touches light and slow as he works him open, the feel of him against his tongue by now a familiar one that Rowan can't get enough of. Like the small gasped exhales Mal makes each time Rowan's tongue flicks over his hole or his lips seal over it.

With one final lick, he rises and slips the panties back in place, the fabric forming a perfect crease between Mal's cheeks.

Rowan secures the cuffs around Mal's wrists first, the motions easy in their familiarity. The thigh cuffs are the same as the wrist cuffs—black leather lined with short fur—but these are larger and have four D-rings around each cuff.

"How high do you want 'em?" Rowan asks. There's no worn hole like the wrist cuffs, which tells him that maybe Mal hasn't used these as often.

"Around my tattoo."

Oh.

The delicate strip of lace tattooed around his right thigh, midway up. Rowan had almost forgotten about it, having seen it so often, but it's the perfect height for the cuffs. As he secures the first cuff over the swell of his quad, it completely hides the lace, leaving only the tattooed knife showing on the side. The second one follows, and the sight of Mal's wrists and thighs wrapped in leather kicks up his heart rate a notch.

"Okay?" Rowan asks, slipping a finger in each cuff to check the tightness.

"Yeah."

The blindfold is next. It's sitting on the bed, right in front of Mal, who picks it up and wordlessly holds it behind him.

And he's not bound yet—hands still free and clear. The blindfold has an elastic strap rather than a tie. Mal could easily put it on himself. But Rowan takes it from him, pulse thrumming in his fingertips as he grabs the smooth black fabric and stretches it over the crown of Mal's head. As he places it over his eyes, the softness of Mal's hair tickles him as he adjusts the strap above his ears.

In front of him, Mal's back rises in a deep breath that Rowan traces with his palms. Feels the solid muscle beneath his hands and the goose bumps that follow.

"There we go. All ready for me now."

With much less force than he normally would, he pushes Mal's chest flat on the bed and nudges his legs apart wider than his hips. And goddamn, the sight of those strong thighs bound in leather and those plump cheeks framed in bright red panties? Going straight to the vault of Rowan's spank bank.

"Look delicious like this," Rowan tells him, squeezing and spreading his asscheeks apart and watching the fabric pull taut, a wet spot in the center from his tongue mere minutes ago.

He tugs Mal's hips back from the bed enough to free his cock from the panties, Mal gasping softly and dipping his head forward as Rowan pumps him to full hardness. The silk feels amazing against his hand, and he can only imagine how it feels against Mal's ass and balls.

"Much as I like seein' you in these, they've gotta go," Rowan tells him, shucking down the panties and letting Mal kick them off. "Next time, wanna see you get 'em filthy. How's that sound?"

All Mal does is moan softly.

"Tell me, Mal."

"Yeah," he replies, voice already husky.

"Good. Next time you feel like gettin' pretty for me, I'm gonna ruin 'em."

From there, he clips Mal's wrists to his outer thighs and hefts his right leg up onto the bed, then digs back in to pick up where he left off. Mal moans, arches his back, and ruts against the bed as Rowan teases him with his lips and tongue until his jaw aches and his cock is straining in his jeans.

It's only then, when Mal's half incoherent in his noises, that Rowan grabs the vibrator. Pulls Mal's cock back from under him, already flushed and starting to leak at the tip—leaking *more* when he touches the tip of the vibrator under the head.

"Mmm, *fuck!*"

"Tell me whenever you're close. You're not gonna come till you show me how good you can be for me."

The vibrations fill the room, drowned out only by Mal's moans when Rowan drags the vibrator across Mal's shaft. Lets it linger under his balls as he strokes over his hole with his thumb. Pushes the tip in and tugs at his rim while he slots his tongue in alongside. All the while seeking out every sensitive spot on Mal's cock and balls with the vibrator. Finding which places make him jump, make him gasp, make him moan the loudest.

In no time at all, Mal gasps, "Fuck, gonna—"

As soon as the words reach his ears, Rowan's pulling away from Mal completely, feeling the other man shake on the bed. Listening to him curse then heave a sigh. Watching him clench his fist and tug at his cuffs.

It's as hot as it is endearing.

"That was only the first one, Mal. Got plenty more where that came from."

"*Hnn….*"

With that he touches the vibrator to Mal's hole, slick with spit and quivering wildly as if trying to keep up with the pulses. But Rowan doesn't let it linger, trailing it back down to his cock, delighting in the jerk of Mal's hips and the continued clenching of his hand.

"Hold yourself open," Rowan tells him.

"Can't…," Mal starts, half muffled from how he's pressed into the bed.

"Try."

He flexes his fingers, reaching toward his asscheek, fingertips barely able to dig in without the cuffs straining around his wrists.

"*Can't….*"

"I got you," Rowan assures, unclipping his wrist from the side D-ring and reattaching it to the one in back, giving him another few inches of slack to spread his cheeks wide and show off more of his hole. "Perfect. Stay like that."

"Oh!" Mal cries out when Rowan squirts a dollop of lube on his hole and sinks in two fingers, keeping the vibrator firmly pressed against his underside of his cockhead.

He's slick and warm, and Rowan's fingers practically vibrate as much as the toy in the excitement of being inside Mal again. He works him open farther, stretching and tugging and gliding his fingers in and out, brushing against his prostate simply to feel Mal clench around him.

"Take my fingers so well, Mal. Look at you, already wanting more, huh?"

"*Yeah.*"

"Take this," Rowan tells him, prying Mal's fingers off his ass and slipping the vibrator into his hand. "Against your hole."

Mal's back muscles flex as his shoulders pinch together and he settles the vibrator against his hole, a soft moan following.

"Good. Keep it there."

Only when the hum of the toy dampens from Mal's grip on it does Rowan move away and start stripping his own clothes. Not for Mal's enjoyment, thanks to the blindfold, but because the pressure against his cock is driving him crazy and the heat radiating off of Mal's body might give him heatstroke. By the time he's shucking down his briefs, he catches Mal silently pulling the vibrator away from him.

"Mal…," he scolds. "Thought I told you to *tell me* when you're gonna come?"

"I…."

"That better not be an excuse. Do it again and you'll be punished, understand?"

His voice is low when he replies, "Yes."

Rowan guides Mal's hand with the vibrator back to his hole while he strokes over the back of his neck and his shoulders, feeling the dip of his spine as his palms explore his back. Reassuring, hopefully. They didn't discuss any kind of punishment tonight. Mal knows that, but he listens to the empty threat nonetheless.

Rowan climbs on the bed, settling to Mal's right and gently guiding Mal's face toward him.

"Open," Rowan says, running a thumb over his slack bottom lip.

Mal's lips barely part, hot breath ghosting over the tip of Rowan's cock, a mere inch away.

"Mmm. Suck," Rowan instructs, slipping his cockhead into Mal's warm mouth. "Pull off if you need to."

He normally wouldn't give Mal the reminder—their understanding of one another's boundaries and limits already familiar enough. But tonight, Rowan thinks he may need it. The way he's responding so easily to everything Rowan says is similar to when he's in or nearing subspace.

So Rowan doesn't fuck his face like he wants to. Keeps his thrusts light and lets Mal's lips dictate the suction and his tongue trail over his shaft however he pleases. Even with his limbs occupied and his sight taken away, his mouth is as talented as ever. Rowan pets his cheek and feels his cock bulge through with every press of his hips.

He could stay here forever, letting Mal suck his cock all soft and slow, but it's obvious that he's grown numb to the vibrator alone, and that won't do. So Rowan pulls out, takes it from him and adjusts the clip back to the side of his thigh. He slips back onto the floor and hefts Mal's other leg on the bed, flipping him onto his back in the process and drinking in the sound of Mal's sharp inhale.

With little effort, he urges Mal to squirm back on the bed, following and settling between his legs.

"Wish you could see yourself like this," Rowan tells him, feeling the taut muscles of his thighs as he spreads his legs and presses them against the bed as wide as they'll go. "All spread out for me. Look fuckin' perfect."

Mal draws a shuddering breath and dips his head back into the bed. For a second, Rowan's gaze is pulled in by the bob of Mal's Adam's apple as he swallows around nothing. His fingers itch.

But he snaps back to the moment, once again annoyed at being so easily distracted by the man in front of him. When he's not even *trying* to be distracting, for fuck's sake.

In this position, it'll be much easier to bring Mal to the edge over and over again.

He starts with the vibrator again, pressed lightly against Mal's balls as he strokes his shaft, hard as he's ever been in his hand.

Finally he grabs the masturbator. Squirts a generous dollop of lube inside it and a trail of it along Mal's shaft that makes his stomach quiver. Touches the opening to Mal's tip and slowly, slowly slips it over his cock, sheathing it all at once.

"*Nnnggg!*" Mal groans.

"Feel good?" Rowan asks, starting a slow rhythm with the masturbator even as Mal's hips start fucking up into his fist.

Rowan sees him nod, but he reminds him, "Words, Mal. Tell me."

"Yes, *fuck….*"

"Good. I wanna hear you. Don't hold back. I'll know if you do."

With that lingering between them, Rowan sets to work, tightening his grip and pumping the toy over Mal's cock in long, teasing strokes. Tossing the vibrator aside and sinking two fingers into Mal's hole once again.

"Ooh! Yes, *shit*...."

"That's it."

Rowan's entranced by Mal's cock emerging from the masturbator. Slick and pink and hot even through the silicone toy. With all the attention he pays to his ass in their sessions, his cock is perfect in its own right. And now the way it penetrates the toy and the way his hips roll up into every thrust has Rowan's mind running wild imagining Mal inside *him*.

Their roles are pretty well established, but they've both made it clear that they get an itch to change things up every once in a while. Fuck, he can picture it perfectly—ordering Mal to fuck him exactly how he wants. Not letting him come until Rowan's had his fill. Letting him finish inside—something no one's ever done.

But Rowan's traitorously wandering thoughts are jolted back to the present when Mal's hands strain against the cuffs, trying to reach his cock, only to be stopped by the rattle of the clasps.

Rowan huffs a gentle laugh.

"If you really wanted, you could reach." He pulls the toy off nearly completely, teasing at the tip of Mal's cock in short, barely-there strokes. "Use those muscles of yours to twist the cuffs around and make me go faster. But I can tell you wanna be good for me and keep your hands to yourself. Isn't that right, Mal?"

The noise that Mal makes is somewhere between a growl and a whine, sitting low in his throat as he flings his head back against the bed in frustration.

"Answer me."

Now Rowan *does* pull away completely. Fingers still pumping away inside, though he should take that away too. But—

"Yes."

"Yes what?" Rowan presses, slipping the toy over the head of Mal's cock for barely a second before pulling off.

"*Nng*, fuck... wanna be good."

A flutter of pride swells up inside Rowan. "I know you do. So you just lie back and quit trying to run the show."

Mal's mouth works like he wants to say something else, but he doesn't. He bites his bottom lip and lets his body relax, even lightening the furious clenching of his hole around Rowan's fingers.

"Good. Now where were we?"

This time, he's not expecting an answer, and he doesn't wait for Mal to offer one before stroking fast and tight around his cock with the toy, the slick sounds bouncing off the walls of the room. He adds a third finger too, pumping them in as fast as the friction will let him.

And Mal's gasping and his back is arching off the bed and his thighs are shaking and his fists are clenching by his side and he cries out, "Gonna…!"

And Rowan pulls off.

"Fu-fuck, *please*!"

"Uh-uh. Again."

WHEN MAL curses, Rowan knows to speed up both his hands.

When he moans, he knows to slow down with the masturbator and press his fingertips firmly against his prostate.

When he writhes, he knows to suck the tip of his cock into his mouth and roll his balls in his hands.

When he can do little more than whimper and mumble some variation of "I'm gonna come!" he knows to pull away completely.

Sometimes he'll leave his fingers buried inside to feel the heat around his fingers and the quivering of his muscles, but he holds them still. Nothing more than a placeholder for his cock.

Mal gets louder each time his orgasm is ripped away from him. A beautiful symphony of moans and gasps and whines that Rowan draws out from him like a conductor, and he feels on top of the world.

And Rowan makes sure to tell him how perfect he is with each one. How good, how gorgeous. Makes sure to pinch and roll his nipples as he comes down from the near-high and stick his fingers in his mouth to let him taste himself and keep his mouth busy.

By the sixth denied orgasm, Mal's skin is flushed pink and glistening with a sheen of sweat, and he's more than earned his release.

"You choose," Rowan starts, watching Mal's chest heaving. "Come like this, or come on my cock?"

Mal doesn't hesitate for a second. "Want you."

There's a little jolt that runs through Rowan's chest at the phrasing. Like Mal actually wants *him* and not one specific part of him.

But he shoves those thoughts aside, not wanting to dwell on maybes when there are a whole lot of *definitely*s happening right now. As in, he's definitely got to get his cock inside Mal again. And Mal definitely wants him to.

Unclipping Mal's wrists from his thighs and hauling him to his feet, Rowan settles against the bench and guides Mal between his spread thighs.

"You're gonna ride me," he tells him.

Mal bites his lip but nods, letting Rowan pull him up so he's straddling him, Mal's cock pressed firmly against Rowan's lower belly and his ass inches above Rowan's own cock. Once he's settled, Rowan clips Mal's wrists together behind his back. He can tell he's wobbly and supports him with a firm hand to his lower back while he slips his erection between Mal's cheeks, slicking his length between his cheeks and positioning himself under Mal's hole.

"Sit."

Slowly, so fucking slowly, Mal sinks down and down and down a half inch at a time, breathing hard through his nose until Rowan's fully sheathed and nearly aching from the heat of Mal's body.

"Fuck…," Rowan breathes, barely audible but so loud to his own ears with the rushing of blood echoing in his head.

He wants to chastise himself for showing his hand, but Mal merely exhales a long, shaky moan in response, and he couldn't care less about the slip.

But he sits there in Rowan's lap. And sits and sits. And *sits*, because that's what Rowan told him to do, didn't he? *God*, he's so fucking good.

"You can move now. At your own pace. And," he says, tugging at the clip binding his wrists together. "You'll get these back if you're good."

Then Mal's rising up, thighs flexing at the height of his ascent and quivering on the way down. As he gains speed, it feels so damn good that Rowan nearly forgets himself. Nearly fucks up into him in an effort to quell the slowly simmering heat that's been building all night. But he reins himself in, focusing on the slick drag of Mal's walls around him and the rolling of his abs as he rides him.

"That's it. Keep fucking yourself until I say you're done."

"I can't...," he says, thighs quivering and pace slowing to little more than a stutter.

"Yes, you can. Make me proud, Mal."

The request works. Mal seems to get a second wind at the prospect of pleasing Rowan—of making him proud—and it's the hottest fucking thing. With every rise and every drop, he brings both himself and Rowan closer to the sweet promise of release. Rowan grabs the masturbator he'd brought with him, slips it over Mal's red cock and makes him whimper.

"Can you do one more for me?"

Mal whines, "N-no. Can't...," but he doesn't stop moving.

Doesn't stop fucking up into Rowan's fist and down onto his cock, so Rowan presses.

"I think you can, Mal. Give me a color."

It takes two thrusts for him to respond.

"Green."

"Good. One more. Then you can come."

After a long night of being on edge, it takes less than a minute to bring him to the brink again. Rowan doesn't even have to move his hand, Mal effectively stroking his own cock from his riding.

"Rowan... I'm...!"

Rowan tugs off the toy and grabs Mal's hips as he rises up, pulling him off his cock and nearly hissing at the cool air surrounding his cock.

"Fuhhck...."

Rowan laments the fact that he can't see Mal's eyes as he shakes through another denied orgasm. He knows well enough from the past few weeks what a sight it is to look him in the eyes when he comes, see the glazed-over expression before his bright eyes roll back and his eyelids squeeze tight. He settles for watching the quiver of Mal's abs as he hovers above him.

"Good. I'm so proud of you," Rowan tells him, stroking his thigh with one hand and petting his cheek with the other. "Sit."

Mal sinks back down as Rowan guides his cock back inside. He starts up his rhythm again, but it's clear he's at his limit.

Taking pity on him, Rowan asks, "Want your hands?"

Mal nods frantically.

"Still gotta use your words, Mal."

"Yes, *please*...."

Rowan quickly unclasps both of Mal's wrists from behind his back.

Immediately, Mal's arms fly around Rowan's neck like a life preserver, pulling himself closer and leaning in so he can fuck himself deeper.

It's a thousand times better. The leverage Mal's able to get with his elbows clamped around the back of Rowan's neck and his short fingernails clawing into Rowan's back is just right for him to rise up fully and drop himself down, a filthy *slap, slap, slap* echoing in the room. It's all Rowan can do to keep the masturbator tight around Mal's cock as his own is fucked raw, an electric charge building in his core with every clench of Mal's hole.

"Fuck, *just* like that, Mal. You close? Tell me."

"Yeah. Yeah, yeah, yeah… wanna…," Mal whines, hips starting to stutter once more. "*Rowan*, please… need—"

"Do it, Mal. Let go. Come for me. Been so fucking good."

When Mal comes, it's with a sob and a shudder that wracks his entire body. He falls into Rowan, blindly pressing his forehead against Rowan's, and before he knows what's happening, Mal's soft lips are pressed firmly against his own.

The impact of his lips vibrates through him like a tuning fork, and Rowan's pretty fucking sure there's a ringing in his ears to match as his chest explodes in surprise. And then he's coming, filling Mal up with their lips smashed together. He inhales sharply, frozen in place and breathing in the musky smell of Mal's sweat.

Fuck. He wants this. He's *wanted* this, but Mal is….

Mal is….

Mal *isn't* in the right state of mind.

Even without being able to see his eyes, he knows that he's *far* from with it right now. It's only been a few seconds, but despite the racing in his mind, his body feels like it's moving in slow motion, fighting against gravity and so fucking *heavy* where there's usually lightness. And when he regains control of his limbs, it's much harder than he thought it would be to cup Mal's cheeks in his hands and gently tug himself away from his warm, plush lips.

The half whine Mal lets out when they finally part nearly breaks Rowan's entire damn heart, but he can't let it get to him.

"Mal…," he whispers, mind reeling and body still tingling from his unexpected orgasm. "Fuck, I can't…. I've wanted to do that since I *saw* you. But not—not now. You can't—you're not in the right state of mind. Do it again when you're back to yourself and I'll kiss you back. I *swear* I'll kiss you back. *Promise*."

He's rambling, tripping over his words, but he needs Mal to know—to *understand*—that he's not rejecting him because he doesn't want him. He's rejecting him because he wouldn't be able to look him in the eye again knowing he'd taken advantage of him in a vulnerable state. As it is, he's glad he can't see Mal's eyes right now, because he doesn't want to know what he might find staring back at him.

Mal makes a tiny, strangled whimper of protest.

"Need you to tell me you understand, Mal."

Thankfully, he nods, a sloppy jerking motion of his head but recognizable as an affirmative nonetheless. He lets his body slump forward into Rowan's chest, arms falling loosely around Rowan's hips.

Rowan scrunches his eyes shut, cupping the back of Mal's neck and squeezing gently, fingers stroking over his short, sweaty hair. He takes it as a good sign that Mal isn't immediately shooting away from him and denying it ever happened, but he knows they're not out of the woods yet.

He feels Mal start to shake against him, a tiny quivering of his shoulders, but it makes Rowan let out a long, uneven breath. He's got whiplash from the kiss, the ringing plaguing his ears earlier now louder than a damn clock-tower bell, but right now, his priorities are squarely on Mal. So he rubs his back as gently as his hands will let him and allows the two of them to sit in the quiet until Mal's breathing evens out and his muscles still.

It's only then that Rowan shifts his hips down enough to slide out of Mal. And fuck, he's still mostly hard. Definitely not as soft as he should be with the shock and intensity of his orgasm. The feeling of his come dripping down back onto his cock is hardly helping the matter either.

"Can you stand?" Rowan asks softly.

Mal nods against his shoulder, and Rowan lightly shrugs Mal's arms away from his hips. With Rowan supporting Mal's back, they stand, and Rowan walks them the short distance to the bed.

He helps Mal lie down on his back and sets to work unclasping the cuffs from his wrists and thighs. But when he gets to the blindfold, he hesitates.

"Gonna take the blindfold off," he says, more to himself than Mal.

But Mal nods again, and Rowan slips the mask off slowly, Mal's eyes still squeezed tightly shut.

Fuck. He wasn't prepared for this *at all*.

He feels stuck amid a swirling mess of *Do you wanna*s and *Can you*s and *Should I*s and *Holy shit, holy shit, holy shit*s in his head, and he doesn't know what the hell to *do*.

But then Mal blinks his eyes open, and Rowan's sucker punched back to the moment.

He looks… God, *vulnerable*? Shocked? Ambivalent? It's hard to tell. Like thousands of years of human evolution has completely left Rowan's brain, and he suddenly doesn't know how to read another person at all.

Rowan mentally runs through his aftercare checklist.

Unbind… get him comfortable… talk him down… soft touches… hydrate… shower… walk… diner….

He cups Mal's cheek, the skin heated under his palm, and swipes away a bead of sweat trickling down from his temple.

And he knows he shouldn't, but he can't help dipping down and brushing his lips against Mal's damp hairline, lower lip catching a stray droplet of sweat poised to fall.

"Did so good, Mal," he tells him, voice low and tone—hopefully—soothing. Rowan feels like a broken record with the number of times he's said that tonight. "Listened and did everything I asked." He brushes the longer locks of Mal's hair away from his face. "Asked for what *you* wanted." He rubs each of Mal's wrists in turn, though there are no visible marks from the cuffs. Presses another light kiss to the inside of his palms.

It doesn't linger, barely more than a whisper of a press, but Mal slowly tugs his hands back to drape heavily across his chest.

Right. Despite what's happened, they're not there yet. Rowan has risked some small kisses to Mal's skin in past sessions, mostly when he's been teasing him, and almost always followed by a hard smack or thrust or bite or pinch or *something* to dampen it. And tonight there's been next to nothing to dampen the action. No spanks or slaps or biting words to take away the fact that Mal broke one of his own boundaries and kissed him.

Rowan lies beside him, ignoring the stickiness on his skin and the cramp in his side, and talks him down. Watching the rise and fall of his chest and his eyes moving gently behind his eyelids. It feels exactly like it did after the gangbang. Like he's talking with little thought behind the words, despite the fact that he's done it multiple times now and knows more or less what to say.

Feels like he's back at square one.

But he keeps going, making sure Mal knows that he did so well for him. That he looked gorgeous. Felt even better. He doesn't mention the kiss. Stays far, *far* away from that particular subject for now.

It normally takes only a few minutes for Mal's breathing to fully even out, but this time it feels like it takes ages. Of course Rowan would give him as long as he needed. Even if their four-hour booking ended, he'd find a way to make sure Mal was okay before they left the club. But he can't deny that he's worried, a sharp thorn of concern wriggling into his side and worming its way up into his chest.

Eventually Mal sits up, elbows resting on his knees and staring straight ahead.

"Okay?" Rowan asks gently, sitting up beside him and trying to catch his eye.

All he gets in response is a quiet, "Mmm," and no eye contact.

Rowan knows well enough not to push him, even though he wants nothing more than to have a giant Undo button that he can slam to go back to the beginning of the night. But that's not gonna happen—he has to deal with the present.

A quick trip to the supply table and Rowan returns to Mal's side to see him now kneeling on the bed, but not doing any of his usual stretches.

Mal accepts the water bottle, taking a single tiny sip. But when Rowan holds out the damp washcloth, he shakes his head. The thorn inches deeper. He wants to clean off the come he can see coating Mal's cock and the lube between his legs and the sweat on his forehead, but…. He knows Mal's stance on Rowan helping clean up afterward.

Then again, he *also* thought he knew his stance on kissing, so he's at a bit of a loss.

"Do you wanna shower?" he asks, hoping to keep some semblance of normalcy to the end of their scene.

"Yeah."

"By yourself?"

There's a dazed-sounding huff of a laugh, which Rowan takes as another good sign. "Yeah, 'm good."

Mal slides off the bed and makes for the door, turning back and grabbing his clothing almost as an afterthought. Rowan follows him into the hallway, both completely naked, and makes sure he sees the door to one of the few private bathrooms he'd only recently learned about close behind Mal.

Rowan returns to the Gold Room, mind completely on autopilot. He does the fastest cleaning job he's ever done and picks up the rest of Mal's things, packing them neatly away in his black messenger bag. When he sees Mal's phone poking out of one of the side pouches, he pauses.

And pauses. And waits for his brain to decide what to do. Snoop or don't snoop. Like he's in a video game and his choice will have consequences.

Because he's fucking *worried*, and he can't stop thinking about the young woman, Amy, who looked so much like Mal, and the timing of everything that happened a couple of days ago and then everything that happened tonight.

He snoops.

Presses the wake button on the side only to find a lock screen with one new notification of a text from "Bitchface" a few hours ago that says *Ok*. Rowan almost misses the background at first glance—a nearly all black photo with a silver circle in the middle highlighting the barrel of a gun pointing straight ahead, a thin wisp of smoke rising straight up. Eerily similar to Mal's chest tattoos.

Rowan quickly puts the phone back in the case and zips it shut. Message fucking received.

He skips his own shower, instead splashing some water on his face and putting on a fresh coat of deodorant in the locker room. As soon as he's done, he stations himself outside the private bathroom stall and waits for Mal to come out.

THEIR CUSTOMARY walk to Sheila's diner is awkward in a way it's never been before. Mal's completely silent save for a few snuffles that don't sound enough like the tearful kind to warrant Rowan asking him anything right now.

He's lost enough in his own thoughts as it is.

Why?

Does Mal think Rowan gets off on taking advantage of people?

Why?

Will this be the last time they meet up?

Why?

Is he unknowingly walking toward his final hour with Mal?

Why, why, why?

Or, on the other hand, will this change things for the *better*? Will Mal be more open to kissing for real now that the proverbial bandage has been ripped off?

Will they ignore it altogether?

No. Rowan can't let that happen. If for no other reason than because communication is so fucking important. *And,* a little voice in his head that sounds suspiciously like a younger, more optimistic version of himself supplies, *I don't want this to end.*

It seems like a lifetime until the familiar neon sign comes into view and they're finally entering Sheila's.

"You go sit," Rowan tells Mal. "I'll get some food. You want your usual?"

"Yeah. Thanks."

Rowan goes to the counter and waits for Sheila to come to him from the kitchen, her customary easy smile etched on her face.

"Hi, honey. What can I get for you?"

"Hey, Sheila. Can I have Mal's usual and a grilled chicken sandwich on wheat? And some waters, please."

"Of course."

She scribbles their orders on a slip—by now thankfully having given up on attempting to give them free meals—and glances over Rowan's shoulder to where Mal's sitting.

"Everything okay over there?" she asks, as if her perception is so strong that she can tell something is off by the slope of Mal's shoulders.

Rowan glances back to see that Mal's head is in his hands, shoulders visibly tense even from the short distance away. "Yeah, it will be."

At least he hopes to God it will be.

Sheila accepts the admittedly cryptic answer, hands him two red cups of ice water, and retreats back into the kitchen. Mal still hasn't told

Sheila anything about their relationship, so he's not willing to divulge anything more to her without Mal's knowledge.

He returns to the table, slides into the booth across from Mal and nudges the cup of water toward him.

"Thanks," Mal mumbles, immediately burying his face in the cup.

Rowan studies him. Tries to analyze every move he makes in the hope that it will shed some light into what Mal's thinking. What he's feeling. There has to be *something*, right? Some reason for Mal falling into him like he had and for whimpering when Rowan had pulled away and put a stop to it. But he doesn't know if that something is going to be something he wants to hear.

When their food comes, Rowan lets his sit until Mal starts eating. He'll let him get some food into his system before he brings anything up.

They eat in silence save for the mellow song playing on the jukebox and the scraping of Mal's fork against his plate. Rowan watches as he tears off chunks of banana pancake with the side of his fork, spearing each little wedge and swirling it around the extra syrup on the plate before actually eating it. There's none of his usual eagerness in his movements, everything slow and cautious. Like he's been fucking sedated or something.

Rowan's own food is surely delicious, but he barely tastes it, only eating half his sandwich and a handful of the fries it came with.

It isn't until Mal's completely finished with his banana pancakes, little else on his plate touched, that Rowan speaks.

"Can we talk about it, Mal?"

Mal sighs before leaning back and fixing Rowan with an emotionless look. He works his mouth like he's testing out how to form the words before he actually says anything.

For a moment, Rowan's worried Mal's going to pull a *Talk about what?* but what he actually says is worse.

"It was a mistake, Red. Just deep in it, y'know?"

Rowan feels himself nodding despite the hollow that's growing in his chest, making him want to collapse in on himself like a black hole. "Yeah. No biggie."

It is a biggie. A very *big* biggie that Rowan's gonna daydream about for the rest of however long he gets to be with Mal—in whatever capacity—like a goddamn loser.

But really, what had Rowan been hoping for? Some grand confession or declaration from the guy he's only been fucking for a few weeks?

"I'm sorry," Mal says abruptly, so softly that it makes Rowan pause his distracted sip of water mid-gulp.

"For…?"

"For… *doing* that." He looks down, shaking his head a little before continuing. "Consent's obviously a big fuckin' deal in general, but especially for shit like this. I shouldn't'a let myself do that, no matter how out of it I was. We didn't talk about it beforehand."

Rowan feels his stomach twist, his dinner threatening to come right back up at Mal's words. He opens and closes his mouth, willing his reply to come to make everything okay. Because fuck, he thought *he'd* taken advantage of *Mal*. By being too shocked to push him away immediately. By coming the second he'd felt his lips for the first, and probably only, time.

Rowan doesn't know how long he's silent, but it's apparently too long for Mal, who continues, "If you wanna stop meeting up, I get it."

"No!" Rowan blurts, far too loud for Mal's near-whispered statement. The one lone patron on the other side of the diner looks up from his coffee at the commotion before shaking his head and flicking the page of his newspaper.

"No, it's fine, Mal," Rowan tells him at a more reasonable volume, shoulders hunched up to his ears. "I'm not against kissing or anything. Actually kinda love it, but not if you're not into it too." He stops to fiddle with his napkin, scrunching it up in his hand. "I just…."

"What?"

"Feel fuckin' guilty for, y'know, blowing during it." His cheeks burn, and he can't force himself to meet Mal's eyes. "You were so out of it, and I feel like shit for basically getting off on it. I don't normally…."

He trails off when he sees Mal nodding in his periphery, clearly understanding what he was going to say. *I don't normally get off on hurting people.*

Somehow, despite the roiling in his stomach, the confession feels good, like a weight has been lifted off his chest. No matter how Mal reacts to it, he's glad to have this conversation rather than let it tear him up inside. But that doesn't mean he's going to tell him how badly he'd wanted to cup his face and lick into his mouth and kiss him senseless. He's gonna take *that* shit to his grave.

"Not your fault, man. Shit's obviously emotional for the both of us, even if no feelings are involved."

The statement hits like a punch to the gut, plunging that thorn of worry straight into his heart.

"Right," Rowan manages.

He'd been worried about this—his chaotic and confusing feelings not being reciprocated. Pretty definitively assumed that was the case too. But to actually have it spelled out, black and white? Far worse than he'd imagined, even in his worst-case scenarios.

He clears his throat, quickly shifting to a topic that feels a little less like swallowing hot coals. "Do you wanna start planning our scenes more?"

Mal takes a deep breath and shifts his gaze to the side, like he's considering. "Not sure that would'a helped. Let's just stick with what we've been doin'."

Business as usual, then.

They've talked about it, cleared the air a bit, but for all intents and purposes, they're gonna sweep this shit under the rug.

Pretend it never happened.

"Hey," Rowan says as they're approaching the club, nudging Mal with his elbow. "Text me if you need anything, okay? Or call, whichever."

"Yeah," Mal replies, though there's a flatness to his voice. He kicks a pebble on the ground, hands stuffed in the pockets of his joggers as they've been during the whole walk back.

"I'm serious. Doesn't matter when."

"I know."

Rowan tries to catch his eye, but Mal's gaze remains firmly downcast. And when they reach the front doors, Mal immediately turns to head to his car.

"Mal," Rowan says quickly, catching his shoulder before he bolts.

Thankfully he doesn't, and lets himself be turned around to face Rowan. When he finally meets Rowan's eyes, there's *nothing* there, and it makes something inside Rowan shrivel.

He doesn't know what more to say. How to express that Mal can still talk to him, especially if he drops because of this, and that he really *does* still want to keep seeing him. But his body knows what to do, pulling Mal in and wrapping his arms gently around his shoulders. Mal stiffens instantly, only relaxing after a long exhale. Even in the sticky summer heat, the warmth of his body is a comfort Rowan didn't know he needed after a tense night.

Mal doesn't hug him back, but Rowan feels one hand slide from his waist to his hip, settling for a beat before dropping back down. A little pleased thrum manages to squeeze itself in among the tangled knots in Rowan's chest, but he takes that as his cue to pull away.

"Text me," he says again.

Mal nods. Clears his throat. Mutters a "Later" and heads straight for his car.

Rowan stands alone on the sidewalk, lit only by the glow of the Menagerie's marquee lights, watching until Mal drives away.

THE NEXT morning, Rowan finds that he's far more rattled by the kiss than he thought he'd be. Well. Truthfully, he *thought* if they ever got to kiss, it would be something as simple as Mal saying, *Hey, I'm cool with kissing and shit now. You wanna?* and that would be that.

No biggie.

Really, the way it *actually* happened tells Rowan a lot about the kind of person Mal is and about what's going on in his mind. Because when he's at his most vulnerable, when he's seeking comfort and reassurance and familiarity, he seeks out a kiss, whether or not he had done so knowingly.

And God, Rowan wanted it *so fucking badly*. Already, after only a few weeks. After only five sessions together, not counting the gangbang. But he'd never forgive himself if he let it continue, and Mal might not have either when he regained his senses.

I'll knock you out if you try to kiss me. That's what Mal said at the gangbang a month and a half ago. Rowan could practically *feel* the hostility in his tone at the time.

He can't help but wonder if he was like this with his last Dom too, or if it's only with Rowan. He thinks back to a few weeks ago—how Mal implied that Rowan had been the first Dom he'd let call him Mal rather than Malcolm.

And the way he'd reacted after the kiss… completely shutting down, even though he'd talked about it with Rowan.

Well. It makes Rowan's heart ache, is all.

The vulnerability that Mal had shown earlier that night during their scene had been all but completely replaced with stoicism by the time they'd discussed the kiss. They'd been doing *so well* too. Their forward progress may have been limited to baby steps with the occasional baby leap, but it was still progress. Now it feels like they've gone backward. And for the first time in a long time, Rowan doesn't see a clear path forward.

It's nearing noontime, and Rowan hasn't heard anything from Mal, so he caves and texts him.

[RC] *Hey, you feeling okay?*

By the time Rowan's getting ready for bed later that night, Mal still hasn't texted him back.

Chapter 7: Tongue Tied

It isn't until late on Monday when Rowan is already in bed that Mal finally texts him back.

[MS] *sorry had some shit going on*

[MS] *i'm good*

[MS] *thanks for checking*

Rowan wants to shout at him. Fucking deck him, actually. Because what the *fuck*? Mal may be the more experienced of the two of them, but what the *hell* gives him the right to stress the fuck out of Rowan? Rowan's been fucking *pacing* the past two days, waiting to hear back from him. Jesus, he's lucky he hasn't had an episode over this.

He's not some goddamn side piece, here.

[RC] *What the fuck Mal?*

[RC] *You couldn't have texted that 2 days ago??*

[MS] *i said sorry man. had shit to deal with*

Rowan wants to punch a wall. He wants to tell Mal that when he stops hearing from people, it's usually because they're on a bender or in jail or dead. He wants to flat-out say he's *worried* and *pissed* and fucking *hungry* for a real kiss after the tantalizing taste he'd gotten.

But as his string of fleeting exes would attest to, he's never been great at communicating emotions.

[RC] *I get if you're busy or whatever but it takes 2 fucking seconds to send a text*

[RC] *I thought you dropped or something*

[MS] *it takes more than a stupid fuckin mistake like that to make me drop*

Hearing Mal call the kiss a mistake again, even if it *is* technically true, feels like a virtual slap in the face.

[RC] *You looked like you were in a fucking trance when we left Mal*

[RC] *What was I supposed to think??*

[MS] *you don't think fuckin anything. i told you i was fine*

[MS] *we're not boyfriend and girlfriend here*

[MS] *i don't owe you shit*

His aggression catches Rowan off guard. Apparently Mal's done being on the defensive. Rowan can practically feel the steam coming out of his own ears as he types out his reply.

[RC] *No shit we're not a couple. But you do fucking owe it to me to tell me you aren't gonna jump into traffic if the reason for it happened with me*

[MS] *it woulda happened with anyone. you're not the hot shit you think you are*

[RC] *I DON'T think I'm hot shit, I was fucking worried asshole*

[RC] *Just because you're the club bicycle doesn't mean you get to ride all over me*

Rowan regrets the text the second he hits Send, and Mal's response takes two full minutes to pop onto his screen.

[MS] *fuck you campbell*

There isn't anything Rowan can say after that.

He knows it's unfair to call Mal a slut when his own wild teenage years aren't too far behind him. Kinda *loves* that he is, if he's being honest.

And he doesn't want to leave it like this, but alongside the new cloak of shame hanging over him, there's still a bubble of anger toward Mal floating around inside him. It may be growing smaller and weaker by the minute, but it's there nonetheless.

He throws his phone to the other end of the bed, watching it tumble uselessly over the bunched-up comforter and clatter to the carpet below. He needs to clear his head. He grabs his running shoes and doesn't bother changing out of his current set of sweatpants and T-shirt before heading out the door at nearly eleven at night.

APPARENTLY, TO Rowan's relief, twenty-four hours is enough for them both to cool off from their tense exchange. Their regular texting starts back up again on Tuesday night with a text from Mal:

[MS] *which one?*

[MS] *img03409.jpg img03410.jpg*

He attaches two cropped screenshots of panties from a website Rowan doesn't recognize—a black pair with crisscrossed straps in the back and a white pair with lace cutouts on the sides.

Rowan accepts the unconventional olive branch.

[RC] *Black ones*

[MS] *thought so too*

Rowan bites his lip, abandons his third rewatch of *The Witcher*, and stretches out on his couch. He types and retypes an explanation for his shitty remark the other day, but erases everything he types. Somehow, he doesn't think *I'm new to this* is a good excuse. So, with a heavy exhale, he settles on:

[RC] *Sorry, btw*

[MS] *yeah me too*

The relief is instant, and the angry bubble in his chest finally pops in a completely lackluster way that makes Rowan wonder why it stuck around so long.

[MS] *not used to not being in control*

[RC] *Thought that was kind of a given being a sub*

[MS] *giving over control and not being in control aren't the same*

[MS] *think you know that by now*

[RC] *Yeah*

He does. Mal allows him to take the reins when they're together because he trusts Rowan enough to do so, but that's a far cry from having no control over yourself. Rowan wants to ask him why it happened and if it had anything to do with the woman that Rowan treated the other day who may or may not be related to Mal, but he feels like their relationship is teetering on the edge of a cliff, too precarious to do anything that might send them plunging over the side.

If they're ever going to get to that stage, Mal's going to have to be the one that leads them there.

[RC] *Just surprised me I guess*

[RC] *You've been doing this a long time*

[MS] *yeah well. surprised me too*

[MS] *not many firsts left to have at this point so*

He doesn't elaborate on the "so" at the end of his sentence, but Rowan's brain is rattling around in his skull like a crash-test dummy's. Because *surely* Mal can't mean that was his first kiss?

[RC] *Wait like your first first kiss??*

The fact that his fingers have typed out and *sent* the message proves that the tact he's been working on developing isn't coming along as smoothly as he'd thought.

[MS] *i'm 28 man not fuckin 15*

[RC] *That wasn't a no...*

[MS] *christ*

[MS] *NO, my 1st kiss wasn't with my fuckin dom in a sex induced haze*

[MS] *not gonna have the chastity pigs after you prince charming*

The laugh that bubbles up from Rowan's chest has him feeling lighter than he has in days. It's nice to be able to laugh at the situation that he's been angsting over for what feels like ages.

[RC] *In this context chastity pigs sounds like some fetish shit*

[MS] *oh ya? you into that farmer brown?*

[RC] *Dunno, you could look hot in a chastity belt*

[RC] *Trapped in a castle and chained to a bed or something*

[RC] *Hard pass on the furry junk though*

[MS] *jesus you're worse than i am*

Rowan can practically hear Mal trying to hide a smile through his message.

[MS] *got a virginity fetish or somethin?*

[RC] *I'd be shit outta luck with you if I did since we met at a gangbang*

[MS] *ya that ship sunk a long fuckin time ago*

[RC] *That's definitely not the right expression Mal lmao*

[MS] *what the fuck ever you know what i mean*

[MS] *so a knight in shining armor complex then?*

[RC] *I do think I'd look pretty good in some medieval armor*

[RC] *Chainmail and feathery helmet and shit*

[RC] *Get a huge lance or something and some fair maiden's token to complete the look*

Mal's next text is an eye roll emoji.

[MS] *don't expect a flower crown from my ass red*

[RC] *I'm sure I could find some stable boy to give me one if push came to shove*

[RC] *Though I would much rather have your ass than some flowers*

[MS] *alright well you can kiss my ass next time, how's that*

Rowan grins to himself, and yeah, that actually sounds pretty fantastic. If Mal's lips are off limits, his ass will have to do. Fake medieval scenario or otherwise.

They chat a bit longer, keeping the conversation light even if mostly still tangentially kink related. Rowan slips in the occasional comment about what's currently happening on the latest episode of *The Great British Baking Show*, which Mal predictably responds to with another eye roll emoji. Once, Rowan manages to wring a cake emoji out of him, followed by a peach emoji and *knew you liked cake, red* that sends an involuntary shudder down Rowan's spine.

As their conversation winds down and it's nearing the wee hours of the morning, Rowan lets himself dip back into the more serious topic they'd been on earlier.

[RC] *I gotta go to bed soon but…*

[RC] *Please let me know if something like that happens again*

[RC] *2 way street, remember?*

[RC] *I know I'm new to this but I'll always try to figure something out*

[MS] *i know*

A minute later, he follows up with another text.

[MS] *i will*

[MS] *for what it's worth i do appreciate you giving a shit*

[MS] *lot of doms don't*

Rowan wants to tell him that his caring has nothing to do with being a Dom, but he'll let Mal think that if it's what he needs to believe. Right now he doesn't think saying *Actually, it's because I like you even though I shouldn't* would go over too well.

[RC] *Of course*

[RC] *Aside from the obvious, was the rest of the scene OK?*

He's careful to phrase the question as if, to him, the kiss *wasn't* the best part of the whole thing, if only for a fleeting moment before the panic set in.

[MS] *wouldn't have gotten that deep if it wasn't*

[MS] *that shit gets to me way more than any other type of play*

As Rowan's head stops swimming from the revelation that Mal enjoyed his praise enough to lose himself to it, his heart lurches at the realization that he probably likes it so much because he doesn't get treated like that in his everyday life. Probably not when he was growing up either, if he was like most South End kids with shitty parents and a street-hardened exterior.

[RC] *I'll keep that in mind next time you're up for it*

Mal sends him a thumbs-up emoji.

Rowan knows that it's kind of a dismissive emoji—a signal that the conversation is over—but it makes him smile anyway.

MAL DOESN'T bring up the kiss again that week, so Rowan doesn't either.

But fuck, he can't stop thinking about it. *Hasn't* stopped thinking about it since Saturday. How badly he'd wanted it—still wants it, even with their tiff still fresh in his mind—and how he'd come the second he realized what was happening. Another knot of guilt coils itself in Rowan's belly, and he can't help but still feel dirty at having basically used Mal in that way.

It's not his fault, and he knows that. It's not even really *Mal's* fault—just one of those things that happens with shit like this.

He wonders if Mal has kissed any of his past Doms. If he's ever *wanted* to kiss any of them. Rowan doubts it, given how visceral his reaction to the thought of it had been when they first met and hashed out their kink boundaries. Still, he rereads Mal's text over and over:

[MS] *it woulda happened with anyone. you're not the hot shit you think you are.*

Rowan doesn't want to get his hopes up that that's a fat lie and that it would *not* have happened with anyone. He already knows that, at least in some capacity, Mal thinks of him as different from his past Doms.

But Rowan doesn't actually know how many Doms Mal has had; all he's gathered from his conversations with him have pointed to "more than a few." One or more of them could definitely have been a romantic partner as well. The thought makes his stomach churn.

He blames it on the lasagna Jay made for him last night.

[MS] *I wanna do some spanking on saturday*

The text comes through while Rowan is chopping vegetables for his lunch salad tomorrow, and when he reads the banner that lights up his phone on the counter, he nearly slips and cuts himself. He should really know better than to be doing anything remotely dangerous when he's within eyesight of his phone, Mal's texts always unpredictable and usually dirty.

Placing the knife far out of reach, he taps out his reply, silently admonishing his rapidly-beating heart for begging him to say *Fuck yeah!* rather than something normal.

[RC] *OK, more than usual you mean?*

[MS] *yeah*

[MS] *and hard*

The *Fuck yeah!* narrowly avoids being sent this time.

[RC] *Do you have a set stopping point or max hits or anything*
[MS] *not really. just till i can't take it anymore*

Rowan ditches his lunch on the counter and jerks off on the couch, coming in barely four minutes to the image of his handprints on Mal's ass.

WITH ALL the drama of the past week, when Saturday arrives, Rowan almost forgets about the shibari class entirely. It's nearly 5:00 p.m. when he jolts up from lazing on the couch and has to scramble to shower and change. Mal had told him to wear something comfortable, so he pulls on some dark gray joggers, a white T-shirt, and his trusty red Nikes before he bolts out the door.

Surprisingly, thanks to his lead foot, he gets to the club a full twenty minutes before the class is scheduled to start. Mal told him he'd meet him at the bar as usual before they went to the class, but he's nowhere in sight.

A sharp *crack!* rings out and catches Rowan's attention. He scans the club, looking for the source of the noise, when it comes again, louder and definitively to the left.

To the VoyEx corner. Color him intrigued.

For the first time, rather than sit and order a drink, Rowan visits the area which he'd only glanced at during his tour the day he joined. The "corner" is actually a fairly large open room tucked around a wall that divides it from the main lounge and bar. There's a small crowd of about ten people forming a semicircle around the main stage, which is bathed in overhead spotlights highlighting two men on stage. Both are fully naked, toned bodies catching the light attractively.

One of the men, clearly the sub, is standing with his legs and arms spread and bound to a Saint Andrew's cross. Thin red welts cover his chest and thighs, angry and long but with no trace of blood, which speaks to the skill of the Dom whipping him with a long black flogger. The Dom reels back and *cracks* it across the sub's chest, the sound of it hitting Rowan's ears before the sub even lets out a peep.

He doesn't know how long they've been at this, but the sub's cock is flushed and hard and the wet from his cunt is dripping down his legs, catching the light as he squirms both toward and away from the flogger.

Rowan watches the exhibitionists and the crowd of voyeurs around him, half of whom are unabashedly jerking off, and lets his mind wander. To whether any of these men are married, to the slice of cheesecake from Addison sitting in his fridge at home, to the text from Clara he forgot to reply to earlier. To Mal. To their argument the other day, to the class they're taking tonight to improve their scenes, to what Mal's ass is going to look like once Rowan gets his hands on it afterward.

Always to Mal.

Rowan's too caught up in him. Too emotionally invested in something that's supposed to be casual and fun, and he can feel it start to weigh on him.

Maybe he should skip a session with Mal—tell him he's sick or something and use one of his four precious monthly visits to the club to seek out the company of some other willing bottom. It might help. But then again, it might make things worse, especially if Mal comes anyway, seeking someone else out too. Caught playing hooky by the principal. His mind is reeling with made-up scenarios that could put soap operas to shame, and he physically shakes his head to bring himself back to the moment.

The thoughts of finding someone else are all abruptly dismissed when he realizes he's barely turned on by everything happening around him, only a tiny blip of desire. A few weeks ago, he'd probably be whipping his dick out alongside everyone else or seeing if the pair on stage were up for a threesome later.

Something a little bit like guilt tugs at his insides as he turns away and slinks back to the bar, the whipcracks and moans fading behind him.

Jeremiah is busy chatting up a group of older-looking men, deftly preparing their drinks without missing a beat of their conversation. Maybe he should see if *he's* up for something.

"You're early tonight," the bartender notes. "Shibari class?"

"Yep," Rowan replies.

"You'll love it."

"Have you taken it before?"

The grin Jeremiah gives him is proud and devastatingly handsome. "I used to teach it."

Rowan's stunned into silence, which makes the other man laugh again.

"Anything to drink before you head out?"

It takes him a solid five seconds to answer. "Can I have a virgin strawberry seltzer? With lime?"

As Jeremiah whips up Rowan's drink, Rowan watches him work, deft hands twirling the glass and flipping a cocktail napkin down on the bar as a coaster.

"Hey, do you only work on the weekends?" Rowan asks as Jeremiah adds a freshly cut lime wedge to Rowan's glass.

He doesn't even know why he's asking, really. Because yeah, Jeremiah is fucking hot. *Especially* so tonight with one of his signature black button-ups pulling tight across his chest, a silver mesh top underneath that shines like chain mail when he turns the right way in the dim light. His hair's gotten longer too—now more of a twist style than the sponge curls he'd had the first few times Rowan had seen him.

"Wednesday through Sunday," Jeremiah replies, gaze raking up and down Rowan's body over the bar top with zero shame. "Why? Trouble in paradise?"

"What do you mean?"

The look Jeremiah gives him is somewhere between pitying and surprised, and Rowan is confused as hell.

"Ah. Listen, I'd love to, but I think we both know that isn't going to end well."

Rowan doesn't have time to dwell on it before Mal's suddenly at his side, one elbow planted solidly on the bar top.

"Yo," Mal says to Rowan, barely glancing at him before he's turning to Jeremiah and sliding an envelope to him.

"Hey, Jer. I snagged those Lizzo tickets for your sister," he says. "Fuckin' scalper wanted eight hundred bucks each."

"Christ… you didn't pay him that, did you?" Jeremiah replies, taking the envelope and stashing it beneath the counter.

"*Hell* no. Told him I'd fuck him up if he didn't fork them over for a better price."

Rowan snorts in the back of his throat, but he doesn't doubt Mal would beat up some random guy for trying to rip him off.

Jeremiah lets out his own laugh, probably thinking the same thing Rowan did. "Thanks. Let me know how much I owe you and I'll Venmo you."

Mal waves him off. "Don't worry 'bout it. Tell her to have a good time and don't bring anyone who fuckin' sucks."

With a kiss to two of his fingers thrown in Mal's direction, Jeremiah heads to the other end of the bar to help a throng of patrons who have emerged, some of whom Rowan recognizes from his little trip to the VoyEx corner.

"You ready, space case?" Rowan hears Mal say next to him, snapping him out of his daze.

Rowan turns to look at Mal straight-on, immediately feeling a heavy swoop of desire that he should have felt watching the men in the VoyEx corner. That he should have felt watching Jeremiah do his thing behind the bar.

"Yeah," he replies, unable to keep the smile completely off his face. "Lead the way."

THE SHIBARI class is held in a large open room on the first floor that would look like a dance studio if it weren't for the thick metal beams crisscrossing the ceiling and dozens of hooks and hardpoints attached to the walls. Rowan wonders what the hell else this room is used for, or if the club really does have an entire room dedicated to group rope bondage.

Already the room is filled with couples scattered around, talking quietly but animatedly. The diversity among them is surprising—not because Boston is particularly homogenous, but because places like this usually *are*. Though the group that Mal picked at the gangbang had been very diverse as well. Seeing how the instructor works with couples of all different shapes and sizes should make for an interesting class.

As they walk in and find an empty table near the front, Rowan can see that a few people eye Mal with surprise and Rowan with what looks like jealousy. It's so easy to forget that Mal—*Malcolm*—is basically a celebrity here. A pulse of pride shoots through him, and he turns away from the gawking faces, even though a small part of him wants to stick his tongue out and chant *nahhh nah-nah boo boo*!

"You've done this before, right?" he asks Mal instead.

"Shibari? Yeah. Haven't done any tying in a long time, though."

"More of a rope bunny?"

Mal gives him a flat stare, but the corners of his lips quirk up as he says, "Fuck off with that term, Firecrotch." After a beat, he shoots back, "You ever done it?"

"Nope. Read a whole bunch about it a little while ago, though. And knot-tying was something we were drilled on in Boy Scouts, so I know my way around the basics."

"Fuckin' Boy Scout," Mal quips.

Rowan snorts, but takes the nickname as a compliment.

He doesn't really know what to expect tonight. They'll clearly be doing some kind of rig, but the extent of it is still a mystery to him. He'd done research a couple weeks ago when Mal first mentioned the class, so he's at least somewhat familiar with the terminology and basic ties. Though like with anything, *doing* is always much different from reading.

So he's mentally prepared for pretty much whatever. He's not, however, expecting Camilla to walk in wearing pastel workout leggings and a sports-bra, tank-top combo with her long blond hair tied up in a high ponytail.

"Welcome!" she trills, taking her place at the front of the room where two large rectangular tables sit filled with dozens of coils of rope. She captures the attention of everyone in the room immediately, a hush falling over the patrons faster than with any schoolteacher Rowan's ever had.

An attractive man with a medium build, light complexion, and brown hair tied into a topknot emerges from the crowd of couples and joins her at the front.

"I'm sure all of you know me, at least you should, but I'm Camilla, and I'll be your instructor tonight." She gestures to the man next to her, "And this is Rory, my demonstration partner. I know we have a mix of experience levels in here tonight, so I'll be as detailed as possible without making everything overwhelmingly technical for the newbies."

She grabs a small remote from the table, and with the press of a button, a projector on the ceiling that Rowan hadn't noticed lights up and displays a large PowerPoint type collage of people tied in all sorts of positions.

"Don't worry, this won't be a lecture," Camilla assures with a laugh. "This'll mostly be for showing different types of rigs and knots rather than have you all crowded around up here."

She launches into a brief but informative history of shibari, and Rowan admits he's only half listening. This is all stuff he's read from various sources already, so he lets himself zone out a bit and finds his gaze drawn to Mal's profile.

The sharp peak of his nose, the cut of his jaw, the pink of his lips— lips that Rowan has felt against his own, if only for a feverish, fleeting moment.

God, he's such a fucking pussy. Jay would drag him to hell and back if he found out Rowan was mooning this hard over a guy he's only known a couple of months, fucked half a dozen times, and accidentally got kissed by once.

A shift in Camilla's voice snaps him out of his self-deprecation.

"Like with any kind of kink play," she says seriously, "the mantra safe, sane, and consensual is paramount in shibari. It's incredibly easy to tie a rope too tight or in the wrong way and cut off blood circulation or even cause nerve damage. The comfort and safety of the person being tied should come before all else."

She walks to one end of the table, pointing out a box and a stack of pamphlets next to the coils of rope.

"This is a basic guide to some of the knots we'll be using tonight, as well as a few different types of ties for nearly every body part," she says, holding up one of the pamphlets. Next she moves to the box and picks up a familiar tool. "There's also a pair of medical shears for each duo. With any kind of rope bondage, they should be accessible at all times in case you need to get your partner out of their binds quickly. Don't assume that you'll be able to untie something quickly enough. It doesn't matter if you're using gold-and-diamond studded silk rope—no rope is worth your partner's safety."

Rowan has never had to respond to an incident involving ropes in his time as a paramedic, but he has had to use shears on more than one occasion to quickly defibrillate a patient or access an injury hidden behind clothing. While Mal may be experienced with this, there's always a chance Rowan will fuck something up and have to cut him free. He hopes that doesn't turn out to be true.

Camilla picks up two differently colored bundles of rope.

"We have two types of rope available tonight: six-millimeter hemp or one-centimeter cotton," she says, holding each up in turn. "Cotton is generally preferable for beginners because of the softness and flexibility. However, hemp is what most experienced riggers use because of its *lack* of flexibility. It makes your rigs much more secure, but it can be a turnoff for some people because of the texture. Hemp generally softens with contact with the body's natural oils, so the longer you use a rope, the nicer it will feel. But then again, some people like the bite of the harsher rope… so it's up to you and your partner what you'll use tonight."

At Camilla's prompting, the couples approach the front and pick out bundles of rope and shears, a quiet but eager buzz in the air. There's a flutter in Rowan's chest as Mal stands up.

"What do you wanna use?" Rowan asks.

"Hemp if you're cool with it. Not really a fan of cotton."

"Sure. Any color preference?"

"Nah, pick whatever," Mal replies, wandering off toward the other end of the table.

Rowan takes in the full rainbow of color choices laid out on the table. A quick scan of the room shows that about half the people chose black rope, while others chose bright primary colors. He tries to picture what Mal will look like in each color, and finds that every single one of them would look fucking amazing, even the browns and beiges that look like they're meant to match skin tones.

He settles on a bright red, the color reminding him of the rope he'd seen in the cabinet during their first scene together. He grabs two coils as Camilla's voice floats softly past his ears.

"Just like old times, huh, Malcolm?"

It makes him snap his head toward her and Mal, and he catches a smile form on Mal's face, followed by a huff of a laugh.

It throws him completely for a loop. Old times? What does *that* mean, coming from Camilla and in this context? He knows Mal has never worked at the Menagerie, so it can't mean that he taught a class or anything like that. So really… that only leaves one possible option, and it makes his head spin.

Coils in hand, Rowan returns to their table, mind racing. He watches the two of them laugh together, the rest of their conversation too quiet to hear. Something that feels a hell of a lot like jealousy twists itself in Rowan's chest, making his fingers clench around the rope until his knuckles turn white.

When Mal returns a minute later, Rowan doesn't hide his gawking.

"What?" Mal asks, eyeing him with his eyebrows knitted together.

"Did you…," Rowan starts, trailing off as he thinks better of prying. It's none of his business, and Mal's made it pretty clear that personal information is squarely off limits.

"*What?*"

Fuck it.

"Did you used to scene with Camilla?"

Mal takes a deep breath and sighs it out through his nose, almost like he'd been expecting the question but hoped it wouldn't come. But he surprises Rowan when he answers.

"Yeah. When I first joined."

"Was she your Dom?"

"No, I was hers."

Rowan knows his eyebrows shoot up, but he can't help it. Mal's definitely a scrappy fucker even as a sub, and Rowan doesn't doubt he would make a good Dom if he wanted to, but he's never expressed any interest in switching their roles. Or in *women*, for that matter.

"I thought you said you weren't bi, though? *Or* a switch?"

Mal rubs absently at his eyebrow, slicking down the already pristine hairs.

"I'm not."

"So were you still figuring shit out back then?"

Mal gazes toward Camilla, where she stands helping a couple pick out which type of rope to use. "Was scared shitless when I first came here. And I didn't wanna… I dunno, admit what I liked. Camilla helped me figure that out after only a couple months together."

"Oh…."

"Think she clocked me right away, though," Mal admits.

"Why's that?"

"Our dynamic was pretty standard, but after a couple sessions she started… pushing back more. Bein' more aggressive and demanding. Kind of a bitch, honestly, but still within our boundaries."

Rowan has a hard time imagining the bubbly woman as being *anything* but perfectly pleasant, but as he's learned with Mal, people can surprise you, especially when it comes to kinks. After all, her twin, Clover, is much more serious, so it isn't actually all that hard to imagine when he thinks about it for more than a second.

Mal lets out another one of those huffy laughs, staring down at the table absently like he's remembering. "One day she suggested we switch, and the rest kinda speaks for itself. Took me longer to admit I wasn't actually into chicks."

Rowan doesn't know what to do with that information, but he glances at the blond, the bitter taste of jealousy in his mouth sweetened only by the secondhand gratitude he feels toward her.

"Everyone ready?" Camilla asks aloud, now that all the couples have returned to their stations.

There are murmurs of *yes* and *yeah*, and Camilla dives in to a thorough yet quick overview of the many types of knots used in shibari—single- and double-column tie, granny knot, reef knot, X-friction, half hitch, square loop…. It seems like an endless list for different situations, a few of which they'd be trying out tonight. But Rowan greedily drinks in the information, committing the names of every tie to memory to practice later on his own.

"A quick note before we begin tying," Camilla says. "Even though it isn't always sexual, shibari is an incredibly intimate act and a profound display of trust, even in the simplest binds, so it's natural to get worked up while practicing. But please keep it in your pants for the duration of the class. If you feel you *need* to leave, you're welcome to."

Once again, Rowan finds his concentration shifting to Mal. If it weren't for the fact that he *wants* to learn this shit, he'd be tempted to drag him upstairs right now.

"We'll start with the single-column tie, which is one of the most useful, in my humble opinion."

Next to him, Mal laughs like it's an old inside joke of theirs—a low snort of a sound in the back of his throat—and it makes Rowan's insides twist more than the rope in his hands.

"Start by folding your practice rope in half," she says, quickly folding the short rope and finding the center of the strands, adjusting the tails to the same length. "This is your baseline for the majority of ties for its security, aesthetic, and safety."

Rory holds one arm out, and Camilla wraps the rope twice around his wrist. "The loop—which is called the bight, as I mentioned earlier—should be facing one direction, while the tail faces the opposite. Cross the bight over your strands, then make a loop with the tail, keeping the bight on top of everything."

She slips two slim fingers under the strands and tugs slightly. "There should always be at least one finger of space between the rope and your partner's skin, but two is preferable in many cases. Unless you have big hands," she says with a wink.

Rowan's eyes flick to Mal, who merely waggles his eyebrows at him. *Got big hands, man.*

He's not going to survive this fucking class, and it's barely begun.

Camilla continues her explanation, blissfully unaware of Rowan's heart palpitating. "Pull the bight under all the strands and through the loop. You always want to *pull* your rope through openings rather than pushing it. If you push, the rope could uncoil or your strands could shift. Finally, hold the bight in place and pull the tail until the knot is tight."

Seems easy enough, Rowan thinks. He's fairly sure he's done this in Boy Scouts, even if the terms used were a little different. There's a shuffling around the room and the light patter of rope ends trailing over the floor as the couples follow Camilla's display. A helpful diagram is posted on the screen behind her, showing stills of each of the steps.

Without prompting, Mal holds one wrist out in front of Rowan. For some reason, the gesture—so easy and done seemingly without a second thought—has Rowan's pulse quickening. This is all about trust. Mal *trusts* Rowan to not hurt him, to let him learn and probably fumble through some shit, all to make their scenes more fulfilling.

It's… a lot to take in. Especially with how fragile their relationship had seemed less than a week ago.

Mal's skin is warm as Rowan wraps the rope around his arm, covering the skull and crossbones tattoo. Rowan's hands work on their own, and in a few seconds, there's a pretty damn perfect knot sitting snugly around Mal's wrist. He turns Mal's hand over, his thumb grazing Mal's knuckles and making the *U* and *G* of his THUG LIFE tattoo disappear for a breath as he sweeps across them. The gasp he nearly lets out at the electricity that zaps through him is suppressed only by the weight of Mal's eyes on him. He distracts himself and checks the tightness, able to fit a single finger underneath.

"That okay?" he asks to be sure.

"Yeah. Figured you'd catch on fast, Boy Scout."

"Questions on that?" Camilla asks aloud. "Great. Go ahead and practice that a few more times until you're comfortable with it."

Rowan tugs the bight, and the knot easily unravels as intended. His second tie is both faster and neater than the first. Mal tugs his arm while

Rowan holds on to the tail, the rope pulling taut in Rowan's hands and halting Mal's movements.

"You must really hate this if you're already tryin' to get away from me," Rowan jokes.

"Couldn't get away from you if I tried."

The statement hits like a shot of cocaine straight to Rowan's brain. For a second, he debates his reply. Cocky? Sincere? Flippant? What the hell does he *say* to that?

"Don't blame yourself. I'm irresistible."

A hum in the back of Mal's throat is the only response he gives before he tugs on the bight himself and frees his arm, then hands the rope back to Rowan. His skin is already starting to redden with the indentations of the rope, and a surge of longing to see more of them rushes through Rowan.

They practice a few more knots that Camilla says they'll need to be familiar with later on—bowlines, X-frictions, square frictions, and half hitches. For some of them, Mal holds the rope taut in between his hands while Rowan makes his ties in the air, the only way to simulate the actual positioning of the rope without incorporating it into a rig. A thrill tingles down his back at how naturally it comes to him and how Mal's spent the first forty minutes not really getting anything out of it other than watching Rowan practice with a soft smile on his face and the occasional pointer correcting Rowan's technique.

When Camilla comes around to survey all the couples and their progress, she stops by their table with a proud-looking smile.

"Guess I don't need to help you two, huh?"

Rowan finishes off a double column tie as she says it, pulling the rope taut. "Think we're pretty good. Malcolm's a good teacher," Rowan tells her, Mal's full name never losing the feeling of strangeness on his tongue.

"Don't be stealing my thunder, mister!" Camilla jokes, pointing a finger accusingly at Mal.

"Wouldn't dream of it, Cam. Much prefer being on this end'a things, anyway."

"I can see why," she says, eyeing Rowan's hands as he undoes the knot.

Her ability to make Rowan both want to preen and shrivel is also something he doesn't think he'll ever get used to.

"You wanna do any more?" Mal asks Rowan as Camilla continues her walk around the room.

"Nah, I think I'm good. I'm sure some of these are gonna be different in an actual rig."

"Yeah. Free tying is good to get the basics down, but when you've got someone underneath it, everything changes." For a beat, Mal meets his eyes before his gaze shifts to the coils of rope still on the table. "Ah, fuck."

"What?"

"Forgot to bring my rope for you."

"Oh, don't worry about it. Next week's fine. Probably wouldn't want to do any tying for a bit anyway till I can practice more."

Mal nods and pulls out his phone, probably to set a reminder for himself.

Back at the front, Camilla clicks over to a new slide showing a chest harness on a female model in four varying patterns. "We'll be doing a chest harness today," she says. "It may seem a little advanced, but it comes together fairly easily and incorporates the ties you've just practiced. I'll give some modifications along the way for anyone not as flexible or comfortable with the position."

Rowan's mouth waters at the thought of getting Mal into the harness.

Camilla turns Rory around, guiding his arms into position. "The person being tied should fold their arms behind their back and hold their forearms, with the wrists turned inward. This will avoid the major nerves and veins in the wrist. If you're not quite there yet, you can simply clasp your hands together."

Next to him, Rowan sees Mal effortlessly clasp his forearms, wrists already turned inward. He's so transfixed by the sharp cut of his shoulder blades and the swell of his triceps that he misses the first step of the harness entirely.

"Cold feet, Campbell?" Mal asks, turning back with a grin that nearly knocks Rowan on his ass.

"You know I run hot, Savaryn," he replies, not nearly as slick in his mind as the words suggest.

But it earns him another dazzling grin and a *tch* before Mal's once again turning his back to him. Trusting.

Rowan draws the folded rope over Mal's arms, the deep red color a pleasing pop against his skin, and coils it around twice more, forming six neat strands. A quick bowline knot tightens the strands around his arms and leaves the bight exposed to allow for quick release if necessary.

"Draw the tail over the left deltoid, just below the shoulder," Camilla instructs. "Be careful to avoid the dip in the arm between the deltoid and the bicep—there are several nerves below that we want to avoid. Now draw the rope around the chest, above the breastbone."

The rope curves around Mal's bare arm and cinches the fabric of his black tank top above his pecs. Rowan's drawn in by the wrinkles in the fabric, but wishes they could do this with him shirtless. Someday, he reminds himself.

With the rope wrapping around Mal's other shoulder, Camilla announces, "Have your partner periodically squeeze your fingers to ensure they haven't lost sensation or strength in their arms."

Dutifully, Rowan slips two of his fingers into Mal's relaxed hand, feeling him squeeze tightly and hoping that Mal can't feel the hammering of his pulse in his fingertips.

"Good?"

"Mmm."

Step by step, Rowan draws the rope across Mal's body exactly where and how Camilla instructs. But the pattern emerges in Rowan's head even before Camilla's words reach his ears. Over, under, pull, tighten, tie. He has to take a second to flip over the pamphlet to double-check how to do the first X-friction, but Mal's talking before Rowan even gets to the correct page.

"Pull the tail through the center line."

Rowan drops the pamphlet in favor of listening to Mal.

"Under?"

"Yeah. Pull it up to my right shoulder… farther… good. Now pull it under all the strands and down toward my right elbow."

"The center line's not straight," Rowan notes.

Mal rolls his shoulders slightly, creating a tiny bit of slack for Rowan to tug the knot closer to the center.

"Thanks. Now up to the left shoulder, right?"

"Yep, then—"

"Down to the left. I remember that part."

"'S a lotta steps, but it makes sense when you do it a few times. Make sure you put tension on the tail before you wrap it around the center line… that's good."

It's endlessly impressive that Mal knows exactly what Rowan's doing by the feel of the rope surrounding him alone. And while Rowan knows how to finish the knot without any further help from Mal, he lets him talk him the rest of the way through.

As he pulls the tail of the rope through the strands across Mal's back, it's impossible to avoid his knuckles brushing down the dip in his spine, the spot Rowan knows is ultrasensitive. Even with the fabric of his shirt in between, Mal shudders gently.

"Feel good?" Rowan teases, already knowing the answer by the dip of Mal's head.

The breathiness of his snappy reply betrays him. "Fuck off."

"Could always head upstairs, catch the next class."

Another trail down his spine, this time more deliberate.

"Gonna have to if you keep doin' that…."

"Oh yeah?" Rowan draws the rope back across Mal's front, the bulge in his sweats pulling Rowan's gaze.

"Such a fuckin' tease, Red."

If it weren't for the fact that they'd probably get kicked out regardless of Mal's friendship with Camilla, and for the fact that this is outside their normal scenes—the nickname a stark reminder of that—Rowan would be tempted to see how worked up he could get Mal before the rig is even finished. Instead he glances up to the front, finding that Camilla already has both of Rory's underarms secured with two lines of rope.

As if sensing his internal panic, Mal guides him through the steps to catch up. Rowan can't help but wonder if Mal has done this exact rig before or if he's *that* familiar with this type of rig. The harness starts to take shape, and it sends a rush straight to Rowan's groin. He knows by the smirk Mal gives him that he's noticed the effect the whole process is having on him. If Mal weren't in the same boat, he might be embarrassed.

Rowan can feel the heat of Mal's body and the goose bumps that pop up under each piece of exposed skin he touches. If only he could run his fingertips over Mal's skin and read him like braille, discern every thought and feeling from just his body's subconscious reactions.

Or maybe he doesn't even need it. Mal's chin dips down nearly to his chest, a stillness settling over him as his eyes start to glaze over in the way Rowan's come to know means Mal is approaching that blissed-out state that all Doms strive for. He won't get there, not by a long shot, but it makes Rowan preen like a peacock nonetheless.

"For the front," Camilla says, "the pattern is up to you and your partner. I'll show the plain version first, with no rope between the breasts, then a second version that is more ornate. For the more advanced version, we'll be adding a fifteen-foot rope extension."

"Which one do you wanna do?" Rowan asks.

"Up to you," Mal replies, snapping out of the daze he'd started to fall into with several quick blinks.

"Hm…." Rowan experimentally places the tail of the rope between Mal's pecs, immediately liking the sight even with his shirt in the way. "Kinda want to show off your tits more."

"*Pft*. Figured you were more of an ass man, Paul Hollywood."

He laughs at the callback to their texts earlier in the week, even as he says in complete sincerity, "I'm an everything man when it comes to you."

His fingers are still on the rope held loosely against Mal's chest. For a second, their eyes meet, and instead of the scoff or dismissal Rowan expects, Mal's lips pull back into a pleased smile.

After attaching another fifteen-foot rope with a box tie, he weaves the strands between Mal's pecs and starts interlacing them to form a braided pattern.

"What do you get out of this?" Rowan asks in a low voice.

For a second, Mal doesn't answer. But when Rowan looks up to make sure he heard him, Mal's eyes are lidded but still manage to bore a hole straight into Rowan's own. It reminds him of the first time they locked eyes at the gangbang all those weeks ago. Intense. Electric.

"Feels secure," Mal says. After a few seconds, he tacks on, "Safe."

"Kind of like a baby being swaddled?"

"If I could smack you for that right now, I would, Firecrotch. But fuckin'… *yeah*, I guess. Don't gotta worry about anything."

Rowan bites the inside of his cheek to stop himself from laughing at Mal's outburst. "That's pretty much what you said about being a sub. They kinda go hand in hand, huh?"

"Mmm." There's a short pause before he asks, "You likin' this so far?"

"Yeah," Rowan responds immediately. "I like being able to focus on something. Working with my hands, I guess. Keeps my mind from wandering to bad shit."

Something about the vulnerable situation they're in—despite being surrounded by dozens of strangers—makes it easy for Rowan to half confess some of his demons.

He's not expecting to have to elaborate, but Mal doesn't take the same opportunity to make a playful jab at his answer, instead following up with "What kinda shit?"

Like whether I'm gonna snap and wind up in the psych ward again. Or not be able to get out of bed for a week straight again. Or risk my patients' lives again. Or stress out my family again. Or....

"Work stuff. Family stuff. And I uh...." He takes a deep breath, finding it easier to speak as he pulls each section of rope taut around Mal's body. "I have some shit I deal with that takes a lot of energy sometimes. Makes me need to stop or slow down and think things through rather than letting my thoughts run wild."

"Shibari's good for that. Kink in general."

"Yeah," Rowan agrees.

Though realistically, he feels like his mind's been nothing but a flurry of activity the past month and a half. But maybe that's not kink. Maybe that's just Mal.

Camilla walks around to survey the class's progress, but she's little more than a blur in Rowan's periphery, his concentration solely on Mal as he checks his lines. A small adjustment here, a tiny nudge there, and from where he's standing, everything looks perfect.

With the rig fully done, Rowan takes a step back to admire his work. It's breathtaking, seeing Mal like that. All trussed up and perfectly still. Every time he's had Mal bound in some way, he's always been struggling against cuffs or Rowan's hands, making a show of it. But now it's as if he's settled into the ties, completely content to simply *be*. The deluge of thoughts cascading through Rowan's mind at all the ways he can get Mal into a full-body rig sends a real shiver down his spine.

"Beautiful...." Camilla's voice floats into his ears, snapping his attention away from Mal. "You're a natural."

The compliment does little for him, even coming from someone as knowledgeable as her. He's much more interested in Mal's thoughts on this particular subject.

"Thanks," he says anyway. "Got a good model."

"Mmm," she hums, eyeing Mal up and down, an appreciative smile on her face.

It's weird is all Rowan can think. And he can't help but see her in a different light now that he knows she and Mal have scened together. That she helped him figure out what he wanted when he was new to the kink scene. Like Mal's doing for Rowan now. The tiny pang of envy that grips at his skin makes him feel like a teenager who didn't get to ask out his crush first before the popular kid got to him.

He mentally slaps himself for it.

"Everything feel okay?" he asks Mal, needlessly straightening already near-perfect lines.

"Yeah. You did good."

"Wish they had a mirror in here."

Mal bites his lip. Shifts his gaze to the side for a beat. Flicks back to Rowan.

"You got your phone?"

In the short time it takes the words to register in Rowan's mind, his heart rate skyrockets.

"Yeah, why?"

"Can take a pic if you want."

"Wh—really?"

"Just don't be postin' my mug to Instabook."

"That's not a… yeah, yeah, course. I wouldn't."

Scrambling to get his phone out of his pocket, he hears Mal huff a laugh.

"Ain't goin' anywhere, man. Kinda tied up at the moment."

Rowan feels his face flush as he unlocks his phone and opens the camera app. "Your legs're still free."

"*Pft.* Won't catch me running unless someone's chasin' me."

"I like running," Rowan replies, as if his hobbies need defending.

"Why does that not surprise me," Mal deadpans.

"How do you wanna…?"

With a jerk of his head, Mal gestures to a blank wall off to the side of the room. Rowan leads the way, waiting for Mal to take his place against the wall as he switches his camera to portrait mode.

As he's about to direct Mal how to pose, the other man half leans against the wall, one leg bent at the knee and foot pressed behind. It creates a tantalizing stretch between his legs, accentuating both the muscular limbs and the thick cock Rowan knows lies beneath the fabric.

Rowan almost forgets to tap the screen to focus on Mal rather than the wall behind him when he sees the sultry, half-lidded look Mal throws his way. He must tap the shutter button a dozen times in rapid succession, unable to take his eyes off the image on his screen to even see if the photos came out any good.

"Want the back too?" Mal asks, a knowing smirk on his face.

Busted.

"Yeah, if you're cool with it."

More like if *Rowan* can be cool with it. Christ.

Mal turns in place, this time standing with his legs shoulder width apart. Even with a tank top in the way, the muscles of his back are prominent beneath the ropes and doing a *lot* for Rowan, making his dick jump for the dozenth time today.

It must be some sort of spidey sense that makes Mal look back at Rowan as he's about to take the next photo, but *fuck* if it doesn't make for an incredible freeze frame. It's slightly blurry with his movement, the strands of rope around his arms the only part completely in focus, but it looks almost artistic in its lack of deliberateness. It would look incredible in black and white.

And Rowan's no photographer, but they look *good*. The kind of photos that would definitely get him banned from any social media site even if it weren't firmly established that these aren't going anywhere but Rowan's own phone.

"You good, Liebowitz?"

Rowan wonders when Mal's going to run out of nicknames for him. "Yeah, 'm good."

"Send me those later."

"I will," he promises, walking back to their table.

"When you're ready, you can start untying your partners," Camilla calls to the room. "Be sure to go slowly and keep checking in throughout to make sure nothing goes numb or is painful. And of course, if you need the shears for any reason, use them."

"You ready?" Rowan asks. "Or do you wanna stay in a bit longer?"

"Can take it off," Mal replies. "Must be gettin' close to eight."

A quick check of his watch tells Rowan that they only have about fifteen minutes until then. He's sure that if they needed it, Camilla would let them stay longer, but Rowan gets to work undoing the rig anyway.

Mal's eyes are closed lightly as Rowan unties him. He's never been tied himself, but Rowan can't help wondering if it's as satisfying having the binds taken off as it is to have them put on. While his fingers work, he watches Mal closely, not often able to drink in the sight of him outside of their scenes. It makes Rowan's head spin a bit, knowing that this gorgeous person chose *him* to share his body with. Even if Rowan's wildest dreams don't come true and Mal's never anything more to him than a sex partner—and maybe even a friend, now—he still feels like Lady Luck is shining on him.

As each section of rope falls away, he rubs the pink skin left in its wake, stimulating the blood flow. He knows he didn't tie anything tightly enough to constrict any major vessels, but he also knows that the delicate web of capillaries sitting below the skin is highly susceptible to pressure.

It's almost clinical, Rowan thinks. He's removed so many constricting objects from his patients' skins at work that his body moves almost on autopilot. Hands gently tugging apart the knots one by one until the red rope gives way to flushed pink skin and soft black fabric.

Sure, there are no sirens or flashing lights or chaotic jostling from dodging traffic while riding in the back of an ambulance, but there's the gentle scratching of the rope against Mal's body, the glint in his eyes from the overhead lights, and the unpredictable rhythm of Rowan's heart kicking his adrenaline into overdrive, and really it shouldn't be all that different.

But it is. It feels like *more* because of where they are and who they are to one another, and the pressure of being perfect almost makes a lump swell in Rowan's throat. He swallows it, reminding himself that even if he fucks it up somehow, Mal's stuck by him so far and hasn't dumped him outside the club by his scruff like a wet dog. It sends a flicker of warmth through him, and he finishes untying the rest of the rig with ease.

Finally free, Mal flexes his fingers and stretches his arms across the front of his chest.

"You good?" Rowan asks.

"Yeah. Here, wind this one up," Mal says, handing him one of the fifteen-foot strands of rope as he grabs the thirty.

He watches how Mal coils it, following suit until they have three neat bundles of rope. Mal takes all three and heads toward the front.

Each couple dutifully places their coils of rope—some neatly tied back up, others in hellish crumpled balls—in a separate bin to be cleaned. Half have marks on their skin and indents in their clothing that mirror the ones on Mal, and Rowan can't help but wonder what the other pairs are going to get up to now that class is over.

As Mal comes back from the front after a brief exchange with Camilla, Rowan feels a swirl of accomplishment and can't wait to tie Mal for real.

But for now, he'll be content with getting him naked again.

With getting inside him again.

"You still up for a scene?" he checks, though they'd already planned on it.

"Yeah," Mal nods and leads the way to the staircase.

ROWAN'S *BUZZING* as they make their way to the Gold Room. He hasn't felt this eager since his first scene alone with Mal.

As usual, Mal sets out the cuffs on the bed, the clinking of the D-rings and clasps making Rowan's cock twitch in some kind of perverse Pavlovian response.

They hadn't planned on using anything else tonight, but Mal's thumbnail rakes rhythmically across the zipper of his bag, and he stares down into it. His gaze is far away, like he's not looking *at* something, but rather seeing straight through the bag to some unknown point in space. Rowan opens his mouth to ask if something's wrong, but then Mal is stuffing one hand inside and tossing a box of condoms on the bed. It makes only the tiniest hollow *thump* against the thick leather pad, but it might as well have been a gunshot with the way it sends a searing pain through Rowan's chest.

"Oh…."

He's not even sure if Mal hears it with how small and pathetic it sounds to Rowan's own ears. Hell, he's not even sure any sound came out at all with the hollow ringing all around him.

He stares at the black-and-gold box for far too long before he feels Mal's gaze on him. When their eyes meet, it's… fuck. Rowan wishes he could see the dark sheen of regret coloring those gold eyes, but there's nothing. No sign of guilt or empathy or anger or *anything* there beyond a silent dare to raise the question that's currently burrowing into Rowan's head and taking over all his thoughts.

It doesn't mean anything. *Of course* Mal has every right to go out and fuck whoever he wants, whenever he wants. Rowan had thought about doing the same only a couple of hours ago. As long as they use condoms until enough time has passed and they get tested next. That was the deal they made. The deal Rowan *agreed to*.

But it fucking *hurts*.

The initial pain of the shock fades quickly, but the ache it leaves behind when he regains his senses is like a week-old bruise. Only really hurting if he pokes it. If he thinks about it too much.

He should stop the scene. He *knows* he should. That's what a *good* Dom would do. A good partner in general. But the thought of getting a half-mewling Mal underneath him again makes it hard to say no. Impossible, even.

Time passes in slow motion, but Rowan manages an astonishingly unaffected sounding, "'Kay."

And with frustratingly shaky fingers, he opens the brand-new box of Magnum Trojans and rips one off the strip, immediately hating how the foil feels in his hands. Knows how much worse the rubber is going to feel around his cock and how dull every sensation will be when he's used to feeling *all* of Mal.

That's exactly what it is, Rowan thinks. A dulling. They'd gotten too close for the parameters of the relationship they'd established, and Mal thought it necessary to pull on the reins. And his way of doing that was fucking someone else. The sour bite of betrayal fills Rowan's chest even though he knows he hasn't earned the right to feel that way. Definitely not yet, if ever.

Rowan's always been quick to anger, one of the many things he hates about his brain chemistry. He's got a pretty low frustration tolerance and tends to lash out as soon as that threshold is met. But he doesn't want that with Mal. Doesn't wanna punish him any more than he would normally for being a brat. Instead he wants to show him how *good* it can be between them—how good *he* can be.

He thinks back to the diner all those weeks ago, how he'd told Mal *I don't like to share* and made him backpedal and state bluntly that they weren't exclusive. The thing is, sure, he's possessive, he knows he is, but like at the gangbang, something about watching others wreck Mal and knowing that he can do it better—longer, harder, faster—gets him endlessly hot.

And they'd planned on a longer spanking session this time— more than a few errant swats like Rowan has done when Mal has been particularly mouthy. So it's going to be hard to make it feel like it *isn't* a punishment.

But Mal had *specifically* requested it. Only two days ago. And Rowan can't help but wonder if he'd slept with whoever else he did before or after that fact. Hell, he could have fucked someone immediately after he'd driven away from the diner last Saturday night and Rowan would be none the wiser. He also can't help but wonder if Mal only chose the spanking to do a complete one-eighty from their last session— the slowness and gentleness of it, relatively speaking—this time wanting something at the other end of his kink spectrum.

More dulling. More pushing away, even though it'd felt like they made progress earlier tonight.

He has to remind himself once again that they're not here for progress. Not the emotional kind, anyway, no matter how badly he wants it.

"Strip."

It's shockingly easy for Rowan to slip back into the role of Rowan Campbell, Dom, as if last week he didn't nearly fall apart at the feeling of Mal's lips on his own.

"Make me."

Mal dips back into his own role as if last week *he* didn't get so overwhelmed by Rowan's words and whatever was going on in his personal life that he'd let himself cross one of his major boundaries.

Business as usual.

Rowan's body moves before his brain does, and in a flash, Mal is faceplanted onto the bed with one of Rowan's hands squarely between his shoulders. The ropes that had held him earlier now replaced with muscle and bone.

"Too easy to rile you up, Firecrotch," Mal grits, half mumbling as he turns his head to stare up at Rowan.

"You think I don't know your bullshit plays by now, Mal? Couldn't be further from the truth."

"Uh-*huh*."

He kicks Mal's legs apart, delighting in the wobble in Mal's knees.

"Take off your fucking shirt."

"How *exactly* d'you expect me to do that like this?"

Underneath him, Mal wriggles, the friction of his body against Rowan's hand scorching.

"Figure it out."

A huff and a grunt have Mal squirming to free his hands from underneath him. With no small amount of effort, he manages to grab the sides of his tank top and tug upward until the fabric bunches up underneath Rowan's palm.

"Move your hand," Mal snaps.

Smack! Rowan's free hand cracks down against Mal's clothed ass, the dull hit still making him jolt forward and let slip an audible gasp.

"My hand's exactly where I want it. Take off your shirt."

There's a grumbling from Mal that isn't gonna fly. Rowan smacks his other cheek, harder than the first.

"Fuck!"

"Quit being a whiny little bitch and take off your *fucking* shirt before I rip it off."

No response this time as Mal reaches back to gingerly shimmy the fabric from under Rowan's palm. He can feel Mal's shoulder blades and back muscles flexing against him. Once the shirt is finally past Rowan's hand, Mal grunts quietly as he stretches to pull it over his head and toss it to the corner of the bed.

"Good," Rowan purrs. He slots himself against Mal's ass, letting him feel his growing erection. "Pants next."

"Are you fuckin'—"

Rowan shoves his hand harder into Mal's back, a silent command to get the fuck on with it.

It's immensely satisfying to see his tattooed fingers curl around the waistband of his joggers and his arms tense as he struggles to strip in his compromised position. He gets the waistband a few inches over the swell of his ass when Rowan stops him.

"Take 'em both off."

Mal huffs, letting the pants snap back into place.

"Only said to take my pants off," he scoffs.

Rowan's response is to grind against his ass and draw out a surprised-sounding gasp, as if Mal had forgotten what the outcome of his compliance would be.

"Gonna be here all day if you take each piece off that slowly. *Move.*"

This time, Mal has the good sense not to make a retort before clutching both his pants and black briefs and starting to shove them over the curve of his ass. Despite his insistence on Mal hurrying up, Rowan does exactly nothing to help him out, one hand still pressed firmly on his upper back and hips flush with his ass. When Mal finally manages to make progress on stripping, it isn't only the hard line of Rowan's cock that it snags on.

Immediately, Rowan grabs the waistbands of Mal's pants and briefs and rips them down to mid-thigh, where his spread legs stop them from falling to the floor.

"Fuckin' slut…," Rowan breathes, seeing the thick base of a plug slotted neatly between Mal's asscheeks.

He presses against it with his thumb, grinding it in a tight circle that has Mal's thighs tensing and a loud "*Unnn…*" escaping his lips.

"You been wearing this all night, huh? Who told'ja to do that?"

"No one tells me to do *shit*."

Rowan huffs an amused laugh. "We both know that's a fuckin' lie. Been telling you to do shit every week for two months, and you keep coming back for more."

He trains his eyes on Mal's ass, and with one hand, spreads his cheeks and sees a distinct sheen of slickness coating either side of the plug. He'll never get sick of seeing the pretty pink hole that clenches around the toy inside. But a churning in his stomach reminds him that someone else got to see this too, at some point in the last week. The rancid taste of bile wells up in his throat, and Rowan knows he has no right to be sickened by it. Has no right to *Mal* because they're *just fuckin'*.

Swallowing, he pushes the bile and his thoughts back where they belong.

"Couldn't even wait for me to prep you," Rowan says. "That how bad you wanted my cock tonight?"

"What can I say? Thought you'd screw around and waste my time."

"Have I ever wasted your time, Mal?"

"Seems like you're doin' it right now."

"*Pft*," Rowan scoffs. He grips the base of the plug and tugs until he feels the pressure of the widest part catch on Mal's rim.

"*Nng….*"

"You want me to fuck you right now? Pull out this plug, use you, then bounce?"

Mal lets out a soft, barely-there moan, like he might actually want that after all.

"Huh?" Rowan insists, twisting the plug back in and pushing hard when it's fully seated. "Fuck you till I'm satisfied and to hell with everything else? Answer me."

A pause, then "No."

It's begrudging and too brusque, but sincere. Not good enough.

"No, what?"

Mal shoves his ass back against Rowan's hand where it's roughly tugging and twisting and pushing his plug.

"Don't want ya to stop."

"Uh-huh. 'S what I thought."

Rowan releases Mal long enough to dip lower and shove his pants and briefs the rest of the way down, then slap the outside of his thigh to get him to toe his shoes off.

Fully naked and with his upper half pressed into the bed, Mal's a fucking sight to behold. Rowan can still see the faint pink lines of the ropes serpentining over his arms and shoulders, and he wants to get him all tied up again.

Reaching forward to grab the cuffs from beside Mal, he can't help but grind his clothed cock again into Mal's bare ass, pressing the plug deeper inside and making Mal gasp.

"Front or back?" Rowan asks lowly.

Mal was only in the shibari rig for an hour or so, but Rowan wants to give him the option of resting his arms if he needs it.

"Back."

The subtle rocking of Mal's hips has Rowan's hand cracking down hard against his left asscheek.

"Fuck!"

He wrenches one arm back, holding it in place against Mal's lower back. But Mal holds his other arm above his head. "Give me your other hand."

Slowly, Mal shifts his arm backward, elbow barely passing his rib cage, but when Rowan reaches for it, Mal yanks it away with a grin that Rowan can see even in profile.

Smack!

Rowan's palm stings from the force of the slap across Mal's ass, directly over the plug. The groan ripped from Mal's throat is cut off as Rowan yanks him to standing, back flush to Rowan's chest and one hand still pressed between them. His fingers dig into Mal's bicep, then trail along his chest, up his neck, and grasp the sides of his jaw to bring his ear directly to Rowan's lips.

"You know…," Rowan starts, voice low as if someone might hear them in the soundproof room. "I know you think you're doin' something here with all this pushing back, but I've got more patience in my little finger than you've got brattiness in your whole body."

With no more fanfare and only the faintest whisper of a huff from Mal, Rowan cuffs Mal's wrists and fastens them together.

"On the bed."

Predictably, Mal gets on his knees, upper body planted into the bed. Rowan lets him sit there. Sweat it out a little as he strips himself of everything but his briefs, because he doesn't know what Mal did with whoever he fucked, but he's not going to take any chances or put Mal in a situation where it takes him out of the scene.

He perches on the edge of the bed, feet planted firmly on the floor, with his back to Mal.

"Come here."

"Told me to get on the bed, didn't ya?"

"Don't be a smartass," Rowan replies, tugging Mal up by the cuffs until he's on his knees. "Or are you waitin' for me to move you myself?"

Over his shoulder, Mal shoots him a wry smile that does exactly nothing to impress Rowan.

"Cute," he deadpans. "Not gonna get you what you want, though."

"Has so far."

"Mmm…," Rowan hums thoughtfully. "I think you're a little too used to getting what you want."

"*Tch.*"

Rowan turns to gaze at him over his shoulder. "Told me you wanted it earlier. So you're gonna have to come get it."

So he leans back on his hands and waits.

It's a standoff.

Sure, Rowan could order Mal to move. Manhandle him easy as pie. But the thought of waiting for Mal to cave, well…. It'll be ten times sweeter.

The tension radiating off Mal behind him is visceral. Even without the benefit of his sight, Rowan can feel the tightness in his shoulders and hear his knuckles turning white from where the grinding of metal tells him he's tugging at his cuffs.

A minute. Maybe two. Definitely not three. That's all it takes for Rowan to hear the frustrated huff and the slick slide of skin against leather.

The satisfaction of watching Mal shuffle over to him on his knees—face flushed, jaw tight, cock bobbing between his legs—is unlike anything Rowan's felt before. No drug that's ever passed his lips has given him a high quite like this.

"Good," Rowan tells him, unable to stop his smug smile from reaching his eyes. "Wasn't so hard, was it?"

Mal stops a foot away from Rowan's thigh. "Fuckin'—*ah*!"

His exclamation comes out a surprised yelp when Rowan pulls him down over his lap and lands a swift smack to each asscheek.

"Enough. Playtime's over."

"Thought it just got star—"

Smack! Smack!

He tugs at Mal's hair to force him to look up at him. "The only words outta your mouth right now should be *more* or a safeword. Got it?"

"Ain't gonna make me count for you, *sir*?"

Smack!

"If you can keep count, I'm not doing my job right."

The first few strikes are easy. Warm-ups to gauge how much Mal can really handle. He knows he can take a lot, but he wants to push him to his limit.

Under Rowan's hand, Mal's skin is warm and heating up by the minute.

"Mmm!" Mal cries out at the first truly hard spank even as his cock twitches against Rowan's thigh.

It's hot as fuck, and Rowan rewards him with more hits, one after another. Nowhere on Mal's backside is safe from his hands—blows raining down on his asscheeks and the crease of his thighs and directly over the plug keeping him open for Rowan's cock later.

With each, Mal groans. Low, high, whining, gasping, growling—the reaction is different every time Rowan's palm connects with Mal's skin. And Rowan commits them all to memory, knowing he's going to jerk off to them for weeks on end.

That and the power he feels having this gorgeous man in his lap, rutting against him.

"Tell me why you wanted this, Mal," Rowan says between two sharp spanks.

"I… *fuck*… I deserve it," Mal breathes back.

"Why?"

"'Cause I…. *Oh*! Fuck, *more*…."

"*Why*, Mal? Tell me."

He wants to hear Mal call himself a brat or spoiled or hell, even a needy bottom bitch, but he's not expecting a sincere confession.

"I sl-slipped. Did something we didn't… I shouldn't—"

It's nearly incoherent. A stuttered mess of half sentences, but… *I kissed you and I shouldn't have* is what Rowan hears. *And then I slept with someone else* is what he doesn't.

This is dangerous—letting Mal ramble like this. He'd said last week he didn't want to talk about the real world during their scenes. Didn't want to use them to work through his personal problems. Which, fine, whatever. Rowan can respect that. Even if it takes everything in him to stop his babbling, he knows that getting Mal *actually* incoherent is dangerous for both of them, for more reasons than Rowan's pride and curiosity.

"Hey, come back to me," Rowan says gently, cupping Mal's cheek and guiding his eyes to meet his own. "You don't deserve it for that. Never for that. Give me a color."

"Green…."

"Good. You need a minute?" he asks anyway.

Mal shakes his head, and with the gesture apparently shakes off whatever vulnerability he'd been about to blurt out.

But Rowan smooths his hands over his red ass anyway, so gently that he barely feels the fine, light-colored downy hairs tickling his palms.

Only when Mal pushes his ass up into his touch and grinds his hard cock into his thigh does Rowan raise his hand again. He gradually ramps back up from one to eleven, each spank harder than the last, dialing it down only when Mal's gasps signal more pain than pleasure.

Every hit is punctuated with a sharp "Hunh!" or "Ohh!" or "Fuck!" that rewires Rowan's brain and makes him salivate. The sounds are nearly as hot as watching Mal's plump ass jiggle beneath the force of his hand. He can't help but knead the thick muscle every few hits, watching the redness turn to white with the perfect indents of his fingers.

By the fiftieth spank, Mal's squirming in his lap. Pushing up and shrinking down, like he can't decide whether the actual spank or the anticipation of the next blow feels better.

Rowan rains down smacks on Mal's ass until each cheek and thigh burn to the touch and his skin is cherry red. Until there are tears streaming down Mal's cheeks and precome dribbling down his cock. The latter drips onto Rowan's bare thigh, and he's struck with the urge to lap it up, to suck the tip of Mal's cock into his mouth and taste him.

But he can't, because Mal fucked someone else.

The petty, nosy part of Rowan wants to know who it was. A friend? An old scene partner? A Grindr hookup? Or maybe he picked up a stranger at a bar. He can't exactly imagine Mal doing that when he's got a top-tier membership here, but he has no clue. Fuck, was it even a man? He'd never have thought it might not be until tonight's revelation with Camilla. And it doesn't bother him, not in principle anyway. What bothers him is the *not knowing*. But he shoves his wandering thoughts aside, focusing back on the man in his lap.

With one final slap, he tugs Mal off of him, pushing back until he's sitting on his heels, a ghost of a wince on his face from the undoubtedly sore area.

"Clean it up."

"Clean… wh—"

"*Me*. Don't be stupid."

He shoves Mal's face down to his own lap like a dog, his hot breath warming the precome on Rowan's thigh. But it's with little kitten licks that Mal laps up his own mess from Rowan's leg, his tongue smooth and wet and making more of a mess than was even there to begin with.

"All of it, or I promise you, the next time my hand touches your ass, you won't enjoy it."

There's a soft mewl followed by two more licks to the inside of his thigh that feel like liquid fire, and Rowan's thigh is clean of every trace of precome.

"Good." He drags Mal off by his hair, not satisfied with having him stop there. He rolls his tongue and spits loudly on his own thigh, the pearly white fluid a poor stand-in for what Rowan would rather see him lick. "Keep going."

Mal's eyes flick to Rowan's, pupils blown, mouth slack. There's a hesitation there that Rowan doesn't like.

"Give me a color, Mal."

His response is instant despite his raspy voice. "Green...."

"The fuck are you waiting for, then?"

A sharp smack against Mal's cheek has the other man yelping and instantly dipping his head, pink tongue darting out to catch the trail of spit trickling down the outside of Rowan's thigh. It tickles, but Rowan tightens his quads to keep from quivering. The sight of Mal cleaning Rowan's own spit off his thigh is enough to have his already hard cock straining in his briefs.

Pinching Mal's jaw between his fingers, he forces him to look up. "Let me see."

Mal's mouth dips open, tongue pink and glistening with his own precome and Rowan's spit.

"Fuckin' filthy. You love this shit, huh?"

As best he can with his face in a vise between Rowan's fingers, Mal nods.

Smack!

Rowan cracks his hand across Mal's cheek, not nearly as hard as he'd been on his ass, but enough to have the other man gasping aloud.

"*Words*, Mal. Not gonna tell you again."

"Yes...." It comes out a garbled whisper of a thing.

"Yes, *what*? Should know by now that one-word answers aren't good enough."

"Love it. 'M so fuckin' hard," he groans, hitching his hips forward and rutting his cock against Rowan's thigh, another dribble of precome leaving a pearly streak.

Rowan *tsks*, collecting the tiny drop of fluid with two fingers and shoving them into Mal's mouth. Mal's surprised "*Mmf!*" is almost as satisfying as the hot tongue that curls around his fingers and sucks the droplet off.

"Filthy…," Rowan comments, but it comes out as praise.

Relying solely on the strength of his arms in this position, he grabs Mal's hips and shifts him away from Rowan's lap, ass up and face down.

Rowan wastes no time in reaching for Mal's plug and tugging gently. But Mal clenches around it, keeping it suctioned inside him.

Smack!

"You want me to fuck you or not?" Rowan scolds him, punctuating his question with another stinging spank. "'Cause I'm good just jerking off."

"Bet you are," Mal mumbles, evidently coming back to his snarkiness after the intensity of the last hour.

Rowan flicks the plug before giving it another tug. It doesn't budge around Mal's walls.

"Maybe go see if Jeremiah's got a break coming up…."

It's a petty, cheap shot, and he knows it. He knows, too, that Jeremiah very much *isn't* DTF, for reasons Rowan doesn't really understand as he found out earlier. But it's enough to get Mal's hole relaxing, and the plug slides out easily.

"Good," he says, a small curl of pleasure at Mal's obvious jealousy swirling in his gut.

Rowan takes a fistful of each asscheek, completely encompassing each and spreading them wide, revealing his slick and waiting hole.

He retrieves the condom from the edge of the bed and tears open the package, the crinkle loud in his ears. He takes off his briefs, rolls the condom on, and rubs the tip of his cock against Mal's thigh—a quick acknowledgment that it's on— before he slicks himself with a squirt of lube. As he slides in, the tight heat that engulfs him even through the condom dulls his earlier heartache and for a split second makes him forget about it entirely.

And when Mal's back bends upward and his deep moan echoes off the walls accompanied by the metallic clinking of his cuffs, well. Rowan's right fucking there with him.

He's been inside Mal over half a dozen times by now, and each time is better than the last. It's easy to get lost in the rhythm of Mal's hips thrusting back against his own, slow at first as he adjusts to Rowan's cock, intensifying in speed and power as he opens up for him.

Rowan pauses his thrusts, basking in the feel of the heat around him for a long moment before pulling all but the tip of his cock out. Mal squirms, attempting to keep up the pace on his own.

"*Nnng, shit*...." Mal complains. "Come *on*."

"Do it yourself," Rowan tells him, widening his knees to plant himself firmly in place.

A huff is Mal's only response, earning him a quick succession of sharp spanks on both asscheeks.

"Fuck! Can't...."

"Don't give me that shit. I don't remember you being this much of a pillow princess when you had ten cocks waiting to fuck you. Mine too much to handle?"

Some unintelligible grumble comes from Mal's throat, and Rowan slaps the side of his thigh.

"What?"

"*No*." After a beat, "Not too much."

"Didn't think so. Fucking cock slut like you is made for this. Now *move*."

Mal pinches his shoulder blades together and clenches his hole in short, fluttering pulses before arching his back and crashing his ass against Rowan's hips, impaling himself fully.

"There ya go. Keep goin'."

The *slap, slap, slap* of skin and sweat and lube is deafening as Mal's speed builds, thigh and back muscles rippling with every sharp thrust.

Rowan's in fucking heaven.

But as much as Rowan likes seeing Mal work for it, he's been in control a little too long. He grips his hips like a vise, pulling him back roughly on his cock over and over until a hoarse, wet scream is ripped from Mal's throat.

"That's it.... Take my cock so fuckin' well," Rowan tells him. He spanks him roughly, not content with the redness disappearing from Mal's ass from his earlier barrage.

Alternating thrusts and spanks has a wall of heat building inside Rowan brick by brick, Mal's gasps and grunts threatening to make it come toppling down in an instant.

"N-no one…," Mal mumbles out of nowhere.

Rowan pauses his thrusts, a spike of concern dampening his lust as he dips down over Mal's back. "What?"

"*Unh*, don't stop…."

With a deep thrust, Rowan picks up a slow but forceful pace. "Tell me what you were gonna say."

A quiver runs from Mal's shoulders down to his thighs, but he stays silent save for a soft litany of moans.

"C'mon, Mal. Tell me."

"No one—*fuck*… no one fucks me like you…."

Rowan has to clamp down on the base of his dick to stop from coming immediately. *And* unexpectedly, for the second week in a row. His pride would never recover if his stamina got *worse* over time with Mal. As it is, his heart's having a hard time keeping up with the stutter step that it's beating into Rowan's ears.

"Yeah," he agrees after the near miss, fucking his full length in at a bruising pace. "And no one ever will."

He doesn't mean it to sound so possessive, but fuck if it doesn't get Mal's hole clenching deliciously around him.

Without breaking the rhythm of his hips, he unclasps Mal's hands from one another and gets in another few deep strokes until Mal's arms thud onto the bed. Only when he hears Mal's soft gasp does he pull out and flip him onto his back, sit on his haunches, and inch forward until the tip of his cock teases at Mal's hole.

They lock eyes, and Mal's chest is heaving, a faint flush on his pecs and hips that makes the black ink of his tattoos shine. He's fucking beautiful.

As Rowan slides back in, there's a palpable shift in the air that's ambrosia on his tongue, and he knows the scene isn't going to end nearly the same way it started.

"Touch yourself."

Mal grasps his red cock and starts furiously jerking off, clearly on edge and nowhere close to matching Rowan's languid rhythm.

"*Slowly.*"

"Rowan…."

"C'mon, Mal. You held out longer than this last time."

It's risky, bringing up *last time*. But fuck it, he's gonna lay all his cards bare.

"Wanna feel you when I come."

Mal's slack jaw and the way his hands forcibly slow around his cock tell Rowan his gamble paid off. As Rowan fucks in, Mal's hand pumps up, fingers flicking over the tip. Out, down, their eyes never leaving each other. It's the hottest moment of Rowan's entire life, and the sweat mussing up his hair trickles down his temple and drips onto his clavicle.

The slow pace has his toes curling underneath him, and he knows he could come from this alone. Easily. *Gladly.*

But he still wants to wreck Mal. Show him that *yeah*, no one else will ever fuck him as good as Rowan can.

He hooks Mal's legs over his elbows and lifts his lower half completely off the bed, pulling a soft "*Fuck...*" from him.

"Tell me when you're close."

It's like his hips have a mind of their own as they piston into Mal. He doesn't feel the sting of his hip bones crashing into the back of Mal's thighs or the strain in his arms or the kink that's going to develop in his neck from constantly shifting his focus between Mal's hole and cock and face.

"Fuck, fuck! Oooh *fuuuck!*"

"That's it, just like that," Rowan pants between thrusts, heat rising to boiling in his core and balls tightening.

"Gonna.... *Rowan, I—*"

"Yeah, *yeah*, come with me, Mal."

It only takes the slightest clench of Mal's hole around him to get Rowan emptying inside the condom with a groan, rhythm and composure completely shattered.

When Mal comes all over his own chest, the look on his face is nothing short of cathartic. *Relieved* in a way that Rowan can't help but think has more to do with the simple fact of having an orgasm. And when he has to bite his bottom lip to keep a grin from spreading, Rowan's chest glows golden.

WHEN ALL is said and done, they lie together on their backs, side by side on the bed. Rowan stares at the ceiling lights that bathe the room in cool white luminescence and make the gold pinstripes of the wallpaper shimmer. He lets himself catch his breath for a moment before propping himself up on one elbow, turning to Mal.

"How do you feel?"

"Mmm… good. Sore," Mal answers quietly, eyes lightly closed.

Gently, Rowan lays a hand on Mal's chest, the dip between his pecs molding perfectly to his fingers. As if he'll startle him, he lets Mal get accustomed to his hand on his skin for a moment before gliding across his body, touch little more than a whisper across his skin.

Like last week, he's afraid of making things awkward or, worse, letting his actions veer too close to romantic. But as Mal leans into his touch, all doubt flies out the window, and Rowan knows that he can't let his budding feelings for Mal get in the way of proper aftercare. Mal *needs* softness after impact play. He told Rowan that during their initial talk, and unless that need changes, Rowan's gotta do it. Even though this is the first scene they've done that has really required it, it's not exactly a hardship.

In fact, it's easy. So easy, even after the emotional sucker punch a couple of hours ago, that it should be concerning. But Mal's sticky-warm skin has completely fucked Rowan up from the inside out, and each sweep of his hand over the planes of his chest and the curve of his hips and the swell of his biceps has a million tiny cracks forming and threatening to burst Rowan at the seams.

In hushed whispers that don't even echo in the stark room, Rowan talks Mal down, by now a familiar process. Rowan's heart swells, knowing that he's done this enough times to even out Mal's breathing in a matter of minutes.

Even then, with Mal lying still beside him, Rowan doesn't stop the light touches. It feels good to be able to touch him like this—like he's wanted to for the past few weeks but has never had an excuse to. He knows how intimate this is and how much more intimate it *could be* if there was anything more to their relationship than sex. For now he lets himself have this as long as Mal will let him.

Rowan's hands wander, and he finds himself idly tracing the thick lines of the tattooed heart emblazoned with *LISA* on Mal's rib cage because it's safer than running his fingers over the skin where his actual heart lies.

"Who is she?" he asks before he can think better of it.

To his surprise, for the second time tonight, Mal sighs deeply but answers, "My mom."

"Are you close?"

Mal reaches his right arm across his stomach, hand coming to rest atop Rowan's as he presses them both to cover his tattoo. The touch is electric and far more intimate than Rowan would have believed possible for such a tiny gesture. He pulls it away before he speaks but doesn't move Rowan's hand from the spot, letting him soak up the warmth of his body through his fingertips.

"We were when I was a kid, yeah. Lost touch when I got older 'cause of a buncha bullshit." He pauses, and Rowan watches his nose wrinkle. "She died last year."

"Shit, I'm sorry, Mal."

"'S fine. Been long enough now."

"Still."

They lie in silence for a few minutes, Rowan continuously stroking whatever soft piece of skin his hands happen to land on. At this point he's not sure he can blame it on aftercare anymore, but Mal hasn't said or done anything to stop him.

He thinks about his own mother. His own messed-up relationship with her. After what Mal shared, Rowan wants to give *something* of himself back, even if it isn't the whole picture.

Before he knows it, he's speaking.

"Mine was a mess. Bailed when we were little and left my older sister and brother to take care of us all. Then showed back up every once in a while like nothin' happened. Tried to be a perfect mom for however long whatever pills she was taking that day let her."

"Sucks, man. She still doin' that?"

"She died a few years back."

"That's rough," Mal says, as if his own hadn't passed far more recently. "Sorry to hear."

Rowan shrugs. "Brain finally gave out on her."

"Drugs?"

"Sorta. She uh…." *Don't tell him. What if he figures it out? It's been a rocky week, but tonight has completely turned things around… kind of. Don't tell him don't tell him don't tell him*—"She had pretty severe depression. Never really took her meds regularly 'cause they made her a zombie. Took just about everything else, though."

He waits for Mal to say something. Some remark that will tell Rowan how he feels about the whole thing. A trial run that he hadn't even planned on. A soft opening. The one good thing about his penchant for blurting shit out is that it'll help to gauge Mal's reaction and determine whether Rowan ever tells him that he's just like her. Well. Not *just*, but close enough.

It's like the air has all been sucked out of the room and shoved into Rowan's lungs, filling him up and waiting to burst out.

But mercifully—

"Genetics fuckin' blow, man."

Rowan exhales for what feels like a full minute as relief washes over him. For now it's enough. Enough to suggest that *maybe* Rowan can tell him about his condition one day without fear of being outright rejected or looked at completely differently. A pleasant warmth settles into his belly where before there had been nothing but permafrost.

Mal climbs off the bed, and Rowan thinks he's going to get ready to pack up, but he slips on his briefs, tosses Rowan his own, and climbs back on the bed.

He sits with his legs crossed, knees high and arms perched on top. Gold eyes train on Rowan as he sits up and shimmies into his own underwear. They don't bother to put on anything else.

"What'd you think?" Mal asks him after a long moment of nothing but a soft stare at Rowan.

"About the scene?"

"Yeah."

The question catches him off guard, something that seems to be happening a lot lately with Mal. It stings a bit too, Rowan's mind wandering down a rabbit hole of questioning why Mal's talking to him about this now and not at the diner like they've done every other time. After how much Mal's already opened up to him tonight, Rowan would be nothing short of devastated if their trips to Sheila's came to an abrupt end. Truthfully, he sees the diner dates as a part of his own aftercare as well as Mal's.

"It was good." He pauses, gathering his thoughts, willing his mouth not to say it was worse—even if only a tiny bit—for having to use condoms. "Different" he settles on. And because he doesn't want Mal to think the worst, he tacks on, "It was hot as hell seeing you like that."

"Got pretty into it yourself," Mal notes. "You ever done that before?"

"Not anything long like that. Just a bit with… y'know, hookups."

He forces himself to meet Mal's eyes after he says it, catching the tail end of a wince from him. The tiniest scrunch of his eyebrows, but it's the only sign tonight that Mal has shown recognition of his other exploits. Or maybe it's for some other reason entirely—Rowan's having a hard fucking time reading Mal tonight.

"Was good. First time, most people don't know how hard to go. Or how long."

Rowan tosses him a smirk. "Thought you'd know by now that I'm not most people."

The corners of Mal's lips pull back into a closed-mouth smile. "Yeah. Figured you'd remind me, Narcissus."

"Oh, fuck off." Rowan laughs, leaning over and shoving at Mal's knee. "I have a text from you from last week declaring yourself the World's Best Bottom."

"Don't even tell me it ain't true. People would commit crimes for my ass."

Rowan doesn't doubt it. Some days he feels like he'd commit a felony for the chance to see Mal outside of the club or diner. To have him visit him at work or go out for a drink outside their normal meetups.

But he rolls his eyes to keep the mood light. "Do you have aloe or something for your world-famous ass?"

"Why, you offerin' to give me a rubdown?"

"Think I just did. I did bring some in my car, though, if you actually need any."

Mal's face softens for a beat before settling on something that looks a little too fond, making Rowan glad he mentioned it.

"I'm good. Got some at home." He eyes Rowan's hands where they're splayed on his lap. "Need some for your hands?" he jokes.

Rowan laughs. "Nah. You've got a peach of an ass. Was like spanking a cushion."

"*Tch*. You say that like it's an insult, Campbell."

"Just the opposite, Savaryn."

THEY TALK for nearly two hours, by Rowan's estimate. About the scene, about the shibari class, about possibilities for future meetups. The occasional sprinkling of other nonsexual topics. It's only when Rowan checks his phone to make sure they haven't gone over their time limit that he sees they've only got twenty minutes till midnight.

"You still up for a diner run?" Rowan asks. "It's pretty late."

"Yeah, I'm fuckin' starving. And I told Sheils I'd get you to eat something besides rabbit food one'a these days."

There's a flutter in Rowan's chest at the thought of Mal mentioning him to Sheila, even as he says, "You're one to talk, Bugs."

"The fuck's that supposed to mean?"

"Your little bunny teeth." He bites his lip teasingly with his top teeth.

Mal kicks him off the bed, but before Rowan stumbles off to his feet, he catches him smiling, his front teeth digging into his bottom lip in a much more adorable and genuine way than Rowan had demonstrated.

"I saw that!" Rowan laughs.

"You didn't see shit, Doc. Put those fuckin' gray sweatpants on and let's roll."

AT MAL'S *gentle* nudging, Rowan orders a bacon cheeseburger with waffle fries but draws the line at the chocolate milkshake that Mal adds to his own order.

Mal heads to their usual booth, and Rowan surreptitiously orders a piece of carrot cake for them to share while they wait for their food. Sheila smiles knowingly and slides the plate across the counter to him, along with two forks.

"Jesus…," Mal huffs when Rowan places the slice of cake on the table, complete with a layer of white frosting topped with an orange-and-green carrot.

But he grabs a fork before Rowan has even fully sat down in the booth, stabbing it straight through the center of the carrot and taking a chunk out of the side. He shoves it fully in his mouth, cheek bulged out to the side as he chews. It's cute, and Rowan knows he shouldn't find it cute that the same mouth that licked his own precome off of him is struggling to contain a sweet dessert, but he does.

Rowan digs in with his own fork, and the cake melts on his tongue. Sheila really is a culinary genius.

He and Mal go for another forkful at the same time, and Rowan quips, "Looks like I got *you* to eat rabbit food this time."

Mal stabs him with his fork, the tines leaving four white dots on his hand that disappear before Rowan's laugh fades from his lips.

WHEN THEIR food arrives a short while later, Rowan has to admit that the burger looks and smells delicious. He squirts a large pile of ketchup on his plate, watching in horror as Mal squirts zigzags of ketchup directly on top of his fries.

"You're such a barbarian," Rowan comments.

"All goes to the same place, Red. More efficient this way."

They eat in relative silence, save for the occasional jab at how the other is eating despite there being no classy way to eat the greasy, messy burgers. All the same, Rowan watches with rapt attention every time Mal's tongue darts out to collect a bit of sauce from his lips.

It feels weird to be at the diner and sharing a meal when they've already discussed their scene. Every other time that's been more or less the main reason to come here—to wind down and hash out anything that didn't work and figure out what did, all while getting some much-needed calories back. And while they've gotten considerably more comfortable with having regular conversations that don't revolve *entirely* around sex, thanks to their frequent texting, in-person is still a different story.

But it isn't awkward by any stretch. Rowan thinks that Mal might actually be the easiest person to talk to he knows, aside from Jay.

As they eat they toss back snippets of conversation. Mal snatches some of Rowan's fries off his plate even though he still has plenty of his own. In turn, Rowan scoops up the tomatoes that Mal picked off of his burger and left on the side of *his* plate.

The meal and the atmosphere and—most importantly—the company are soothing in a way that fills all the spaces in Rowan's body and mind. There's a soft rock song playing on the jukebox that Rowan doesn't recognize until he hears Mal softly humming the chorus.

Ah, "Summer Breeze." He's not even sure Mal knows he's doing it until his eyes meet Rowan's over Mal's chocolate milkshake. And Rowan knows he's smiling like an idiot—can feel his cheeks start to hurt from it. Quickly, Mal clears his throat and wipes his already-clean mouth with the back of his hand.

The display is enough to make some deeply buried part of Rowan awaken and long for something he never thought he'd get to have.

Someone to come home to, someone to cook with, someone to wrap his arms around at night. Something that goes beyond the shallow things he's called relationships in the past. A life. A *love*. And fuck, Rowan wants it. It isn't clear how long he daydreams of it, but the song has changed at least twice by the time the bus girl drops off the check at the table.

"I'll get the bill," Rowan says when Mal goes to grab the slip. "You paid two times in a row a couple weeks ago."

Rowan's half standing and about to slip out of the booth to pay when Mal's quiet voice stops him.

"She wanted to name me William," Mal says, apropos of nothing, that same distant look in his eyes from earlier in the evening threatening to bore a hole through his plate. As if sensing Rowan's confusion without even looking up, he adds, "My mom."

"Oh."

He hums absentmindedly, eyebrows raising as if he'd suddenly realized that he'd blurted out something inappropriate. When he looks up at Rowan, his expression melts from worried to neutral, apparently seeing no judgment or shock on Rowan's own face as he sits fully back down in the booth.

"How did she settle on Malcolm, then?"

"She didn't," Mal scoffs. "My old man did. Larry."

It's the first time Mal's mentioned anything about his father since all those weeks ago when Sheila hinted that he wasn't exactly an upstanding citizen. Something about not judging someone for the sins of their father, she had said. Rowan waits, sensing that Mal has more to say.

"She came home with a blank birth certificate. Course Larry wasn't at the hospital. Mom said she liked William, and that they could call me Billy for short. Larry said he wasn't gonna have a son with a bitch name. Said everyone would call me *Willy*, and that his son wouldn't be a fag." He pauses momentarily to shake his head. "Plot-fuckin'-twist, I would'a been one no matter what they called me. But Malcolm was the name of some dead relative or whatever, and he thought it sounded tough, so he made her write that."

"And *Larry* isn't a bitch name?" Rowan jokes, attempting to lighten the mood. Though he files away Mal's father's name in the back of his mind in case it ever comes up again.

Another snort from Mal, but he continues talking, easily the most he's spoken in a single sitting. "He was a fuckin' idiot."

Something about the vulnerable half confession makes Rowan want to push, a lingering question in the back of his mind from weeks ago left unanswered by Mal's story. "So how does using your full name at the club come into play?" Rowan asks, dots still not quite connecting.

"Kind of a… fuck you to him, I guess," Mal tells him after a minute of semiawkward silence.

Maybe it's the familiarity of the diner that gives Mal the courage, or maybe it's the way he'd opened up about his mom, or maybe it's something he's been holding back for so long that the dam had to burst at *some point*, and Rowan's the unknowing recipient of it.

"Felt like retribution or some shit… goin' by my full name at the club. Like he'd have a fuckin' meltdown if he knew his favorite son was gettin' railed by a bunch of dudes who all only knew him as Malcolm. Just kinda stuck with it after that."

His *favorite* son. Meaning Mal has brothers at least. The jury is still out on sisters with shitty boyfriends. Rowan wants to ask but doesn't dare push his luck *too* far. Not when Mal's actually opening up about himself.

Whatever the case, Rowan chooses his words carefully. "The first time we came here, Sheila kind of implied that he's a dick."

Mal snorts, quickly covering it up by chugging the last of his water. "Piece'a shit's more like it."

"Mine was the same," Rowan confides, bolstered by the knowledge that all of their parents were terrible.

"Yours was an abusive racist homophobe?" Mal shoots back, brows flat.

Rowan's face reddens. "Oh… uh, no. Just a regular old drunk and liar and thief. Sorry. Sucks."

"Yeah, well…. He croaked a few years back. Rest in fuckin' pieces."

He knows deadbeat dads aren't exactly a rarity, but the fact that Mal seems to share the same sentiment about his dad as Rowan does about his own is weirdly comforting.

"You ever actually tell him?"

"What, that I was willingly gettin' gangbanged on the regular?" Mal's eyebrows practically hit the ceiling. "*Fuck no*, man. Homophobe or not, that's the kinda shit you don't tell your parents."

"*Jesus*, obviously not." Rowan shudders at the thought, but in reality, he thinks both his parents wouldn't bat an eye if he told them about any of his sexual exploits. "I meant that you're gay."

Mal sniffs and looks to the side, avoidant. But "Yeah."

When he doesn't add anything more to it, Rowan hedges, "Didn't go well, I'm guessing?"

"Fuckin' understatement...."

Again, Rowan thinks he isn't going to keep talking on his own, but he's not sure if this is something he should let lie, or if he should let his curiosity win out and push for more detail. But even if he doesn't share anything else, Rowan can piece the picture together himself. Homophobic, violent dad finds out his favorite son is gay? Pretty much a recipe for some bad shit. He's thankful that even for how shitty his own parents were in their own ways, they never made him feel ashamed of who he is.

Shockingly, Mal *does* continue, after a long bout of silence. "Beat the shit outta me for it. Was fuckin'... seventeen maybe? Told me before I became a *man*, I had to come on a *fag-bashing* run. Like it was a fuckin' normal family tradition."

"What, just pick any gay guy you see and beat him up?"

Mal pauses, taking a deep breath before continuing. "Some new family moved in, couple blocks from us. Larry somehow found out the kid was gay, or he prob'ly fuckin' assumed he was for whatever reason. Couldn't'a been more than, like, *fourteen* for fuck's sake. Told him I wouldn't do it, and he called me a pussy and demanded to know why."

"Shit," Rowan says, stunned. "A fuckin' *kid*?"

"Yeah. I fuckin'... lost it. Told him he was a fuckin' psycho and that if he wanted to bash a fag so bad, he'd have to start with me."

Rowan's eyes widen, quickly followed by a rush of sadness, pride, and fear mixed all together in an ugly cocktail that makes Rowan's stomach lurch.

"Jesus."

"Mmm. Got a few good ones in on him at least."

At least. As if a few punches were worth whatever hell Larry put him through both before and after Mal's confession. Even though he's still practically a fucking *stranger*, that instinct to want to protect him—even retroactively—surges up and makes Rowan's fingers shake.

"I'm so fuckin' sorry, Mal."

Mal simply rolls his eyes, but not unkindly. "It's fine, Dr. Phil. Was a long time ago, and I've already been to therapy and shit for it. 'M good."

The therapy comment surprises Rowan, but pleasantly so. When he thinks about it for a moment longer, though, it makes sense. Mal seems remarkably levelheaded in the way that only working through your childhood traumas with a professional can achieve.

"HAVE ANY plans this week?" Rowan asks idly on their walk back.

There's a warm breeze drifting between them, and the stars are out in full force, the sprinkling of dim lights as bright as they can be in the light-polluted Boston sky.

Mal quips, "Yeah, icing my damn ass."

"Oh, fuck you! You asked for it."

"Got a bag of peas callin' my name."

"I'll bet you twenty bucks you don't actually have a single vegetable in your house, Bunnicula."

"You're one to talk, Casper. Do *you* got anything that comes in a box or can?"

"Think I have some bags of mixed nuts layin' around."

"*You're* a bag of nuts."

If only Mal knew how close to the truth that statement actually was, he might not be joking around with Rowan like this.

"Great comeback. I see your talent stops with numbers, Shakespeare."

"Shakespeare was a douchebag," Mal states definitively, like he knew the guy personally, and he went to the grave owing Mal money.

"What could possibly make you think that?"

"Anyone who wears frilly collars and leggings is a douchebag in my book."

"So everyone in the sixteenth century, then?"

Mal snorts in agreement.

"And besides," Rowan continues. "Pretty sure all your jeans *are* leggings with how fuckin' tight they are."

"Can't deny they look good, though."

"Got me there."

Mal stuffs his hands in his pockets, and Rowan idly wonders if he's cold in only his joggers and tank top.

"You?" Mal asks.

"Me what?"

Rowan doesn't have to turn his head to see Mal's eye roll. "Plans?"

He chooses to not acknowledge that Mal didn't *actually* tell him if he had real plans or not.

"Working. Seven to three every day."

"What, no one's allowed to get hurt outside those hours?"

Huffing a laugh, Rowan says, "Nah, if they do, they're fucked."

"Some paramedic you are." Mal shoves him gently in the arm, making Rowan stagger a foot away before bouncing back with his own light push.

"I'm fantastic at my job, dick."

"Fantastic dick, that's for sure."

Rowan laughs again but takes the rare compliment. "Going to babysit my brother's two kids on Thursday too. Caleb and Jacob."

"How old?"

"He's a year older than me."

"Wh—no, the fuckin' *kids*. Jesus, Red."

Rowan's face turns about as bright as the nickname.

"Right. Uh, Caleb is three, and Jacob just turned one."

"Sounds like a fucking nightmare."

"I love 'em. They're cute as hell at that age. How 'bout I send you a pic of us?"

Mal's quiet, mouth snapping shut from whatever reply he'd been about to make. Like maybe he realizes at the same time as Rowan does that that's toeing a line that they'd agreed to set in stone at the beginning of their sexual relationship. Even after opening up somewhat about their pasts tonight, it's still another step closer to that line.

"The fuck would I want a pic of your ugly mug for, huh?" Mal says eventually, but it's soft.

"Could send you a dick pic instead," Rowan offers, trying to lighten the suddenly tense mood.

"That's more like it."

By the time Rowan looks up to catch Mal's profile against the yellow streetlights, they've reached their destination. And this time Rowan hesitates. Every other week, there's been a clear decorum dictating how they should separate—a wave, a chaste *see ya*. Last time, a one-sided hug.

But for the umpteenth time tonight, Mal surprises him by dipping into a quick side hug that has every nerve on Rowan's right side lighting up before he's across the street and shouting, "See ya next week, Firecrotch."

As far as partings go, this one is much better than the last, but somehow it feels much worse.

As Rowan lies in bed that night at nearly 2:00 a.m., once again staring at the blank expanse of his ceiling, he doesn't know what to think about anything. Mal's attitude toward him has been a fucking roller coaster this past week. Crawling up, spiraling down, and throwing Rowan for one loop after another. He only hopes that Mal opening up to him tonight means that he's started to trust him with *more* than his body.

Though that trust apparently comes at the *cost* of his body. The new physical barriers that they need to have in place for the foreseeable future is an unfortunate price to pay for getting closer to Mal, though it's one Rowan's almost glad to pay.

But what keeps him awake long into the night is wondering if he'll ever get to have both simultaneously. Eventually he falls into a deep sleep, dreaming of jasmine petals fluttering in the wind.

Chapter 8: The Shape of You

The rest of the weekend and into Monday passes by in a blur. Rowan feels like he's on cloud nine, not quite believing how much Mal had opened up to him on Saturday. There are still plenty of questions rattling around in his head, but he feels a sense of peace that he hasn't since they started their arrangement. A sense that they're actually *something* to each other—enough of something to share a portion of their pasts.

With that peace, though, comes a profound sense of want. What started as a fleeting thought at the diner a few days ago has blossomed into a full-blown rom-com style longing.

He selfishly thinks of all the things he wants to say to Mal. *Once a week isn't enough. I wanna see you more. Talk to you more. What if I upgraded my membership? You're worth the money. Or what if we saw each other outside the club? Would that be so bad? I promise I won't cross any lines.*

Even as he thinks it, though, he knows that he couldn't keep that promise if he were ever really tested. It makes him sweat, thinking about how Mal might react to all of it.

On Tuesday, Rowan is stuck washing the rig with Addison. It's hot as hell outside, and Rowan has shucked off his uniform shirt in favor of the plain white tank top he wears underneath. Even so, with the physical exertion of soaping and scrubbing the outside of the ambulance alongside the harsh sun beating down on him, he's sweating profusely.

Addison is faring better, somehow managing to get away with only a thin sheen on her forehead, though her wild, curly brown hair is suffering from the humidity.

They've only had one call today, to help an old woman who was suffering heat exhaustion during an ill-advised walk in the park. The rest of the Back Bay, it seems, had the good thought to stay home in the air conditioning. Rowan has to wipe the sweat from his brow repeatedly, wishing that he, too, could be home in the cool air.

"This sucks," Addison remarks for the tenth time in as many minutes.

"Yeah," Rowan replies, spraying his hands with water from the hose and cooling off the back of his neck. "Gotta keep the boss lady happy, though."

Addison snorts and scrubs the soapy sponge around the back doors.

Rowan finds himself getting lost in the motions, the monotonous physical labor letting him slip into a daydream of ink and lace. The memories of Mal whining his name as Rowan fucks him or spanks him or gags him flood through him, making his head spin and his cock give an inappropriate throb in his slacks. He recalls every one of their sessions these past couple months, marveling at how good they've gotten at taking each other apart. How well they *fit*.

The only thought that overshadows everything they've done is everything they haven't. Rowan desperately wants to feel Mal's lips on his own. For *real* this time. He wants to wrap his hands around Mal's throat—more than merely a gentle graze of fingertips as he's done countless times—and watch his eyes roll back. He wants to hear him scream until he's hoarse and feel him whimper his name against the crook of his neck. He wants to leave bruises on his hips and bite marks on his chest and fingerprints on his thighs. See his skin blossom with pinks and reds and purples that will linger for days and weeks to come. So anyone else Mal fucks will see that he's been with someone who knows how to take him apart better than they ever could.

He wants *so goddamn much*, and he knows he's being unrealistic. But the thoughts flow through him like a tsunami—the more he tries not to think about it, the more the waters recede until inevitably, they rear up and come crashing down onto him in one giant, unyielding wave.

It's been happening all too often the past couple of months, and Rowan's constantly on the verge of drowning in the torrent that is Mal Savaryn.

The hazy waves of heat simmering on the pavement make him think he's hallucinating when the object of his daydream appears on the horizon like a mirage. But rather than fade into nothing, Mal's form gets sharper and more defined the closer he gets. Rowan sputters, utterly flabbergasted, and it isn't until he hears Addison's disgruntled shriek of "Hey!" that he realizes he's sprayed her right in the face with the hose.

Mal's stride is purposeful, and it draws Rowan's gaze away from his coworker.

"Holy *shit*, is that the guy?" Addison asks, suddenly and excitedly whispering in Rowan's ear.

"Jesus," Rowan gasps, taking half a step away as he feels a spray of water droplets hit his bare shoulder as Addison wipes off her face. He doesn't know if it's the way he's frozen in place or the way he's gawking that tells Addison who it is, having never given her any physical description of Mal. Maybe she's *that* good at her job and can sense his heart hammering in his chest.

"The guy I'm *fucking*, yeah."

"Damn. Congrats, Rowan.... I don't know which one of you is hotter."

Rowan does.

Addison's ogling is wildly apparent, even though Rowan isn't looking at her. "What's he doing here?" she asks.

"No clue," Rowan says, finally dropping the hose and wiping his wet hands on his pants.

With a still-wildly fluttering heart, Rowan realizes this is the first time he's seen Mal in the daylight. And *fuck*, his eyes are impossibly gold. Honey and caramel and all sorts of other things coming to mind. He remembers seeing them for the first time at the gangbang—finding the color so vibrant even in the dimness of the club. But in the sunlight, they *shine*. He's dressed mostly the same as he always is—tight black jeans and a maroon shirt that has Rowan staring as much as Addison has been, though this is far from the first time he's seen him.

"Hey," Mal greets, casual as ever, as if he hadn't shown up unannounced to Rowan's work.

"What're you doing here?"

Mal rolls his eyes. "Nice to see you too."

"Uh, this is Addison. My coworker," Rowan says, gesturing to the woman on his left and nearly hitting her in the shoulder as he does.

"Nice to meet you…?"

"Hey. Mal."

"I'm gonna go—" Addison starts, thumbing vaguely in the direction behind her.

"See ya," Rowan cuts her off, thankful that she didn't ask to hang around. But as she leaves, the realization that Mal has met, however briefly, someone in Rowan's life outside of the club rattles around in his brain.

When Addison disappears into the station, Rowan asks, "How'd you know where I work?"

"Only one station this side of town."

"Gotcha."

There's a beat of silence, the two of them taking in each other's appearance as if they're seeing each other for the first time.

"Here," Mal says, handing him a large brown paper bag, the top folded over neatly, concealing the contents.

Rowan's eyebrows knit together as he takes the bag, opens it and peeks inside, instantly snapping it shut when he sees the rope Mal promised he'd bring him, two bundles of neatly coiled black hemp.

"Oh, thanks. You didn't need to come all the way here, though. Could've waited till Saturday."

Mal bites his lip. "Yeah, well. Said I'd give it to ya. Practice on yourself if you want, just not on anyone else." He says it like it's the most obvious thing in the world, but Rowan doesn't miss the slight apprehension in his voice or the way he glances quickly to the ground. Scuffles his shoe a bit.

"What do you mean 'anyone else'?"

"Anyone else you sleep with."

"Mal, I'm not sleeping with anyone else."

He makes sure to mirror Mal's wording and not say "seeing" someone else. Because he and Mal aren't. Seeing each other, that is. But they are. Sleeping with each other, that is. They're just fuckin'.

For a brief moment, Mal looks quietly pleased, but says, "You could, though."

Rowan shrugs. "So can you."

So did *you*, he thinks. It's on the tip of his tongue, almost tumbling out of his mouth, but some part of his brain stops him. The part that had reined him in when Mal pulled out the box of condoms last week. The part that wants to not fucking blow this before he even has a chance to see if it's gonna go anywhere.

"Yeah...."

His discomfort is palpable, and Rowan tries not to let the little burst of smugness in his chest take root. He quickly changes the subject for both their sakes.

"Are you on lunch break right now?"

"Yeah. You hungry?"

Rowan grins. "Always."

ROWAN QUICKLY makes his way into the break room to grab his wallet and phone out of his locker and tucks Mal's rope safely at the bottom of his backpack.

"Gonna take lunch now," he announces, slamming the metal door shut. "Be back in an hour."

"*Just* fucking, huh?" Addison quips, mischievous twinkle in her eye.

Rowan flips her off as he retreats, but his face still burns hotter than the midday sun.

THEY WALK to a café five minutes away, the sun beating down so hard that it keeps them mostly quiet to avoid expending any unnecessary energy.

As they enter the blissfully air-conditioned café, Rowan instantly dislikes it. It's modernly decorated with quirky succulents and inoffensive, bland artwork on the tables and walls. Everything is painted in muted neutrals that wash the whole place out and give nothing interesting to focus on. There's none of the retro coziness that he's come to associate with Sheila's diner across town, but it smells like basil and freshly baked bread, and he thinks it'll be okay.

They find a table for two in the corner of the café, a mercifully secluded spot in an otherwise pretty busy restaurant. Less than a minute later, an overly chipper waitress pops by their table and hands them two laminated menus, then gives them a few minutes to look them over. Despite the bougie feeling of the café, Rowan has to admit that all the dishes look delicious. Over half the menu is vegan or vegetarian, and from the numerous pictures, everything is loaded with fresh-looking veggies.

"Jesus, they got any actual food here?" Mal grumbles as he surveys his own menu.

Rowan laughs. "How have you survived this long?"

"Fuck off, Red. I'm healthy as a clam."

Lips pulling back into a small smile, Rowan resists the urge to once again correct Mal's idiom in favor of teasing.

"Oh, I know. I'm plenty familiar with your stamina."

And your six pack, he thinks. *And muscular thighs and sharp hip bones and firm biceps and tight ass and....*

"Ready to order?" the waitress asks, breaking Rowan out of his thoughts by placing two glasses of water in front of them.

Rowan orders a turkey-bacon and avocado wrap, which makes Mal scoff a little and mutter "Hipster..." under his breath.

Shockingly, Mal orders a salad. A buffalo chicken salad smothered in bleu cheese dressing, but there's at least some green on his plate. Rowan wants to think he's having some kind of positive effect on him.

With a smile, Rowan orders a piece of strawberry cheesecake for them to share.

"Your eyes are so fuckin' green," Mal says after a beat of silence.

"Uh, thanks?"

"Don't mean to be a little bitch, just... never seen 'em in the sunlight before, yanno?"

Yeah. Rowan *knows*.

"Was thinking the same about yours earlier," Rowan confesses, butterflies burrowing into his belly.

It all feels a little too much like a high school date for Rowan's liking. Not that he ever really *went* on any of those when he was that age, his love life limited to risky hookups with the few gay or questioning guys behind the bleachers in high school.

While Rowan's been thinking of their visits to Sheila's diner as dates for a while, it's really only been a placeholder word in his mind. A stand-in for "a fundamental way to refill their depleted energy levels" and "a part of their mutual aftercare sessions." But now... neither of those options is a viable excuse. It's simply the two of them choosing each other's company over being alone.

When their food comes, Rowan's stomach gives a demanding growl.

"Can't believe you eat this shit regularly," Mal grumbles, food stuffed to one side of his cheek as he chews a bite of his salad.

"Literally no one is making you eat salad, Mal."

"Didn't wanna deal with your judgy ass stare if I got a cheeseburger."

Rowan huffs an incredulous laugh. "Why the hell would I judge you? And since when do you *care*?"

"I *don't* care, Firecrotch."

It's the least believable lie Mal's ever told. Still, Rowan finds it cute that Mal values his opinion enough to try to eat healthier.

"'Sides…," Rowan muses, plucking a crouton out of his wrap and crunching it. "You look good stuffing your mouth with meat."

Mal chokes on a bite of salad, a tiny spray of dressing dusting the table between them.

"Jesus Christ…," he mutters, pawing at the mess with a handful of napkins.

"Wow, didn't think that'd be enough to get a reaction outta you." Rowan laughs, helping Mal move glasses and condiment dispensers to clean between them.

"Fuck you, man."

But his clipped tone is betrayed by the small smile Rowan can see playing out on his lips, pink and soft-looking in the early afternoon light.

Mal sucks his fork clean, jabs it straight into the strawberry cheesecake, and takes a big bite, spurning his earlier green-eating attempts in favor of a delicious dessert. It's a little mind-boggling how comfortable he and Rowan have gotten with swapping bodily fluids when they've never even properly kissed.

Rowan can only laugh, set aside his own *actual* food, and dig into dessert alongside Mal.

ROWAN'S FUCKING horny. Ever since he had lunch with Mal two days ago, he hasn't been able to stop thinking about him. He won't lie, he *is* satisfied with hooking up with Mal once a week, but fuck if he doesn't want more. At this point, he's not even interested in hooking up with anyone else. He wants more Mal. Always more Mal.

His cock throbs in his briefs, and goddamn, it's only been a couple of days since he saw him and a couple of hours since he last texted him, but that itch is back that only Mal seems to be able to scratch.

Before he knows it, he's got one hand down his pants petting at the soft red curls above his cock and the other typing out a message to Mal.

[RC] *Can I send you sth?*

[MS] *assume it's somethin dirty if you're askin permission*

[RC] *Yeah*

[MS] *better be good campbell*

He sucks in a shuddering breath, shucking down his sweats and briefs and finally getting a hand around himself. The steady pulse of his cock in his hand is the only thing dulling his rapid heartbeat as he spreads his thighs and tightens his core and snaps a few photos.

Rowan's never been good at selfies, but goddamn if he can't take a killer dick pic. He sends the best to Mal, his cock flushed and dwarfing even his large hands.

[MS] *fuck man*

[MS] *what the hell you been fantasizing about that's got you that hard*

[RC] *You*

Fuck, backtrack, backtrack, backtr—

[RC] *In the harness the other day*

[RC] *Was hot as fuck*

But… would it really be so bad? If he leaned into it a little? This casual flirting thing they've had going on since the start really has only grown the longer they've known each other.

[MS] *oh yeah?*

[RC] *Yeah. Been practicing with the rope you gave me*

[RC] *Think we can start using it soon if you're cool with it*

[MS] *if it gets you goin like that then hell yeah let's do next week*

Rowan has to grip the base of his cock to avoid an embarrassingly early finish from the barest of touches and the thought of tying Mal for real.

[RC] *Been wanting to tie your legs. Get you spreadeagled for me*

[MS] *fuck yeah*

[MS] *love that shit*

The heat swirls in Rowan's belly. Coils low as he pumps himself to images of Mal tied up and completely exposed for him. Pink hole twitching under Rowan's lips and tongue and fingers. Hard cock leaking and face flushed and muscles straining.

God, Mal gets him going like nothing else.

Rowan's lost to the sensation of his hand around himself when he feels more than hears the *bzz, bzz* of his phone.

[MS] *img03450.jpg*

One hand fumbling to unlock his phone, Rowan nearly doubles over when he sees what Mal sent him.

He's kneeling on the bed, photo taken from behind with his thighs spread, cock hanging heavy between his legs, and his two middle fingers shoved deep inside his hole. The *H* and *U* of his THUG tattoo completely hidden from view, replaced only with the shimmery sheen of lube.

[RC] *Holy fuck Mal*

[MS] *thought you'd like that*

[RC] *Wanna be in you so bad*

[RC] *Look so fuckin good*

[MS] *couple more days*

[MS] *gotta deal with those big hands of yours till then*

[RC] *Such a fucking tease*

But despite his light response, Rowan is thinking *I don't wanna wait. I wanna see you now. Touch you now. Show you how fucking bad I want you all the time.* Rowan's body is on fire, curling in on itself as he works his cock, with Mal's photo nearly scorching his retinas. But fuck if he isn't gonna drink in every gorgeous detail of it. The messy white bedsheets. The softness of his skin. The corded ropes of his muscles. The mosaic of his tattoos. The—

Bzz, bzz.

[MS] *img03451.jpg img03454.jpg*

His phone's never been slower loading the images, but when it finally does, an excruciating three seconds later, he's treated to the sight of Mal sinking down onto a long thick dildo. The first pic with the pink tip kissing his hole, and the second with him fully seated down to the realistic balls at the base.

Don't want you to fuck anyone else. Just me. Just me just me just me.

[MS] *i gotta make do too*

[MS] *silicone can't fill me up the way you do*

The pain of clenching down around himself sears through his lower body, but it's dulled by the thrumming underneath his skin.

[RC] *Jesus that almost made me cum*

[MS] *good*

[MS] *want ya to*

[MS] *get off thinkin bout me*

[RC] *Send me more*

[MS] *mov00439.mp4*

The position's different. This time Mal's on all fours with his ass facing the big wooden headboard. Fucking himself hard and fast back onto the dildo now suction cupped onto it. Curving spine bowing and dipping with his movements that has the heat and breath in Rowan's chest rising and falling with each one.

Fuuuck.

[RC] *You're so fuckin hot holy shit*

[RC] *Fuck yourself faster for me*

[RC] *Wanna be able to hear that headboard cracking against the wall from here*

This time, there's no response, Mal apparently lost in his own world of pleasure. Rowan returns the favor nonetheless, stomach tight but giddy as he films his fist flying over his pink cock, barely able to show any finesse or skill in his desperation to finish the video.

He barely has to open Mal's video again and scrub to somewhere near the end before he hears the faintest muffled whimper of "Rowan…," and he's tumbling over the edge to oblivion.

And when Rowan comes, it's with Mal's name pulled from his lips.

Breaths still not yet evened out, he sends the video and a photo of the trail of come streaked from his cock to his chest to Mal. A testament to what he does to him and a glimpse of what he's been missing while they're forced to wear condoms.

Two minutes later, he gets one of Mal's own spent cock and come pooled in the sheets beneath.

[MS] *think you just made me see god red*

[MS] *christ*

[MS] *send more of that shit next time*

[RC] *Hell yeah*

Five minutes after that, Mal sends a pic of the dent in the wall from his headboard.

As June melts into July, Mal finally gives Rowan the all-clear to start barebacking again. The first thing he does is get his tongue in Mal's hole and his mouth around his cock, the musky taste of him sweetened by the fact that, for now, Mal doesn't seem to be sleeping with anyone else again.

And when he presses into him bare for the first time in over a month, he doesn't even care that he lasts half as long as he normally does.

With the way Mal mewls and clenches around him and comes only a heartbeat after Rowan fills him, he doesn't seem to care either.

THE FIRST week in August has the heat rising to sweltering even in the late evening, and Rowan is thankful for the cool air inside Sheila's diner. By now, Rowan has had every dish on the menu—and some off, thanks to Mal's connection with Sheila. He decides his favorites are the turkey burger and the tomato soup with grilled cheese.

"So, uh…," Mal starts, breaking their otherwise quiet meal. He fiddles with his milkshake straw until Rowan meets his eyes. "'S my birthday next weekend."

Rowan's ears perk up. "Oh yeah?"

"Mmm."

For a moment, Rowan's heart sinks, but he asks, "So do we need to skip next week?"

"Yeah, but…. Was gonna see if you wanted to come out."

"Out?"

"Goin' to a bar with Camilla, Clover, and Jeremiah."

There's a swelling in Rowan's chest that should absolutely concern him.

"Yeah, I'd love to."

Somehow, his voice remains unaffected despite the rushing in his ears.

"Cool, I'll text you the details."

Rowan grins and snags Mal's milkshake to take a quick sip, the cold liquid on his tongue doing nothing to quell the heat simmering in his veins.

THE REST of the week, Rowan agonizes over whether to get Mal a birthday present. It wouldn't be weird, he thinks. They're friends. With benefits, sure, but Rowan's comfortable saying that even if they don't really hang out outside of the club, he considers Mal a friend. Probably his best friend if he's being honest. Which says as much about their relationship and how well they get along as it does about Rowan's lack of a social circle.

He lays back in bed, scrolling absentmindedly through Amazon, finding nothing but cheap junk he thinks Mal would scoff at. It isn't until he gives up and Googles *birthday gift for fuck buddy* that he finds a site that makes his eyes light up.

Perfect.

THE SATURDAY of Mal's birthday rolls around, and Rowan has never taken longer getting ready in his life. He feels like a teenager going to prom, primping and pruning and going through his entire wardrobe to find the perfect outfit.

Eventually, he settles on gray semiformal slacks with a black button-up and his casual oxford shoes. The address that Mal had texted him was for a club in Cambridge that Rowan's never heard of, but from the photos online looks fairly upscale. It's a little surprising, given Mal's penchant for shitty beer and small-town diners, but he has a feeling it wasn't Mal who made the final choice.

He spends what feels like ages getting a perfectly smooth shave and taming his hair for the humid night. With nearly half an hour to spare and a tornado ravaging his insides, Rowan sets his GPS and heads for the club.

He arrives at the same time as Jeremiah, Camilla, and Clover, and when he sees them in the foyer, he's glad he put so much effort into his appearance. For all Rowan's self-confidence, this group is unnaturally beautiful and dressed to the nines.

If Rowan didn't know that Clover and Camilla were twins, he'd never have guessed it from their wildly different appearances tonight. Camilla is sporting her signature long silvery hair, pinned back and flowing to her mid back. Her makeup is nothing short of full runway glamour, all sparkles and bold dark colors. She's sporting a slinky dark green dress with one bare shoulder and one full-length sleeve.

Next to her, Clover's natural blond waves and subtle makeup are more reminiscent of old Hollywood starlets. This is the first time Rowan has seen her without her customary tailored business suit, though the navy-blue jumpsuit she's wearing and classy silver jewelry still give her that same air of authority Rowan has come to associate her with.

Jeremiah is in black slacks and a black mesh top accented with large maroon fabriqué roses. The look is completed with bold accent jewelry in both silver and rose gold, and his hair in his typical flawless sponge curls, his fade newly tidied since that last time Rowan saw him.

"Rowan!" Camilla beams when she finally sees him. "It's so good to see you in the real world!"

Rowan laughs. "Hey, everyone. Good to see you too. Not gonna lie, though, it's a bit weird."

"I'm glad he actually invited you," Clover chimes in.

"I know!" Camilla says.

"We had a running bet going," Jeremiah says casually, as if their topic of conversation isn't sending sparks down Rowan's spine. "Speaking of, Clove, you owe me twenty bucks."

"Damn, I'd hoped you'd forgotten. I'll buy your first drink," she concedes.

"And mine!" Camilla adds cheerily, slapping her sister on the shoulder.

"You shouldn't even get one seeing as *I* was the one who finally convinced him," Jeremiah adds, directed at Camilla.

"Okay, okay, we're making Rowan uncomfortable," Clover says in a chastising tone.

He hadn't even realized his face felt hot until she'd said it, but he's glad for her distraction. After all, he's never been one for being in the spotlight. But even with the lighthearted teasing at his—or really, Mal's—expense, Rowan likes them all more than he already did.

They make small talk until Mal shows up ten minutes later, causing Rowan's jaw to hit the floor. He's dressed in all black, tight, ripped jeans accentuating his shapely legs and—though he can't see it right now—surely hugging his ass nicely. He's got on a black button-up shirt unbuttoned to reveal a hint of his toned chest and his tattoo, accentuated with a thin gold chain. A chic-looking belt and his black boots complete the look, and goddamn, Rowan's seen him in all sorts of outfits by now, dressy and casual alike, but he looks hot as *fuck*, and Rowan wants nothing more than to jump him right in the middle of the club.

But from behind him emerges someone that makes Rowan's jaw hit the floor for a *different* reason as he does a double take. And not because of her similar all-black attire, an oversized blazer with the sleeves cuffed to her forearms showing off the long-sleeve lace top underneath and revealing the twin snake tattoo he'd seen that had instantly reminded him of Mal.

It's the woman he'd helped with the injured arm several months ago. What was her name? Amy?

"Holy shit, you're that EMT," she says, mirroring Rowan's thoughts and shaking her long, messy ponytail off her shoulder.

Rowan's shock at seeing her and at her recognizing him months later is enough to keep him from correcting his title.

"Wait, how the *fuck* do you two know each other?" Mal interjects instead of any type of greeting.

She leans into Mal's side. "Mal, he was with the ambulance when Jared…." Rowan connects the dots at the same time Mal does.

"No shit? Small fuckin' world. Well, Campbell, this is my sister, Bitchface. Bitchface, this is m—Campbell," he crudely introduces them.

"Amy," the woman says, holding out her hand and glaring at her brother. "And it was Rowan, right?"

Rowan's surprised she remembers, but, "Yeah. How's your arm doing?" he asks, shaking her hand gingerly while his own is nearly crushed with her firm grip.

"All good. Was just a sprain."

"And, uh…."

"He's gone," she says, inferring Rowan's next question. "Rest in fuckin' pieces."

Rowan's eyes widen. He doesn't put it past this firecracker of a woman to actually kill someone. *Or* to sic Mal on him on her behalf. The sour look on the man in question's face tells Rowan he might not be too far off on that line of thinking.

But potential felonies aside… holy *shit*. Everything about the scene when Mal kissed him makes sense: Why he'd gone radio silent for days in a row before requesting more praise than normal. Why he'd been so distracted that he'd done something outside his normal boundaries. Why he'd slept with someone else afterward.

He doesn't yet know how close Mal and Amy are, but hell, if any one of Rowan's siblings got abused like that, he'd be a fucking mess too.

"Mal! Happy birthday, darling!" Rowan hears from behind him.

For a moment, the name that Camilla calls doesn't register with Rowan, being so used to hearing her calling Mal *Malcolm*.

But when it *does*, Rowan's stunned into silence. Everything makes sense now. These aren't just random people that Mal happens to see on a fairly regular basis when he's at the club. These are his friends. His *family*. Of *course* they're going to call him what he wants to be called. His stomach twists as if he's on a Tilt-a-Whirl at the thought of what that makes *him* to Mal.

As everyone hugs and wishes Mal a happy birthday, Rowan catches snippets of conversation.

"Hey, sweets," Jeremiah says to Amy, hugging her tightly. "Jules said you two had a good time seeing Lizzo?"

"Fuck yeah, she was incredible. Your sister's wild as hell, though. Can drink me under the table."

"Don't tell me that," he says with a laugh, though he looks secretly proud.

Rowan's not sure how Amy fits in with the rest of Mal's friends, doubting that she's a member of the club herself, but it goes to show how close Mal is with both her and his friends.

"Speaking of…," Amy says, eyeing the group. "Why are we not drunk yet?"

"Shots!" Camilla declares, slinging an arm around both the Savaryns and tugging them off toward the bar.

And with that, Rowan's crowded around Mal at the bar with one shot of tequila burning his throat, six *thunk*s of empty shot glasses ringing in his ear, and two golden eyes boring holes into his own.

"Happy birthday, darling!" Clover shouts, giving Mal a side hug.

Jeremiah flags down a bartender, leans across the bar, and whispers something to her. She smiles and, a moment later, places a shot glass with shimmery blue liquid straight down in front of Mal, adding a shot of something clear on top. With the *whoosh* of a blowtorch, the shot bursts into a deep blue flame before the bartender pours on a lighter yellow drink and the fire erupts into a sparkling, crackling blue-orange flame while the drink transforms into a swirling sea of bright purple.

"The *fuck* is this, Jer?" Mal shouts, picking it up and holding the flaming purple drink two full feet away from his face.

"A phoenix. Quick, make a wish!"

As Mal bows his head to blow out the flame, lips puckered into a sweet O shape, he once again locks eyes with Rowan. The cheering around them as the fire is extinguished with a puff of air is completely lost on Rowan, gaze focused solely on the cords of Mal's neck as he throws back the shot.

"Tastes like a fuckin' flower...," Mal says, but there's a smile tugging at his lips as he slams the glass onto the bar top. "All right, someone get me a real drink!"

As if by another feat of magic, an old-fashioned materializes next to Mal's hand, Camilla winking at him across the top of what looks like a Long Island. Everyone else orders, Rowan settling on a beer on tap, and gets their drinks with loose fives and tens tossed onto the bar top for each one.

"I got us a table and started a tab," Jeremiah calls to the group, ushering everyone to a secluded table with a small white Reserved—Savaryn placard on it. Prime real estate, being so close to both the bar *and* the dance floor.

The music is something vaguely synth-pop that Rowan would normally hate were it not for the alcohol already working its way through his bloodstream and loosening his metaphorical tie.

"So how did you guys actually become friends with Mal?" Rowan asks no one in particular, settling down in between Mal and Amy.

There's a cacophony of laughter, and the man himself launches into an explanation, as if to set the record straight from the get-go.

"First time I went to the fourth floor, I decked a fucker for gettin' too rough and ignoring safewords."

"Decked him? Mal, you nearly put the guy in the fucking *hospital*," Camilla says, but it's with a proud twinkle in her eye.

"He fought back! The fuck was I s'posed to do? Bend over again?" Mal takes a deep drink of his old-fashioned, picks out the orange zest and flicks it onto the table. "Fuck *that*."

"So I knew him from scening with him, as I think you figured out at the shibari class a few months ago," Camilla says. "Then he near-paralyzes another member and—"

Clover continues, "And after *that* little incident, Mal waltzes straight into my office, this horrible, bloody cut on his eyebrow and knuckles to match, and goes, 'Yo, Dandelion, shit's gotta change around here.'" Clover and the others pause to laugh. "We sat down with him the very next day to make some major changes and renovations to the club."

"Like what?" Rowan asks, curious.

"The policy against more extreme types of play was probably the biggest," Camilla says.

Choking and breath play, Rowan mentally fills in the gap. He's a little surprised given Mal's apparent love of choking, but it does make sense from a business standpoint.

"Yeah," Clover agrees. "Along with vetting new members, making sure people respect safewords, and requiring monthly STI screenings."

Rowan can practically feel Mal's flush next to him, and it's cute as hell that he's embarrassed. The little swoopy feeling in Rowan's stomach rears its annoying head.

They chat for a while, idly swapping stories of the club and their personal lives and whatever else happens to come up. It's nice. A sense of friendship and belonging that Rowan hasn't felt in… well, *ever*, if he's being honest.

He used to be popular in high school before he dropped out for some half-baked plan of joining the military at seventeen using Jay's identity. He used to be *sane* before his brain freaked out on him and made him start seeing things that ultimately made him go crazy and landed him in a psych ward. From then on he's had… nothing. No one. Except his siblings and too many exes who never really meant anything.

Now, he has…

"Mal," Jeremiah starts seriously. "In honor of your birthday, we've got to do the customary—"

"Fuck no!" Mal interjects.

"Aww, c'mon, Mal! We have to!" Clover adds.

A quick glance to Rowan tells him that whatever *custom* they have, it's not a good one. Or at least it's an embarrassing one that Mal doesn't want him knowing about. Rowan's immediately on board.

"I'm game for whatever it is," he says.

"Never Have I Ever!" Camilla shouts, clapping along with each word like a cheerleader.

The laugh that bubbles out of Rowan's chest is genuine, and he knows that with this group, this high school game is bound to be wild.

"Jesus," Mal mutters.

"Who goes first?" Rowan asks.

Jeremiah answers for the group. "Birthday boooy!"

Next to him, Mal groans. "Fuckin' clowns…. Fine. I've never—"

"You gotta do it right!" Amy interrupts at the same time as Clover starts booing "Noo—"

"Fuckin' *fine*! *Never* have I *ever*…," Mal lilts mockingly, "graduated high school."

Everyone but Rowan drinks, and he's immediately as red as the lights currently illuminating the dance floor, assuming he's going to be judged for his lack of typical education. Or worse, asked *why* he had to go back for his GED a couple of years after he should have graduated.

"No shit?" Mal asks. "How the fuck'd you become a paramedic?"

Shrugging, Rowan answers, "GED."

"Up top, Campbell."

Rowan returns the surprising high-five. "You too?"

"Mmm," he hums, swirling his old-fashioned.

"Southie solidarity!" Amy cheers, taking her own sip.

"The fuck? You graduated in the top like… ten percent, bitch. Made sure'a that shit."

Oh? That perks Rowan's ears up, piques his interest. Any shred of Mal's history that he can learn about, he'll lap up like an eager puppy.

"My turn!" Camilla says. "Never have I ever bartended."

"That's dirty, baby doll." Jeremiah glares, taking a drink.

A drink that Rowan mirrors. 'Cause he *has* bartended before, even though he wasn't legally old enough to do so. *Or* in his right mind.

"Rowan! Where did you bartend?"

Camilla's voice is far too chipper for the story that accompanies the answer to that question.

"Uh, a bar when I was younger. Nothing exciting."

He's gotta learn to lie better. That sounded dodgy as shit.

"Okay," Clover says, thankfully drawing away the attention from Rowan. "Never have I ever waxed any part of my body."

"Oh, come on!" Amy complains. But thankfully Rowan doesn't drink alone—he's got Jeremiah, Amy, and Camilla on his side.

"Looks like you and me are *au naturel*, Mal!" Clover laughs.

Amy barks a teasing laugh. "Please, I've got more hair on my chest than he does."

"Ey! Ain't there a rule against shitting on me on my goddamn birthday?"

"Speaking of…," Jeremiah says with a smirk. "Never have I ever been shit on."

"Like by something besides an animal or a human baby?" Rowan asks, making the table erupt into laughter.

There's an awkward pause as everyone looks around to see if someone drinks, but when no one does (thankfully, in Rowan's humble opinion), they burst out laughing once more.

"All right, no more gross shit until we're drunker!" Amy declares. "Never have I ever made out with a woman."

A communal shrug has every one of them taking a sip.

"Seriously?" Amy looks around, baffled. "Et tu, Rowan?"

"It was a one-time thing," he explains.

"Same," Mal says.

Clover flashes her brilliant smile, adding, "Not for me! Dunno who you thought you were playing with, Ames."

The *thump* of the music is drowned out by the beginning of tipsy laughter.

ON THEIR second round of drinks—everyone else ordering another cocktail while Rowan sticks with the first beer he's had since the tequila earlier—the game turns predictably dirty. It's a welcome distraction from Mal's thigh pressed heavy and warm against Rowan's own, far closer than he needs to be for the size of the table.

"Never have I ever… given a blowjob," Clover smirks, watching as the rest of the group groans and takes a drink.

"Well, that's fuckin' dumb," Mal grumbles. "How 'bout… never have I ever worked at a sex club."

Clover, Camilla, and Jeremiah all drink with a roll of their eyes. While everyone is distracted, Rowan takes a tiny swig of his beer, avoiding Mal's eyes when he senses him staring at him.

But—

"Really?" Amy interjects, words slightly slurred, apparently not having any of the tact that the rest of the group does when slightly intoxicated.

Something a little too close to shame makes Rowan's fingertips swell as he clinks the beer glass with the side of his fingernail.

"Yeah," he confesses, attempting to sound nonchalant. "It's a long story."

And not one I particularly want to tell in front of all these tentative new friends, he thinks. *Or Mal.*

He knows that, most likely, no one here would judge him for his past—for being out of his mind and on too many unprescribed pills to name and fucking everyone in a ten-foot radius—but the self-doubt runs deep in his veins, and some habits are hard to break on a whim. Hard to share during a silly game.

"We've all got our skeletons," Jeremiah says, absentmindedly thumbing at the crook of his elbow.

The gesture is a familiar one to Rowan—something he'd seen countless times when nameless men used to offer him *something stronger* than weed or booze or ecstasy or coke. Something that would *Make you feel like you're floating, baby.* He shudders at the memory. And he'd never have guessed that Jeremiah used to use, but he's glad that he seems to have gotten out.

"My turn," Clover says, breaking the tension. "Never have I ever… gone skiing."

"Who the fuck *has*? We're in the middle of the city," Mal quips.

No one drinks, and the group laughs after a round of curious eye contact.

"All right, you're up, Red," Mal says, any semblance of order they'd been following at the beginning of the game now completely shattered as they bounce around the circle, calling one another out randomly.

"Hm… never have I ever… owned more than one dildo."

"Oh fuck you," Mal retorts, taking a deep drink.

To his surprise, the rest of the group drink as well.

"Looks like I'm in the minority on that one," Rowan laughs.

"Fucking did *not* need to know that, Mal," Amy scoffs, face scrunched in disgust.

"You think I wanted to know that about *your* skanky ass?"

"Oh, fuck you, dick!"

"That's what the dildos are for, bitch."

Jeremiah intervenes with a laugh, "Settle down, you two. Cam, you haven't gone in a while."

"Hm… never have I ever stripped for money," Camilla says, grinning wickedly at her sister.

"You bitch," Clover says, taking a quick swig of her drink. "I was in *college* and *broke*!"

Rowan would kill for either of those excuses as he takes his own sip, the beer now gone warm from how slowly he's been nursing it. Fuck.

Tonight is *really* dredging up a lot of shit that he didn't think would come up *ever*. He knows, logically, that he could lie, but well…. He's never been very good at that particular skill.

"I'll be damned, Campbell," Mal says next to him. "Is there anything you *haven't* done?"

Rowan shrugs, trying to play off his racing heartbeat as indifferent. "Guess not."

"And you never stripped for me?"

"Uh…."

Because what the hell does he *say* to that, other than *We don't really do that, Mal,* or *I gladly would as long as you weren't paying me anything.*

They've sexted plenty of times now, sending each other pics and videos with barely a second thought anymore, but stripping is… deliberate. Deliberately *intimate*, Rowan guesses. Even with his history of doing it "professionally" when he was a coked-out teenager, he'd promised himself years ago that if he ever did it again, it would be for someone he wanted to show off to and not to put food in his belly or poison in his veins.

Not as part of a nonromantic *just fuckin'* arrangement.

But thankfully, Jeremiah swoops in and saves the day with "Never have I ever been in a gangbang."

The rest of the Menagerie employees howl with laughter and bang on the table, chanting for Mal and Rowan both to drink.

"Fucking *gross*, Mal!" Amy squeals, pretending to avert her eyes as if Mal's going to get ravaged right in front of her.

"I fuckin' told you not to come, skank!"

The Savaryns continue their bickering, but the rest of the game goes by largely without incident. Thankfully without any more skeletons of Rowan's smashing through the layers of closets Rowan's locked them in.

Rowan learns that Mal is allergic to grapefruit—which Rowan drinks with in solidarity due to the interaction the citrus has with his meds—Camilla is older than Clover by seven minutes, even though she acts like the younger of the two, Jeremiah has his master's in psychology but prefers bartending, and Amy used to run track in high school, among many, *many* sexual things about everyone, most of which Rowan probably shouldn't know.

Only when Mal announces that he needs another drink does it end, and another round of drinks materializes by their side without the excuse of a game to sip down.

"OH, THIS is my *jam*!" Camilla squeals as the opening melody to some pop song pumps through the speakers, reaching across the table and waggling her fingers at Amy. "Come dance with me, love!"

"I've got you, birthday boy!" Jeremiah claims Mal, dramatically twirling out of his stool.

"Looks like that leaves me and you, Rowan!" Clover grins, taking a somehow still elegant sip of her cocktail despite the three she's had already. "Lezz-a-gay!"

Her impression of Super Mario makes the whole group explode into giggles as the table empties and half fumbles their way to the dance floor. Pairing off, they each take on their own distinct style. Realistically, he knows they're probably all good dancers, but they're here to have a good time, pride be damned.

Clover is a riot. The song playing is some kind of pop-rap mashup, and she bangs out hit after hit of terrible dance moves, starting with the Egyptian and working her way to the sprinkler. Rowan laughs and mirrors her, occasionally throwing in his own freestyle that has the both of them grinning and out of breath.

Next to them, Amy and Camilla are taking things a *bit* more seriously, at least attempting some kind of conventional club dancing, all swaying hips and pumping arms. It makes Rowan smile when eventually they give up on being serious and start undulating and attempting to moonwalk.

Inevitably, Rowan's gaze shifts to Mal and Jeremiah. He finds them doing something a *little* too close to grinding. They're not even *touching*, for fuck's sake, a respectable gap between them for Jesus, but it still makes a mean, sour swirl of jealousy rise in the back of Rowan's throat that nearly kills the pleasant buzz he has going on.

"All right, quit hogging him!" Camilla calls out, dragging Mal away from Jeremiah to waltz with him, horribly mismatched to the current rock song playing.

From then on, Mal bounces between each of them, arms flailing wildly and legs stomping out of rhythm no matter what type of music is playing. He's intoxicating to watch as the gorgeous smile blossoms on his face with each and every song, each and every dance move. From little sways of his hips to tiny shimmies of his shoulders, Rowan can't take his eyes off of him.

When he finally gets to Rowan, his cheeks are flushed a pretty pink, and the tips of his neatly coiffed hair are damp with sweat, and he's fucking beautiful. But like everyone else, he thrashes around wildly a meager two feet from Rowan, and even with his erratic and silly movements, Rowan can't stop watching. It makes a grin break out on his own face as he dips down into a low squat, bouncing back up a little too close to Mal and shimmying in front of him.

He's literally been inside the man countless times by now, but his heart still flutters at being in such close proximity to him. He doesn't think he'll ever be over the butterflies that have taken up permanent residence inside his chest ever since he met Mal all those months ago.

With static and sound driving their group closer together, they form one giant mass, goofily bouncing and swaying to whatever song comes on next. For each one, someone knows all the lyrics and belts them out, the rest of the group forming a sad semblance of a mosh pit around them and providing off-key backup vocals.

It's the most fun Rowan's had in a long time, limbs loose and head empty in a good way, feeling the music pulse through him and let him breathe for the first time in a long while despite the humidity on the dance floor.

BACK AT the table, it's only Mal and Rowan, and he has to admit it's nice to get him alone for a bit, the rest of the group seemingly content with continuing to dance. It's like a little sanctuary for the two of them.

"You a lightweight or somethin', Red?" Mal asks, clearly having noticed that Rowan's still sipping on the dregs of his first—and only—beer of the night.

It's obvious that Mal's a little tipsy. He's not at the point where his words are slurred or his gaze is unfocused, but there's a slight slowness and a looseness to his movements that tells Rowan he's got a pleasant buzz going.

So maybe this is the perfect time to tell him about his mental issues. Maybe he's inebriated enough that he won't think too hard about it. What's that saying? Drunk words are sober thoughts? Maybe it's the best way to gauge how Mal will feel about Rowan's depression with booze loosening his tongue. After all, he'd already seemed chill about it when he thought Rowan was talking about his mother having it.

But at the last second, words on the tip of his tongue, he chickens out. This isn't some past trauma that he dealt with long ago and has had plenty of time to recover from. This is something he still deals with on a daily basis. And it's something that could absolutely make Mal think differently about him. It wouldn't be the first time Rowan's lost someone over his diagnosis, and he can't bear the thought of that happening with Mal.

"Yeah, somethin' like that."

"So uh—" Mal takes a piece of ice out of his empty drink and chomps on it loudly. Watching his mouth work on the cube is distracting, but Rowan manages to catch the tail end of him asking, "—all that shit true? During the game?"

Rowan sighs heavily, but for all Mal's opened up to him the past few months, Rowan figures he owes it to him to give him *something* back. "Yeah."

"Can piece it together. You don't gotta elaborate."

"It's fine, just… went a little crazy when I was younger. Working underage in clubs, bartending and dancing, and uh…." The words don't come as easily as he thought. But somehow, in the darkness of the bar and the way Mal's lit by the dim light of the lamp above them, the sincerity in his eyes… it feels easy. "Workin' the back of the house. I wasn't in a good place back then. Lost in a lotta ways and couldn't really get out. It took my whole family staging an intervention to get me some help, and I finally got my shit together, got my GED, and managed to work up to getting my job. Straightened my shit out."

"Glad ya did," Mal tells him when he's done his mini spiel. No judgment whatsoever in his eyes. "World's a better place with you helpin' people."

"Thanks, Mal."

"Fuckin' Superman…."

Rowan lets out a weak laugh, but he's truly touched by Mal's words. It warms him more than any alcohol he *can't* have ever could.

"Can't fuckin' believe you met my sister before," Mal mutters, thankfully changing the topic and not pressing Rowan for any more details of his past escapades.

Rowan follows his eyes where they're trained on Amy and the rest of the crew dancing. Flashes of red and yellow and blue lights that illuminate each of them like a strobe light, one after another after another.

"Wasn't exactly in the best circumstance, but…." He reaches over and scoops out an ice cube from Mal's empty drink, thoughtfully chews on it, and tastes the bitter bite of whisky. "Y'know, I thought she might'a been related to you."

"The fuck? How?"

Rowan shrugs. "You look a lot alike, for starters."

"*Pft*. I take offense to that, Campbell."

Even as a gay man, Rowan knows that Amy is gorgeous and that Mal's joking despite his snorted reply.

"And you have the same tattoo. Kind of, anyway. The snakes."

"I forget about that one sometimes," Mal confesses, referring to his own double snake tattoo on the back of his ankle.

"Yeah, well… I see a lot more of you from behind than you do," Rowan teases.

"Oh, fuck off."

There's an easy smile on his face, and Rowan doesn't want to pop their pleasant bubble, but….

"Was uh…." He clears his throat, gets a fucking grip. "Was she the reason you were kinda spacey that week? When you wanted to do a praise-heavy session the first time?"

One deep breath and eight *pops* of knuckle cracking later, Mal responds. "Yeah." He wipes his fingers through the condensation ring left by his empty drink on the tabletop. "Always get kinda fucked up where she's concerned."

"I know the feeling," Rowan sympathizes, picturing his two older and three younger siblings and all the hell he'd go through to keep them safe. *Especially* little Marc, the youngest of them, though the most levelheaded.

"Basically raised her." Quiet, subdued, and Rowan has to strain to hear Mal over the thumping bass music. "Jamie and Scott, my brothers, they fucked off pretty early on, in and outta juvie then jail for dumb shit.

So it was just me and Ames most'a the time, dealin' with Larry. When I moved out after I came out to Larry, I took her with me. Couldn't let her stay with that fucker alone."

"She's close to your age, though, right? What, two or three years younger?"

"Two. Always kinda felt like I had to be her big brother *and* both her parents growin' up, y'know. 'S why when anyone fucks with her, it gets to me. Feels like I failed her or some shit."

"You were just a kid yourself, Mal. You didn't know what you were doing. 'Sides, she can make her own choices."

"Still feels like it's my fuckin' fault."

"If it helps, she turned out good," Rowan tells him, meeting his eyes from where they'd been unsubtly focused on the V of his exposed chest. "So did you."

The smile that Mal throws his way nearly stops Rowan's damn heart.

"All right, no more depressin' shit on my birthday," he declares when Rowan's own smile grows naturally. "You dance, Red? For real?"

"Yeah."

"C'mon."

Rowan's skin prickles where Mal grabs at his wrist, slides his hand down until their fingers lazily interlace and then *tugs* Rowan toward the dance floor. The crowd parts for them and closes behind them, and all of a sudden, the sanctity of their table is gone, and they're surrounded by nameless faces, yet still in a world entirely of their own.

And look…. Rowan knows how to dance. He spent long enough dancing in seedy clubs in his youth to have picked up more than a few tricks. Now that he's older and *saner*, he knows even better how to move his body in any number of ways. So yeah, he knows how to dance. He *does*, but when Mal grabs on to the lapels of Rowan's shirt and presses their lower halves together in a slow grind, it's clear that *dancing* isn't on his mind.

Not like he'd been doing with the others. Silly. Goofy. Cute as hell. No, Mal's leering at him with an intensity that Rowan has only ever seen from him when he's about to act up during their scenes. When he wants to get destroyed by Rowan. Maybe this time Rowan's gonna get *his* shit rocked.

The thumping music makes Rowan's jaw vibrate, and the friction of Mal's jeans against his own clothing burns his muscles as they start to move together. Slow, so goddamn slow to the bassy music, but deliberate. Filthy. And goddammit, much more of this and Rowan's going to get hard. Right here in front of all these people.

But fuck, Mal's so attractive. The light cascades onto him, illuminating sharp cheekbones, a pointed nose, and long, curling eyelashes.

It shouldn't surprise Rowan that Mal's a good dancer. The guy *knows* how to move his body; that much was made abundantly clear from their very first scene together and every one since.

The staccato of the percussion-heavy song guides their movements, Mal undulating and grinding against him in heavy swirls and suggestive thrusts. It's for his own sanity as much as Mal's sake that Rowan grabs him by the hips and spins him around, tugging his ass back against his hips. 'Cause if Mal keeps looking up at Rowan like *that*, all lidded eyes and plush lips, Rowan's not sure he could stop himself from kissing him.

And here he wouldn't even have subspace as an excuse.

He wonders if Mal thinks about their accidental kiss as much as Rowan does. Wonders if he wants a real one as much as Rowan does. But as Mal's firm ass collides with Rowan's hips, all thoughts of the kiss are wiped from his mind.

It isn't until a familiar song comes on that Mal really ramps it up. The bouncing, lilting melody has them starting a dirty grind to the beat of the music. It's "The Shape of You" by Ed Sheeran. A perfect analog for how Rowan feels about Mal.

Mal grinds his ass back against Rowan, Rowan's hands magneting to his hips to guide his movements while the song encourages following his lead.

They dance in sweeping rough circles as their bodies press impossibly closer together, Mal's hands closing over Rowan's and dragging them over his body. Pressing forward into the heat of Mal's ass as desperately as Mal's pressing back against him. Guided by Mal, Rowan's hands roam over his chest, feeling the hard planes of muscles and the soft curves between them. And like the song says, Rowan loves Mal's body. Can't get enough of it as they grind together to the beat.

He chances a pass up Mal's neck, fingers tangling in the gold chain and inadvertently tugging it against Mal's throat. It's an accident. Really it is. But Mal dips his head back against Rowan's shoulder and moans up at the ceiling, and, well…. The second time's not so accidental, Mal's hips finally stuttering in their steady rhythm.

Rowan releases the chain, replacing the harsh metal with the soft pads of his fingers, Mal's Adam's apple bobbing against him. Feeling the rapid thrum of his pulse even over the vibrations of the bass and the sporadic jostling of the couples around them.

The song all but fades out as their hips and hands move on their own. Mal flings his arms back to clutch at Rowan's neck as his back arches, a rush of cool air filling in the gap between them. It's too much. Rowan pulls him back flush against him and gasps at the lightning that crackles through his core. He's so fucking turned on, feeling the soft tickle of Mal's hair on his lips and the firm weight of his body against him.

And then Mal's turning in Rowan's arms, clothing dragged askew as he invades Rowan's space, invades his body and mind and continues his filthy grind again from the front.

Fuck, Mal's hard. Rowan knows he can feel how hard Rowan is too.

It's too much. *So much*, and God, Rowan wants him. Fuck public decency. He wants nothing more than to hike Mal up into his arms and fuck him against the nearest flat surface. Hell, he'd even drop to his knees right here on the dirty floor and suck Mal off if it meant getting some kind of relief from the throbbing in his veins.

It's going to be hell waiting a whole week to be inside him again.

Chorus after chorus, verse after verse, their dancing gets more and more intense. Much harder to control as they meld into one another. Hands everywhere and thoughts only on the other. Heat wraps around Rowan, threatening to boil him from the inside out as he pulls Mal closer, hands dipping into his back pockets and squeezing his ass.

Another moan from Mal grazes his ear, hairs on the back of his neck rising like he walked through a phantom. Their movements get messier, sloppier, the more into it they get, and by the time the song ends and fades into the next, they're all but panting into each other's open mouths. Staring at one another, drinking in the sight of sweaty and flushed faces, and Rowan swears Mal's eyes dip down to his lips.

And then he leans forward and—

"Gonna go get a drink," Mal shouts in Rowan's ear, hot breath tickling at his earlobe and making him shudder. "Want anything?"

Disappointment curls itself in Rowan's belly.

"I'm good. Gonna go back to the table for a bit."

Mal nods, and in a flash, he's disappeared into the crowd, and Rowan's left in the middle of it, cold and achingly hard.

But he shakes it off, wandering to the other end of the bar to flag down a glass of water. When the cold glass is placed down in front of him, he takes a long, deep drink, the cool liquid a lifesaver for his dry throat.

He downs half of it before he sees Jeremiah and Mal talking across the bar, blissfully unaware of Rowan watching them through the gaps in the ceiling-high shelves of liquor.

Even with the pair yelling loudly over the thrum of the music and his probably better-than-average ability to read lips thanks to his job, he's still only able to make out snippets of what they're talking about.

"… laid on your *birthday*?" Jeremiah shouts. "Just ask…."

"… *not* askin' him…."

Rowan's heart thuds in his chest. Did Jeremiah tell Mal to ask him to fuck? Because yes. His answer is *hell fucking yes*, if Mal will only ask the question.

But the rest of their conversation is cut off when they're pushed aside by a group of drunk bachelorettes. When Rowan finally returns to the table with his half-empty glass in hand, alone, it's like the exchange never even happened.

MAL'S BEEN eyeing him across the bar, where he's now been planted with Jeremiah and Amy for the last half hour. Rowan knows, 'cause he's been eyeing him right back from the table where *he's* sitting with Clover and Camilla. Despite that enough time has passed since his only real drink, he still feels tipsy enough that the lingering stares are sending wave after wave of heat and want coursing through him.

Rowan's not listening to what the Monroe twins are saying. Something business-related, maybe. Maybe something about some hot woman at the bar. Rowan is *mm-hmm*ing and *yeah*ing along at what he hopes are appropriate times when it feels like they're talking to him, but his attention is solely on Mal.

Specifically the heated, glazed-over look he gives him over the rim of his beer bottle. How his fingers slide along the curved neck of the brown container, slick with condensation.

Rowan's waiting for it. Some sign that Mal wants it as bad as Rowan does.

But it's gotta be Mal. It's his birthday after all.

Ask me. Ask me, ask me, ask—

There.

With a glance over his shoulder and the quirk of one neatly sculpted eyebrow, Mal has Rowan excusing himself from the knowing stares of the twins. Has him trailing Mal into the bar bathroom, an invisible string tugging at his chest and winching him forward.

They shouldn't do this. Even as his legs carry him forward, Rowan knows they shouldn't do this. They've been sexting at least once a week between their scenes, but this is…. Well. It's crossing a big line from *just fuckin'* to… something else. There's hardly an ounce of blood left in Rowan's brain to think about what that *something else* might be, which means it must be a good idea after all. Even if a bar bathroom is a far cry from the comfort of a bed, this will be the first time they've hooked up outside the confines of the Menagerie.

And fuck, he wants it.

The second the door to the bathroom swings shut, a tattooed hand latches on to his shirt and drags him into the largest stall. Their hands are a blur between them, fumbling to get each other's jeans unbuttoned and relieve the mounting pressure that had built up earlier on the dance floor. The stall door creaks open, hitting Rowan in the shoulder. He slams it shut and flicks the lock, attention immediately back on Mal as he shoves him against the door.

A spark zaps between them when Mal presses their foreheads together, ragged breaths mingling across the tiny gap between their lips.

"Tell me your words," Rowan demands, ripping his gaze away from Mal's mouth.

Mal's fingers still on Rowan's zipper, face pulling away as he looks up at Rowan, lidded eyes widening.

And fuck, did Mal not think this was going to be a scene? Was he expecting a regular hookup? Through the fog in his brain, he realizes that he may have fucked this up entirely.

But Mal answers after a tiny, shaky breath. "Green's good to go, yellow's pause, red's full stop."

"Good."

As soon as Rowan works open Mal's button and zipper, he spins him in place, pressing his chest against the stall door and hearing it rattle on flimsy hinges.

"*Unh….*"

Fingers raking against Mal's lower back, Rowan shoves his jeans down over his ass, revealing lacy white panties that stretch tight across his cheeks.

"Fuck…," Rowan whispers, cupping Mal's ass in his hands and watching the delicate holes in the fabric spread under his palms. "These are new, huh?"

"Bought 'em the other day."

"Mm… thought it was your birthday, not mine."

Mal's chuckle turns into a moan as Rowan drags his hands around the front, feeling his hard cock beneath the panties.

"Felt you earlier, when we were dancing…."

A press, a drag, a moan, and Mal hitches his hips forward into Rowan's touch.

"Were so fuckin' hard, just from a little grinding."

Rowan slips one hand under Mal's panties, feeling the heat of his bare skin and the softness of his neatly-trimmed pubes.

"Was that 'cause of me, or would you have gotten that turned on with anyone?" Rowan asks.

"*Nng….*" Mal's chin dips, the crown of his head *thunk*ing against the cubicle door.

"Tell me, Mal."

With a few pumps of Mal's cock, Rowan wrings the answer out of him.

"You…," he breathes. "Fuck, get me goin' like nothin' else."

"Thought so."

Spurred on by the revelation, Rowan shoves Mal's panties down to join his pants where they've crumpled to the floor.

The scent of strawberries fills Rowan's nose, his mouth watering as he takes in the plug nestled between Mal's asscheeks.

"Planned this, huh?"

It's phrased as a question, but Mal doesn't answer. Doesn't need to really. The panties and the plug and the fucking *strawberry lube* speak volumes on their own. And normally Rowan would make Mal answer him, but this is a far cry from their normal scenes.

He tugs the plug out slowly and tosses it on the pooled panties at Mal's feet, the black silicone contrasting with the white lace. Rowan's cock aches as he finally frees himself, spreading Mal's asscheeks and rutting against his slick hole.

"You're so fuckin' wet…," he notes, kneading Mal's cheeks while his cockhead catches on the rim. "Can picture you fucking yourself open, wishing it was me."

Two fingers slip inside, drawing a punched-out breath from Mal. The heat between his legs is tantalizing, beckoning Rowan to slip his cock between his thighs and rut against the underside of Mal's own hard cock as he opens him with his fingers.

"Fuck…," Mal groans, reaching back to paw at Rowan's side.

Right then the bathroom door swings open, the thumping music and din of voices outside crescendoing to a deafening volume, then quickly fading back to a dull hum.

Mal's fingers flex white where they're pressed against the stall door. Even with the hitch in his breath, the shifting of his ass back against Rowan's cock is anything but subtle. Rowan takes it as his cue to slide into Mal to the hilt, slapping a hand around his mouth to stifle the moan he knows is coming. He feels Mal's lips vibrate against his fingertips.

The sounds of the unknown man a few feet away dissolve into nothing as he lets Mal adjust to his cock. Only for a moment until he feels him clenching around him, milking his cock for all it's worth. He fucks into him deep, with one hand still covering his mouth and the other bruising his hip. And when he pulls out fully, then thrusts back in with enough force to make the door hinges rattle, Mal whimpers loud enough to be heard over the sound of running water in the background.

"Not a fuckin' word, Mal," Rowan whispers in his ear, grinding into him. "Unless you want the rest of the club to know what a slut you are for my cock."

Beneath him, Mal shudders and reaches up to clench his knuckles on the top of the stall door. Shoves his hips back and groans against his fingers.

"*Pft*," Rowan snorts, even as his stomach churns with anticipation. "Have it your way, then."

His muscles are on fire as he fucks into Mal at a brutal pace, not caring about the cacophony of slick skin slapping and sweet moans echoing off the tile.

As he fucks him, it's immediately different than every one of their scenes. The thrill of being in a public place, away from the sanctity of the Menagerie, and knowing that Mal had planned this—that he'd *chosen* to be with Rowan when he could have easily had his pick of any number of men in the club—gets his heart racing faster than his hips.

"Ohh, *fuck*," Mal groans on one particularly hard thrust.

"That the spot?"

"Yeah, *fuck* me…. Harder."

"I got you."

Time passes slowly as the heat rises in the stall and in Rowan's core, but in the blink of an eye, Rowan's on the verge of coming. He holds off, wanting to give Mal a birthday fuck he'll never forget, and manages to get Mal's knees shaking beneath him and his knuckles turning white against the top of the stall door.

"God, look at you," Rowan praises, grinding his hips into Mal's ass and reaching around to grasp his leaking cock. "So fuckin' good for me, Mal."

"Feel so fuckin' good…," Mal moans. "Fill me up like nothin' else."

"No *one* else."

"*Nng!*"

He pumps Mal's cock in time with his thrusts, but the tight heat encompassing Rowan's own cock is too much to bear.

"Gonna come inside you. Tell me you want it—wanna hear you."

"Yeah, *fuck*, do it. Fill me up…."

His heart and his head and his hips race toward his finish, and with a shuddering exhale that racks his entire body, he empties inside Mal in hot pulses. For a long minute, he allows himself to rest his forehead against Mal's neck and catch his breath as he softens inside of him.

"Rowan…," Mal whines, shoving his ass back against him.

After slapping his ass, Rowan finally pulls out and dips down to retrieve the plug from its resting spot atop Mal's panties.

"Gonna keep all this inside you," he says, pushing the plug into Mal's used and leaking hole.

"Fuck...."

"Though," Rowan muses, spinning Mal in place by the hips, "be a shame to waste this strawberry lube."

Rowan drags the plug back out and grasps the sides of Mal's face. "Open."

Mal's eyes dip half closed, pupils blown wide as he parts his lips and sticks his pink tongue out a fraction of an inch. The sight makes Rowan's spent cock dribble onto his slacks even as he drags the plug across Mal's lips, eyes rapt as a streak of his own come is lapped up by an eager tongue. And when Mal's lips close around the toy and hollow out in a filthy *suck*, Rowan nearly gets hard again as his blood rushes south.

"So good for me," Rowan coos, thumb stroking his cheek as Mal cleans off the plug.

"Mmm...."

"That's good, open."

Mal complies, cheeks flushed and hairline sweaty. As Rowan tugs the plug back out, a dribble of spit and come follows that he swipes at with his thumb and sucks into his own mouth. The taste is bitter on his tongue, but Mal's moan is sweet.

"Fuck...."

Rowan feels the heat radiating from Mal's body as he slides the plug back between Mal's cheeks. "Keep that inside you. Consider it your birthday present."

Another soft groan is his only response before Rowan drops to his knees and swallows Mal's cock down to the root.

"*Ohhh...!*"

Fingers rake through his hair and tighten with each bob of his head and flex with each flick of his tongue. It's been far too long since he's had Mal's cock in his mouth, their scenes frequently playing out the other way around.

It barely takes any time at all before Mal's groaning, "Shit, gonna… Rowan!"

"Mmm...." A silent signal to *do it*.

As Mal's come floods Rowan's mouth, it feels like they've reached a milestone that has Rowan greedily drinking him down. His cock starts to soften in his hand as he laps up the last few drops of come before tugging Mal's panties back up and letting the elastic snap around his hips.

"Goddamn…. Happy fuckin' birthday to me."

Rowan huffs a laugh through his nose and stands, fastening his slacks before cupping Mal's cheek in his hand and meeting his eyes. His fingers burn where their skin meets, but not nearly as much as the sparks that sizzle between their shared gazes. Mal dips his head to Rowan's shoulder, one hand resting firmly on Rowan's hip.

And this part… it's a little hard to navigate, isn't it? Because how the fuck do you do aftercare in a public bathroom?

"C'mon," Mal says, pulling away and tugging up his jeans before Rowan has a chance to think about the moment that passed between them. "Think everyone else is prob'ly gettin' suspicious."

THE REST of the group shares knowing smirks—Amy making an exaggerated gagging noise—when they eventually make their way back to the table.

"That was a birthday gift from all of us," Jeremiah says, making the rest of the group burst into laughter.

"Oh, fuck off," Mal says, corners of his mouth pulling up even as he tries to wipe the smile off his face.

For the next hour or so, they wind down, a number of inside jokes from the night popping up and making them all dissolve into one fit of laughter after another. It's nice. It's fun. This little family Mal has assembled for himself and invited Rowan into is something he's going to treasure for as long as he gets to have it. By the end of the night, Rowan has to agree with what Clover said at the beginning.

He's *so* glad Mal invited him.

HAVING SAID their goodbyes to the rest of the group, Rowan and Mal walk together to the small parking lot behind the club, the midnight sky unusually sparkling with stars.

"Hey, before you go," Rowan says as they near their cars. "Got you something."

"Already gave me a birthday gift," Mal quips.

Rowan snorts. "A *real* gift, dick."

"Didn't need to do that, man."

"I wanted to. And it's not much. C'mon." He gestures for Mal to follow him to his car.

He opens the passenger door when they arrive and retrieves the carefully wrapped package. It's a small white box with black twine that Rowan had painstakingly woven around to resemble some of the shibari rigs they'd done over the past few months. A little cheesy, maybe, but he's proud of it. And when he hands it to Mal, the amused smile that blossoms over his face is completely worth it.

"Fuckin' Boy Scout," Mal mumbles, but there's a small smile on his face as he dutifully begins unwinding the rope.

When he sees the small goldmine of miniature Reese's cups inside, he snorts, but Rowan can tell he's pleased.

"You tryn'a fatten me up, Campbell?"

"Nah," Rowan laughs. "Although… if it went to your ass…."

"Fuuuck off, my ass is fantastic as it is."

"Can't argue there." Rowan gestures to the box when it looks like Mal's going to put the lid back on. "There's something else too."

Mal digs through the chocolate to find the tissue paper Rowan had neatly folded around his other present. He places the box down on the trunk of Rowan's car and gingerly unwraps the paper until he reveals the jockstrap Rowan had custom ordered last week and paid out the ass for expedited shipping.

"Holy shit…," Mal whispers, pulling out the jock and examining the fabric.

It's solid black with golden threads woven through the back and thigh bands, the pocket in front outlined in the same golden thread in an intricate pattern. When Rowan found the site, he'd pulled out his credit card on the spot and selected a pattern that would both complement Mal's complexion and—inevitably—remind him of the Gold Room. Of Rowan.

Mal's stunned into silence, running his thumbs over the straps and holding it up in the dim yellow light provided by the streetlamps. Even in the low light, Rowan can see the thread glimmer.

"Figured I should finally pay you back for that one I shredded during our first scene," he explains when Mal doesn't respond further.

Rowan remembers the day fondly, though he'd be lying if he said he hadn't harbored a twinge of guilt this whole time for having ruined Mal's clothes. Even though he *had* said he could ruin it.

"Thank you, Rowan," Mal says finally.

It's the sincerity and the breathiness in his voice that gets to Rowan as much as it is the fact that this might be the first time Mal has actually used his name outside of sex and not one of his many nicknames for him. It catches him so off guard that it takes him a long moment to realize that the warm feeling encompassing him isn't just pleasure at the name, but rather Mal's chest pressed against his own and his arms wrapped tightly around his back.

It's far from the first time Mal's hugged him of his own accord, but those other times had been fleeting, with barely any contact. This is *intimate*, if Rowan dares call it anything. Somehow, their bodies pressed flush together like this feels more meaningful than every time they've been connected sexually. But before Rowan can even properly enjoy the hug or fully respond back to it, there's a sharp inhale, and Mal releases him.

"See you next weekend, yeah?" Mal says, backpedaling toward the other end of the lot where his black Charger is parked.

"Yeah. Happy birthday, Mal."

THE WHOLE night replays in Rowan's mind like a film reel. Grainy and slightly out of focus but loaded with unforgettable images. Unforgettable feelings too. The way Mal felt pressed against him on the dance floor and in the bathroom stall and in the parking lot. The way he'd shared bits of himself with not only his closest friends and family, but with Rowan too. The way he hadn't judged when Rowan had shared some of his own sordid past.

They'd said their goodbyes in the parking lot less than an hour ago, but Rowan hears his phone vibrate on his nightstand.

[MS] *can still feel you*

Fuck, Rowan wants to say. *You can't just say shit like that, Mal.*

[MS] *half of it fuckin leaked out on the way home*

Or like that.

[RC] *Can't decide if that's hot or gross*

Really, Rowan knows which, but Mal changes the subject to something a little more heartfelt.

[MS] *thanks btw*

[MS] *for the gift. and for comin. it was fun*

[RC] *I'm glad you like it. And I had fun too*

[RC] *Your friends are all crazy lmao*

[MS] *yeah but i'm stuck with em*

Rowan hears the fondness in Mal's words as if the man were speaking them aloud.

[RC] *Gonna be hard to top tonight for your 30th though*

[MS] *i'm sure we'll find a way red*

Despite his exhaustion, it takes Rowan a full hour to fall asleep, eyelids flickering with threads of shimmering gold and white lace.

CHAPTER 9: RED AND GREEN

ROWAN CAN'T get last night out of his head: Mal's birthday. The opening up and sharing, yeah. The grinding and the near-choking with Mal's necklace, definitely. The risky fuck in the bathroom, most of all. He knows they crossed a line by fucking like that. Keeps telling himself that, but somehow it *still* doesn't seem like it was a bad idea.

Only… he can't get over how Mal reacted when Rowan had asked him for his safewords. He'd seemed… surprised? While everything else is becoming grainy and hazy, Rowan remembers that moment clear as crystal. Mal's hands had fumbled on Rowan's zipper, and his voice before he answered hadn't been as steady as Rowan would normally require from a typical scene.

All that leads him to believe that Mal was *expecting* a normal hookup and not a Dom/sub scene. And while their fucking *was* closer to the former, they still had that aspect of power imbalance; the thing that they both crave and seek out from one another week after week. So Rowan didn't do anything wrong, right?

What was he supposed to do? *Not* ask about it and have Mal think that if something went wrong, he didn't have a say in stopping? Even as the thought crosses Rowan's mind, he knows it's not true. Mal would say if something bothered him or if he didn't like something. Would probably put a dent in Rowan's face with those knuckle tats, honestly. If there's one thing he's learned about Mal in the time they've spent together, it's that he's a scrappy fucker with a razor-sharp tongue and the muscles to put his money where his mouth is.

He's never heard Mal safeword before—not even a yellow— so truth be told, he doesn't know how he would actually react in that scenario.

But hell, Mal probably should have *told* Rowan straight-up that he didn't want to do a scene if that was the case, and Rowan would have been perfectly fine with that and adjusted accordingly. Wouldn't have pushed as much, maybe. Been so rough. Not that it was a particularly hard-core scene in the slightest, but still.

The only thing that Rowan can think of to explain Mal's confusion is simple: Mal was expecting a regular hookup and did a mental double take when he thought Rowan wanted to do a scene. Which means… would Mal be *open* to regular hookups outside the confines of the Menagerie? Outside their Dom/sub arrangement? Fuck, Rowan would *love* that. For months now he's been lamenting the fact that he can't see Mal more often. That he can't fuck him more often—every goddamn day like he wants to. Like Mal deserves.

And he'd finally thought the perfect opportunity came up to be *more* than what they are, and Rowan unknowingly screwed the pooch and slid them back down the hill of intimacy they've been steadily climbing.

But Mal had seemed so normal after they fucked. Rowan's body can't forget the way Mal had rested his forehead on his shoulder, caressed his hip. The way he'd been all smiles when they'd returned to the group. The warm feeling of his arms around him after Rowan gave him his present. The texting afterward. The planning for the future, a full *year* in advance.

So now he's all confused again. Hates feeling like this more than anything. So unsure when he's used to being in control or, at the very least, having a decent understanding of what the hell's going on in his life. But now…. It's nothing short of emotional whiplash, and Rowan does not know how to handle it.

The next thing he knows, Rowan's in his car and driving aimlessly, hoping to find something like an answer to his confusion somewhere on the pavement of Boston's rigid streets. Twenty minutes later, he finds himself staring up at the unlit marquee lights of the Menagerie. It's undoubtedly closed now, but the thought of going inside makes his head spin, and he knows it wouldn't have helped him.

So he turns around, intending to go back and sulk at home like he should have been doing all along, when the smell of bacon wafts in through his open window and another familiar sight comes into view.

Sheila's diner.

Fuck it. He pulls into an empty spot that thankfully doesn't require him to parallel park and makes his way into the all-too-familiar diner with the jingling of a bell.

There's nothing unexpected about the diner—not anymore—but he's not expecting to see Sheila herself front and center, pouring a cup of steaming hot coffee for one of the patrons at the countertop. For a second, his brain tells him that she's some kind of ghost that's doomed to be here forever.

"Rowan!" She beams when she sees him walking up. "I'm surprised to see you in the daylight."

"Could say the same for you," he says. "I thought you worked nights."

She laughs. "Oh no. Just Saturday nights. I'm here during the day the rest of the week."

Well, that makes much more sense than her being a disgruntled spirit or whatever tall tale Rowan was concocting. Though he does wonder if it has anything to do with that being the night that Mal comes here after he goes to the club.

"What brings you here?" she asks.

"Just in the area." It's not a complete lie, after all. "Thought I should finally try your coffee."

She places a fresh white mug in front of him and fills it to the brim, then places a miniature pitcher of milk down next to it. He normally takes it black, but today he decides to treat himself by adding two sugars and a generous splash of milk.

"Anything else I can get ya? I'm out of apple pie, but I have some lemon squares that are killer. Go right to your thighs, though you look like you can spare the bulk."

"Sure, that sounds great. And can I get a veggie egg-white omelet, please? Wheat toast?"

"You got it, hon."

As Sheila leaves to put in his order, Rowan sits at the counter and takes in his surroundings. It's definitely weird being here in the light of day rather than nearly midnight, when the only sources of light are neon signs and fluorescent lights. The natural sunlight from the large wall of windows streams in, illuminating the bright red stools and benches, the subtle sparkle of the material making them shine. The retro-looking photo frames gleam and reveal old fifties-style posters that Rowan's never really taken the time to notice before, his attention usually solely on Mal.

It really is amazing how comfortable he's gotten here, the sights and sounds and smells making him feel at home. What's sad is how much he misses having Mal here with him. How empty it feels when he's not here, despite there being many more patrons than every other time they've come here.

But the breakfast rush thins out while Rowan waits for his food, and he finds himself once again in a nearly empty diner, much closer to what he's used to. And when Sheila brings him his lemon square, he finally finds the opportunity to ask her something he's been wondering about the past few months.

"So I've been meaning to ask, but how did you know Hank?"

She scoffs and leans against the counter, one hip cocked to the side. "Bah, that old drunk wandered in here one night high as a kite, lookin' for handouts."

Rowan snorts. "Sounds about right."

"He took one look at my name tag and got all sentimental about some ex-girlfriend of his. Then asked if I was gonna shove anything inside him. I didn't bother asking, and he didn't bother explaining."

Rowan winces, also not wanting to know what the hell Hank was talking about, though he figures it had to do with Sheila Mapleton, who Hank lived with when Rowan was a kid.

Sheila continues her story. "I took pity on him and gave him some coffee and a sandwich, and the next thing I know, he's out the door with his food and my tip money. Swindled me outta food a couple more times throughout the years."

"Shit, seriously? I'm sorry, Sheila."

Fucking Hank.

"Not your fault. Besides, it was years ago, and I'd already emptied the tip jar when my bussers and waiters went home, so there was only a few dollars in there."

"He died a few years ago, and somehow I'm surprised to still keep finding people he's screwed over."

Her face is pitying, but her tone is anything but. "Sorry to hear that."

"It's fine. He'd been drinking himself to death since before I was born, so he had it coming."

She hums thoughtfully and leaves to help other patrons.

Rowan takes his first sip of coffee, and it really is delicious. Hot and fresh, with a hint of sweetness. He wishes he and Mal could come here during the day. Maybe now that they've broken that invisible barrier once, it'll happen more often.

He can't deny how weird it is being here without him, in this place that Mal had introduced to him. Already in his everyday life, more or less everything reminds him of Mal. Bottles of antiseptic at work with a bright caramel label? Same shade as Mal's eyes in the sunlight. Shorter-than-average guy with dark hair walking down the street? Could be Mal. Someone curses out the cashier at the grocery store? Mal would have chewed that guy the fuck out.

He's everywhere. Go figure that Rowan would try to solve his problems with Mal in a place that practically *smells* like him. Like cinnamon and worn leather.

Taking a deep breath, followed by a deeper sip of coffee, Rowan weighs his options. He could tell Jay about Mal. He trusts his older brother more than anybody on the planet, but…. But he knows Jay would respond with a snarky *Jesus Christ, Rowan,* or something similar, and tell him to either nut up and tell Mal how he feels or quit seeing him, cold turkey. Band-Aid approach.

The rest of his family wouldn't really give him much better advice. Aubrey would probably tell him something similar to Jay, her long string of exes hardly making her a helpless romantic. His younger siblings might be worse. Clara would probably swoon a bit and say he should go after him, assuming he could get her to listen to someone else's problems for five minutes to explain the situation. Rory would probably ask if he has any priors now that he's turned traitor and become a full-blown cop. And Marc…? Well, Marc would probably actually give him some good advice. But he's already had to suffer the embarrassment of asking him how to set up a Grindr profile in the past, and some wounds cut a little too deep.

He hadn't even realized he'd started eating the lemon square that Sheila brought him when she stops by and drops off his food, the pastry nothing but crumbs on the tiny dessert plate.

"Anything else I can getcha?" she asks.

"I'm good, but… can I ask you somethin' else, Sheila?"

She cocks one round hip against the counter, half leaning on it. "Shoot."

"It's kinda… personal, I guess. I wouldn't bring it up normally, but I kinda don't want my family to know 'cause they'd give me shit for it."

"Family's like that," Sheila laughs. "You won't find no judgment from me, honey. Whatever it is, I've either been through it myself or know someone who has."

"I uh... sorta like this guy. A lot. But we're not really... we're friends, I guess. But I don't know if he actually likes me back or if I'm just makin' shit up. And if he doesn't, I don't wanna fuck anything up by telling him."

He feels like a teenager asking his parents for advice on his crush, but something about the woman seems so caring and nonjudgmental that Rowan isn't bothered by it.

"How long have ya known him?"

"Few months."

"Hmm...," she muses, setting her sole focus on Rowan. It's a little unnerving being the center of attention of her small but alert hazel eyes. "How often do you see each other?"

"Usually once a week for a few hours." He pushes the home fries around on his plate, adding, "But we text pretty much every day."

"And do your conversations ever turn romantic, or are they strictly platonic?"

Rowan feels like he should be leaning back against a chaise lounge in a therapist's office.

"They're all over the place, I guess. Honestly most of the time they're a little... uh... not-safe-for-work, if you catch my drift. But then other times it'll be completely ordinary stuff."

"Well, that changes everything," she says, finally pulling up a stool from somewhere under the counter and taking a seat opposite him. "You're sleeping with this friend?"

Rowan's cheeks are undoubtedly as bright as the cherry-red seat cushions. "Yeah. That's... kind of how we started becoming friends."

Mercifully, Sheila's soft huff of a laugh is nothing but kind. "No need to get embarrassed, honey. I'm old, not dead."

"Sorry. I know, just... not something I make a habit of shouting off the rooftops, y'know?"

Her response is an affirmative hum.

"So you've been sleepin' with this guy for a few months, developed a friendship, talk every day even if you only see each other once a week— which, keep in mind, hon, is a miracle as you get older, even at your age. And now you caught feelings but don't know if he did too?"

The bite of omelet that Rowan had shoved in his mouth while she was talking is burning hot, but he manages to swallow with most of his taste buds intact. "That sums it up, yeah."

"How's the sex been? Different?"

He wishes he could blame the new wave of redness on the heat of his food.

"Yeah? Kinda…. I mean, I don't want to call it *intimate*, but it's definitely closer to that than it was before. But we don't…." He shakes his head. *She's heard it all*, he reminds himself. And he trusts that she won't judge him for sounding like an awkward teenager. "We don't even kiss or anything. Well, we kinda did once, but it was an accident and hasn't happened since." He doesn't bring up their *almost* kiss on the dance floor last night. "So it all still feels a little…."

"Impersonal?"

"Yeah, exactly. And I don't want to risk losing what we have by trying to make us become more. Especially if he doesn't want that."

She nods in understanding. "'Cause if he doesn't, it's never gonna be the same between you two."

Rowan sighs, nodding. He is glad that Sheila gets it, even if it makes the ache in his chest throb at hearing someone else say the words out loud.

"Seems to me like you're at a crossroads, Rowan. You have to decide if he's worth pursuing and potentially losing completely. From the looks of it, and don't take this the wrong way, you look like you've been beatin' yourself up over this for a while now."

The ketchup he'd doused his omelet with helps soothe the burn of her words, but only barely.

"I feel fucking stupid, is all. For wanting more. But like… I know I'll be pissed at myself if I don't try. There's been all these little moments the past couple months that make me think I'm not way off track here, but I can't gear myself up to potentially lose him."

"My opinion? If you're wonderin' about it this much, he probably is too."

Hope surges in Rowan's chest, dampening the ache.

"You think?"

"There's gonna be times when these things are completely one-sided, but if there's been signs that make you think you've got a shot, I say trust your gut." There's a sparkle in her eye as she points to his plate.

"Finish that first, though. You never want to confuse a gut instinct with hunger. Made *that* mistake with two ex-husbands."

Rowan erupts in genuine laughter, the first time he's done so since Mal's birthday last night.

"Thanks, Sheila."

She rips his bill off of her pad and slips it under the lip of his now-empty plate. "Anytime, sweets. I'm not even gonna try to fight you on this anymore," she adds and laughs, tapping the check.

"I think Hank got enough handouts for the rest of the Campbells combined," he tells her.

"And Rowan?" Sheila says as he stands to leave.

"Yeah?"

There's a knowing smile on her face that has Rowan's stomach doing preemptive somersaults.

"When you're ready, tell him. In all the years I've known him, I've never seen Mal so happy."

For the umpteenth time this morning, Rowan's cheeks flame. But this time, he can feel the telltale pitter-patter of butterflies throwing a rave in his belly and a tingle all the way down to his fucking toes. He wishes he weren't so transparent, but well… who the hell else would he have been talking about?

When he leaves, he tips her extra. Both for the advice and to make up for what Hank did years ago. Not that it means much now, but it makes him feel better.

THREE WEEKS have passed since Mal's birthday. Since Rowan talked to Sheila. The crisp, cool September air is a welcome relief from the blistering heat outside and the heat *inside* Mal's body that stays with him week after week, long after they've parted.

Rowan's gonna tell him.

Ask him?

Tell him.

He needs to find the right time. The right words.

I think we should—

The past couple months, I've been feeling—

What if we—

When I'm around you, I feel—

I know you feel it, too—
I like you, I like you, I l—

He scribbles them down in his mind and erases them over and over with a firm shake of his head. So many "I" statements. His psychiatrist would be proud if Rowan weren't too gut-wrenchingly embarrassed to say any of this shit out loud. One of his many character flaws is that he's always been terrible at talking about his feelings. Maybe it's his brain chemistry, or maybe it's from growing up Southie, where sharing your weaknesses—real or perceived—was a sure way to get your ass kicked.

Maybe that's why he's always had such bad luck in relationships, and why he *doesn't* want to fuck up this one.

This… arrangement.

He's gonna tell him tonight. At the diner. Just needs to find the right words, the right time. When they're walking home? Yeah. That way if it goes south, they both have a quick getaway.

The words will come to him when the time's right, he's sure of it. It's gonna be great.

ROWAN'S GOT Mal trussed up on the bench, calves roped to his thighs, legs wide. Spread-eagled for Rowan like he'd been wanting to get him for months. Face down on the bench, arms outstretched, muscles taut.

It's the most intense position they've done by far, and Rowan's mind reels with the trust that Mal is showing him. The clicker in Mal's hand has been silent save for the single *click* for "green" when Rowan's asked for a check-in.

All he hears instead are moans. Sweet, guttural, broken moans that vibrate around the breathable ball gag in his mouth.

It's a trade-off. One moan for every one of the beads Rowan pushes into Mal's hole, two for every one he drags slowly back out.

And as much as he craves Mal's moans, it's been too long since Rowan's heard his voice. Fuck, an hour? Fifteen minutes, maybe? He's lost all track of time, relying solely on the alarm on his phone to alert him if they're close to overstaying their time limit. He stuffs the last two beads into Mal's ass, toying with the loop at the end and circling it around his hole before rounding to Mal's front, carefully unclasping the gag from behind his head. Soft hair sweaty under his fingertips.

As the gag comes free, slick with spit, Rowan cups his cheeks, gingerly rubs at the redness on the sides of mouth from the bite of the gag's leather strap.

"So good for me, Mal. Tell me how it feels."

"Full...."

"Yeah? What else?"

Rowan pets over his shoulders, feeling the coils of rope one after another under his hands like speed bumps interrupting the smooth expanse of Mal's arms.

"Feels... *fuck*...." Mal's voice is raspy as he clears his throat. "Feels like I'm floating."

Mal's very much *not* floating. Not with forty feet of rope securing his limbs, anyway. He's well and truly rigged in place, unable to even push back the slightest bit against Rowan's prying hands. But fuck if that doesn't go straight to Rowan's dick—getting Mal right where he wants him, knowing that he wants to be there as badly as Rowan wants him there.

Every time Rowan gets Mal into that headspace—gives him that the safe, secure, *floaty* feeling—it's a direct shot of dopamine straight to his brain. There have been very few sessions that he's failed to get him there, something that Rowan prides himself on. It's the ultimate high that Rowan seeks out as much for Mal as for himself.

"Gonna fuck you like this," Rowan tells him, stroking his cheek. "And you're gonna sit here and take it like I know you can. You gonna be good?"

"So good, wanna be good...."

"You are, Mal. Always."

The beads come out one by one, a slow and steady pull that has Mal's hole stretching wide and clenching shut over and over. When they're all out, Rowan smooths his palm over Mal's hole, spread wide for him and twitching at the contact.

"Please...," Mal whines.

It's amazing how far he's come. From adamantly refusing to beg for anyone, now freely begging for Rowan's cock without prompting and at the tiniest hint of contact.

He's so fucking good.

"Shh...," Rowan coos. "Thought you wanted to be good for me?"

"I do."

"And you know I'm always gonna take care of you, right?"

"Right."

Smack!

"*Hhn!*"

Mal's asscheek vibrates and reddens with the force of Rowan's hand on him.

"So quit beggin' for it like I'm not gonna fuck you in five seconds."

With that, he slides into Mal's waiting hole, matching groans bouncing off the walls. The sight of Mal bound before him drives Rowan's hips forward, slow at first, then gaining speed with the breathy moans pouring from Mal's lips.

As much as Rowan loves heaving Mal around like a rag doll, having him perfectly still and unable to move is as much of a turn-on. He loses himself in the sensation, in the heat, in the bliss that is Mal's body, and lets himself drown in the din of slick skin and guttural groans.

And Mal may not be able to press back into him like he usually does, but it doesn't stop him from clenching around him, milking Rowan's cock for all it's worth. He'd once called himself the "world's best bottom," and Rowan swears he's right. Like he's sucking Rowan's soul out through his goddamn dick, and it makes him grip Mal's hips harder and pound into him faster.

Too soon, he's nearing his end, the room all but spinning and his body throbbing head to toe.

"Gonna fill you up."

"Yeah, *yeah*...."

"Wanna feel you come on my cock first."

"Can't... need—"

Smack! Smack!

"C'mon, Mal. I know I'm hittin' that spot. Focus."

"*Nngg*...."

Rowan slows down his thrusts, grinding his hips in tight circles and drawing back only an inch or two before drilling back in, working Mal's prostate.

"Fuck!"

"Know you can do it. Wanted to be good for me, 'member?"

"Yeah... want to... more, *please*...."

"I got you."

Rowan gives him everything. And in a dozen more thrusts, Mal's moaning beautifully, a crescendo from a soft mumble to a near shout as he spasms around Rowan's cock.

"Fuckin' *perfect*, Mal, God...."

And Rowan's right there with him, emptying inside Mal, body bowstring taut as he milks his release. The pleasure courses through him in waves, in time with the rhythmic pulsing of Mal's walls around him, perfectly in sync.

He pulls out slowly, watching in wonder as Mal's open hole winks at him and a dribble of Rowan's own come trickles out and drips onto the bench below.

Fuck. It's almost enough to get him hard again. If there's anyone able to make Rowan's body defy biology, it's definitely Mal.

Rowan grabs a damp cloth from the supply table and gingerly wipes the come and lube from between Mal's cheeks and thighs and the come from his cock where it's softening among his pubes. Something Mal's only really allowed him to do the past two months or so, after their more intense scenes, and Rowan takes the job and the gesture seriously, wiping thoroughly yet gently.

Rowan unties Mal like he's unwrapping a gift. Gingerly and with a precision that frees him quickly and efficiently. He flings each coil of rope over the bench, not bothering to wind it yet as he guides Mal to standing, then leads him to the bed. It's clear his legs are shaky from disuse, but he manages to stay upright and lies flat on his back on the leather bed.

The rope indentations zigzag along Mal's legs and arms, sweet pink to violent red from how hard he'd strained against the binds in some areas. Rowan rubs them gently, hands massaging Mal's skin to stimulate the blood flow. Pressing, pulling, sweeping, up and down and across. As he works him over, Mal's head dips softly back to the bed, eyes lightly closed.

"Feels okay?"

"Mmm. Yeah.... 'S good."

Rowan shifts to his legs, stroking his shins and his knees and his thighs, past his groin and up to his hips, then all the way back down to complete the circuit.

By the time Mal's breath has evened out and his skin has mostly returned to its normal color, Rowan's got a smile on his face that won't go away.

ROWAN IS still coasting on the high of their session on the walk back from Sheila's diner. He's gonna tell him. The marquee lights of the club are visible over the horizon, half a mile away, give or take. Plenty of time for a heart-to-heart. A confession and a plea.

"So…," Mal starts before Rowan can even open his mouth.

Rowan's pulse races, body a live wire and suddenly too alert for the quiet night.

But….

"My old Dom's gonna be back in town next week."

There's that chill in the air again, the first week of September signaling the end of summer, and it passes straight through Rowan's body like a ghost.

"Yeah?" Rowan asks, because what else is he supposed to do with that information?

"Said he wanted to do a scene together."

Rowan's feet don't stop moving, but he's pretty sure his heart does.

With a shuddering breath, he feigns nonchalance. "Okay? Go for it. You know you don't need to ask me, Mal."

Bitterness laces his tone; he knows it does, but it can't be helped. Not when he was seconds away from telling Mal that he wants to be more.

"I want you to be there. If you're cool with it."

Oh.

"To… watch? Or join in?"

"Prob'ly just watch. He's not big on sharing, but he's a big exhibitionist."

Last Rowan checked, you can't *share* something that doesn't belong to you in the first place. He chances a glance over at Mal, and he can faintly see the marks on his wrists and forearms from the rope.

Rowan lets himself be silent until they get to the next block. It's fucking weird hearing Mal talk about his old Dom. Rowan's predecessor. It feels like asking if your new boyfriend is cool with watching you sleep with your ex. And yeah, whatever. They don't have those titles for each other. Their arrangement still lets them sleep with other people, if they want. But the thing is, Rowan *hasn't* wanted to in a long time. And he thought that Mal was finally on the same page as him with that.

But it seems like Mal had his own agenda for their walk back tonight. Maybe this whole time Rowan's only been seeing what he wants to see. Maybe he's been interpreting Mal's actions the past few months as intimate when they should have been classified as something else. Something more platonic.

He thought they had something, is what it boils down to. And now he feels a lot like an idiot for thinking that.

"Are you gonna do the scene with him whether I'm there or not?" Rowan asks, and he knows it's pettiness and an unhealthy dose of spite that's making him ask.

But, mercifully, "No."

So Rowan's at a crossroads again, isn't he? Mal clearly wouldn't have brought it up if some part of him didn't want to do a scene with his former Dom again. But he also doesn't want to do it without Rowan there. For… what? Exactly? To show Rowan what a *real* Dom is like? It's been a while since he had doubts about his ability to dominate Mal, but now the worry rears its ugly head and comes straight to the forefront of Rowan's mind. He doesn't know how long Mal was with this guy before Rowan, but he must have been good enough to warrant a scene when the guy happens to be in Boston for a weekend vacation or a business trip or whatever.

A big part of him wants to say no. Now that he feels like he and Mal have gotten to the point of being nearly exclusive, he's finding it real hard to give that up. But that's the thing that he has to keep telling himself: No matter how much he wishes they were, they're *not* exclusive. Not yet. Maybe not ever if Rowan freaks out and gets all clingy and possessive like he's wont to do.

So maybe this is the cost of getting there. Watching someone else take his place for one night. Who knows? It could even be hot as hell. He's gotten off on thinking of the gangbang more times than he can count— seeing Mal with all those men. Maybe this won't be any different.

But even as he tries to rationalize it, he knows that it's different now. *They're* different now. Their dynamic at the very least, if not their actual selves. Hell, Rowan knows he's changed in countless ways since he started his arrangement with Mal.

What exactly those ways are, though, he's not sure he could put into words. His life feels like *more* now that he has Mal in it. It's in the little things, he guesses. A pep in his step on the way into work, a penchant for humming along to the schmoopy songs on the radio, a feeling of well-restedness the morning after waking from syrupy sweet dreams. Little things that could single-handedly cure his depression in one fell swoop if only he could grind them up and wash them down one at a time with a glass of water. He hasn't felt this good in a long time, and for once, he's not even waiting for the other shoe to drop.

At the very least, he can anticipate how good it'll feel to show Mal what a kickass Dom he has become.

The Menagerie looms over him by the time he finally gives Mal an answer.

"Okay. Text me the details."

He makes a break for his car with little more than a "See ya" and a wave goodbye.

THE SESSION is booked for the Green Room. Rowan remembers enough from his English literature classes before he'd tested out of them that the irony of being in a room associated with *envy* isn't lost on him. This will be the first time he's had to see Mal with someone else since the gangbang all those months ago. And while he knows that Mal has at least slept with other people—the condom incident still fresh in his mind, far away as it is—seeing it is a whole 'nother story.

The normal sashay in his step when he's walking into the club is all but gone, replaced with a sluggishness that should have him turning tail and heading straight back home. If Camilla notices his drastically different demeanor when she checks him in—which she almost certainly does—she doesn't mention it. She simply smiles and gives him directions to the correct room.

When he finally gets to the room, Mal's already there with another man. Standing—fully clothed, thankfully—and talking. The guy's not what Rowan expected, but he immediately dislikes him. The man is an inch or two taller than Mal, an inch or two shorter than Rowan. He's dressed in black slacks and a blue button-up with a starched white collar. Black belt. Shiny black shoes. Rolex watch. Dark brown hair that's starting to hit the salt-and-pepper stage putting him somewhere probably in his forties, maybe late thirties depending on his genetics.

He looks like a fucking accountant, Rowan thinks. Then he remembers that *Mal* is an accountant and throws that theory out the window. A CEO or something, then.

"Hey!" Mal says when he spots Rowan.

Though, Rowan guesses, he's *Malcolm* now.

"Hey," Rowan says, closing and locking the door behind him.

"Rowan, this is Steven. Steven, Rowan." Much more formal than when he'd introduced him to Amy at his birthday.

Steven. Probably spells it S-t-e-p-h-e-n like an asshole. Such an ordinary fucking name for an ordinary-looking guy. Definitely not someone who deserves someone extraordinary like Mal. Rowan shakes the guy's hand and finds it too clammy and delicate for his liking. Like this guy's never worked with his hands a day in his life, and it doesn't bode well for his ability to be a good Dom. How he managed to bag Mal is a mystery.

"Nice to finally meet my replacement. I'd wondered how long it would take Malcolm to find someone new."

His voice is a low purr that makes the hairs on the back of Rowan's neck stand up.

"Not too long, it seems," Rowan replies, though in truth he has no idea how long before the gangbang Steven left.

Steven snorts lightly through his nose and eyes Rowan up and down. Scrutinizing. Rowan feels his blood heat up in his veins, but returns the favor, keeping his face completely impassive.

"All right, put the rulers away," Mal quips with a roll of his eyes.

And yeah, Rowan knows what Mal's saying, but all he can think is that this guy better not have a bigger dick than he does.

"So how's this going to work?" Rowan asks. "Do you have a plan for the scene?"

"Pretty standard stuff—gagging, wrist restraints, and spanking."

"I assume we're going to do it raw like usual?" Steven asks, a glint in his eye.

"Condoms," Mal replies curtly.

Rowan's heart swells.

"Shame, but all right."

There's a thick leather armchair in the corner, several feet from the same platform bed that's been in all the other rooms so far. Rowan takes his cue from Mal's nod to retreat to the chair, where he'll have a front-row seat to watch Mal get fucked by someone else.

As Rowan drops down into the chair, the air in the room suddenly shifts.

"Clothes off," Steven instructs.

There's a bite to it that tells Rowan the guy knows how to order others around, but the cadence of it makes it seem more like he's used to ordering around the hired help. But Mal complies, and with a swift nod, he deftly strips out of his black button-up shirt, letting it fall to the floor, followed by his shoes and the rest of his clothes.

Seeing Mal naked predictably spikes Rowan's pulse, but he's a far cry from being as hard as he would normally be if he were in Steven's position. The same goes for Mal, Rowan notices. There's a pulse of interest between his legs, but he isn't fully hard yet. Rowan chalks it up to nerves, maybe. But then, Mal hadn't even batted an eye when he'd gotten on his knees for ten men a few months ago, so this might as well be a regular old Saturday night for him. Or maybe he's bored already with Steven.

In a practiced set of motions, Steven binds Mal's wrists behind his back with leather cuffs. Something Rowan's done more than a dozen times himself by now. His fingers twitch with the phantom sensation of cool metal and soft leather as Steven pushes Mal onto the bed.

Mal is facing Rowan, eyes heavily lidded. Intense. The look alone makes him throb in his jeans. Steven climbs on the bed behind Mal, barely looming over him. He shoves his hips against Mal's bound hands.

"Get me out," Steven tells him.

"How d'you expect me to do that?" Mal quips.

Rowan tries to force down his laugh, but it comes out a garbled sound that he tries to cover with a cough.

"Same way you've done a hundred times, you little slut."

The realization of how long they've been together—exaggerated or not—hits Rowan like a freight truck, and suddenly he's not laughing anymore. That's at least two years if the number is to be believed. Despite his own connection with Mal and their chemistry, Rowan feels himself shrivel a bit. But he shakes it off. Mal wanted him here for a reason. And

Rowan owes it to him to at least *pay attention* and enjoy the show, as much as he'd rather be up there himself.

Mal fumbles with Steven's pants, eventually working him free. Steven shuffles around so his back is facing Rowan and Mal is turned three-quarters of the way to him. Still perfectly in view. From the glimpse he'd gotten, he can tell that Steven's cock is average. Nothing special in either the girth or length department. How a size queen like Mal got by with it is a mystery. Rowan knows for a fact that it's not *all* in how you use it. Size *does* matter. Or maybe Mal *became* a size queen after Rowan. That thought sends a rejuvenating rush of possessive pride through Rowan that he doesn't even try to shake off or ignore.

He's so lost in his thoughts that he didn't even notice Steven wrapping his cock and shoving it deep in Mal's throat. He hadn't even gotten fully undressed, his already undone slacks now shoved halfway down his thighs.

Rowan can't lie that the sight of Mal sucking dick gets him going, even if he has to fight off the curl of jealousy in his belly. Mal's a goddamn natural. Taking Steven deep, jaw slack and breathing raggedly through his nose as Steven fucks his mouth. His mouth was fucking—

"Made to suck cock," Steven grunts.

For once, Rowan agrees with him.

He spreads his legs wider and palms himself, his growing erection in desperate need of attention. But he won't take it out yet. As much a tease for himself as for Mal, whose eyes are glued to where Rowan's hand strokes rhythmically over his bulge. Even with another man's cock in his mouth, he's still got all his attention focused on Rowan.

And fuck if that isn't the hottest shit.

With a sharp hiss, Steven mutters, "Watch the teeth. You're getting sloppy."

As if Mal's head game isn't top tier, even if—hell, *because*—he gets filthy and sloppy with it when he really gets into it. Like he's getting into it now. He adjusts his stance so he can get a better angle, legs spread wide and head dipped low, bobbing freely and with lewd slurping noises that go straight from Rowan's ears to his dick. Rowan sees that Mal's hard now, cock hanging heavy between his spread legs.

It's torture to not jump up and suck his beautiful thick cock down, Steven be damned. He palms himself harder when Mal pulls off with a gasp, a thin trail of spit connecting his lower lip to the tip of Steven's cock. It's now that Rowan would pet his face and tell him how good he was.

"You've gotten rusty, Malcolm" is what Steven tells him instead.

Last week, Mal sucked him off so well that he nearly saw stars and had to pull off to avoid blowing early. And *that* is rusty? Rowan thinks that Steven either has no idea what good head is, or he's being an asshole for the sake of being an asshole. Something that Rowan knows doesn't usually make someone a good Dom.

"Is that how he likes to be sucked? Badly?" Steven asks, tearing the condom off and tucking himself away before chucking the condom in Rowan's general direction.

Rowan nearly gets up and throws it back at him.

"N—" Mal's eyebrows knit together for a beat before he answers firmly, "No…, Sir."

"And you've nearly forgotten my title. *Tsk, tsk.* Let's get that mouth of yours shut before you make a bigger fool of yourself."

Even when he's being rough and mean with Mal, Rowan's own admonishments never come with the harsh bite of cruelty underlying them that Steven's seem to.

They've used a breathable ball gag a few times, but Steven grabs a long piece of black cloth from the bed that Rowan hadn't noticed.

"Open your mouth," he tells Mal.

"Make me."

In his seat, Rowan smirks.

But Steven clicks his tongue again, spins Mal in place, and forces the gag in his mouth, tying it tight across the back of his head. Mal lets out a groan as the fabric tugs at the corners of his lips.

"Still acting out, I see," Steven notes.

Like being a brat isn't Mal's default state the majority of the time he scenes. It's practically his signature fucking personality trait in bed. Part of Rowan can't help but wonder if Mal's changed since he was last with Steven, or if Steven really didn't know him at all.

Steven adjusts Mal's cuffs so they're clasped in front of him, then pushes him down on all fours, still facing Rowan.

"Think it's time we see if you can still take it like you used to."

After climbing off the side of the bed, Steven stands beside Mal, stroking roughly over his back and ass.

The first spank is hard, straight to Mal's ass.

"Mmm!" Mal groans.

Mal's head dips, breaking eye contact with Rowan for the first time since they got started. More hard spanks in quick succession, the sound reverberating off the green walls. He grunts or groans into the bed with each spank, fingers clenched together and turning pale white, tattoos all but popping off his knuckles.

Steven didn't even ease Mal into it, which Rowan knows he prefers.

Mal's grunting grows more frequent, but varies in its volume from the barest squeaks to throat-rattling groans. Something about his noises sounds stilted, though. Not quite what Rowan is used to hearing week after week. Not like the sweet sounds he's committed to memory.

Steven keeps spanking, stopping every few hits to adjust himself in his jeans. Clearly enjoying *him*self, while Rowan's all but gone soft.

As Rowan watches, his mind reels. Does Steven know what Mal's favorite positions are? Probably. Does Steven know that Mal's toes curl before he comes? Maybe. But does Steven know why Mal goes by Malcolm? Most likely not. Does Steven know that he raised his sister by himself to get away from his abusive father? Definitely not.

Rowan knows all those things and more. He knows that Mal hums along to classic rock songs when he's in a good mood. He knows that he's Southie through and through—and proud of it—even though he lives in the Back Bay now. He knows that he likes pretty lace panties and that his eyes glimmer in the sunlight like diamonds.

Rowan wants to see Mal's face. *Needs* to see his face. Because this is… well, intense doesn't quite capture it. He needs to know that Mal is enjoying himself. He's used to hearing his groans muffled through a gag, even, but the sounds he's making are shy of *actual* pain. And he's pulling away from every impact, squirming in his restraints in a way that Rowan can't place but that looks different from his normal squirming.

"Has this little bitch made you soft, Malcolm?"

Mal's full name is poison on the man's tongue. Rowan can only imagine what it would be like to hear him call him *Mal*. Rowan has no idea what he ever saw in this guy.

"No, Sir." His voice is garbled through the gag, the words barely intelligible.

"I think he has. You used to be so good for me. Now you're distracted. *Weak.*"

Rowan's fingers dig into the armrests, angry half-moons scratched into the soft leather. He bites back the response on the tip of his tongue, saliva and the bitter taste of unplaced anger flooding his mouth. Mal's the strongest fucking person that Rowan knows.

"Or is this all just because your new toy's here, watching?"

Rowan can't understand Mal's reply, quiet and jumbled as it is.

Smack! Smack! Smack!

An ugly knot of jealousy coils itself in Rowan's belly, threatening to rise up and burst out of his chest. Mal finally raises his head again to meet Rowan's gaze, eyes brimming with wetness. The cloth gag digging into the corners of his mouth is damp with spit and snot, and Mal's lips twitch as he looks pleadingly toward Rowan.

Something's not right. This isn't a look he's seen from Mal before, no matter how deep in it he's been. He's made him cry before, but it didn't look like this. *Then* his features were relaxed, body loose and moaning freely. *Now* he looks tense, on the verge of quivering. Rowan sits up straighter, nerves tingling, ready to intervene. And then he sees what Mal's been mouthing through the gag.

Red.

He's calling to him.

He's *safewording*, but no sound is coming from his mouth except muffled whimpers.

Smack! Smack!

Each spank is like a gunshot, sharp and punctuated.

But then, finally audible—

"R-rcd. *Red*!"

And Steven doesn't stop. Definitely hears the word from right next to Mal if Rowan could hear it across the room. Another hard spank echoes in the room, this one a shotgun blast that makes Rowan's blood run cold.

"Hey," Rowan hears himself say. Too quiet at first, then as Mal calls out again, louder, firmer, *angrier*, "Hey!"

Steven's only response is a gritted, "Shut the *fuck* up, he's *mine*," as he raises his hand again.

In an instant, Rowan's across the room, and before he knows what's happening, his fist is flying. All at once, he hears the satisfying *crack*! of the man's nose and the *thump*! as his knees give out and he crumples to the floor.

Steven makes a garbled noise of pain from below, but Rowan's entire focus is on Mal. He kneels down in front of him, locking eyes with him as he quickly unties the knot from the gag and flings it to the floor.

"Okay?" Rowan asks, frantic, cradling Mal's head between his hands.

Mal nods jerkily, a tear spilling over and rolling down his cheek before disappearing under Rowan's thumb. He swipes it away, rubbing Mal's cheek softly.

Rowan frantically unclasps Mal's wrists as he leans toward Steven and growls, "I'm no bitch, asshole. And Mal doesn't *belong* to anyone."

Steven only groans in response, hands clasped over his nose as blood gushes around his fingers.

With Mal fully released, Rowan scoops up his clothes from the floor in one hand and takes Mal's arm with the other, guiding him out of the room and down the hall.

He opens the door to one of the recovery rooms, Mal silent at his side but swaying gently. Rowan's never been in this room before. They've never needed it, thankfully. He guides Mal to the queen-size bed he sees off to the side—an *actual* bed with clean white sheets and a puffy duvet—and gets him settled on it, clothes placed by the headboard.

He doesn't want to leave Mal alone in this state, but he also doesn't want Steven to fuck off and disappear before he faces any consequences for his actions.

"You okay for a minute?"

Mal nods, mumbles a "Yeah," and Rowan's out the door.

Rowan's eyes are wild as he races down the three flights of stairs to Clover's office. Pounds his fist on the door twice and flings it open without even waiting for an answer.

Clover's typing something on her computer, but she snaps her head up at Rowan's impromptu entry.

"Just punched some fucking asshole in the Green Room. Steven? He ignored Mal's safeword."

"Holy *shit*," Clover says, standing abruptly. "Do I need to call an ambulance or the police? For him or for Mal?"

"I don't think so. I'm going to check on Mal again. The guy's nose is definitely broken, but he'll live as long as he doesn't cross my path again."

She rushes out of her office, walkie-talkie in hand. "Enrico, fourth floor, Green Room, code yellow."

The crackle of the walkie fizzles out as Clover leads Rowan back up the stairs to the fourth floor, taking the steps two at a time before heading straight to the Green Room, the security guard she'd paged reaching the room right before her.

Rowan doesn't go in with her, leaving her to deal with the asshole herself. Instead he rushes back to the recovery room to check on Mal. When he spots him, he's kneeling on the bed, motionless save for the slow side-to-side movements of his head and the steady rise and fall of his bare chest.

"Hey," Rowan says quietly, closing and locking the door.

He watches as Mal's gold eyes blink open, pupils shrinking the tiniest amount as they adjust to the dim, warm lights.

"Hey."

Rowan climbs onto the bed beside him, noting that he's pulled on his briefs but nothing else, and takes in the room for the first time. It's nice. Pleasantly warm, a stark contrast to the cool chill of the normal playrooms. Soft cream-colored walls with dim yellow lights. Two plush couches off to one side, tasteful beige furniture covers lining the cushions and armrests. Lush plants in each corner with a small bubbling water feature on the side wall and a fully stocked supply table with the usual items plus a large basket of all types of medical supplies. Rowan thinks that Mal's case is more mental than physical, but it's nice to have the supplies here just in case.

"Never realized how fuckin' shit he was," Mal grumbles, settling down cross-legged on the bed.

Rowan envelops him in a tight hug and feels Mal melt into it, face buried into Rowan's shoulder.

"I'm so sorry that happened, Mal. But I'm proud of you for stopping it when you did."

They pull apart, Rowan keeping contact with Mal's upper arm. For both of them.

"We used to have people watch us all the time," he says, voice a little distant, eyes cast off to the side. "Was wicked hot back then, but now…."

"Now it felt wrong."

"Yeah."

Mal meets Rowan's eyes for a moment, the contact lingering and intimate in the dim light.

"D'you want to lie down?"

The deep breath that Mal heaves out could go either way, but he tilts to the side and falls down onto the bed, jostling the mattress under Rowan slightly. For too long Rowan stares at Mal sprawled on the bed, having wanted to get him in an actual bed for so long that he feels guilty for enjoying the sight under the circumstances. But he looks fucking beautiful outlined in white, stark black tattoos painting a lovely contrast. Rowan swallows down his desire and lies down at Mal's side, turned to face him.

As he watches his profile and the steady rise and fall of his chest, the soothing sounds of the bubbling water feature help to steady his heart rate, still thundering away from the chaos of the past ten minutes. Tentatively Rowan brings a hand to Mal's cheek, stroking at the soft hairs behind his ear. They lay in silence for an unknown amount of time, Rowan's thumb starting to ache from the repetitive motion.

"Wanna talk about it?" he asks, breaking the near silence.

"No." Mal places a hand over Rowan's, stilling his movements. "Not right now."

Rowan takes that as a sign that Mal will want to talk eventually. And he'll listen when he does. For now he can be here for him.

Mal sighs. Rolls onto his side. Tentatively rests his head against Rowan's shoulder with one arm slung across his stomach. His breath catches in his throat, heart rate quadrupling underneath Mal's cheek. Part of him hopes Mal can't tell. Part of him hopes he can.

As much as he's longed for this, Rowan can't shake the feeling that the position is only because Mal is in such a vulnerable place right now. Nevertheless he wraps an arm around Mal's shoulder and strokes his skin delicately, feeling the gentle rise and fall of his chest. His skin is warm, and Rowan allows himself to sigh into the contact.

Mal breathes softly.

The water fountain bubbles.

Everything is still and comfortable, and Rowan knows that they're like this because of a serious situation, but he wants so badly to enjoy the moment that he nearly lets himself forget. He lets himself imagine that they've woken up together, made love in the early morning light, and are enjoying the aftermath together. Not huddled together in a recovery room at a BDSM club after Mal's been practically violated.

Eventually, Mal stirs. He lets out a tiny mewl that Rowan wants to bottle up and save for a rainy day.

"Okay?" Rowan asks quietly, barely more than a whisper.

"Yeah. Thanks."

When Mal lifts his head, Rowan instantly misses the contact. Goose bumps pebble up along his arms as Mal swings his legs off the bed and sits upright.

Mal reaches for his clothes, pulls on his shirt first, movements slow and methodical. Hair mussed and shirt lines etched onto his face where his head was pressed against Rowan's shoulder.

"Do you want to get something to eat?" Rowan asks as Mal finishes getting dressed.

"Not tonight. Just wanna get home."

They stand facing one another, Mal's eyes flitting everywhere but Rowan's.

"Okay. You good to drive?"

"Yeah, I'm good."

There's a beat of silence that stretches on for an eternity. Rowan wants to hug him, but he hesitates. Despite their near cuddling moments ago, he's not sure if the touch would be welcome or met with trepidation. Instead he settles on trailing a hand down Mal's arm, stopping and squeezing his palm in what he hopes is a comforting and reassuring gesture.

"Text me when you get there."

Mal's hand flexes when Rowan lets go. Finally Mal meets Rowan's eyes, his so golden brown and so beautiful even in the dim light.

"I will."

A LITTLE over twenty minutes later, as Rowan is pulling up to his apartment complex, he finds a text message from Mal.

[MS] *home*

[RC] *Ok good*

[RC] *Call or text me if you need anything ok?*
[MS] *i will*

This time Rowan believes him.

He collapses into bed, utterly exhausted and mind a hazy mess of thoughts and emotions. His body feels heavy and useless—a sack of flour left at the bottom of the pantry and slowly leaking out through a pinprick hole. It's a feeling he's all too familiar with, and he can only pray that he only needs a good night's sleep to get back to feeling normal again.

THE NEXT day, Clover asks Rowan and Mal to meet her at the club to discuss the incident. It's strange being at the club in the daytime. While it's normally closed, she'd come in specially for the two of them, greeting them at the front door and unlocking it before ushering them inside. She leads them through the empty club, flicking on lights here and there to illuminate the way to her office. The air feels different somehow. Thicker, maybe. Or maybe it's the anticipation and dread congealing in Rowan's stomach and rising up to his throat.

Sitting in Clover's office under the harsh fluorescent lights, Mal looks about as well as Rowan feels. Rowan notices him glance at his bandaged hand, then quickly flick his eyes away once Rowan curls his fingers into a fist in his lap.

"So," Clover starts, lacing her hands together behind her desk. "As you both know, fighting is against the club's rules and usually results in membership suspension."

Rowan's heart sinks as he chances a side glance at Mal, his expression hardened.

"But given the circumstances—Mal, your safeword being ignored—we're obviously not going to take any further action."

The relieved sigh Rowan heaves is palpable in the quiet room.

"And Steven?" Mal asks, voice stern.

"His membership is revoked with no chance of renewal," she says, a slight smile in her eyes and voice.

"Thank Christ," Rowan says.

"I'm sorry that happened to you, Mal. And you, Rowan. We obviously do our best to avoid these types of situations when we vet prospective members, but this seems like an out-of-the-ordinary circumstance."

"Is he gonna… press charges or anything?" Rowan asks, his temper from yesterday soothed and the potential consequences of his actions finally sinking in.

"No."

"Woulda killed him myself if he tried anything like that," Mal says, a fierceness in his voice that makes Rowan's heart catch in his throat.

He wouldn't put it past him.

Clover meets each of their eyes, and the moment she switches from *friend* back to *manager* is evident. "There's obviously no making up for this, but your membership fees will be waived for this month. Is there anything else we can do to help rectify this for you both?"

"Long as the fucker's banned, I'm good."

Rowan nods in agreement. "Me too."

"Okay," Clover says, jotting something down on her computer. "Is there anything else either of you want or need from me today, then?"

With two simultaneous shakes of their heads, Rowan and Mal heave mutual sighs of relief.

"How'd he look yesterday?" Rowan asks, curiosity rising.

"Oh, his nose was definitely broken. You did a serious number on him," she laughs. Probably inappropriate for the club manager, but what-the-fuck-ever.

"Good," Mal replies for them both. "Should'a hit him again."

"Enrico had to wrestle him out the door with how much he was putting up a fight."

"Damn. Enrico's a big guy too."

"Mm-hmm," Clover agrees. "We had a short but to-the-point conversation. Once his temper calmed down, he seemed to realize what he had done, even if he was unapologetic about it."

Her eyes harden, and Rowan knows that she would have the same reaction even if it wasn't one of her best friends who this happened to.

"Guy's a piece of shit. Can't believe I never saw it before," Mal laments.

"You did nothing wrong, Mal," Rowan tells him, reaching across to lay a hand on his knee.

"Agreed." Clover nods. "It's a difficult situation, but I think the both of you handled it the best you could. We have a few legal issues to deal with on our end, but nothing either of you has to worry about. For all intents and purposes, it's done and dusted."

Rowan hums thoughtfully. In truth he probably could have *not* resorted to physical violence, but well, fuck that guy. He wasn't going to sit idly by while Mal was being subjected to something he didn't want.

"Thanks, Clove," Mal says.

Rowan gives his own thanks, and the pair of them walk out of the club with Clover, who locks the door behind them.

Clover pulls each of them into a hug. It's warm and sincere, a comfort that Rowan appreciates, and he finds himself relaxing into it. She smells like lemongrass and pear, like she did when they'd danced together on Mal's birthday.

The night that probably started this whole situation in the first place.

When Clover leaves, Rowan and Mal stand outside the door to the Menagerie, taking each other in.

"You wanna go for a walk?" Mal asks, surprising Rowan.

"Sure. Let's go."

They set off with no particular destination in mind, quiet for the first few minutes. It's chilly enough out that Rowan's glad he brought his green jacket with him—Mal's got his own light denim jacket on, the rustling of the fabric drawing Rowan's focus as they walk.

The Back Bay passes them by, all quaint brownstones with wrought-iron fences and yoga studios and cafés decorated with flowers and handwritten chalk signs. Eventually the buildings fade away and small patches of lush green greet them, lit by the early morning sun. The foliage has only begun changing, greens shifting the slightest bit to umber and yellow.

A small, clean park comes into view, completely abandoned at this time of the morning. The brightly colored merry-go-round squeaks, and the plastic-wrapped chain swings rattle in the wind. They settle on the wooden swing set, the black seats dipping under their weight.

"So I went to Sheila's the other day," Rowan says, breaking the silence with the spur-of-the-moment admission.

The other day, a couple weeks ago, whatever. Immediately he wants to kick himself. This wasn't how he wanted today to go. He's not sure he even *wants* to tell Mal how he feels anymore, after everything that happened yesterday. At least not today. He isn't sure how Mal would react to the confession so soon after such an emotional evening.

"Oh yeah? Takin' over my stomping grounds, huh?"

Mal's teasing voice pulls Rowan back from the edge, and he huffs out a laugh. Moves his feet a bit to sway against the breeze blowing past his cheeks.

"Nah, just went for a drive and got hungry." It's not a complete lie. More like a gentle omission of the truth. "Was weird… being there without you," he admits.

"Yeah?"

"Mmm."

Mal kicks off from the ground, starting up a gentle swing with each pump of his legs. Rowan watches him while he sways.

"How'd you find that place, anyway?" Rowan asks. He figures it'll be a safer subject to talk about than yesterday.

At first, Mal doesn't say anything. Simply swings higher and higher, until he's nearly level with the top of the swing set, the wooden frame creaking ominously. On one particularly big swing, Rowan thinks he's going to go all the way over. But then he stills his legs, letting gravity pull him back to earth in progressively smaller, sweeping arcs. He heaves a sigh as he finally stills next to Rowan, stirring up the wood chips on the ground with his feet.

"When I left with Amy, I didn't know where to go," he says, voice nearly drowned out by the wind. When it calms down a minute later, he continues, staring straight ahead into the jungle gym across the park. "Didn't really have any other family that wasn't connected to Larry in some way, so we took the T all the way here. Walked for what felt like fuckin' miles lookin' for a hotel or something and wound up at Sheila's since it was the only place open. Turns out the Back Bay doesn't really do seedy, cheap motels."

Rowan snorts in acknowledgment, but lets Mal continue.

"So we walk in, two pathetic-ass-looking runaways. Might as well have been soaked through with rain and shivering for how sad we must'a looked. Anyway we ordered some food with the money I'd stolen before we left and ended up sitting there for *hours*."

"She didn't kick you out?"

"No." Mal turns to look at Rowan, eyes full of disbelief still, after all this time. "Said she heard us talkin' and wonderin' where we were gonna go. 'Bout me gearing up to steal a car to crash in for the night. But instead, she fuckin' just… took us in."

"No shit?"

"Yeah. Let us stay the night in her office. Had a pull-out couch and blankets. And a fuckin' safe and everything sittin' right there."

"You weren't tempted to steal it?" Rowan asks.

Mal sways side to side in his swing. "She told me she emptied it the other day, but if the cash was all there in the morning, she'd give me a job and let us stay."

"Jesus, I knew she was nice, but that's actual saint shit."

Mal hums. "I know. Couldn't believe it. But you bet I didn't touch that fuckin' safe. Started workin' there the next morning. Got Amy enrolled in a new school using the diner's address, which thankfully no one fuckin' questioned back then."

"What'd you do for work?"

"Started washin' dishes and shit. Bussing tables, cleaning, cooking sometimes when they were short-staffed. She couldn't pay much, but she let us eat whatever we wanted, which was almost worth more with how expensive food is here."

"Sounds like you had it pretty good."

His nod of agreement is evidence enough, but he adds, "Yeah. Fuckin' sucked sharin' a pull-out couch with my sister, though."

"I know the feeling. Had to share beds with all my siblings at one point or another."

Huffing a little laugh and twirling himself around in a circle, crisscrossing the chains, Mal commiserates, "Fuckin' Southie, man."

"How long'd you stay there?"

"'Bout a year."

Rowan whistles. "You finally save up enough to move out on your own?"

The wind howls, blowing a small pile of fallen leaves around the swing set. Mal dips down and picks one up, pulling the crunchy pieces off of the veins one by one.

"Couple months in, I started lookin' at her ledgers and saw she was massively in the fucking red. Helped her adjust her pricing, make some changes to the menu, and negotiate with her suppliers so she'd actually start makin' some real money."

"Damn, Mal."

"Started saving up then," he adds.

Rowan doesn't know how to put into words how he's feeling. He's a little blown away, to be honest. First Sheila's, then the Menagerie? Mal may have a trauma-and-street-hardened outer shell and an attitude that could scare the collar off a priest, but he has a heart of gold. Seems like he always has too. Rowan wants so badly to see more of it.

"What?" Mal asks, eyeing him suspiciously.

"Nothin'. Just… you're a good person, is all."

The compliment doesn't sit well with Mal, who turns to unsuccessfully hide his blush from Rowan, dropping the now leafless stem to the ground.

"Yeah, well…."

"I mean it."

Mal laughs gently, the sweet sound nearly swallowed by the wind. "I know you do, Red."

The nickname jars him a bit after last night. After hearing Mal whimper the word with tears streaking down his cheeks. But more than anything, he finds it comforting that Mal still has it in him to use it in a positive way. In a way just for Rowan.

They sit on the swings until the sun is overhead, Mal occasionally going for bursts of swinging while Rowan can't quite muster the energy to do more than rock one way or another. All the while, they make small talk. It feels a lot like in the beginning, the two of them avoiding talking about any particularly heavy subject in favor of people-watching and idle chitchat about music and TV shows.

It's nice, and Rowan doesn't exactly want it to end. But a family of a mother and three kids shows up to the playground, the kids making a beeline for the swings, only to be disappointed to find them occupied by two adults. Rowan takes it as their cue to leave.

"You ready to head back?" Rowan asks, slipping off the swing.

"Yeah. You got somewhere to be, or you wanna get somethin' to eat first?"

Rowan grins. "I could eat."

IT ISN'T until he's finally back home late that afternoon that Rowan realizes he hadn't taken his evening pills last night or his morning ones today. He curses to himself, setting an alarm in his phone for tonight.

One day of missed doses won't do any harm.

He's okay.

Chapter 10: Release

"Whoa, what the hell happened to your hand?" Addison asks as soon as Rowan walks into the station on Monday morning.

He'd done his best to clean it up, but there are still obvious bruises and cuts on his knuckles, thanks to Steven's nose cartilage.

"Long story," Rowan tells her, hoping to end the conversation there as he drops his backpack in his locker.

"Uh-huh. And we've got a long shift. Spill, mister."

Rowan sighs. Thinks about how he can word this to make it seem like he *didn't* punch a guy in the face for ignoring a safeword during a BDSM scene. Sighs again so Addison will know how put out he is by telling her even a shred of the truth.

"Had… an altercation."

"Well, that wasn't a long story at all. With who?"

He can hear the concern in her voice even through the nosiness.

"Just some guy."

"You went out and got in *an altercation* with *some guy?*"

As she reiterates it, Rowan winces, knowing he's digging himself in deeper. Again, Rowan sighs, moving to sit next to her on the open rig. She takes his hand, grabbing some gauze and antiseptic even though Rowan had long since done that on his own. Rowan watches as a curl draped over her forehead bounces with the dabbing motions she's making across his knuckles.

"It wasn't Mal, was it?" she asks lightly.

"No. Not… exactly."

She perks up, meeting his eyes for the first time this morning. "Was it *because* of him?"

"Yeah. Kinda… I kinda punched a guy for hurting him."

"*Jesus*, Rowan. You're not gonna get sued, are you?"

"No. He deserved it."

The small smile playing on her lips looks proud. "Good. The last thing you need is to go to jail over something like that."

"I don't think I have to worry about that, thankfully."

"He fight back?"

"Nah. Was a huge pussy."

Addison's laugh is a loud bark of a thing that spreads warmth through Rowan's chest, replacing the cold dread he'd felt at the beginning of their conversation.

"What did Mal say about it?"

"We haven't really talked about it… but I think he felt guilty that I did."

"How come?"

Rowan ponders it for a minute. "He doesn't really like being helpless, I don't think. Or feeling like someone needs to come to his rescue."

"Did he need it in the moment, though?"

She doesn't ask for details, which Rowan appreciates.

"I thought so." Another deep sigh. He winces as Addison tapes up his knuckles, the flayed skin catching on the tape. "I didn't even *think*, Ads. Just fuckin' flew off the handle and broke the guy's nose without a second thought. Thought I might'a been…."

Losing control. He doesn't say it. She gets it anyway, nodding.

"You've been good, Rowan. Haven't had an episode in a while. Least not one that you've had to call out for."

"Yeah. I've been okay."

There's a comfortable silence between them as Addison fiddles with Rowan's hand then pats him on the arm, signaling that she's finished.

"So, you full-on white-knighted for the guy, and you're *sure* you're just fucking?" she teases.

This time, Rowan doesn't bother answering her.

IT'S TUESDAY night when Mal calls Rowan. His phone buzzes in his pocket as he's unlocking his front door from a particularly rough day at work. The shift was grueling and long, with call after call after call coming in, leaving them barely any time to return to the station to take a break in between each one. It felt like an endless cycle of pain and discomfort, mentally ill patients, and pranks gone wrong. He doesn't even bother looking at the caller ID as he blindly swipes at his phone, expecting Jay or Aubrey or even his boss calling him back in for a double.

"Hello?"

"Hey."

Mal's voice startles Rowan, freezing him in place in his doorway momentarily.

"Hey," he says, finally snapping out of his daze and entering his apartment, dropping his backpack on the stool in the kitchen, and tossing his keys on the counter. "What's up?"

"Wanted to see if you could talk. You got a few minutes?"

He sounds so different on the phone. Quieter, somehow. Softer too. Rowan likes it.

In truth, he's exhausted. But he's not going to turn down a chance to talk to Mal. Especially since this is the first time he's ever called Rowan. *And* because of what happened with Steven a few days ago.

"Course. Everything okay?"

"Just thinkin' about the other day."

Rowan kicks off his shoes and immediately flops down on the couch, his body weight heavy as he sinks into the plush cushions.

Rowan's silent for a beat. "Yeah?"

Mal's silent for a beat. "Yeah."

And Rowan doesn't really know how to navigate this. Doesn't know where Mal's head's at or what he wants to talk about exactly, but he isn't offering any information. So he's at a bit of a loss here.

"You feeling okay?"

He can start there, at least. See if Mal's doing all right or if he's about to go into some sort of mental breakdown. If he does, Rowan's not sure how or *if* he can even handle that himself. But no matter what, he knows that he owes it to Mal to try.

"Yeah, I'm all right."

"Did you drop?" Rowan asks gently.

"Nah. I'm more pissed than anything. Been a long time since I had to fully safeword during a scene. I'm used to pulling yellows every once in a while, but…." He's quiet for a moment, and even through the phone, Rowan can feel that his gaze is somewhere far away. "I dropped that first time, y'know."

"Huh?"

"After the gangbang."

"Shit, really?"

The admission throws Rowan for a loop. Especially why Mal is bringing it up now of all times, months later. But he can go with the flow. Whatever Mal wants to talk about, there must be a good reason for it.

"Yeah."

"Had that happened before?"

"Never like that. It used to a lot when I first got into this shit 'cause I didn't know any better, and when I *did* know, didn't wanna admit I needed anything… *soft* or whatever. But it hadn't happened in years till that night. Felt like garbage all week."

Rowan's hit with a memory, a flash of clarity. Him meeting Mal at the club for the first time after the gangbang. Rowan asking how his week was. Mal taking a long time to answer with a simple, "Okay" or "Fine" or whatever he'd actually said. It nearly breaks Rowan's heart that he had waited this long to tell him the truth, but he's glad he trusts him enough now to tell him.

"What was different about that time? I thought you'd done scenes like that before."

"I did. That time it was kinda… jarring, I guess, gettin' used by a bunch'a strangers, then havin' you be all soft and shit. Messed with my head."

The admission hits him in the face like an icy splash of water. An unbidden wakeup call that has a chill running down his chest and dripping off his limbs.

"Fuck, I'm so sorry, Mal. I had no idea. I wanted to make sure you were okay."

"I know. Not your fault. It wasn't until the next morning anyway. When I was alone."

"Why didn't you tell me?"

"Didn't wanna freak you out, I guess. Kinda some heavy shit to drop on someone right away."

"Maybe, but that's what we both signed up for."

"Yeah," Mal sighs, the phone crackling with grainy static. "I know I shoulda communicated it, even though we just met."

"So it was only me being too gentle right after that caused it?"

"Not entirely. I guess I realized I liked havin' you touch me 'n wanted more of it. Even though we agreed to meet up, still couldn't get it outta my head that I'd never see you again, so it made the drop worse."

It's a punch to the gut and a kiss on the lips at the same time.

"When we met up the week after, were you still feeling the same way?"

"Till I saw you again."

Rowan laughs softly, hoping that Mal doesn't take it for unkindness. "Dunno how to feel about being both the cause and the cure for you dropping."

Thankfully, Mal snorts in response. "Got a knack, man."

There's a muffled rustling on the other end of the line, like Mal's changing positions. Rowan imagines him lounging on his own couch, settling in after a long day at work. He wonders if Mal has a home-office setup or if he uses a laptop at the kitchen table. He wonders if Mal *has* a kitchen table.

"Why bring it up now?" Rowan asks, still absentmindedly wondering about Mal's home setup.

A long exhale on the other end of the line brings Rowan back to the moment. "'Cause I don't want it to happen again."

"What can I do?"

"Just… talk to me. Wanna talk about it. Don't really know where to start. This shit's never happened to me before."

"Me neither, if that makes you feel better," Rowan offers.

"*Tch.* Thanks for the solidarity."

Rowan hums in amusement and starts picking at the stray pieces of blue yarn on the throw blanket that Aubrey had knitted for him during one of her new hobby sprees.

"Have you been sleeping okay the past couple nights? Getting enough to eat and drink, too?"

Rowan knows how to take care of people, even if he struggles with it himself sometimes.

"Slept like a rock on Saturday and Sunday night. Not so good last night." He laughs lightly, and it's a beautiful golden sound that has Rowan pressing the phone against his ear harder, as if it'll make Mal do it again. "Think you know I never have a problem eating."

Smiling into the phone, he realizes sadly that Mal's not here beside him to witness it. He clears his throat. "What happened last night? Like, bad dreams, or tossing and turning, or…?"

"Dreams, I guess. Sorta like… scenarios playing out in my head? I dunno. Couldn't… couldn't stop my brain from picturing it going down much worse than it did. Prob'ly think I'm fuckin' crazy, hallucinating shit."

Rowan swallows the newly formed lump in his throat. He knows all too well about crazy and about anxiety-induced hallucinations and probable PTSD. But Mal doesn't know that yet, and now's not the time to bring it up—not when Rowan's supposed to be a source of comfort for him.

"You're not crazy, Mal. You went through something traumatic. How your mind and body react to it doesn't say anything about you as a person."

And if Rowan's reminding himself of that fact at the same time, that's just a bonus.

"Yeah."

The silence between them stretches on for a tad longer than comfortable. Rowan's about to say something, anything, when Mal speaks again.

"How's your hand today?"

"It's seen worse," Rowan says with a laugh.

"Hit the guy pretty hard if the sound of his nose was anything to go by."

Rowan laughs lightly. "Yeah."

"Wish I could'a seen it," Mal laments.

"Are you… okay that I did that?"

"Hell yeah, man. Fuck that guy. Why do you ask?"

"I didn't want you to feel like… like I had to rescue you or some shit."

"Kinda did, though. Not like I could'a done much in the position I was in. Or the… the state of mind."

All Rowan can say to the relief that washes over him is "Okay."

It's quiet for a few moments. Rowan listens to Mal breathe softly on the other end of the line. He wonders if Mal's still on the couch or if he's moved. Maybe he's sitting up in bed right now, back against the headboard and legs crossed at the ankles.

He wants to ask him where he is, what he's doing, what he's wearing—to paint a better picture for himself as they talk. But he's too worried that it would sound like he's trying to start something, and something else comes out anyway.

"Why'd you wanna do a scene with him?" Rowan blurts.

The question maybe catches Mal off guard, because he takes a long few seconds to respond.

"'Cause I needed to see."

"See what?"

"If you and I actually had somethin' real or not."

Rowan's pulse hammers in his veins.

"And do we?"

It's hard to keep the edge of hopefulness out of his voice. He wonders if Mal can hear it anyway.

"Uh… yeah."

His heart soars. Maybe Sheila was right after all.

Rowan wonders if it's easier for Mal to talk like this. Talk about *feelings* when they're not face-to-face. Merely voice-to-voice with miles of space between them.

"He never…," Mal starts, backtracking almost and taking a deep breath that crackles through the phone. "He never used to be like that. Never ignored a word like that before."

The moment before is barely acknowledged, but Rowan will take it anyway.

"You said you used to have people watch you a lot. What was different this time?"

"Prob'ly you bein' there. You've got a… vibe, man."

"A vibe?"

"Like… a presence, I guess."

"Mal, are you saying I've got Big Dick Energy?"

Mal covers his laugh with a scoff. "Fuck off, Red. You know what I mean."

It's not pride or ego that makes Rowan agree with it. He and Steven clashed from the second he met the guy.

"So you think he was jealous? Why?"

"New situation, I guess?" Mal asks more than says. "Never really had anyone there that pulled my attention more than him."

It's the highest of compliments.

The blue threads continue to pile up as Rowan asks, "But everything else was the same besides that?"

"Yeah. It was the same shit we always did. Talked to me the same way when we were actively scening as he did the other night. Fuck, *you* talk to me like that. Just… felt different. Wrong, I guess. Can't explain it, man."

Rowan thinks that he probably can.

"So where do you wanna go from here?" Rowan asks.

"Whaddya mean?"

"I mean for us. I don't want to jump straight back into any intense stuff this weekend if either of us is gonna be rattled."

"Yeah, prob'ly a good idea. Do…." Rowan can picture him shaking his head. That pretty pink flush he gets every once in a while coloring his cheeks and ears and neck.

"What?"

There's a deep breath before Mal speaks again. "Do you wanna grab a drink or something on Saturday? Same time?"

Rowan's head spins. He has to lie down fully on the couch to prevent himself from falling back onto it. *Like a date?* echoes in his mind, but he forces himself not to blurt *this* particular thought out loud.

"Yeah, that'd be great."

Rowan Campbell has successfully played one thing cool in his life so far, and he thinks it earns him a congratulatory pat on the back. He'd do it if he could get his limbs to move.

They talk until Rowan's phone is hot against his cheek and his battery threatens to give out. When they finally hang up, it's close to midnight, and Rowan barely manages to pry off his work uniform before crawling into bed.

ROWAN BREATHES as deeply and evenly as he can while he gets ready to go out with Mal.

This time there's no good excuse for why they're going out other than to spend time together. No birthday, no getting to know one another's kinks, nothing. They could have easily skipped a week or two entirely and not seen each other, though the thought of that makes Rowan's stomach lurch. He hasn't gone without seeing Mal at least once a week since they started their arrangement several months ago, and the thought of it happening now—even hypothetically—is a little too painful for him to bear.

They meet outside the bar, a decent little hole-in-the-wall in the Back Bay, somewhere that seems much more suited to Mal's liking than the club they went to for his birthday. The floor's only slightly sticky with beer, with the occasional peanut shell or two strewn about, dark walls filled with signed photographs of famous patrons, and some rock song playing over the speakers. The bar is fully stocked with every type of liquor, from cheap brands to the top-shelf stuff that Rowan isn't sure he'd ever be able to justify buying.

"I'll get a table," Rowan says to Mal. "Grab me a beer? Whatever doesn't suck."

Mal salutes him. "One Bud Light, comin' up."

"I'll kill you if you get me a Bud Light, Mal."

Mal only laughs and stalks toward the bar.

Rowan finds them a table for two tucked away in a corner, much like their usual spot at Sheila's diner. The dim overhead lights cast the area in a warm yellow glow. A few minutes later, Mal appears by his side, placing a bottle of beer in front of each of them.

Mal had gotten him a Blue Ribbon, and he has to laugh as Mal takes a sip of his own beer.

"Thought I said something that doesn't suck?"

"Bitch, I know it's your favorite," Mal says, flicking the side of the bottle. His nail makes a tiny *tink*! against the glass that has Rowan grinning.

"What're you drinking?" Rowan asks, not recognizing the silvery label or the dark liquid inside.

"Some kinda local stout," Mal says, turning the bottle so Rowan can read the label. "They only sell it in-house, but it's pretty good. You wanna try?"

"Sure."

Mal slides the bottle over to him, the glass bottom making a *skriiitch* noise across the wooden tabletop, a ring of condensation streaking along the way.

When the near-black liquid hits his tongue, Rowan's first inclination is to grimace at the heaviness of it, and he hears Mal laughing gently as he tilts the bottle back farther. Tries not to think too hard about how it had Mal's lips wrapped around it moments ago as a more pleasant aftertaste of coffee settles in his mouth.

"First sip's always fuckin' weird, but it's got a good aftertaste," Mal tells him.

Nodding in agreement, Rowan slides the bottle back to Mal and wipes his mouth with the back of his hand. "'S good, though."

"Kinda weird not being at the club tonight," Mal says after a few moments.

Rowan hums. "What's the longest you've been away from it?" he asks, knowing that Mal's been going there for a long time, practically since the moment he was old enough.

"Few months. After Steven fucked off to Florida, I took some time off."

"Wow," Rowan says, slightly awed.

"What?"

"Just, that's not that much time to take off after, what, almost ten years?"

"Seven. That a problem?" The challenge in Mal's narrowed eyes is obvious.

Rowan feels nervous sweat pebble up on his forehead, something that's never happened with Mal. Leave it to his stupid mouth to fuck things up.

"No! Definitely not. Hell, you know most of what I did when I was younger, which is worse than having consensual sex at a BDSM club for years."

Thankfully, Mal's eyes soften. "I guess."

For once, Rowan's glad that his sordid past gives him an out. He looks around for a distraction, taking another long pull on his beer.

"You play pool?" Rowan asks when the couple previously occupying the table clears it.

"You sure you wanna take me on? I'm pretty good," Mal replies cockily.

It makes Rowan's heart pitter-patter in his chest.

He puts on his own sense of bravado.

"Used to hustle pool with Jay when we were teens," Rowan says, standing and heading to the pool table.

"Oh yeah, tough guy?"

"Mmm. Swindled more biker dudes than I can count outta their cash."

Mal laughs, a little incredulous, a little fond, and it has Rowan's heart racing.

While Rowan chalks the cues, Mal expertly racks the balls, one ball in the front, eight ball in the middle, alternating stripes and solids everywhere else. The *click, click, click* of the balls cracking together as Mal rolls them in the triangle takes Rowan back to swindling said bikers and drunk tourists out of cash when he and Jay would sneak into bars with fake IDs to make some extra money.

As confident as he is in his pool skills, Mal has a tendency to surprise the hell out of him, and he's not exactly sure he can beat him.

They play a quick match of Rock, Paper, Scissors to determine who gets to break, Mal huffing when Rowan beats his rock with paper. The warmth of his hand as he covers Mal's fist with his flat palm is searing, and he pulls away quickly, as if his faux paper might actually burn to ash at the touch.

Rowan dips over the table, and with a loud *crack*! the balls scatter, two striped balls sinking into two of the corner pockets.

"*Tch*," Mal scoffs. "Beginner's luck."

"You wish, Savaryn."

His next shot is a mess, nothing lined up neatly enough for him to sink anything.

Rowan grins as Mal leans over to take his own shot, admiring the way his jeans hug his ass.

"I see you starin' at the goods, Red."

The orange five ball sinks into the pocket.

"Looks like you have to go again. How unfortunate for me," Rowan teases as Mal leans obscenely over the pool table, far more than necessary to make the easy shot.

"Can see how bent outta shape you are about it."

They take turns, sometimes sinking two or three shots in a row, sometimes missing their marks entirely, but constantly throwing teasing jabs back and forth. Idly sipping their beers as they eye each other from across the green felt table.

It's ridiculous how attracted to him Rowan is.

Rowan wins the game, coolly sinking the eight ball into one of the middle pockets. Mal insists on best two out of three, and he wins the second game on a technicality—Rowan forgot to call the pocket for the eight ball because Mal was doing this *thing* on the cue with his hands that looked obscene and got Rowan all kinds of flustered. Mal laughed at him and reracked the balls. Fucker knew exactly what he was doing and the effect it would have on Rowan.

In the end, Mal wins the match but offers to buy Rowan another beer anyway. He's already had one, but another couldn't hurt. He'll have to pace himself.

After the display of Mal practically humping the pool table and parading his ass around in those tight jeans of his, the sight of him bringing the beer bottle up to his lips and taking a long swig, eyes fluttering closed in contentment, is more than Rowan can handle. He forces himself to look away, taking a tentative sip of his own beer as he leans back in his chair.

"What happens if you drink too much?" Mal asks, noticing the tiny sips Rowan's been taking.

Rowan picks at the label on the side of the bottle until it's nearly completely off on one side.

"I get fucked up really easily. Get drunk really fast, or if I go too hard, end up puking my guts out and spending the rest of the next day with a killer hangover."

"Too bad. I'd love to see you drunk."

"*Pft*. No you wouldn't. I'm a nightmare."

"Oh yeah?"

"Mmm. Real clingy and shit. Sappy too. Basically a drunk girl in a bathroom."

"Now that I *gotta* see someday."

Mal's smile is soft, so goddamn soft that it makes Rowan's insides churn. He doesn't have the heart to tell him that if he gets drunk, his meds basically stop working. He'll let Mal have his little fantasy. Part of him is glad for it. For not being able to drink anymore, especially around Mal. He knows that if he did manage to get drunk around him, he'd be hard pressed to stop himself from going and doing something stupid like admitting he's in love with him.

Oh.

Oh *fuck*.

There's a jolt in Rowan's stomach that makes his arm fly out and knock over his beer bottle, then frantically pick it up before the entire thing spills out on the table.

"Jesus, you okay, Red? You have one too many already?" Mal asks, eyebrows screwed inward in concern and lips pursed in a questioning pout that Rowan wants to kiss. Mal takes a handful of napkins from the dispenser and starts wiping up the mess while Rowan has a panic attack.

That can't be right. Can it? They've only known each other for a few months!

But even as he thinks it, Rowan knows deep down that it's true. He's fucking head over heels for Mal and his beautiful face and his razor-sharp humor and his tantalizing tattoos and his—

God fucking dammit.

Mal's still looking at him with that same look etched onto his face, and Rowan wants to smooth over the crease between his eyebrows with his thumb.

"I'm good, just thought I forgot to pay a bill," he lies.

Mal seems to accept the answer, shrugging and taking another pull of his beer as he pushes the wadded-up, soggy napkins to one side of the table. Even the simple motion has Rowan tracking his hands, thinking absently of how good they feel on his skin. How good Mal makes him feel *all over, all the time*.

"Should put that shit on auto pay," Mal suggests after a minute.

"Yeah, I'll do that."

The time passes by in a blur of laughter and casual touches that make Rowan's senses go haywire, and all of a sudden, it's last call, and he and Mal are paying off their tab and heading out into the cool autumn air.

They part with a hug that leaves Rowan breathless despite not being nearly crushing enough to cut off his air supply.

By the time Rowan slogs home, he's exhausted and riddled with confusion and anxiety and maybe a bit of acceptance.

When Rowan falls asleep that night, it's with a full heart but heavy limbs and heavier eyelids.

ROWAN FEELS it in his bones before his mind can really process it. Like the slow creaking of overtrodden wooden floors, his joints ache and struggle to move with the fluidity that he's used to. The days get longer and longer until they blur together completely, morning and night meaningless against the closed curtains in his bedroom.

He should have seen this coming. He barely manages to text work that he won't be coming in for the next few days before it really hits. It's been a while, but the sinking feeling is all too familiar.

The days come and go, and by the time Saturday rolls around, Rowan can't even dredge up the energy to plug in his long-dead phone to send Mal a text. If only he could overcome the inertia of the heavy weight sitting on his chest, he'd be fine. If only he could get out of bed, walk across the room, grab his phone from his backpack, plug it in, wait, wait, wait—

He knows Mal will be pissed—might even be *worried*—but he can't bring himself to care enough to do anything about it.

All he wants to do is lie in bed, curled under the covers.

At some point, he thinks Jay or maybe Clara comes by, but he's too wrapped up in thoughts of worthlessness to pay attention. Too glued to his bed to even lift his head or turn around at the worried "Rowan?"s that drift into his ears from across the room. It's hard to tell what's real anymore—what's a solid, tangible thing and what's a construct that his mind has fabricated to try to fuck him over.

It's been a few days, and Rowan's barely managed to overcome the heaviness in his bones long enough to get up, take a piss, and drink some water straight from the tap with cupped hands.

Hasn't managed to eat anything more than a packet of peanut butter crackers, but the thought of cooking anything—even one of the microwavable meals he's got in the freezer—seems an insurmountable task that makes his head hurt.

But despite his deep exhaustion and the weariness he feels from too much sleep and too little sustenance, all he can think about is Mal. Things have been going so well between them. They've grown undeniably closer over the past few months of scening, and especially after Mal's birthday a couple of weeks ago, and it feels like they're right on the cusp of something big. So of course it was only a matter of time until the shit hit the fan. Until Rowan's illness reared its big ugly head and fucked everything up.

He doesn't even *deserve* Mal, honestly. Someone like him should be with someone extraordinary, not someone deeply scarred like Rowan is. Someone who can love him the way he deserves and not with some half-baked semblance of love like Rowan must be feeling. How he ever thought that Mal could like—hell, *love*—him back must be the Ninth Wonder of the World.

Hot tears prick at his eyelids, shriveling up as they roll down his cheeks and stain his pillowcase.

NEARLY A week later, Rowan finally musters up the mental and physical strength to grab his phone and plug it in long enough to get it to turn on. He ignores the copious amounts of text and missed call notifications—though he does notice that over half of them are from Mal—and scrolls through his contacts to find Mal's name. He hesitates, thumb hovering over the Call button.

Should he even bother him? What if his texts and calls are all telling him that he's pissed that Rowan missed their session and that he wants to stop scening with him? Rowan's anxiety flares behind his eyelids, and he quickly scrolls to the texts from Mal.

[MS] *hey are you coming?*

[MS] *it's 830 man if you're late it's cool just lmk*

[MS] *wtf red it's 9 i'm not gonna wait around here forever*

[MS] *did something come up last night?*

[MS] *mfer are you ghosting me?*

[MS] *quit being a bitch and text me back*

[MS] *is everything ok?*

[MS] *i don't see your name in the obituaries so i assume you aren't dead*

[MS] *are you there?*

[MS] *why is your phone going straight to voicemail*

[MS] *can you please let me know if you're ok?*

[MS] *rowan???*

[MS] *what the fuck is going on? you're sick??*

[MS] *call me*

[MS] *please*

Rowan jabs the Call icon at the top of the text window.

Mal answers before the second ring.

"Hey!" Mal's voice comes through the receiver, and Rowan can hear the worry lacing his tone.

"Hi, Mal."

"Are you okay?" The words come out in a rush, each one hitting Rowan in the gut like a bullet.

"I'm okay. Sorry for going MIA," Rowan tells him with a halfhearted laugh that Mal ignores.

"What the hell happened, man? Your coworker—Addison?—told me you were sick but wouldn't give me any details."

For a moment, Rowan's stunned. "You went to my work?"

"Yeah, course I did. Thought you fuckin' ghosted me or… died or something."

"Not dead. Definitely didn't intend to ghost you, either."

"What happened?"

"I was sick. Didn't mean to worry you."

"I w—" Mal starts, and Rowan's glad he doesn't finish because it's clear he *was* worried. Worried enough to text and call him a couple dozen times and even go to his work. "What had you so sick that you couldn't even text me back, Rowan? The flu or something?"

"It's…."

Rowan takes a deep breath and exhales slowly. One, two, three in, four, five, six out. He hadn't wanted to tell Mal at *all*, but with everything that Mal's shared with him, it seems wrong to hide it from him any longer. And to be honest, a big part of him is tired of hiding it. He's wanted Mal to be more than a hookup to him for a while now, and trusting him with this is the first real step to getting there. Now instead of feeling backed into a corner like he thought he might feel, he wants Mal to know. To *understand.*

"It wasn't a cold or anything. I'm…." He tries again. "I've got depression. Like my mom had. Major depressive disorder, it's called. Got diagnosed when I was a teenager. Later got diagnosed with PTSD from all the shit I did when I was younger. Makes me go crazy sometimes. See things. Get angry. Feel like shit, you name it."

For a long moment, there's nothing but silence on the other end.

And finally, when Rowan's lip is bitten raw with worry, Mal replies, "Okay."

"Okay." No shock or disgust or any of the dozen other things Rowan had been expecting to color Mal's voice.

"But you're okay now? Just had… like, an episode or whatever?"

"I… yeah." His head's spinning with questions he wants to ask. "Couldn't get out of bed or do much of anything. Sometimes it gets worse than the usual run-of-the-mill depression I've got."

"You on meds for it? I remember you said your mom wasn't."

"I am. I'm good about taking 'em, mostly. But the past few weeks have been kinda rough. Y'know… emotional."

There's a sharp breath in on the other end of the line. "Was it cause'a…."

Steven.

"Partially, yeah. Didn't really think it affected me all that much till I felt like garbage."

"Fuck, I'm sorry, Red."

"Not your fault. I shoulda… shoulda told you a while ago."

Mal doesn't tell him that Rowan doesn't owe it to him to tell him about his life, but Rowan hears it anyway in the strangled sound he makes. But what Mal says is, "Why didn't you?"

Rowan shrugs before he realizes that Mal can't see him.

"Guess I didn't want you to think I was batshit crazy or, like… not able to be a good Dom or something."

"Well, I know you're batshit crazy, knew that shit after the gangbang," Mal jokes.

Rowan snorts out a soft laugh, the first time he's done so in well over a week. It feels good to laugh again. To laugh with Mal again.

"And you've been… fuck, the best Dom I've ever had, so I dunno what you were worried about, man," Mal adds.

The sincerity of the statement makes a puddle of warmth ripple in Rowan's belly.

"Yeah?"

"Yeah. Just… tell me next time, yeah? If this happens again."

"I will," Rowan promises.

He remembers the promise he made to himself all those months ago: That if his disease ever compromised their arrangement, he'd tell Mal about it. And he did. Even if not as quickly as he would have liked, he did still manage to keep his word. Rowan takes his own promises very seriously, having grown up without a lot of that in his life—words meaning things.

"Can I…," Mal starts, trailing off as if he'd bitten his lip.

"What?"

"Can I see you? Today? If you're up for it."

Rowan takes a shaky, surprised breath. "Maybe not today. I'm kinda… kinda gross. Haven't really showered or anything in a few days," he admits. Though by now it's been at least a week. "Tomorrow, though?"

"Yeah, that'd be good." There's no judgment in Mal's voice, for which Rowan is eternally grateful. "I'll text you."

"Okay," Rowan replies, unable to wipe the smile off his face.

"See you, Red."

"Bye, Mal."

WHEN TOMORROW comes, Rowan wakes with a sense of peace that he hasn't felt in weeks. A calm that he feels in his body as much as in his mind. Equilibrium restored. A large part of that, he thinks, is due to finally telling Mal about his depression. It feels like a ten-ton weight lifted off his chest, leaving him so light that he may float off into space.

He downs his newly adjusted pills with a glass of water from his nightstand that he doesn't remember putting there. He'd called his doctor right after he called Mal yesterday—which really shows where his priorities lie—and she'd only been slightly worried. It wasn't that bad of an episode, all things considered. He's had much, much worse in the past—to the point where he'd been close to actually trying to off himself—and the fact that he was still *kind of* on top of his meds when the depression really started to set in had helped. It can never be completely avoided, something it had taken him a long, long time to come to terms with after he was diagnosed, but it can at least be mitigated.

The warm shower water feels glorious on his skin. As he lathers his body wash and scrubs himself clean, he rinses away the sweat and the grime and the shame of being bedridden for a week.

It's always the first step to feeling better after a depressive bout. The first step to feeling *human* again. A nice long shower.

The second step is human interaction.

Mal.

It'll be good to see him again. Rowan's actually looking forward to it, the first thing he *has* looked forward to in a couple of weeks. Sometimes it seems like Mal's the one thing he never gets tired of, even when his body is screaming at him that he's exhausted. It's a good feeling. Even if there are nervous butterflies jittering in his stomach, he's missed being excited about things. Excited about *life*.

THEY AGREE to meet at Sheila's diner, a comfort after the past week and change that he didn't know he needed.

As soon as he walks inside the diner, he finds Mal sitting at their usual booth. When he hears the doorbell jingle at Rowan's entrance, Mal looks up and immediately stands, then speed walks over to Rowan.

Before Rowan can even get his bearings, Mal's wrapping him in a warm, tight hug.

"Hey," Mal breathes into his neck. "You okay?"

"I'm okay."

"Kinda look drained."

Rowan laughs. "Well, we can't all look perfect all the time, Mal," he says, cupping Mal's chin between his thumb and forefinger and tilting his beautiful face up for closer inspection.

Perfect as always.

Mal smirks but shrugs away from the touch with a shiver that Rowan barely notices. "Fuck you, man."

"Hey, that was a compliment." Rowan drops his hand, the contact of his palm on Mal's stubbly chin and the residual feeling of his arms around him warming him to his core.

They pull apart completely, as if realizing at the same time how close they'd been standing even after the hug had run its course. Rowan thinks he sees the faintest hint of a flush on the back of Mal's neck as he turns and waves him over to the counter.

Sheila's not here today, but they order from one of the waitresses, each getting an omelet—meat lovers for Mal, veggie for Rowan—coffee, and a blueberry muffin on the side.

They dive into the muffin as soon as they sit down, the sugary and tart treat melting on their tongues.

Conversation is light between them. Nothing serious. Nothing heavy or life-changing. It's nice being face-to-face with another person again. Especially when said person has a face like Mal's. A tone of voice like Mal's. A sense of humor like Mal's.

Their food comes out steaming hot and looking every bit as delicious as it always does. Rowan digs in, pan-seared veggies spilling from the cheesy center of his omelet.

"So depression, huh?" Mal says casually around a forkful of home fries.

"Yeah," Rowan sighs.

"Have you always known you've had it?"

Rowan sets his silverware down, knowing this is going to be a story that takes him a few minutes to get out.

"I got diagnosed when I was sixteen. Didn't know anything was really wrong at first. I ran away from home and joined a hard-core orthodox church group and had my first big episode while I was there…." Rowan stops, laughing a little incredulously at the memory. "Started seeing demons and shit and was convinced they were after me, then stole all the cash in the tithe box and went AWOL."

"Holy shit."

"Yup."

"And you didn't get arrested?"

"Not then. The police caught up to me eventually, though. Managed to avoid jail because my brother told them I was mentally ill and unable to take care of myself."

"Jesus."

"Yeah. Had to spend a month in a psych ward, drugged outta my mind. Reminded me a lot of my mom, actually. How she said her meds made her feel."

Telling Mal all of this feels good. Like an undue burden finally being released and freeing Rowan from the crushing weight of it. To his credit, Mal doesn't judge or look pitying like Rowan had half been expecting.

"Was that before or after you worked at a club?"

Rowan's surprised Mal remembered from when he'd shared snippets of his story at Mal's birthday, but he sighs again and answers, "Before. After I got out of the hospital, I went pretty much straight to the clubs. Worked underage, front house, back house, you name it."

A cold trickle of shame rushes through Rowan, still not quite dispelled even after over a decade.

"I'm sorry," Mal says, and it sounds so sincere that the cold shame warms to a soft glow in Rowan's belly.

Rowan shrugs. "Thanks. It wasn't… a great time in my life. But I'm better now."

"Good. You're… stable? That the right word?"

"Stable, yeah. Take my meds regularly and adjust them when I need to."

Rowan stuffs some home fries in his mouth, the butter and spices a shock to his taste buds after barely any food the past week.

"How often do you… get depressed or whatever?"

"Can't tell ya," Rowan says regretfully. "It's sporadic. I'm always baseline depressed, but the meds help with that and mitigate the worst of the symptoms. But when something particularly emotional happens, there's a chance of it getting much worse. Crashing, kind of. And sometimes my PTSD makes me go a little crazy if something sets me off. I get irritable and tend to go into an almost manic state, acting out and engaging in risky behaviors. It's almost cyclical between the two of them. Highs and lows."

"And it usually lasts a week or so?" Mal asks, eyebrows once again knitted together.

"Depends. This episode lasted about that long, but I've had better, and I've had worse." Rowan shrugs apologetically. "Sorry I can't give you any real answers here. It's always different. A week is usually about right before I get my meds adjusted, and then things settle back down."

"No, it's okay. Just tryn'a understand."

They're quiet for a few minutes while they eat their food.

"Does this… change anything?" Rowan asks.

"What?"

"Any of that, I mean. Does it change stuff between us?" Rowan's almost afraid to ask, noticing how quiet his own voice has become.

But Mal answers right away. "Course not, man. Already said you were the best Dom I've ever had. Doubt you're the first one to have mental health issues I didn't know about, either."

"Okay. Good." Rowan can't help the slow smile that spreads across his face.

There's a rhythmic tapping on the table that Rowan belatedly notices comes from Mal's fingers anxiously tapping away.

"I'm dyslexic," Mal blurts out.

For a moment, Rowan's stunned. "Huh? Really?"

"Yep. Can't read for shit on paper. Takes me forever. The letters all get jumbled around."

Something clicks in Rowan's brain. "Is that why you do audiobooks and work with numbers mostly?"

"Yeah. Makes it easier. I can read shit on a screen just fine, but something about having a piece of paper in front'a me is like I'm havin' a fuckin' seizure."

Mal's admission softens the blow of Rowan's own admission. He didn't need to tell him something personal like that. Something that doesn't really affect their scenes together—like all the other times Mal's told him about his family or his past—but he did. Just to, presumably, make Rowan feel better.

It warms his heart far more than the still-steaming omelet ever could.

"Genetics suck," Rowan empathizes.

Mal clinks his coffee mug gently against Rowan's before taking a slow sip. "Yeah, they do."

Rowan smiles and takes a sip of his own coffee.

There's a comfortable silence between the two of them, only the soft music of the jukebox and the scraping of their utensils on their plates filling the air. Mal's the one to break the silence, asking the question that Rowan's been waiting for him to ask since they came here.

"Do you think you'll be good to start scening again, or do you need some time off?"

"Maybe not tonight, but for next week I'll be fine."

"You sure? We don't have to jump back into anything."

Mal's concern warms Rowan's belly, but it isn't necessary. He's ready. Maybe not for anything extreme yet, but—

"I was thinking…." Rowan says. "Wondering if you wanted to switch things up for next time."

"Switch things up how?"

"Having you top. Ease us back into things, y'know?"

Mal appears stunned, his mouth hanging open a fraction. He snaps it shut, visibly swallowing, throat bobbing prettily.

"Y-yeah. *Hell* yeah."

And maybe it doesn't make sense, diverging from their norm on the first session together again, but Rowan wants it. Make sure that *Mal* knows he's in control after Steven, even under the guise of giving it up to Rowan. To give up a tiny bit of control himself. Take some of the pressure off.

But mostly, he wants to feel Mal like that. He's been thinking about it nearly constantly the past few weeks, each time he thrusts into Mal's ass or wraps his hands or lips around his thick cock. Picturing Mal sliding into him, filling him up, *coming inside him*. He wants to feel something again, and he wants that something to be Mal.

SATURDAY FINALLY rolls around. He's mostly back to normal, only a lingering sluggishness paired with a slight buzzing under his skin from the adjusted meds, but he feels good.

Feels *ready*.

The butterflies in Rowan's stomach must be migrating, because he can feel them fluttering rapidly all throughout his body.

It's been a long time since he's bottomed. He can't even remember *when*, exactly, only that he didn't enjoy it all that much. Part of him is worried that this time will be no different, but a bigger part of him tells him that it's going to be different simply because this is *Mal*.

Mal, who he…. Loves. Fuck, it still doesn't seem real. Still feels weird as hell to admit that, even to himself. And to think that a week ago, he'd been feeling sorry for himself and thought Mal didn't even like him back. Now here he is, fully admitting his feelings. *Accepting* his feelings too. He thinks about it as he takes probably the longest and most thorough shower of his life before leaving, only teasing himself the slightest bit, but not fully prepping himself. He wants to save that for when he's with Mal.

AT THE club, he finds Mal already at the bar, half a beer sitting in front of him. Rowan's usually always the earlier of the two, Mal typically showing up either on time or a few minutes late to their sessions.

When he meets his eyes, he looks eager. *Giddy*.

"You ready to do this, Savaryn?" Rowan asks, taking a swig of Mal's beer.

"Damn straight, Campbell."

Mal's nearly vibrating out of his skin by the time they make it to the Gold Room, slamming the door behind him and locking it as soon as the latch clicks shut. He hurries over to the bed and dumps out his bag unceremoniously and with a fervor Rowan hasn't seen him with even when they first started scening.

"What's got you so excited?" Rowan asks with amusement, picking up the cuffs from the pile of stuff on the bed.

"I'm pent up, man. Haven't had anything but my right hand in *weeks.*"

The confession warms Rowan's belly as the words reach his ears. Mal hadn't slept with anyone else in the time that Rowan had been depressed and they'd chosen to take another week off. It shouldn't mean much, but it *does*, and Rowan feels as tingly as Mal looks.

"Let's change that then, hmm?" Rowan responds, inspecting the plug Mal has brought with him.

Apparently he doesn't want to be empty even when he's topping. That's plenty fine by Rowan. The plug is made of smooth black silicone, shaped like a dildo, on the long and thin side—at least compared to Rowan. The base tapers to a thin stem then flares out wide, forming a sturdy base that's sure to keep it in place.

"Strip yourself, then undress me," Rowan tells Mal, wasting no time exchanging pleasantries.

Mal complies, nearly ripping off his shirt and shimmying out of his jeans at lightning pace. He nearly forgets to remove his boots first, the fabric of his jeans catching on his ankles before he dips down to hastily unlace them and kick them off toward the bed. His tight black briefs come off last, his already hard cock bobbing free as soon as the material slides over the tip.

"Good," Rowan tells him, though he's sure his hungry eyes on Mal's body say it all.

When Mal steps toward him, Rowan can feel the heat of his body in the small space between them even through his clothes.

Mal sets to work undressing Rowan with a much greater sense of precision and grace than he'd done with his own clothing, folding each piece and placing it on the bed without being asked, like he's done every time he's undressed Rowan.

Now fully naked, Rowan sits on the edge of the bed, drawing his long legs up and spreading them wide. In this position, he feels so *exposed*, but more turned on than he can even put into words.

"On your knees," Rowan tells him.

Mal dips down obediently, landing on his pile of clothes on the floor.

"You're gonna open me up. You can choose: mouth or hands. But you only get to use one, understood?"

Mal makes a small, pained sound like the thought of being restricted to only his mouth or his hands kills him, but he nods anyway.

"What am I gonna tell you?" Rowan demands.

"Words," Mal says, head bowed slightly and voice breathy. "I understand."

"Good, get to it."

Rowan dips his head back to stare at the ceiling lights. There's a brief, anticipation-laced moment where Rowan drops his upper body to the bed and doesn't feel anything at all, waiting with his legs spread before Mal.

Then the soft tickle of Mal's hair against Rowan's inner thigh. A hot breath against his hole. Lips pressing off to the side of where he wants them. Rowan knew he'd choose his mouth. Mal's got an oral fixation that any partner would kill or die for.

Mal starts out tentatively, a small kitten lick with the tip of his tongue over Rowan's hole. Teasing, testing. After the first lick, Mal moans against him and digs in more firmly, tongue lapping feverishly. It sends an electric jolt up Rowan's spine.

As Mal's eager tongue opens him up, Rowan groans. He can't remember the last time someone rimmed him. It might have only happened once, and he was undoubtedly too coked out to even recognize it was happening, let alone enjoy it. But Mal's mouth is delicious, smooth and hot and so goddamn talented that Rowan feels himself melting into the bed, legs jelly and threatening to flop down off the edge.

He feels Mal's hand squeeze his asscheek, then a thick finger slide into his hole alongside Mal's tongue.

Rowan barely stops himself from moaning, from gasping at the stretch, before remembering the rules he'd put in place. "That better not be your hands I'm feeling, Mal. You know the rules."

Mal's fingers slink away, and Rowan instantly misses the stretch. He probably needs it, given that it's been forever and a day since he last bottomed, but Rowan wants to feel the burn of Mal opening him up with his cock. Needs to feel something again after too long feeling nothing.

Rowan reaches back, grabs the bottle of lube from the pile on the bed, and shoves it down toward Mal.

"Let's put those hands to use, hmm? Finger yourself. Make sure you're nice and open for your toy."

Mal pulls away from Rowan's hole, his heat leaving as a rush of cool air makes Rowan's hole pucker.

"I didn't say you could stop," Rowan tells him, pulling him back in with his heel. "Keep going."

Mal moans, going back to work without a fuss, his tongue hot on Rowan's skin. The moment Mal breaches himself with his fingers, Rowan can feel it. There's a little stutter of his tongue before he delves inside completely, fucking his tongue into Rowan's hole undoubtedly at the same pace as he's fucking himself.

There's a slick squelching noise emanating from below, but Rowan has no idea if it's coming from Mal's fingers or tongue. Either way, it feels fucking incredible, hot and wet and making Rowan's toes curl against the edge of the bed.

"That's it, fuck, Mal. Should'a had you do this a long time ago."

Mal hums against him, the vibration of his lips hitting Rowan just right. It makes him forget that he's supposed to be doing something other than lying on his back with his legs spread in desperation.

They've got a plan. And that plan involves Rowan getting fucked.

"That's enough."

When Mal doesn't pull back, Rowan yanks at his hair, missing the contact immediately as Mal's jerked back with a wet gasp.

"Wanted to keep going," Mal says, a dazed sound to his voice.

Rowan feels his eyes softening as he tugs Mal up between his legs. Brings a hand up to stroke at his cheek.

"I know. Did so good for me. But now I'm gonna sit on that thick cock of yours, 'kay?"

"Y-yeah. Yes."

Rowan slips off the bed, his legs wobblier than he thought they'd be and his hole achingly empty with the loss of Mal's tongue.

He guides Mal onto his back on the bed, cuffing his wrists gently and tugging them back behind his head. He fastens the cuffs to a hook underneath the bed, Mal's hands resting delicately on the edge.

All stretched out for him, Mal is gorgeous. His abs and obliques and pecs pulled taut and on display, and Rowan knows he could spend the rest of his life running his hands and lips and tongue along each ridge and still never tire of it.

And fuck, Rowan *loves* him. He's gonna bottom for someone he loves, and it feels like it might as well be the first time ever. His heart stutters in his chest.

Gingerly, he coaxes Mal's legs up and slides the plug into his slick hole to keep him full. When the base nestles against Mal's ass, he lets out a long, low moan, hips grinding down onto the bed in an attempt to work the plug deeper inside himself.

Rowan laughs. "Even when you're topping you can't resist being filled, huh?"

"Mmm…," Mal hums.

Rowan teases the toy, pressing hard with his thumb and dragging in slow, languid circles, grinding the toy against Mal's walls. Mal lets out a low groan that Rowan feels vibrating through his fingertips.

"Hmm," Rowan muses. "Sounds to me like I should fuck you, you're so desperate for it."

"N-no! Wanna feel you…." Mal pants, squirming against his restraints.

"Oh yeah?"

"Yeah… been—*fuck*! There!"

"Been what?"

"Been thinkin' about it."

"Tell me what you've been thinking about, Mal."

Mal's legs thrash wildly as Rowan starts pumping the plug in and out, each thrust a hard press that has Rowan's own hole clenching.

"You," Mal breathes.

Rowan laughs through his nose. "I'd hope so. What about me?"

While Mal strokes Rowan's ego, Rowan toys with the plug in Mal's ass, now twirling it in long, slow, sweeping arcs that drag across his hole.

"Your ass… fucking you… bet you'll be—*hnng*!—be so tight."

"Keep going."

"Felt it on my tongue. So fucking tight…. Tasted so good…."

"It's been a long time since anyone fucked me. Did'ja know that, Mal?"

"*Nnng*… no."

"Gonna make it so good for you. Sit right on your fat fuckin' cock and ride you till you're beggin' me to come. That sound good?"

Mal's moan is answer enough, but Rowan still feels a rush of pride and lust when he whimpers, "*Yes*… so good…."

With one final push, Rowan nestles the plug all the way into Mal's hole, making sure that it won't fall out.

He meets Mal's eyes, little more than thin slivers of gold that are nearly swallowed by blown black pupils. His cheeks are flushed a pretty pink color, and his dark brows are furrowed, probably from the pain of how hard he's biting his lower lip.

Rowan swings a leg over Mal's hips, straddling him and feeling his cock slide between his asscheeks. Mal's thick and hot behind him, Rowan's eyes fluttering at the contact. His belly swoops with a heady wave of desire, legs trembling as he reaches behind him to stroke Mal's cock, spreading precome and lube from the bottle Mal had used earlier.

He rises up, locking eyes with Mal as he lines up and slowly, slowly starts sinking, legs shaking with the effort of not dropping straight down. As soon as the tip pops past Rowan's rim, he sees stars, vision dotting white at the stretch. But it feels *good*, exactly what he needed after an exhausting couple of weeks. He sinks farther onto Mal's cock and further into a blissed-out headspace that he barely registers when he's fully seated, only noticing the sharp press of Mal's hip bones against the back of his thighs.

"Fuck…," he gasps, unable to stop himself.

Mal echoes the sentiment, arching his back lewdly off the bed and squirming so that his cock creates a maddening pressure against Rowan's walls. And fuck, Rowan's so *full*. His heart and his hole and holy *shit* does it feel good. The burn hits just right, a slow sizzle in his belly that spreads to his limbs. Rowan knows instantly that this is going to be better than every other time he's bottomed, few and far between as those times were.

Because it's *Mal*. Mal's cock filling him up, Mal's toned chest spread out beneath him, Mal's cutoff whimpers filling the air and being swallowed straight into Rowan's lungs with each shuddering breath.

"Rowan…," Mal gasps, eyes wide like he's straining to keep them open.

Rowan runs a hand up Mal's chest, feeling each ridge of his abs beneath his fingertips.

"Tell me how it feels, Mal."

"*Good...* fuck. Feel so hot and tight. N-need...."

"Whaddya need?"

"Need you to move, *please....*"

Rowan squeezes Mal's pec, thumbing over one pert nipple and making Mal jolt up, cock driving impossibly deeper into him.

"Yeah? How bad d'you need it?"

Mal mewls. "So bad... feel so fuckin' good."

On shaking legs, Rowan rises up halfway, then grinds back down and feels the stretch all over again as Mal's cock spears back into him. Rowan's jaw drops, slack against his chest as he rises up farther and drops down with a lewd *slap*!

"Fuck, Mal... you're hitting so deep. Can you feel it?"

"*Yeah*, holy fuck...."

It's unlike anything Rowan's felt before. Satisfying and filling and *ful*filling in a way that he feels down to his goddamn bone marrow.

He picks up the pace, legs rising and falling and generating a slow but steady rhythm, occasionally rocking back and forth and grinding when the pressure of Mal's cock inside him is too much to take. Finally, after what feels like ages, Rowan lets out an audible gasp, fingers clenching furiously around Mal's waist as he grinds Mal's cock against his prostate.

"Ohhh...," Rowan moans. "Right there."

"There?" Mal echoes desperately.

"Yeah, fuck.... Feels good."

Mal groans, straining against his cuffs. "Wanna make you feel good."

"You always do, Mal."

Their eyes lock, and Rowan can't help but run a hand across Mal's cheek, melting at the way Mal nuzzles into it, eyes fluttering shut. It's too intimate, and Rowan doesn't want the contact to end. But he forces himself to, knowing that he can't handle any more heartache from how badly he wants them to be more than what they are.

He shifts his efforts, focusing now on the feeling of Mal inside him. Rowan's thighs are straining as he rides Mal to his heart's content, filling him in all the right ways. It feels so fucking good, hitting Rowan deep and stretching him wide over and over as fast as his legs will let him. Nailing his prostate on every thrust and sending pulse after pulse of pleasure coursing through him.

Mal fucks up into Rowan as best as he can, short, stuttering hitches of his hips that meet Rowan's ass each time he rises. It reminds him of the day Mal kissed him—how he'd been fucking up into the masturbator with wanton abandonment before collapsing down onto him. And God, Rowan wishes it would happen again. Wishes he could feel Mal's lips for real and hold him close and kiss him breathless.

Breathless, like he's getting now just thinking about it. His limbs are aching with exertion, but he feels the pleasure in the base of his spine, and he doesn't want it to end anytime soon, but he's getting close. He can tell by the quiver of Mal's thighs beneath him that he's nearing his end too.

"Rowan, please… wanna… need to touch you."

Rowan dips forward, breath ghosting against Mal's cheek as he reaches to unclasp Mal's wrists from behind his head.

Immediately, Mal's hands latch on to Rowan's hips, nails digging into the skin in a way that makes Rowan's belly curl with the possessiveness of it. They breathe into each other's space, a bubble all their own that Rowan's sure will pop if he exhales a little too hard, eyes locked and sparks crackling between them at the intensity of their gazes.

"Fu-fuck… gonna… Rowan, I need—"

"I got you," Rowan says, hands raking up Mal's chest, squeezing at his pecs and ghosting over his neck. Hips never losing rhythm. "No one's come in me before. Wanna feel it. Feel *you*. You gonna give me what I want, Mal?"

"Yeah… wanna…."

He wasn't sure he even *would* feel it. But as Mal spills inside him, he feels the warmth, the *fullness* with every pulse of Mal's release, and it's the hottest fucking thing that's ever happened to him.

And when Rowan comes moments later, with a desperate cry as he releases across his fingers and Mal's chest, it's with one hand over Mal's heart and the other around his throat.

CHAPTER 11: CHOKE ME

ROWAN AND Mal bask in the afterglow of their scene, sated and warm and utterly spent.

It's been two weeks since Rowan bottomed, three since he told Mal about his depression, and he feels better than ever. They've been taking things easy the past two weeks, their scenes more praise than degradation or humiliation. More intimate too. Soft touches and free-falling whimpers and so, so much emotion that it makes Rowan's heart swell almost painfully in his chest.

Rowan wants so badly to tell Mal how he feels. He's sure now that Mal feels *something* for him, so there isn't really that lingering inkling of doubt anymore, but something still holds him back. It's mostly to do with the fact that Mal hasn't made a move yet to initiate anything more. He's definitely the bolder of the two, at least when it comes to sexual things, so Rowan thought that would translate to romantic things as well.

So often during their scenes or their now-frequent phone calls, the words are on the tip of his tongue. He's so close to blurting out *I'm in love with you* nearly every time he sees Mal that it's becoming a real problem. He's bitten his tongue more times than he can count to stop it from slipping out without his permission.

But would it be so bad? Would Mal react badly? Shove him away with a scoff and a look of disgust? Or would he welcome him into his arms and cradle his face and kiss him till he's breathless?

Despite how intimately Rowan can confidently say that he knows Mal after months of scening—after months of *friendship*—he honestly can't predict how he might react. And that's what scares him most of all. What makes him bite his lips and tongue and the inside of his cheeks until they're raw and red. The *not knowing*.

THEY'RE AT the diner, enjoying a well-deserved dinner, when Mal says something that makes Rowan's heart stop in his chest.

"I want you to choke me."

"What?"

"We've been dancin' around it for months, man. I can tell you wanna do it as bad as *I* want you to do it."

"Mal, we can't—" Rowan starts, about to remind Mal of the club's rules against choking and breath play which he clearly very well knows, when Mal cuts him off.

"Come over."

And Rowan's…. Rowan's brain stops. Because did Mal just ask him to…?

"Come… over? Like to your apartment?"

Mal rolls his eyes, but Rowan can tell it's in that fond way of his. When Rowan's being an idiot and doesn't realize it. "Yeah, dumbass."

Rowan knows all the signs of heart attacks in men—shortness of breath, the feeling of a heavy weight crushing your chest, dizziness, nausea—and he's in great shape, but he's not ruling it out as the cause for the stuttering tightness behind his ribs. He wants to do a stupid dance and shout *Dear fucking God,* Yes!, But all he can think to do is sit there gaping, and all he can think to say is: "But I don't know where you live," like Mal was going to make Rowan guess that information rather than giving him his address.

"Jesus Christ, Red," Mal says, pinching the bridge of his nose between his thumb and index finger.

He pulls out his phone, types a quick message, and Rowan's phone vibrates a few seconds later.

"Next week? Same time?" Mal's tone sounds somehow both hopeful and fearful.

"Ye-yeah. Course."

Rowan shoves a french fry in his mouth and can't keep the smile off his face.

As SOON as Rowan wakes the next morning, he takes his meds and Googles *sexual asphyxiation.*

He's aware in theory how to do it safely, partly from having done it in the past, and partly from his training as a paramedic. Avoid the trachea, the larynx, and the hyoid bone and squeeze gently at the carotid arteries to slow the flow of blood to the brain. Always press on the sides of the neck, never the front. He's done it a little bit with some partners in the past, but this is *Mal*, and Rowan doesn't want to risk his well-being for anything.

There are dozens of articles on it, some sketchy and some legitimate. He opens a few tabs and begins reading: The history behind it, the cultural taboo around it, the inclusion (or exclusion) of it in some BDSM circles… there's *so* much information. Some of it he can tell immediately is crap, reminding him of when Mal had sent him a list of BDSM books to read and warned him against stuff that was total bullshit.

He reads the copious warnings carefully. There are common side effects, including muscle weakness, loss of coordination, dizziness, and coughing, which can be expected if done for too long a period of time. Then there's the chance for permanent brain damage, lung damage, artery damage, or even death in some cases (though most often when done to oneself). The list goes on and on and makes his head spin. He won't lie, he *is* worried about the potential consequences, and those warnings should be a full-stop deterrent, but….

The thought of getting Mal to a state of extreme bliss—that rush of dopamine and serotonin and endorphins straight to the brain—is so tempting. It's tangible, literally right at his fingertips. Rowan wants to get him to the point of giving complete control over to Rowan and trusting, trusting, trusting him to see him safely through to the other side. And he knows that Mal wants it as badly as he does. Asked him to *come over* so they could do it away from the Menagerie in the safety and privacy of his own home.

Rowan remembers way back to their first meeting after the gangbang. About how Mal had said he goes to the club—never invites anyone over to his apartment—because it *keeps shit separate*. That must mean that things between him and Rowan *aren't* separate. Must mean there's something more, right? Rowan would bet his life on it.

Or, he thinks painfully, Mal just really wants to get choked out. Break his own rule badly enough to have Rowan come over rather than breaking the club's rule against choking and breath play.

Rowan shakes the negative thoughts out of his head. He knows by now that he and Mal have something special. Mal admitted as much to him on the phone a few weeks ago, and they've only grown closer since then. Their scenes have continued to evolve from largely impersonal, like they were at the start, to more and more intimate, and it sets Rowan's heart ablaze knowing how far they've come since they first met each other.

He keeps reading, watching a few videos he'd found on a kink-related Reddit page that shows how to choke someone out safely—well, saf*er*.

Once he's comfortable with the motions in theory, he tries them out on himself. Wraps his hand around his own throat and positions his thumb and the rest of his fingers on opposite sides of his neck, gently starting to squeeze until he can feel his pulse in his fingertips. In barely a minute, he feels the light-headed rush that everyone online swears is better than an orgasm. In truth, it doesn't do much for him—kind of makes him panic a little bit, honestly—but he can easily see how the tingling he's feeling from his cheeks down to his toes could be pleasurable.

He can easily see *Mal* finding it pleasurable. Getting off on the danger of it as much as the physical sensations. And all at once, Rowan feels his cock stir. He releases his neck, trails his hand down his body and over the hardening bulge in his briefs. It shouldn't be so easy to rile him up, but God, even the thought of Mal gets him going like nothing else. As he loses the battle to not jerk off—twice in a row—he pictures what Mal's face will look like when Rowan finally gets a hand around his neck.

ROWAN WANTS so badly to tell someone about Mal. About how he *asked him to come over*, but the harsh reality is that he can't exactly do that without revealing that they've only been seeing each other at a BDSM club.

He thinks about telling Jay, but there are some things that family shouldn't know, even if he'd known about Rowan's illicit club days when he was younger.

He thinks about telling Addison, but he doesn't think he'd live down the humiliation of admitting the same thing to her. And she *doesn't* know about his past.

Hell, he even thinks about telling Aubrey, who's as open about sex as Rowan himself is, but he's really only mentioned Mal to her in passing *as a friend*, and he doesn't want to get into the whole story.

Which is why he finds himself at the Menagerie on a Thursday night. He already knows that he's not going to need to use one of his four monthly visits this Saturday—because he'll be *at Mal's*, his brain reminds him helpfully—so he doesn't care about wasting it on seeking advice.

He's never been here on a Thursday before, but the place is *packed*. As Rowan makes his way to the bar, he's leered at constantly and groped no fewer than five times, some probably unintentional as he moves through the throng of people, but some *definitely* intentional.

"Hey, Jeremiah," Rowan says, plopping down at the one empty seat at the bar.

Jeremiah looks up and beams that bright smile of his, throwing up a finger to signal one sec as he expertly mixes a cocktail.

Another bartender that Rowan's never seen before comes over to take Rowan's order, pours him a plain seltzer with cut-up lime wedges and sets it down on a napkin in front of him.

By the time he's three sips into his drink, Jeremiah slides over to him and leans across the bar, half shouting over the din of the music and chatty patrons.

"How's it going?" he asks.

"Good, you?"

"Busy as hell," Jeremiah laughs. "But great. What brings you here on a Thursday?"

"Wanted to see if I could get your advice on something."

Jeremiah checks his Apple watch. "I've got a break in about ten minutes if you can wait till then."

"That'd be great. Thanks."

The ten minutes fly by, mostly taken up by Rowan fielding advances by twinks and daddies alike and letting his thoughts fade into nothingness under the heavy bass of the music. He swears it's more attention than he's gotten in his entire life, but absolutely none of it interests him. Not when he's got Mal to look forward to now.

Jeremiah waves at him and gestures for Rowan to follow, Rowan taking a last sip of his drink before sliding a five under the napkin and pushing it closer to the edge of the bar. He follows Jeremiah through swinging double doors behind the bar, past a bustling kitchen area, and into an employee lounge that's blissfully empty and quiet. A few tables and comfy-looking chairs are strewn about the middle, with a fridge in one corner and countertops filled with all the necessities, plus an expensive-looking deluxe coffee machine.

"Don't tell the twins I let you back here," Jeremiah says conspiratorially.

Rowan laughs and says, "I won't," but wonders if they would actually care if they *did* know.

As Jeremiah grabs a protein bar out of his locker, Rowan sits at one of the round tables.

"So what's up?" the other man asks, taking a heaping bite of his bar.

Rowan feels a twinge of guilt for taking up his time, but steadies his breathing with a long, slow breath.

"Mal asked me to come over."

It's said in a rush, a blurted-out thing that he's been bottling up for the past week. As Rowan half expected, Jeremiah's eyebrows shoot up to his hairline, and he stops chewing on his snack altogether.

After a brief moment and an audible swallow, Jeremiah says, "Holy shit."

It reminds Rowan of the time after the gangbang when he'd told the then-stranger that he and Mal were going to be starting a Dom/sub relationship.

"I'm kind of freaking out" is all Rowan can say to explain why he's here, taking up Jeremiah's break.

The smile he gets in return is kind—not pitying—for which Rowan is eternally thankful.

"Am I correct in assuming he wanted to break one of the club's rules?"

Rowan's eyes widen a fraction. "Yeah, how'd you know?"

"Mal is one of my best friends, and we've known each other for years now. It's not exactly a secret that he likes getting choked out, even if he *is* the one who suggested banning it from the club in the first place."

There's a twinge in Rowan's gut that he doesn't like. "So, he's done this before, then?"

"Nah, not even close. Anytime we've talked about it, he's been *extremely* intent on mentioning that he keeps his personal life separate from his sex life."

The twinge turns into a cascade of warmth and churning rapids.

"Oh."

"You don't sound thrilled about that. I thought you were into him as more than a scene partner?"

"I am!" Rowan insists, too loudly for their quiet conversation. "I'm just…." Rowan sighs, unsure how to phrase his qualms.

"Just what?"

"Worried if it doesn't work out. If he doesn't want something more."

"I think the fact that he's inviting you over speaks for itself, Rowan. Again, from what I know, he doesn't do that. Not even to do something outside the club's rules, no matter how badly he wants it."

"Yeah?" Rowan's voice is hopeful, giddy.

"Mm-hmm," Jeremiah hums. "And I obviously don't know too much about your sex life together, but Mal's been different ever since you two started scening."

"Different how?"

"Less grumpy. More open. Dare I say, *happier*."

Sheila's words from weeks ago echo in Rowan's mind. *In all the years I've known him, I've never seen Mal so happy.*

"He makes me happy," Rowan confesses, feeling like a blushing teenager.

"I think you're good for each other. Not that you need it, but you've got my blessing."

"That means a lot, actually."

"I don't think you have anything to worry about. Just make sure you know how to do whatever specifically he's asked for safely, and anything that happens beyond that is a bonus." He takes another bite of his bar, half chewing before adding, "It obviously means something that he's asked you to come over, so run with it. Let yourself have it."

Rowan's stomach churns again at the thought of something *more* happening on Saturday night. But Jeremiah's words successfully cure his fears, and now he finds that he's immensely looking forward to this weekend.

"Thanks, Jer."

"Anytime."

ON FRIDAY night, Rowan's phone vibrates with a message. When he opens his text thread with Mal, he's greeted with an artsy, slightly out of focus photo of Mal's neck. The picture is cropped above the cut of his jaw and below his clavicle, the corded muscles of his neck and shoulders on tantalizing display. Rowan's mouth waters.

[MS] *can't wait till tomorrow*
Fuck.
[RC] *Me neither*
[RC] *Gonna make it so good for you*
[MS] *i know you will*
[MS] *been dying to feel those big hands for real*
In an instant, Rowan's hard in his sweats.
It's going to be a long twenty-four hours.

ROWAN LETS himself take a few deep breaths inside the foyer before he presses the button to be buzzed into Mal's apartment building. From there, it's a quick elevator ride and he's face-to-face with Mal's door. It takes him a good minute to quell his nerves to knock, and Mal must be wondering if he got lost.

In a matter of seconds, Mal's flinging open the door, looking comfortable in a plain white T-shirt and black sweats, but with an eager glint in his eye.

"Hey," Mal greets.

"Hey," Rowan replies, stepping inside and toeing off his shoes, kicking them off to the side where a shoe mat lies filled with Mal's boots and sneakers.

Mal gestures to the space around him, adding, "Well, this is it. I'd give ya a tour, but there's not much to see."

Mal's apartment is clean and tidy. Almost suspiciously so. Like he'd shuffled everything around a dozen times and eventually shoved anything out of place into some too-full closet that's going to spill everything the moment it's opened. It's a pretty standard layout, the front door opening into the living room with the kitchen off to the left and a short hallway, where presumably the bathroom and bedroom are, to the right.

The walls are apartment-standard white, the furniture all shades of black and brown and gray, made of leather and soft-looking fabric and dark-stained wood. He doesn't have a kitchen table, but there is a small island off one end of the counter that has two wooden barstools tucked in underneath it. Rowan pictures Mal eating breakfast here in the morning, and it fills him with a sense of warmth.

"Want a beer?" Mal asks, shuffling off to the kitchen before Rowan replies.

"Sure."

Rowan steps further inside, taking in his surroundings.

It's minimally decorated, some framed movie and band posters comprising the majority of the decorations. A couple of unframed candid photos of Mal and Amy and the staff of the club strewn about the twin bookshelves in the living room, curled at the edges. What looks like an urn next to a small black-and-white photo of a young Mal and a dark-haired woman Rowan doesn't recognize. On top of the photos, there's a plant or two here and there, mostly succulents and low-maintenance plants by the looks of it, one pothos in particular vining all along and down the side of an end table in the living room. There's a small desk in one corner with a beast of a computer on the floor and three monitors side by side on the desktop, which must be where Mal does his work.

It's cozy and simple. It's *Mal*, and part of Rowan still can't believe he's being let into this side of Mal's life, so different from the gilded glamor of the Menagerie.

Mal passes him a Blue Ribbon, twisting off the cap before he does.

"How was your day?" Rowan asks, taking a sip.

"Eh, not bad. Did some chores, cleaned up a bit. Lounged around and tried not to spend the entire day jerking off. Usual weekend shit." Mal pauses to take his own drink, a much deeper sip than Rowan had taken. "You?"

"Same, except I failed at the not jerking off thing."

Mal laughs and rolls his eyes. "Better not have blown it all before tonight, Red."

"Nah, I'm good. Can get it up again pretty quickly. Besides, that was hours ago."

"Yeah? You think of anything in particular while you were jerkin' it?"

Rowan gives him a pointed look. "May have gotten off to the pic of your neck that you sent the other day."

Mal's eyebrows shoot up in surprise. "Of all the filthy shit I've sent you over the past few months, *that's* what you got off to?"

It's Rowan's turn to give Mal a surprised look. "You said yourself that you could tell I wanted this as bad as you did."

"Knew you were a fuckin' vampire or somethin'," Mal says, grinning. He's got the cutest little dimples in the middle of his cheekbones that Rowan wants to run the pad of his thumbs over.

"Pft, your ass is paler than mine, Mal."

"So? No way your Irish ass doesn't burn like a motherfucker."

"You got me there. Though yours gets pretty damn red when I spank you."

All at once, Mal splutters, the beer in his mouth spewing across the table, little droplets hitting Rowan in the arm.

"Thought I was gonna make you choke in a different context, but all right," Rowan says with a laugh.

Once he stops coughing, Mal laughs, a warm golden sound that makes Rowan squirm. "C'mon, enough chitchat," he says, placing the still half-full bottle down and nodding to the hallway where his bedroom lies.

This is it.

Rowan follows Mal into his bedroom. Like the rest of his apartment, it's neat and minimally decorated. A queen-size bed sits in the middle, a nightstand with a lamp on each side. The comforter is a dark navy, two pillows on each side of the bed making it look like something out of a hotel, except that the comforter is folded at the bottom of the bed, exposing the white sheets underneath. There's a bureau off to the side of the room, scattered with belts and deodorant and other personal effects. Next to it, a bifold closet is partially ajar, giving Rowan a glimpse into the rows of neatly lined-up hanging garments and a hamper with a piece of clothing partially hanging out. It reminds Rowan a lot of his own bedroom.

"You wanna use anything tonight?" Rowan asks. "Cuffs or toys?"

"Nah. Gonna be intense enough without anything else. Let's work up to it for next time."

Rowan's heart stutters at Mal already anticipating a *next time* when they haven't even gotten started yet.

They stand at the foot of the bed, staring at one another for a beat. Then another. Then another. It's awkward until Mal laughs, shoving Rowan gently in the chest with his palm.

"C'mon, tough guy. Show me what you got."

Rowan laughs in response, the tension instantly dissolved between them.

Normally, he'd order Mal to strip off his clothes right now, like he's done a dozen times before. Call him selfish, but he wants to undress Mal himself tonight. Let himself live in the fantasy that this is spontaneous and has more meaning than a preplanned BDSM scene.

He feels his spine straighten as he looms over Mal, who's looking up at him through long, dark lashes, lips parted. Rowan cups the back of Mal's neck, tugging his body toward him in one firm motion, chests pressed together.

Mal lets out a tiny whimper, and Rowan can feel the start of the hardness in his lap.

Rowan covers one hip with his free hand, stroking up under his shirt to the side of Mal's ribs. He's hot to the touch, burning Rowan's fingertips as he trails across bare skin. He releases his grip on the back of Mal's neck, Mal's breath leaving him in a *whoosh* as Rowan strips off Mal's T-shirt, yanking it over his head. He allows himself time to take in his tattoos, the flowers and pistols spread across his chest and shoulders, the smattering of smaller tattoos gracing his arms and chest, the hint of vines growing on either side of his hips from under his sweats. The LISA tattoo on the side of his ribs.

Tucking his thumbs into either side of Mal's sweats, Rowan slides them down, letting them pool onto the floor and coaxing Mal to step out of them. He leaves his briefs on for now, teasing the inside of his thighs with light strokes as Mal's head dips forward to his chest and his breathing grows ragged.

"Quit teasin' me," Mal tells him.

Rowan grabs either side of his face, pinching his cheeks between his thumb and forefinger.

"Gonna tease you all I want."

To prove his point, Rowan cups Mal's cock, hard enough to get the other man to jerk his hips forward at the contact, but too light to provide any real relief.

Mal moans softly but presses on when Rowan pulls his hand away. "Brought you here for a reason."

"Uh-huh. And we're gonna get to that when I say we are."

Rowan lets his hands travel back up and ghost over Mal's neck, the corded muscle taut under his palms. He feels his own cock stir in his jeans.

"Words are gonna be tricky tonight," Rowan says casually, though they feel heavy in his mouth. "You'll make sure to tap out if you need to, yeah?"

"Yeah, course," Mal assures him.

The moment lingers, a brief cooldown in the otherwise steamy atmosphere of Mal's bedroom.

Any other time Mal has been gagged during their scenes—made unable to speak, anyway—they've used a clicker. But Mal didn't want to use one tonight. Wanted to be able to fully let go and not have to worry about holding on to the thing during the scene. They've already talked about Mal tapping out—"I'll fuckin' smack you if I need to, man," Mal had said—but Rowan wants to double-check. Wants to be *sure* that it'll happen if it needs to happen.

He locks eyes with Mal, pupils already dilated in the dim, warm light cast only by the two bedside lamps, and finds nothing but excitement and sincerity. No doubt or anxiety or anything else that would give Rowan pause.

He blinks, breaking them out of the still moment and crashing back to reality. The reality that he's going to get his hands around Mal's throat for the first time. Rowan pushes Mal's chest, watching with rapt attention as Mal falls gracefully backward and hits the bed with a soft *whump*. The bedding rustles underneath him, as soft and supple as Mal's spread thighs. He'd been longing for the day he'd get Mal in an actual bed, and now that that day is here, he hardly knows what to do with himself.

So he settles on what he knows, crawling onto the bed after him and raking his hands up and down Mal's legs and thighs, fingertips digging into the lace tattoo on his upper thigh, watching the skin turn from black and white to red and pink. If Rowan were trying to show Mal his love of him as a person through his love of his thighs, he's sure it would come across and leave little doubt.

He teases Mal until every inch of his thighs and chest and arms and neck are flushed pink. Until his nipples are as hard as his cock. Until there's a generous wet spot on the front of his briefs. Until his breathing is ragged and his voice is strained.

"Hurry the fuck up, man… I'm halfway to blowing already," Mal whines after apparently too long.

Rowan smacks him hard on the inside of his thigh, the flesh jiggling underneath and turning a bright scarlet with the force of his handprint.

"Patience, Mal."

But Rowan caves after only a few more minutes of exploring Mal's body, mostly because he wants to get the show on the road as well. If he was a stronger man, he'd spend all night drawing sighs and whimpers from Mal's lips.

With fingers hooked under the elastic waistband, he tugs Mal's briefs over his hard cock and down his legs. Underwear gone, he shuffles closer between Mal's spread legs, slotting his knees under Mal's thighs. His cock is hard and flushed pink and dripping greedily from the tip onto his lower stomach, making the soft strands of pubic hair glisten with moisture. Rowan runs a finger through the precome and brings it to his lips.

"Tastes good," Rowan tells him.

"Fuck…," Mal breathes, jaw slack and eyes lidded.

Rowan watches Mal's eyes dip down to his own cock as another bead of precome wells up at the tip.

"You wanna taste?"

Mal nods, face flushed.

Rowan grabs Mal's hand, gathers a drop of the precome on Mal's index finger and guides it back up to his mouth. The pearly liquid all but dissolves on Mal's tongue as he sucks his own finger into his mouth.

"Mmm…," Mal hums.

"So fuckin' hot, Mal. How 'bout you get my fingers nice and wet for me, hmm?"

Rowan slips two of his own fingers into Mal's mouth alongside his, feeling Mal's tongue immediately coil around his digits and soak them in saliva.

"That's it, just like that."

As Mal sucks on Rowan's fingers, Rowan gives his cock a few cursory strokes. He can feel Mal's moan vibrate through his fingers and down his wrist, a direct line to his own sorely neglected cock. Their eyes meet—Mal's lidded and heady—and Rowan can feel his own pupils dilate further.

Once Mal's got Rowan's fingers nice and coated, Rowan pulls them out and immediately dips them between Mal's cheeks and circles his tight rim in teasing spirals until he's able to slip inside to the first knuckle.

Above him, Mal moans softly.

"Give me the lube," Rowan instructs.

Dutifully, Mal reaches to the bedside table and then passes a bottle of lube—the same Good, Clean Love brand that they use at the Menagerie—to Rowan.

As Rowan opens him up with his fingers, it's all he can do not to rock forward and thrust into the mattress. He's more turned on than he can ever remember being in his *life* watching Mal gasp and listening to him whimper as Rowan stretches him. He's got Mal's legs hiked up over his thighs, lower back arching off the mattress as he thrusts onto Rowan's fingers.

"Rowan, wanna see you…," Mal whines, apparently not content with Rowan still being fully clothed.

Laughing gently but not unkindly, Rowan withdraws his three fingers from Mal's hole, pulls off his T-shirt, and tosses it onto the pile of clothes on the floor.

"That good, your highness?"

"All of you…."

Mal sounds like he's halfway to being fully fucked out, not like he's only been caressed and fingered for twenty minutes or so.

Rowan could argue the point that he shouldn't be taking orders from his sub, but it's not that kind of mood tonight. Not really. And Rowan would be lying if he said he didn't want to be naked in a *real* bed with Mal fucking *yesterday*.

So he gets off the bed, keeping eye contact with Mal as he unbuttons his jeans and steps out of them, pulling his socks off in the process. Grabs at his hard cock through his briefs for a moment before shucking those off too. He stands before Mal fully naked, and the hungry look in the other man's eyes pulls him back to the bed like a magnet.

He takes his place between Mal's spread legs once more, shuffling forward as far as he can. With a generous coating of lube, he takes both their cocks in one hand, stroking them together and making a keening cry spill out of Mal's mouth.

"Oooh, *fuck*!"

"Thought you might like this. Feel good?"

Mal nods frantically.

"C'mon, Mal. Wanna hear how much you like it."

"Feels so fucking good… big hands around both'a us."

"Yeah, know how much you like my hands, Mal. Tell me all the time."

Likes that they're big and can span most of any one of Mal's body parts—his torso or his hips, sure, but especially that he can completely encircle Mal's wrists with plenty of room to spare. That he can completely cover Mal's neck.

Rowan's instantly harder than he thought possible, fucking into his fist and feeling the slick slide of Mal's cock against his own. It's hot and firm, and he can feel every vein and every twitch as he rubs them together, hips and fist working overtime to chase the pleasure.

Mal's jaw falls slack once more, hitting his chest briefly before his entire head thrashes back against the pillows and his thighs tighten around Rowan's waist. It looks and feels and sounds like Mal's seen God, and it sends Rowan's ego into overdrive.

"Shit… gonna…. *Please*, don't wanna—" Mal mumbles, one arm slung over his mouth and muffling his words as he writhes against the bed.

But Rowan gets the gist anyway, quickly removing his hand and watching Mal's chest finally deflate in reprieve.

"Can't have you coming too soon," Rowan laughs. "Haven't even gotten my hands on you where we both want 'em yet."

Rowan runs a hand up Mal's torso, feeling his taut abs quiver under his touch. He skirts his fingers to Mal's neck, ghosting over his clavicle and the hollow of his throat. Mal's body is racked with a shudder as he moans.

Rowan slides back onto his heels, slicking his cock in lube and wiping the excess on the sheets before pushing Mal's legs up to his torso.

Their eyes meet as Rowan slides into him in one long motion, eyes fluttering shut at once again being inside Mal's tight heat. It's a feeling like no other, one that threatens to drive him insane each and every time. A heavy, gut-wrenching feeling that hits him in every single cell in his body. At first he keeps the pace slow, letting Mal adjust once more to his size and girth. When he feels Mal's heels dig into his lower back, driving him forward, he picks up the pace ever so slightly.

Rowan fucks into him languidly, right hand resting on Mal's clavicle.

"Rowan… choke me," Mal rasps.

He looks so desperate yet so *eager* that Rowan relents at once, a thrill rushing through him. This is it. The moment he's been waiting for. The moment *Mal's* been waiting for.

Rowan wraps his hand around Mal's throat, fingers spanning the entire width of his neck. He's done this before, plenty of times. Mal and he both get off too hard on it to keep entirely away from each other, but to actually get to *squeeze*, to dig his fingers in and see Mal's reaction to the real deal? He can hardly wait.

But he hesitates, stilling his hips and his hand. From here Mal's neck looks so fragile. So pale and thin that all it would take is one wrong move and....

"You won't hurt me," Mal whispers to him.

Rowan feels Mal's Adam's apple bob beneath his palm. Feels Mal's muscles ripple under his fingertips. Feels Mal's chest rise and fall under his wrist.

And he squeezes.

Gently to begin with, until there's the first sign of Mal's mouth parting in a perfect O.

Then firmer. With more confidence as Mal's skin tints from peach to pink to red. As his eyes roll back in his head and his eyelids flutter shut. As he clenches impossibly hard around Rowan's cock.

Rowan fucks into him hard and fast, and he chokes him with a firm, steady grip that has a hoarse, wordless rasp of a cry dripping from Mal's lips.

Rowan's other hand caresses the side of Mal's face until he manages to open his eyes wide enough for Rowan to see the gold nearly completely blacked out.

That's all it takes, really. A few minutes of sustained thrusts and squeezing and Mal's whole body is shaking beneath Rowan. He knows he's hitting him deep, hitting him right where he wants it, and cutting off the sweet supply of blood to his brain and getting him right to that dizzying state that Mal so desperately craves.

Mal comes violently, with a wordless cry as he spills across his own stomach, a sticky mess that smears across Rowan's lower belly as he fucks hard into him.

At once Rowan releases his hand from around Mal's throat, and he watches the color rush back to his face. Mal takes great gasping breaths and pulls Rowan down by the back of his neck, pressing their foreheads together and breathing hot into the space between them like Rowan's going to provide all the oxygen Mal'd gone without for the past few minutes.

"Fuck, Mal…" is all Rowan can say as he squeezes his eyes shut and comes in long, thick pulses that must fill Mal to the brim.

The strength of the orgasm nearly takes Rowan's own breath away, forcing him to gulp down the air in the scant space between them to stop his limbs from shaking. He's still inside Mal, but he can feel his cock softening and the come and lube leaking out onto the bed, and he knows he needs to pull out soon. But he wants to lie here, inside and surrounded by Mal, basking in the afterglow. He allows himself the luxury for a minute, maybe two, before he forces himself to pull out and roll over onto his back next to Mal, chest still heaving.

"I think that's the hardest I've ever come," Mal says, voice still hoarse.

Rowan laughs. "Gonna have to do this more often, then, if you wanna top it." He props himself up on one elbow, turning to Mal. "How are you feeling?"

"Mmm," Mal hums softly. "Good. Great. Knew you'd be fuckin' perfect at it, Red."

"I'm glad. Was really hot seeing you like that."

"Ditto."

Rowan caresses Mal's neck softly with his fingertips, the red welts in the shape of his fingers already starting to take shape. He knows they won't last until tomorrow—he wasn't choking him *that* hard—but they'll last for a few hours at least. Rowan's tempted to ask if he can take a photo to remember this night and everything that it's entailed so far.

Mal's breathing slowly returns to normal, along with his pale complexion. Rowan watches the rise and fall of his chest, focusing on the solid lines of his tattoos with each exhale and on his musculature with each inhale. In profile, he's beautiful. All sharp nose and delicate eyelashes and high cheekbones and mussed hair with traces of sweat drying at his temples.

They lie there in silence, occasionally sneaking glances at each other. Rowan continues his touches along Mal's chest and arms and neck if for no other reason than he wants to touch him. Wants to still be connected to him in some way. The only sound in the room is the gentle, soothing pitter-patter of rain hitting the windows outside, and Rowan thinks he hasn't ever been this content in his entire life.

"Think I wanna change my safewords," Mal says after a long few minutes of nothing but slow and steady breaths.

"Yeah?" Rowan replies, curious.

"Yeah. Use actual words instead'a colors."

The admission surprises him. Rowan remembers something about Mal saying he didn't need to think about his old math teacher when he was in bed, which is why he uses colors in the first place.

"How come?"

Mal hesitates, rubs at his eyebrow with his index finger before meeting Rowan's eyes. He rises up on one elbow, partially leaning over Rowan, the look in his eyes unreadable but determined.

When he answers, his voice is softer than Rowan's ever heard it before.

"'Cause now I associate red with you… and I don't ever wanna think of you as a bad thing."

A lump forms in the back of Rowan's throat that doesn't seem to want to go away no matter how much he swallows around it.

"Mal…."

"You always keep your promises?" Mal asks in a whisper.

"Always."

It doesn't register with Rowan why he's asking until Mal's free hand comes up to cup Rowan's cheek, warm palm gently resting on his skin.

Time moves in slow motion.

Vaguely, Rowan registers Mal leaning closer, leaning *in*, but it isn't until his soft lips are pressed against his own that he realizes what's happening. He sucks in a sharp breath through his nose, an undignified whimper erupting from the back of his throat. Rowan's brain finally gets with the program, and he kisses Mal back. Slow and soft and filling Rowan's entire body to the brim with butterflies and fireworks and cotton candy. Mal's plush lips moving against his own beat every single scene they've ever done. His kiss beats the high of getting him into subspace and making him come by a landslide.

Rowan wants to roll them over, press Mal into the mattress and kiss the life out of him until both their lips are chapped and their spit runs dry, but this isn't the time. He thinks that maybe Mal needs to be in control right now. Set the pace. Later. Rowan can take over later, because there's gonna *be* a later, he's sure of it. With the way his heart is pounding in his chest and the way Mal's shifting his weight to straddle Rowan's hips and get closer, closer, there's *definitely* going to be a later.

They kiss for what feels like hours and seconds all at once. Exploring each other's mouth softly with lips, then more eagerly with tongues, a mutual gasp at the first touch. Mal tastes like fire and cinnamon sugar and something that makes Rowan's toes curl and his belly twist itself into knots.

When they pull back, Mal's eyes flutter open slowly, gilded honey even in the dim lights of his bedroom.

He's beautiful, perfect, *gorgeous*, and Rowan's never wanted to keep kissing someone so badly in his entire fucking life, his lungs aching for the taste of him.

"Stay," Mal whispers, lips still brushing against Rowan's.

Rowan nods silently, pressing his forehead against Mal's and letting his eyes drift shut as his lips find Mal's once more.

IT'S EASY, navigating being in Mal's space. Far easier than he thought it might be in the spare seconds he'd given to thinking about it between kissing Mal. They slip their briefs back on and pad barefoot across the plush carpet of the bedroom to the bathroom.

Side by side, they wash their hands and faces and wipe the come off of their stomachs. They brush their teeth in tandem—Rowan borrowing an extra toothbrush that Mal had stashed under the sink—like they've been doing it for years. Rowan takes his pills he always carries with him with a cup of tap water, completely unashamed of doing so in front of Mal for the first time.

It feels so good, so *domestic*, that it fills Rowan with amber and sunlight in a way that he's never felt before.

Together they change the soiled sheets, working side by side so easily that Rowan's heart soars with every corner they tuck in. It reminds Rowan of that first time they cleaned up the bed together after the gangbang—working as if they've been cohabiting each other's space for years, not months.

They climb into bed, Rowan on the left and Mal on the right, again so natural and uncomplicated that Rowan questions why he was ever worried about them working out in the first place.

They face each other, talking about nothing important as their eyelids droop closed and the promise of sleep takes them. Mal leans forward, drawing Rowan into a simple kiss that makes Rowan melt.

Mal rolls onto his other side, letting Rowan wrap his arm around his waist and pull him close against his chest. Rowan feels him sigh before relaxing completely into the mattress, warm and pliable and the best thing Rowan's ever felt in his arms.

Like that, they fall into a deep, peaceful sleep.

WHEN ROWAN wakes in the morning, it's the warmest he's ever felt.

For a brief moment, it doesn't register *why* he feels this way, until he tries to turn over onto his side and is greeted with Mal's peaceful face. Mal's right arm is flung across Rowan's stomach, curling protectively around his side. His face is nuzzled into Rowan's shoulder, one cheek smooshed up so his lips are parted slightly, a thin wisp of drool in the corner. Hair ruffled within an inch of its life.

He's by far the most beautiful thing Rowan's ever seen, and he looks his fill to commit every part of this moment to memory.

Gently he brushes a lock of hair away from Mal's forehead, the thin golden strips of light streaming in from the windows illuminating his perfect face. The action makes him stir, a soft trilling moan of sleepiness rising up from the back of his throat.

"Morning," Rowan whispers, voice scratchy with disuse.

"Mmm, mornin'," Mal rumbles back.

Rowan runs a hand through Mal's soft hair, strands sliding silkily through his fingers. With a shudder that racks his entire body, he realizes he wants to wake up like this every single day for the rest of his life.

He cups Mal's chin and draws him in, when Mal stops him.

"*Mmf*, I've got morning breath, man," Mal complains, hand over his mouth.

"Don't care. Been waiting forever to kiss you."

Mal does not, in fact, taste like morning breath. He tastes like nothing much at all and too much all at once. Tastes like *Mal*, and Rowan thinks that it might be his new favorite taste.

They kiss slow and languid, Rowan running his tongue along the seam of Mal's lips before delving inside, licking behind his teeth.

Mal moans, opening his mouth wider as he melts into the kiss. After a lifetime, Mal pulls away.

"Rowan, want you…."

"I got you, Mal."

Rowan kisses him once again before coaxing Mal to roll over onto his side, his ass pressed firmly against Rowan's morning wood. With a little finagling, they work their briefs off in a tangle of limbs, Mal pressing back against Rowan and grinding his ass into Rowan's hard cock. It sends a pulse of desire through Rowan, making him buck his hips forward.

As Rowan reaches over to the nightstand to get the lube, Mal hikes up one leg, spreading himself wide for Rowan. After squeezing lube onto his fingers, Rowan wastes no time in working Mal open. He's still so slick and open from last night that it takes only minutes for him to get Mal panting and writhing in Rowan's arms.

"C'mon…," he whines.

"Always so impatient," Rowan says and laughs, dipping forward to kiss Mal's neck as he continues to finger him.

"Mmm, fuck…."

Rowan sucks a bruise on Mal's neck as he pumps himself, spreading the lube on his cock. And as Rowan slides into him, he gasps and feels his abs tighten as Mal's heat envelops him. Mal moans, a bright and beautiful sound in the quiet of the room. His head dips toward his chest, and Rowan takes the opportunity to kiss behind his ear as he pulls out and thrusts back inside.

"Oh fuck… feel so good, Mal…."

"Rowan, fuck me…."

A swoop of desire fills Rowan's belly as he fucks into Mal in deep, slow thrusts. A breathy sigh greets every thrust as his hips press hard into Mal's ass. Mal hikes his leg higher, gripping under his knee to open himself more to Rowan, allowing him to slip impossibly deeper inside.

They move together, hitches of hips and breath as Rowan slides in and out of Mal's heat. He chases his pleasure, clutching on to Mal for dear life, as if he'll vanish if Rowan doesn't hold him tightly enough.

"Fuck! There…," Mal moans.

Rowan obliges him, alternating grinding against his spot and pistoning into him, turning him into a moaning mess in his arms. It's like his hips have a mind of their own as he fucks him, Mal clenching around him eagerly and with abandon. He's sucking him in deeper, deeper, undoubtedly bruising his ass as he drops his leg and reaches back to pull Rowan closer.

The position is good—incredible, even—hitting deep and hard and letting Rowan feel Mal's muscular back pressed firmly against his chest. But it's been too long since he's seen his face. Too long since he kissed his lips.

"Mal, turn over. Wanna see your face."

Rowan pulls out and they swap positions, Mal on his back with Rowan nestled in between his legs.

He can't look anywhere but Mal's face as he slides back in, watching that perfect mouth part in pleasure. Fully seated, he dips down, catching Mal's bottom lip between his own, tugging gently with his teeth.

He keeps the pace slow, drawing whimpers from Mal's lips as he kisses him deep. And fuck, it's all so perfect, so warm and filling and fulfilling that he can't help the words that escape him.

"Fuck, I love you," Rowan whispers against his lips, hips moving on their own as his body fills with emotion.

He hadn't meant to say it, but weeks—hell, *months*—of keeping it to himself has felt like a lifetime.

Mal gasps, a sweet little hiccup of a sound that Rowan's going to remember for the rest of his life. He pulls Rowan down for a kiss that's mind-blowingly tender, and feels more than hears Mal whisper, "I love you too."

Rowan shudders into the kiss, eyes squeezed tightly closed as his chest constricts and his breath leaves his lungs in a *whoosh*. He wants to breathe in the residual oxygen from Mal's exhalations so he can say that a part of him has been inside every single one of his cells.

It doesn't take much after that. A handful of hard, deep thrusts has Rowan's belly coiling tight and Mal clenching around him, and with mutual gasps they come together, shuddering in each other's arms. It's easily the best orgasm Rowan's ever had in his life, and if the keening moan that Mal lets out as he comes across his chest is any indication, the same can be said for him.

They lie together, silent and sated, softly stroking whatever part of the other's skin they can reach. Planting kisses here and there, on shoulders and foreheads and lips and hands because they can now. Rowan can feel the warmth seeping out of every one of his pores.

"I'm so glad I met you," Rowan sighs.

Mal hums, curling into Rowan and snuggling into his chest. The casual display of intimacy is almost more than Rowan's heart can bear.

"Me too, Red." He's quiet for a moment, breath coming down into soft little puffs out his nose. "You ever think we'd end up here, back at the gangbang?"

Rowan laughs softly. "I wanted it. From the start. But I didn't want to get my hopes up, you know?"

"Yeah," Mal agrees with a nod of his head against Rowan's chest. "I know exactly what you mean."

It feels like they've done this whole thing backward, to be honest. Started with impersonal sex and ended with love, or something a hell of a lot like it. Rowan's never been in love before, but he can't imagine it feels like anything but filling his entire being with Mal.

They don't talk about what they are. Rowan, at least, doesn't feel the need to label anything when what they have is still so new, so tender and raw.

But Rowan knows in his fucking *soul* that what they have is real. Solid and sure and so damn *right* that no matter what happens, they're going to make it work. They've been through so much together the past few months that it feels like they can take on anything that comes their way. And they'll do it with the other at their side.

In his wildest dreams, Rowan never would have thought that a routine call to save someone's life would end up saving *his* life. Never thought that it would lead him *here*, in Mal's bed and Mal's arms. But he wouldn't change a thing.

Epilogue

It's been six months since their first kiss. Six months since their mutual *I love you*s, and six months since they became… *them.*

And they've been the best six months of Rowan's life.

He's all but moved into Mal's apartment by now—his being the nicer of their places—and it all feels so domestic that it sets Rowan's chest on fire. He stays over on weekends and some weeknights when he feels like making the slightly longer commute to work the next morning. Clothes and toothbrushes and face wash and extra meds left over there just in case, and Rowan can feel Mal on the brink of asking him to move in fully.

As much as he doesn't want to rush things between them, he can't imagine finding anyone that gets him better than Mal does. Can't imagine finding anyone that makes his heart skip a beat on the daily when he looks at him with that fond gaze or kisses him with those soft lips. So he'll wait, but he has a feeling he won't have to wait too much longer before the question is posed.

By now Mal has been introduced to the chaos that is the Campbell family, and he fit in right away, especially with Rowan's younger siblings. They viewed him as a *cool, mysterious bad boy* who's way too cool and mysterious to be dating their loser brother, but nonetheless they accept him and their relationship in a heartbeat. He's clashed a bit with Jay here and there, but their petty squabbles usually dissolve into good-natured jabs that die down after a beer or two. Even Aubrey likes him, for all her advice against catching feelings for a fuck buddy.

For once everything in Rowan's life seems perfect. He's happy, and this time there is no but. No caveats to his feelings. No other shoe waiting to drop that threatens to ruin his contentment.

It's all perfect.

They still go to the Menagerie. Their sex life has improved exponentially since they've gotten together, but every once in a while, they get an itch to go back. Even worked out a new membership option with Clover to allow them to come as guests for a small fee rather than paying the exorbitant monthly membership rates.

So once a month or so, they find themselves back in the Gold Room. Back to where it all started, more or less. It feels good to slip out of the comfort of their bed and back into the gritty, sensual underworld and let loose for a couple of hours.

Sometimes, they even make a game of it. Pretend that it's the first time. The first scene. Like they don't know each other inside and out and backward and forward by now. Like they're two near-strangers meeting once a week to give and take control.

But underneath, they know that their bond is unbreakable. They know that love courses through every bratty remark, every hard, answering spank. And it makes it that much better, that much *hotter*, to pretend otherwise.

Mal and Rowan both know that if Mal safewords—*meringue* for pause and *apple* for stop (green apple, Mal insists, not the red ones, because green apples are disgusting)—that Rowan will stop immediately and cradle Mal in his arms and kiss away any tears that may have spilled and tell him that he loves him to the moon and back.

So much love underneath it all.

TONIGHT FOR the first time, they visit the VoyEx corner. They'd talked about doing it for a while now but hadn't yet worked up the courage to actually do it. But they finally decided on it and booked a slot on the stage—wanting to make sure that no one else claimed it first.

When they walk over, hand in hand, there's already a crowd forming around the empty stage, Mal still drawing in gaggles of onlookers long after he's stopped scening with anyone but Rowan.

"Jesus," Rowan remarks under his breath.

Mal laughs. "You can say that again. Horny fuckers."

"They see your name on the Events calendar and go fucking nuts."

"Let 'em. Only one person I care about driving nuts anymore," Mal says, squeezing Rowan's hand tighter.

Rowan smiles and squeezes back.

They'd specifically requested a Saint Andrew's cross for tonight, and the staff of the Menagerie did not disappoint. Smack in the center of the stage is a large, leather-padded, X-shaped black cross, cuffs already in place in each of the four corners. Mal sets his bag down and goes to work swapping out the cuffs for his own fabric-lined ones while Rowan lays out the lube and toys they've brought tonight—nipple clamps, a vibrator, a prostate massager, and a clear masturbator.

They're going all-out tonight.

The crowd around them thickens, more and more men gathering around despite the fact that nothing interesting is happening right now. A couple of them have even started jerking off, completely unashamed. Rowan knows that's the point of this whole area—to get off watching strangers getting off—but *Christ*. Save some for the good stuff.

One guy looks like he's halfway to blowing already, leering greedily at Mal's clothed ass as he switches the cuffs. An ugly coil of jealousy twists itself in Rowan's gut, but he has to remind himself that Mal is *his* now, and that what they've got can't be shaken by some middle-aged businessman with an average-at-best cock.

When everything is set up, Rowan runs a hand down Mal's back, rubbing gently at the dip in his spine above his ass.

"You ready?" Rowan whispers to him.

"Always."

"Good. Then strip."

He raises his voice, aware of the crowd around them. They're here to put on a show, after all.

Mal complies immediately, no fight in him at this point, only eagerness. He strips off his shirt first, pulls it over his head in a swift motion before he chucks it over to the supply table where his bag sits. His shoes and socks come next, kicked off in a somehow attractive, flawless manner that Mal always seems to be able to pull off. Finally he gets to his jeans, shucking them down without preamble, revealing what's underneath.

Tonight, he'd wanted to wear the jockstrap that Rowan bought him for his birthday. The gold threads shimmer in the overhead lights, accentuating the bulge between his thighs. The straps frame his ass perfectly, digging in tight enough for the soft fat on the sides of his hips to bulge out a bit over the sides.

Rowan grabs him by his hips, tugging him forward flush against his chest. Someone in the crowd whistles, a high-pitched wolf call that makes Rowan surge forward into Mal, grinding his hard cock against his thigh. The attention feels good. Whether it's more for Mal or for himself or for the both of them combined, it doesn't matter to Rowan.

Pressed hard against Mal's body, he stares down into Mal's gold eyes, slowly but surely being encompassed by black and blinking up at him. He sees the love there, reflected back at him, and it makes his knees weak. He manages to keep them both upright despite threatening to buckle and guides Mal back to the cross. He cuffs first his wrists, then his ankles, kissing the inside of his thigh as he dips down to each leg.

With Mal all trussed up, Rowan steps back to inspect his sub. He's gorgeous, the hard planes of his body taut and begging to be touched. So Rowan does, running his hands over every inch of exposed skin that he can reach. The heat of Mal's body fuels him, as do the dozens of pairs of eyes that he can feel boring into him from behind. But this worship of his boyfriend's body isn't for show by any stretch—it's something he'll gladly do for the rest of time if Mal will let him.

He doesn't interact with the crowd at all. This may be a performance, a show, but it's mostly for them. For him and Mal. While they both love being watched, Mal admittedly more of an exhibitionist than Rowan, they could easily go without. Could easily focus on each other and forget the rest of the outside world ever existed.

Rowan doesn't do anything like ask the crowd what to use on Mal first. Because he *knows* what he wants to use on Mal first. He picks up the clover clamps from the table and saunters back to Mal with the clamps jangling in his fingers. Mal breathes hard through his nose when he sees the clamps, something they've introduced over the past couple months of their relationship after their brief dalliance with them during one of their first scenes. Something he *really fucking likes*. He squeezes his eyes shut as Rowan opens the first one, poised above Mal's hard nipple.

"Watch," Rowan tells him.

Mal's eyes flutter back open, and Rowan forces him to look down as he fastens the first clamp around one pert nipple. Mal moans, loud and unabashed, squirming in his restraints.

"Good. Now the other."

Open. Clamp. *Moan.* Louder this time now that both nipples are subject to the same onslaught.

Rowan tugs gently on the silver chain connecting the two clamps, causing Mal to jerk forward off the cross, hips and chest jutting out as far as they can from where he's bound. Another small tug has him crying out, gasping a moan, and wringing his hands.

"Feels good?" Rowan asks, though he knows the answer.

Mal nods frantically.

Smack! Rowan's palm rains down on Mal's left pec, just shy of where his nipple is turning red from the clamp.

"Fuck!"

"*Answer me* when I ask you a question."

"Y-yes. Feels fucking good."

"Better."

Rowan crouches down beside Mal, raking his nails down his chest and thighs on the way as he settles on his knees. He runs a palm over Mal's bulge, the black-and-gold fabric of his jockstrap stretching but not revealing its contents. Mal groans and tosses his head back as Rowan gropes his ass, massaging each cheek in his hands. It isn't until Mal's greedily hitching his hips back that Rowan reaches for the lube and the prostate massager.

Mal's never been a big fan of vibrators, but they bought the toy a couple of months ago, and it made Mal come harder than he pretty much ever has in three minutes flat, so it's the perfect toy to tease him with tonight.

Because Mal needs to last the whole night without coming until Rowan lets him. Rowan has edged him plenty of times by now, but this will be the most intense session by far. Not only because of the numerous toys he brought with them, but also because of the added stimulation of dozens of pairs of eyes watching their every move. Eyes that Rowan can feel on him as he works a lubed finger into Mal's hole. Mal moans, hips jutting forward in an attempt to work Rowan's finger deeper inside him.

Smack! Rowan rains a hand down on the inside of Mal's thigh.

"Hold still."

"Make me." The challenge is clear in Mal's voice.

Rowan uses his free hand to grab Mal's hips, shoving him back against the cross with a *thud*! that's audible even over the lowly thumping club music and a few collective groans from their audience.

"You're not exactly in a position to be a mouthy brat," Rowan tells him, shoving a second finger inside.

Mal mewls. He tries to rock his hips forward, but he has no leverage, and Rowan's grip on him is too strong. Rowan can see the hard line of his cock through the jockstrap, and he watches with rapt attention as his cock jumps as soon as Rowan's fingers spear into his prostate. A loud moan is ripped from his mouth, cutting off whatever snarky retort he was about to make.

Rowan laughs low, fucking into him and brushing against his prostate on every other stroke, reveling in Mal's gaspy moans and the desperate hitching of his hips under Rowan's palm. He digs his nails into his hip, knowing that Mal likes the bite and the crescent-moon indentations that will be left over for at least the rest of the night, if not longer.

"Gonna fill you up," Rowan says. "Get this perfect ass open for my cock. Have you begging for it by the time I'm done."

"We'll see about that," Mal retorts, though it's low and breathy.

Rowan smacks his thigh again, the sharp *slap*! of it echoing in the corner. He slicks the prostate massager in lube before sliding it into Mal's hole and nestling it right against his sweet spot. Rowan flicks the remote, the toy buzzing to life and making Mal jump at the sensation. He can barely hear the low *zzt, zzt, zzt* of the pulsing setting as it whirs away inside Mal's body.

"Let's see how you do with this first. Then we'll see about you begging."

"Oooh…," Mal moans, head craned back, exposing the long column of his neck to the stark overhead lights.

Rowan lets him stand there for a few moments, adjusting to the sensations. He runs his hands up and down Mal's bare torso, feeling the dip and swell of his abs under his palms, tugging absently on the chain connecting the nipple clamps when Mal's still for too long. It draws these tiny whimpers from Mal that head straight to Rowan's already hard cock and make something feral coil in his belly.

He bends down, tonguing over Mal's clamped nipples, the metallic bite of the clamps cold on his tongue, but Mal's flesh hot. Mal writhes underneath him, straining against his bonds. Rowan presses him back against the cross with a hand to his rib cage, nearly covering the entire length of his abdomen. Despite that Mal's a full-grown man, it'll never cease to make Rowan go fucking insane that he's *that* much smaller than Rowan that his hand can span half of his torso.

He can feel Mal's moan vibrate through his rib cage.

Rowan leans in, breathing in Mal's scent deeply as he shakes against the cross, all sweat and musk and *Mal*. A smell he'll never get tired of.

"Rowan," Mal gasps, pulse hammering loud enough for Rowan to hear. "C'mon…."

"C'mon what?" Rowan replies, a small smile tugging at his lips.

"Need more…."

"Funny that you think you've earned more already."

Mal mewls, a frustrated, garbled sound in the back of his throat. Rowan tugs on his nipple clamps, drawing a gasp from the other man.

"You'll get more when I say you get more."

"Not fair…," Mal complains, torn between pressing into Rowan's hand and pulling away from the pain.

Smack!

Rowan slaps Mal's outer thigh hard, skin blossoming red from the impact.

"*Nng!*"

"That's enough whining."

"I wouldn't have to—"

Smack! Smack!

Two more sharp blows against his thigh, Rowan's palm stinging with the force of the hits.

"Shut the fuck up."

Rowan reaches back, pressing hard against the prostate massager and driving it deeper into Mal's ass.

"Fuck!"

"That's better."

Mal moans again, hands balling into fists in his cuffs and teeth digging into his lower lip.

After a long while of teasing touches, Rowan takes pity on him, dipping his hand inside Mal's jockstrap and releasing his cock from its confines. He's so fucking hard, leaking profusely, and Rowan slicks up his hand and pumps him once, twice, spreading the precome around his cock.

He grabs the masturbator, slicks it with lube and brings it to the very tip of Mal's cock, teasing the edge of it at his head. Mal's hips fly forward, instantly trying to get more of himself into the toy, a gasped moan escaping his lips.

His abs flex and strain as his hips undulate in the desperate attempt to fuck deeper into the toy. It's like his body can't decide between shifting his hips back onto the prostate massager and forward into the masturbator, making him twitch wildly and rock forward and backward with little coordination. It's the hottest fucking thing Rowan's ever seen. If he could spend the rest of his life watching Mal in the throes of pleasure, he'd do so in a heartbeat.

Rowan works the masturbator over Mal's cock in torturously slow pumps, deliberately ignoring Mal's moans and bitten-off pleas for more. He throws in the occasional twist, tightening his grip around the toy as he eases it toward the tip of Mal's cock.

In no time, Mal's babbling.

"Rowan… gonna come—"

"Don't," Rowan orders. "If you come, I'm not stopping."

Mal whines, eyes screwed shut as he fights through what must be the overwhelming pleasure from the massager inside him and the masturbator working quicker and quicker over his cock.

"Fu-fuck! Gonna…!"

Rowan pulls away the masturbator immediately, watching as Mal's body shudders from the sudden lack of stimulation.

"Fuck!" Mal whines, hips thrusting against nothing.

Rowan presses him firmly against the cross as Mal's cock twitches in the air. A few excruciatingly slow moments pass as Mal's body calms down and his eyes blink back open.

"Good," Rowan praises, trailing a hand down the side of his cheek.

Rowan tugs the fabric of the jockstrap to the side, exposing Mal's balls. He retrieves the vibrator from the table, turns the wand to the lowest setting, and nestles the head behind Mal's tight balls.

The buzz dulls as it touches Mal's sensitive skin, making him jump.

"Ohhh!" he gasps.

A few sessions with Rowan had changed Mal's initial stance on vibrators. Now he's whimpering freely, taking everything that Rowan's giving him and all but begging for more.

Rowan works the masturbator back over Mal's cock, setting up a languid pace. In no time, Mal's shaking again, body a trembling mess as Rowan speeds up the masturbator. His cockhead pokes out through the opening with each pump, slick and pink and making Rowan's mouth water with the need to taste.

He trails the vibrator across Mal's perineum, not quite touching his hole but practically feeling it clench in anticipation.

Mal nearly comes again when Rowan places the vibrator under the tip of Mal's cock, pumping away with the masturbator at the same time. But he doesn't because he's so good for him. Rowan can tell how badly he wants to come—muscles taut and quivering, breath heaving with every touch of the vibrator and every pump of the masturbator.

He brings him to the edge three more times, pulling away when he hears the telltale gasping moan that signals that Mal's about to come.

"That's it, baby. I want one more."

"Can't, Rowan…," Mal whispers.

"I know you can. One more."

"*Nnng….*"

Rowan cranks the speed of the vibrator and prostate massager up as high as they'll go, the sound audible even over Mal's ragged breaths and the slick sounds of men jerking off behind them. He strokes the masturbator furiously, vibrator trailing around his cockhead and over his balls and back to his hole.

Mal's hoarse moan rises in a crescendo that spikes Rowan's heart rate through the roof.

"Fu-fuck…!"

"Don't come," Rowan warns.

"*Please…,*" Mal begs.

"I said *no*. Don't disappoint me."

Rowan works him faster, until the point where it looks like Mal might actually combust if he's teased any more. He can see his fingers and toes curl in his peripheral vision, and he finally lets up as Mal's stomach clenches violently.

"Fuuuuck!"

"That's it. So fuckin' perfect."

He withdraws and turns off all the toys and dumps them on the table. Rowan cups Mal's chin in his hand, turning his face toward him, whispering low in his ear.

"Can I kiss you in front of them? Show them how good you are for me? That you're mine?"

They'd already talked about it, but—

"Y-yeah," Mal breathes.

And Rowan slots his mouth over Mal's, slipping his tongue inside in a filthy, sensual kiss that makes him throb and Mal's knees buckle. Rowan grips under his ass, supporting his weight as he takes him apart with his lips and tongue. There's a groan somewhere behind them and a gasp or two, but Rowan ignores everything but the feeling of Mal's talented lips on his own, giving as good as he gets.

When they part, a thin trail of spit connects their lips, Mal's jaw slack and his eyes hazy and lidded. Rowan wipes the spit away with his thumb, running it along Mal's lower lip and feeling Mal shudder slightly beneath him.

"So good for me, Mal," Rowan tells him in a low voice that only he can hear.

Mal gives another full-body shudder at the use of his name. Here, he's used to being Malcolm. He's been going by his full name here since he joined almost eight years ago, and earned a lucrative reputation under it. Rowan doesn't care what other people call him. Because with Rowan, he's always been *Mal*. Something that none of these assholes watching him and getting off to him will ever have.

But at the same time, he loves showing Mal off. Loves showing how fucking good and gorgeous his boyfriend is, even if no one here knows that they're anything beyond Dom and sub to one another. He knows that he's the one going home to Mal nearly every night. He's the one who gets all sides of Mal, beyond this hypersexual, physical side. He gets the quiet moments, the funny moments, the joyful and sad moments alike. He gets *all* of Mal, and he wouldn't trade him for anything.

Fuck. He needs him, and he *wants him*, so badly it makes his chest ache.

Rowan bends to swiftly uncuff Mal's ankles. His own cock is so fucking hard and straining against his jeans that he feels like he might actually explode if he doesn't get inside Mal right now.

He rips his shirt off, tossing it to the side before unbuttoning and unzipping his jeans and pulling his cock out through the slit in his briefs. With a cursory slicking of lube, he grips Mal by the underside of his asscheeks, hoisting him into the air.

Mal yelps, eyes flying to Rowan's, widening a fraction before slipping halfway closed in a heated gaze that makes Rowan's cock throb where it's sliding against the back of Mal's balls. With a quick check to make sure Mal's weight is fully supported and he's not hanging by his wrists, Rowan shifts his hips and in one swift motion, slides up and into him.

The inferno of Mal's body is a welcome relief to the chill running down his spine caused by Mal's loud groan. He gives him a moment to adjust before pulling out and fucking back in, a sharp thrust that creates a low *slap*! that's swallowed by the men and the music in the background.

As he fucks into Mal, he sends a quick prayer that the cross is as thoroughly mounted as it looks. His pace builds and builds and builds, a lewd crescendo that pulls moan after moan after moan from Mal's lips, voice hoarse with the strain.

The chain connecting Mal's nipple clamps rattles with the strain of Rowan fucking Mal, hitting Rowan in the chest periodically. A cool burst of metal on his heated skin. In his arms, Mal's a moaning wreck. Rowan knows how much he enjoys being manhandled, and this is right up his alley. He clenches tight around him, milking Rowan's cock with every drop down.

Time ticks by too slowly and too fast all at once as Rowan loses himself in the feeling of Mal surrounding him. His arms begin to strain under Mal's weight, but he pushes the pain aside, focusing entirely on the spot where they're connected.

At this point the rest of the club is drowned out along with the ache in his arms. His mind zones in on his boyfriend, and Rowan pushes his body to its breaking point to give it to him harder, faster, *better*, pouring every ounce of strength and love into each thrust.

"Fuck, Rowan...," Mal moans. "G-gonna... need to.... Please let me come...."

Rowan knows he wants a hand around his cock. But he also knows that he can't do that for him without dropping him. So he presses closer, Mal's cock trapped between their bodies and dripping with precome and lube and sweat.

"Do it, Mal. Know you can. Show me how good you are by coming untouched."

Mal groans, a deep, low sound that has Rowan's own orgasm nearly ringing the alarm bells in his brain, and in a dozen more thrusts, Mal's coming, spurting between them and slicking their already damp skin.

His walls ripple around Rowan's cock, sucking him in deeper as he quakes in his arms. Rowan chases the pleasure, fucking deep into Mal's body with wanton abandon. It doesn't take much. He's so turned on by having Mal in his arms and dozens of eyes at his back that it takes only a handful more thrusts before Rowan's spilling inside him, body tingling like a live wire.

"Fuck…," he gasps, still thrusting with aborted half thrusts, the pleasure of Mal's ass quickly slipping to overstimulation the longer he stays inside.

He forces himself to still as his cock softens, Mal long since gone slack in his arms. He slips out with a rush of come and lube no doubt trickling down Mal's legs as he gingerly lowers him to the ground.

Once sure that Mal has his footing, Rowan unwinds himself from Mal's body and tucks himself away, uncaring of the mess now staining the front of his jeans and his briefs. With a hand to the side of his face, Rowan drags Mal's eyes to meet his own. Rowan kisses Mal one last time, staking his claim for all to see. A gentle peck on the lips, but lingering. Pouring his love into a single kiss that has his limbs shaking all over again, this time with the weight of something more. Mal's eyes flutter open when they part, and there's a small smile on his lips that makes Rowan's heart thud painfully in his chest.

God, he'd kill for that smile.

Rowan uncuffs Mal gingerly but quickly, massaging each wrist and stimulating the blood flow in his arms as Mal lowers his arms from above his head. He places a gentle kiss on the palm of each hand. Mal wobbles a bit once he's freed, Rowan catching him easily and holding him close to his chest until he regains his balance.

"Did so good for me, Mal. So fuckin' perfect," he whispers.

Rowan unclips the nipple clamps quickly, both at the same time, knowing by now that Mal prefers the Band-Aid method rather than a slow release when it comes to the clamps. After wearing them for so long, he knows that removing them hurts almost as much as the initial sting of putting them on. Knows, too, that Mal's nipples will be sensitive for *days* after, a fact which he's going to take full advantage of starting tomorrow night.

Once Mal is finally freed of the cross and all his toys, the crowd begins to disperse with satisfied murmurs. A bunch of happy customers, it seems. Rowan feels a tingling swell of pride in him.

Rowan and Mal clean up their belongings and wipe down the cross quickly, working in tandem. When they're finished, Rowan leads them to the recovery room where Mal collapses onto the bed with a heavy, contented sigh. Rowan joins him, tugging Mal toward him and relishing in his body heat as Mal curls into his side.

He kisses the top of Mal's head, whispering sweet nothings in his ear while he comes down. Mal hums lightly, reaching for Rowan's hand and interlacing their fingers.

"Love you," Mal whispers.

"Love you too," Rowan replies, voice and heart light.

It feels good. Feels right, having Mal like this. Rowan is so lucky to have him.

They'll settle down for a while, get their heart rates and minds back under control and wait for the rush of endorphins to subside. Then they'll go home, cuddle up on the couch with some shitty movie on in the background and talk about nothing in particular. Eventually they'll make their way to bed and fall asleep in each other's arms.

A perfect ending to a perfect day. Rowan doesn't think he's off base saying he hopes it'll be the ending of all their days for the rest of their lives. But for now, he's happy with what they have.

They'll always have the Menagerie.

It'll be here when they need to get away, when they need to come home. It started as an impersonal place to lose themselves, but they never expected to find something else along the way. And now, they have so much more than a club.

They have each other.

And that's worth its weight in gold.

Keep Reading for an Exclusive Excerpt from
If You Let Me by Saria Bryant
Coming This Summer
from Dreamspinner Press

CHAPTER ONE

SPRING BREAKS had never been more than a week of Jasper locking himself in his room and keeping quiet. How enjoyable the week was always inversely correlated to the number of times he saw his father, which meant spring breaks were usually shit.

This year was different. Now that he'd moved in with his cousin Amber, her fiancé Terrance, and their three housemates, he no longer had to sneak around his own home to avoid verbal or physical blows. This year Jasper intended to enjoy himself, especially while he had a small break from both college and his part-time job. Which was how he ended up standing inside a kink club on Saturday night.

He scrubbed his palms against his slacks—a bit too small since they were borrowed from Matt, one of his housemates—for the fifth time since getting out of the car. The club was far classier than other clubs he'd been to, but then, none of them had catered to anything more than dancing and drinking. The bar was well-stocked with every kind of nonalcoholic drink imaginable, and there was a sitting area with posh leather sofas and dark-wood, live-edge coffee tables. Black-and-white photos were interspersed along the walls, but he was too far away to make out anything more than the shapes of bodies.

Amber and the others—Terrance, Keith, Matt, and Reiko—had already vanished into the play area, and while he was curious what was in there, he wasn't ready to cross that threshold yet. Despite the fetish videos he'd watched and his growing curiosity about bondage, seeing all this up close and personal was something else entirely. Especially when Amber had invited him along only a few hours ago.

Instead he went to the bar and ordered a soda, wishing he was a few months older and could have downed some liquid courage. Then again, Amber would probably kill him if he got drunk just to try something new with a stranger. He wasn't *that* stupid, thanks.

He took his drink to a comfy armchair and settled in to people-watch, ignoring the little voice in his head piping up with a *You're stalling.* Maybe he'd get lucky enough to catch someone's eye while lingering in the sitting area. He sipped his drink with a soft snort. *Yeah, right.*

People weren't wearing as much leather as he'd expected. Most were in casual clothes, but there were a few who dressed the part: leather pants, corsets, fishnet. He caught sight of a man wearing a collar with a leash attached. A shiny silver collar that glinted against his dark skin.

Jasper watched him as his partner led him into the dungeon, absently touching his own throat as he slumped further into his chair. No way was he going to get anyone's attention sitting in the corner like this, but the thought of going in there alone made him feel like puking. He wasn't entirely sure if that was the excitement or the nerves, or both. With a sigh he pulled his phone out, finding a game to keep himself occupied until his cousin was done.

At least he'd gotten out of the house for a bit. He could even call it experiencing something new. If he ignored the heat of self-loathing in his gut for getting all the way here and chickening out.

He'd only finished half his soda when someone sat in the chair next to him. From the corner of his eye, he caught the dark fabric of an expensive suit. Someone way out of his league. Probably waiting on someone. Probably *straight*. Such a travesty.

"Seeking pain or pleasure?" a quiet voice asked, and it took Jasper a moment to realize Mr. Suit was talking to *him*.

Jasper glanced up, choking on his soda and nearly shooting it out his nose. Dark hair, hazel eyes, and a face that belonged on a *Forbes* issue about the hottest entrepreneurs of the decade. "Uh, what?" he asked, pinching his stinging nose, his eyes watering. *Real smooth, dumbass.*

Mr. Suit raised an eyebrow, and Jasper kissed his chances of making a good impression good-bye. "Are you here to play?" he asked, glancing at the white band on Jasper's wrist. The band had a red line through the center that marked him as a guest, new to the scene, and "vanilla." Because Amber was a bitch.

Jasper sat up, nerves fluttering in his stomach. "Maybe? Are—" He cut himself off, taking in the rest of Mr. Suit's appearance: mussed but effortlessly styled hair, expensive watch, shoes so polished he could nearly see his reflection. Definitely out of his league. "Are you offering?"

"Depends." Mr. Suit tilted his head and offered his hand. "I'm Vincent."

"Jasper," he replied, shaking Vincent's hand. "And pleasure. Definitely pleasure."

Vincent smiled briefly and let go. "In that case, why don't we talk?" He stood and motioned to a set of doors near the bar.

"Sure," Jasper said, hating how he was suddenly breathless. No way was he this lucky. "Holy shit, he's hot," he whispered as he stood and followed Vincent into another lounge, this one empty aside from chairs and tables.

This was fine. Have a talk with the gorgeous guy who hopefully wanted to play with him.

He totally had this.

CHAPTER TWO

VINCENT MOTIONED to a chair at one of the smaller tables, then sat across from Jasper. Once they were settled, he leaned back and crossed his legs. "What kind of pleasure are you seeking?"

Jasper wrapped both hands around his glass and bit his lip, shifting once in his seat and then stilling like he was trying hard not to fidget. "What do you mean?"

Well, that partly answered the question of how new to the scene Jasper was. The white band had caught his eye on his way out, and the way Jasper had been absorbed in his phone was not an image he liked to see in his club. He wasn't sure who'd brought Jasper in—few of the members even had guest access—but maybe he should rescind that completely if this was the result. He didn't mind members bringing in their friends, but abandoning them was a dick move.

"Some people enjoy being tickled," Vincent said. "Or having hot wax dripped over their bodies. Others are more interested in sexual release." He tilted his head when Jasper shifted in his chair again. "What is it that brought you to my club rather than a seedy strip joint?"

Jasper cleared his throat. "I-I kinda want to know what being tied up is like."

"Kinda? Is that a 'I like thinking about it, but don't really want to experience it' kinda, or a 'please tie me up and torment me' kinda?" Vincent asked, holding back a chuckle when Jasper squirmed.

"I've never done any of this before." Jasper glanced up, his blue eyes bright in the low light. "But I want to. I'd like to try. With you."

Vincent couldn't exactly say no in the face of that eagerness. Especially since he didn't like the idea of someone so inexperienced getting in over their head. He did everything he could to keep his club a safe space, though there were more than a few hard players among the members.

"All right." He clasped his hands in his lap, tapping his thumbs together. "Do you have a safeword?" he asked. When Jasper shook his head, he continued, "Are you familiar with the stoplight system?"

"Yes…. Sir."

Vincent smiled. "Good," he said, glad when Jasper smiled back and finally seemed to relax. "So tell me how you'd like tonight to go."

"Besides being tied up?"

"Once you're tied up. Do you want to be naked? Touched, kissed, fingered?"

Jasper licked his lips. "Y-yeah. All that."

"Anywhere you don't want to be touched? Anything you don't want done?"

"Tickled."

Vincent chuckled. "No tickling. How about aftercare?"

Jasper shrugged. "I don't think I really need it?"

"Is that a question?"

"No. I think I'm good without it." He glanced towards the door with a grimace. "Do we have to use the dungeon?"

Vincent followed Jasper's gaze as he considered. The rooms upstairs were for select members, but there were no rules about guests not being allowed, though maybe that had been an oversight. Not that he had any reason not to trust those he'd screened, but then, few as green as Jasper ever made it to his club. At least not alone. "No," he said. "If you'd prefer a private room, we can go upstairs."

"Yeah." Jasper drained the last of his soda. "That sounds good."

"This way, then."

Vincent stopped by the security room on the second floor. Ian was on duty as part of the night's security team, and he eyed Vincent in surprise when he poked his head in. Vincent had said he was going home an hour ago, and technically this was supposed to have been his day off to begin with. "I'll be in room two."

Ian saluted and didn't bother to hide his grin when he caught sight of Jasper. "Yessirrr," he drawled.

Vincent stifled a sigh and counted himself lucky when Ian didn't wink. He turned and continued down the hall.

Room two was one of their tamer rooms by far. There was a bed near the far corner, a sofa, a low table long and wide enough to tie someone down on, and a large wingback chair with a cushion in front of it. Next to the bed was a small chest with basic necessities and toys and a mini fridge stocked with water. A door in the adjacent corner led to a bathroom.

Vincent closed the door behind Jasper and shrugged out of his jacket. He draped it over the end of the bed, then turned to face him. "So. To reiterate, you'll be tied up. Naked. I can touch you, kiss you, and finger you. No tickling. And at the end, you'd prefer to get off, yes or no?"

"Yes. Definitely yes." Jasper let out an unsteady breath where he still lingered by the door. He took a step forward and stopped. "What is it you want in return?"

Vincent raised an eyebrow. "Tonight is about you. I'll show you a good time and hopefully bring your fantasy to life."

"That's it?"

"Were you expecting me to only do this if you gave me a blowjob?" he asked, frowning when Jasper shrugged. "That's not how this works, Jasper. I'll only do what you've given me permission to do, and if you decide you don't like it, you give me the word. No sex or sexual favors in return. Understood?"

When Jasper nodded, Vincent turned the chair and sat facing him. "Let's get started, then. When you're ready, strip."

CHAPTER THREE

JASPER FLEXED his fingers and stared as Vincent sat with an expectant expression. "Strip," he repeated.

Vincent really expected him to strip in front of a stranger? Just like that? Even if he'd agreed to it, he'd expected *something* to happen first. Like making out, maybe. Or at least being naked *together*. Not to be watched like he was a stripper, though that could be kinda hot too.

"You do know how to undress yourself, don't you?" Vincent asked, sounding amused.

Jasper glared, a brief flare of indignation stamping out his nerves. "Fucker," he grumbled, swallowing hard when Vincent raised an eyebrow. That might have been all he did, but somehow that conveyed a warning all on its own.

He cleared his throat and muttered under his breath as he accepted that he was really about to do this. Then he toed off his shoes and socks and stepped closer to the chair. He was hyperaware of Vincent's eyes on him as he toyed with the bottom button of his shirt.

"Changing your mind?"

Jasper took a breath and shook his head. "No."

"No, what?"

"No, Sir."

"Good boy," Vincent purred, and *damn* if that didn't do pleasant things to Jasper's stomach. "When you're ready, then."

Jasper resisted the urge to roll his eyes and shrugged his shirt off, then tossed it in Vincent's face and kicked his pants aside. His boxers followed his shirt, and he smirked as Vincent dropped them to the floor with narrowed eyes.

Now that he'd committed to this, he sure as hell was going to have fun. It was either that or let the nerves paralyze him.

He let out a slow breath as he was left standing there. Naked. While Vincent sat and studied him, like he was some kind of statue to be admired.

He refused to fidget. This was some kind of test, he knew. He'd been around his cousin and her housemates long enough to at least know that much. He may not understand all the finer subtleties of the whole kink thing, but hopefully he knew enough not to make a fool of himself.

Vincent finally let out a soft hum that sounded like approval and stood. He moved across the room to the chest and pulled out a long strip of black silk. "Hands behind your back."

Jasper clasped his hands behind him. He glanced over his shoulder as Vincent adjusted his arms until they were bent at the elbows, his hands clasping his forearms instead. The feel of the cloth winding around his arms set off a spike of panic in his chest, but he breathed through it. When Vincent finished, Jasper found he couldn't budge his arms an inch, and the panic intensified enough that he squeezed his eyes shut.

Shit. This was such a bad idea. He didn't even know this guy!

Vincent gripped Jasper's biceps and pulled until Vincent was pressed flush against Jasper's back. "If you say Red, I untie you, you get dressed, and you can go back downstairs," he murmured into Jasper's ear. "Understand?"

Jasper licked his lips and forced in a deep breath. And then another. He could do this. He could get free whenever he wanted, right? That was how this was supposed to work, at least according to Amber. "Yes," he whispered.

"Good. Then give me a color."

Jasper swallowed, surprised when Vincent didn't move at all until he said "Green." He shivered as Vincent hummed again and finally moved his hands, sliding them down Jasper's arms and over his chest.

That felt nice. For some reason, he'd expected a rougher touch. To be manhandled and pushed around, and he couldn't stop the hitch in his breath when Vincent merely skimmed his palms over Jasper's skin.

"You said you didn't want pain," Vincent said. "Does that mean you don't like things rough either?"

"I don't mind rough," Jasper murmured, cracking his eyes open to watch Vincent's hands. "But I don't see how pain can be pleasurable."

Vincent chuckled. "I see." He moved a hand up to Jasper's nipple, circling a finger around it. "Maybe I'll show you sometime," he said, rubbing the nipple between his fingers and then squeezing it.

Jasper bit back a groan as his head dropped to Vincent's shoulder, sure he'd fall over if Vincent weren't standing there. Why was it so hard to keep his balance with his arms trapped behind him? "You assume there'll be a next time." He tried to sound taunting, but the words came out breathless.

"Not enjoying this?"

Jasper valiantly tried to think of a smartass response, but then Vincent found both his nipples and tugged, and coherent thought abandoned him. He whimpered, his knees threatening to give out on him too. The low, rich sound of Vincent's laugh in his ear didn't help in the least. "Fucker," he moaned.

Vincent *tsk*ed and pulled his hands away. He tangled his fingers in Jasper's hair instead and gave a sharp tug. "You have a strange way of showing your appreciation. Don't tell me you don't know at least basic etiquette."

Jasper shivered, surprised at the intensity of the arousal that shot through him and pooled in his gut from the tug. "Yes," he said, moaning at the pointed jerk Vincent gave his hair. "Yes, Sir."

"Good boy," Vincent said, releasing him. He dragged blunt nails down Jasper's back and stepped around him, glancing down with a smirk. "You sure seem to be enjoying yourself."

"Fuck you, Sir," Jasper replied lightly, because he could.

Vincent snorted, then grasped Jasper's chin, and tipped his head back. "I should have known you'd need a gag," he said, pressing two fingers past Jasper's lips. "For now this will do."

Jasper's eyes widened, and he let out a muffled curse around Vincent's fingers. What the hell? He tried to pull away, but Vincent held his chin in a firm grip, moving his fingers in and out in quick thrusts. When he finally pulled them away, they were slick with saliva. Jasper hardly had time to tell Vincent off for putting his *fingers* in Jasper's *mouth* before those same fingers were rubbing against his entrance.

"Oh fuck," he gasped. He arched into Vincent with a strangled whimper as a single finger pressed into him.

"I would have enjoyed playing with you more, but you obviously have no desire for foreplay," Vincent said, as if he were commenting on the weather. "I might have even sucked you off, but if all you want is a quickie, I'll give you what you want."

Jasper squirmed as Vincent nudged his finger deeper, his hips jerking forward at the thought of Vincent's mouth on him. No way would Vincent really do that. Would he? "No. Wait," he groaned, trying to get away from the finger and only managing to rub against Vincent. "Please."

Vincent stilled with a soft hum. "Please what?"

Jasper squirmed as embarrassment crawled through his veins, dropping his forehead to Vincent's shoulder. Bastard. Of course he was the perfect few inches taller. "Please…. Foreplay."

Vincent hummed again as if considering it, then pulled his hand away. "I don't think you've earned it."

Jasper swallowed, a strange warmth spreading through him. He wanted Vincent to tell him he'd earned it. He wanted—he very much wanted—to earn it.

He turned his head, carefully nuzzling against Vincent's neck. "How can I?" he asked, momentarily distracted by how good Vincent smelled. Sandalwood and citrus. "Sir."

Vincent slid his fingers into Jasper's hair again and pulled. Not hard, disappointingly, but tight enough that Jasper swallowed a groan. Vincent studied him with his intense hazel eyes for a moment before loosening his grip. "Ask nicely for what you want."

Heat crept into Jasper's face as he imagined all the things he could ask for. He never thought he'd ever be in this kind of situation in real life. Standing in a private room in a fetish club. With an actual Dom. If there was anyone on the planet he could actually ask to indulge any of his fantasies—

But he was already tied up. Kinda. He wasn't sure he could handle adding blindfolds or gags tonight.

His attention flicked to Vincent's lips, and he tipped his head back. "Will you kiss me?"

"With pleasure." Vincent's fingers caught Jasper's chin, holding him steady as he closed the distance between them.

And *fuck,* Vincent could kiss. He kissed Jasper with intention. Like kissing was his sole purpose of existence. Maybe it was all part of being a Dom, but Jasper could get used to it *far* too easily. No one had ever kissed him like it was a luxury rather than a means to an end. By the time Vincent's lips ghosted across Jasper's jaw and moved to his neck, his apprehension at being bound and helpless faded. Forming in its place was something else he was all too familiar with.

Infatuation.

He stared at the ceiling and fought the sudden urge to laugh. Fuck, what was *wrong* with him? He'd sworn off anything close to relationships after the last one ended in a dumpster fire. Like hell he was going to even *think* about getting involved with Vincent. As if it were even possible. This was a one-time deal. A bit of fun before the next semester started.

"Planning on kissing me all night?" he asked, his voice hitching as Vincent's teeth grazed his neck. "Thought you were going to make my fantasy come to life?" Taunting the guy who had him tied up was probably a worse idea than letting a stranger tie him up in the first place, but at least it helped him keep his feet under him, instead of throwing himself at said stranger like a dumbass.

Vincent chuckled and lifted his head from Jasper's neck. "Your mouth ever get you into trouble?"

Jasper grinned, his smartass response cut off by Vincent claiming his lips again. At least Vincent seemed to have a good sense of humor. And *gods*, he was such a good kisser. To the point that Jasper chased after Vincent when he pulled away.

"In the chair," Vincent said, his voice a bit rougher.

Goose bumps broke out on Jasper's arms; Vincent sounded as wrecked as Jasper felt. He barely even considered protesting as he took a seat.

Vincent stood in front of him and let out a slow breath. "Good boy."

Jasper shivered at the warmth that traveled through him from the praise. He tipped his head up as Vincent touched his cheek and leaned into Vincent's palm, still surprised by the gentle touches.

Vincent guided Jasper back against the chair with his fingertips against Jasper's chest, then traced his thumb along Jasper's lower lip. "Relax," he said. He hooked a hand under Jasper's knee and lifted it up and over the arm of the chair before leaning down.

Jasper squirmed at the awkward position, his eyes widening as Vincent secured something around his leg, above his knee. He let out a strangled sound as he tried to pull his knees back together, only to have his leg kept in place by the restraint.

"Shh," Vincent soothed, running his fingers through Jasper's hair. "I thought you wanted foreplay?" He pinched Jasper's nipple, then secured his other leg to the opposite arm.

Jasper whimpered as Vincent stepped back, his skin tingling as Vincent's intense gaze took in every inch of him. He was utterly exposed and helpless and… fuck. He liked it. Something not quite panic and more intense than excitement coursed through him, settling in his gut. Whatever it was, he relaxed into it as easily as a warm bath.

It was liberating. This…. This was what he'd been wanting without really knowing how to get it.

Vincent ran his fingers through Jasper's hair again with an approving murmur. "That's it. Now the real fun can start."

Jasper shivered and had a momentary thought that maybe he should be worried but decided to hell with it.

He had a safeword for a reason.

Scan the QR code below to preorder now

J.P. CARUSO is from Massachusetts' North Shore, where she lives off of iced coffee year-round. With bachelor's degrees in graphic design and biology, she's transitioned from a career in art to a career in science with aspirations of becoming a pathologist. When she isn't working, she's playing survival-crafting videogames, drawing spicy art, or practicing krav maga and muay thai kickboxing, in which she is a first-degree black belt.

Primarily a M/M romance writer, J.P. has been in love with love her whole life, and she has been honing her writing skills since she was a teenager. Her first foray into writing was through fanfiction, and she has participated in numerous fandoms throughout the years. Since then, she has written everything from TV commercial scripts to poetry to scientific manuscripts. Her fiction writing features detailed world-building, feel-good character development, flowing descriptions, and poignant turns of phrase.

Follow her on Facebook, Twitter, Instagram, and TikTok for news and gratuitous cat photos. All links can be found on her website, jp-caruso.com.

FOR **MORE** OF THE BEST **GAY** ROMANCE